The Fourth Amendment
A Novel

by SM SMITH

Other Works by SM Smith

Storm in the City: Two Short Stories
Prequel to The Fourth Amendment

Contact SM Smith:
brooklyn25518@gmail.com

ISBN: 1508719128
ISBN 13: 9781508719120

Dedicated to Heidi, Alex, Sabrina and Garrett

AUTHOR'S NOTES

1. This is a work of fiction. Names, characters, places, events, and incidents either are the product of the author's imagination or are used fictitiously. Any resemblance to actual persons living or dead, commercial entities, schools, professional sports teams, events or locales is entirely coincidental.
2. Major League Baseball has mandated that all its teams install metal detectors at their stadiums for the 2015 season.

TABLE OF CONTENTS

THE FOURTH AMENDMENT TO THE CONSTITUTION OF THE UNITED STATES

The right of the people to be secure in their persons, houses, papers, and effects, against unreasonable searches and seizures, shall not be violated, and no Warrants shall issue, but upon probable cause, supported by Oath or affirmation, and particularly describing the place to be searched, and the persons or things to be seized

PART 1

"The fault is not in our stars, but in ourselves..."

Julius Caesar
by William Shakespeare

"Let's go Yankees," twenty year old Anatoly Turken wisecracked. Standing in the compact kitchen of the cramped two bedroom apartment that he still shared with his parents in the Russian enclave of Brighton Beach, Brooklyn, he anchored a sixteen ounce water bottle, displaying the familiar Poland Springs label, to the countertop with his left hand. Slowly, very slowly, he poured a clear, viscous liquid from a bright red container into a funnel that emptied into it. The spicy aroma of tonight's dinner, roast chicken, garlic potatoes and borscht, normally would have distracted Anatoly, he adored his mother and her cooking, but not today. Anatoly's blue eyes burned with the intensity of a true believer, while his hands, calloused from hours hoisting heavy crates on the loading dock of his father's furniture store, never faltered. The work had sculpted Anatoly's wiry, six foot frame, stretching taut his sleeveless, black Brooklyn Nets tank top. Mikhail Prokhorov - oligarch, politician, athlete, playboy, and owner of the Nets - was his idol. When the Poland Springs bottle was full, Anatoly screwed the green plastic cap on tightly, pushed down the drinking spout, fitted the plastic cover on top, and resealed it with clear plastic wrap. He grabbed a blue floral dish towel from the rack next to the sink and dried the sweat from his hands. The squeals of children splashing in the gushing fire hydrant rose from the street through the kitchen's lone window, open wide to provide some minimal respite from the June heat wave. Anatoly rubbed his head, blond hair trimmed so tightly that he could appear bald at times, and surveyed his handiwork. He had assembled four Poland Springs bottles, all similarly filled, in a neat row.

Vladimir Unchkin, two years younger than Anatoly, nodded approvingly, as he usually did whenever in Anatoly's company. Vladimir was a full head shorter than Anatoly and much thinner. His gray "Brooklyn Basketball" tee shirt, another variation of Nets' merchandise, hung loosely on his frame, while his baggy jeans sagged to reveal red boxers and an occasional glimpse of his butt crack. Vladimir's mother had died of cancer two years ago, and his father was still drinking away his grief. Not surprisingly, Vladimir frequently rang the Turken doorbell near dinner time. Peeking through a shaggy mop of brown hair, his green eyes flickered between the bottles and the chicken roasting in the oven.

"What time does the game start? Do you think we can eat before we go?" he asked in rapid fire succession.

"I can't fucking believe that you are thinking about food," Anatoly replied, turning to stare down at his young friend. "Today is Russia Day - Independence Day for our country. Mr. Nakitov wants us to make a statement that the whole world will notice."

"What's for dinner? Can't we eat first?" Vladimir persisted.

Anatoly just sneered in reply. "Help me load up," he said, picking up one of the two blue and white pinstriped backpacks on the tiled floor. He grabbed a yellow bath towel from a stack on the counter, laid it flat, and then placed one of the bottles in the center. Then he gingerly wrapped the towel around the bottle and placed it in the first pack. Anatoly exhaled loudly when the bottle was at rest. "Two in each pack. We need to take them on the subway to the stadium," he explained.

"Where did you get the stuff?"

"Never mind where I got it. We used it last night and it works," Anatoly replied, feathering the second bottle into position.

"Sidney's Cleaners?" Vladimir asked incredulously.

"Sidney's causing trouble again. We did the job at 2AM so no one would get hurt. Mr. Nakitov just wanted to send a warning."

"Shit," Vladimir mumbled.

"I researched it all on-line too - FreedomFighters.IO. It's based in the Middle East." Anatoly added proudly.

"They got websites for this?"

"*Mudak*, the Internet's not just porn, you know."

"I like porn. Did you see the video of that pixie gymnast doing her balance beam split on the Ukrainian hockey player?" When his question did not elicit a response, Vladimir added, "She really curved his stick," laughing at his own well-worn tagline.

"Your brain is porn-fried." Anatoly reached into a brown cardboard box and pulled out two coils of spaghetti thin yellow wire, each with a silver blasting cap, the size of a cigarette, on one end and an orange plug on the other. "These are detonators. I bought them on-line too," he bragged.

"On Amazon?"

"No. On the FreedomFighters' site. They label everything as mining supplies and ship all over the world." Anatoly returned the detonators to the box. "Let's finish up," he said.

Vladimir reached for a towel with his left hand and a bottle with his right.

"No!" Anatoly screeched, recoiling a half step back from the counter. "*Medlenno*, slowly - one step at a time." He locked his fingers around Vladimir's right hand and returned the explosive-laden bottle to its place. "Just go to the stairs and look out for my mom. She should be coming home from Aunt Volga's soon. I'll finish up here," Anatoly said, heart still pounding from his friend's carelessness.

"OK," Vladimir said, shuffling away.

Anatoly's searing eyes followed Vladimir out of the kitchen before he returned to work. After storing the two loaded packs in the hall closet, Anatoly flopped down on the overstuffed living room couch to watch TV. Within five minutes, he heard the intercom ring from the lobby, Vladimir's signal of his mother's return.

"Watching TV? Don't you have anything better to do?" Anatoly's mother, Ariana, said as she bustled through the living room. She had been pretty but was starting to show the mileage of a hard life - graying hair, thickening waist, and worry lines encircling her eyes. Her grandfather had fought the Nazis at Stalingrad, and survived, but then had the poor judgment to agitate for more freedoms in Russia. Stalin had rewarded him with a one-way ticket to Siberia and his descendants had been out of favor with the Soviet government ever since. Ariana had immigrated to America with her parents when she was ten years old and never looked back.

"Hi ma," Anatoly replied without turning around.

"Your cousin Joseph goes to school at night now, you know."

"We're going to the Yankee game tonight."

"That's in the Bronx."

"Yeah, mom, we're taking the subway."

"Dinner's almost ready. You should eat first."

"I'm not hungry. I'm watching the news," Anatoly replied, still fixed on the television where a reporter solemnly noted the escalating military situation in the Ukraine. A snippet of a video of the Russian President addressing the Russian parliament flashed on the screen.

"I'm hungry, Mrs. Turken," Vladimir chipped in as he followed Anatoly's mom into the kitchen.

Ariana fastened a blue apron around her once-white sleeveless sundress and grabbed two potholders to protect her hands as she removed the chicken from the oven. "Set the table. Get the milk. I can't do it all myself," she said, although she often did exactly that. Anatoly was her only child and she had always doted on him.

The pleasing smells from the kitchen finally lured Anatoly away from the TV. "We've got to eat fast, Mom," he said, sitting down at the faux marble table in the front foyer that served as the family's dining room.

"Never a problem with this one," Ariana replied, nodding towards Vladimir who had already filled his plate. "Here, eat," she said passing the chicken to Anatoly.

"What about dad?"

"He's working late. I'll fix him something when he gets home."

"He's always working," Anatoly said, adding a large spoonful of potatoes to his plate. "What does he have to show for it? Mr. Nakitov just bought a new Mercedes. He's got a penthouse apartment. Everyone in the neighborhood respects him."

"I don't want to hear about that gangster at my table."

"He's a businessman, mom, and a war hero. A new Russian."

"The new Russians are just like the old Russians. Stalin, Brezhnev, Putin - they are all the same." Ariana's frustration bubbled to the surface. Countless times, she had described the realities of life in their homeland to her son, but he persisted with his fairy tales.

"You'll see. Putin will make the *Rodina* great again." And I will restore our family name after all these years, Anatoly thought, but dared not say aloud. Instead, he started to hum the Russian national anthem.

"Enough of that nonsense. Your country is right here. It's called America. Now eat or you'll be hungry at the game." Ariana rose and began to clean up while the boys finished their meals. She wrapped two pieces of chicken in cellophane and headed to the hall closet. "I'll put these in your packs for later."

Anatoly spit up a mouthful of the purple borscht as he lurched to head off his mother. "I'll take them," he said. "Come on, Vladimir, let's go. We don't want to miss the first pitch." He picked up both packs and held one out to Vladimir. Vladimir looked longingly at the leftovers on the table, but knew that he had to go. He sidled to the door, slowly placed the pack over his shoulder, and followed his friend downstairs.

Once they were on the street, Anatoly put his pack on the ground and pulled out two red baseball caps with the interlocking NY logo of the New York Yankees. He put one on his head, brim forward but cocked to the right, and then handed the second one to his friend. "Wear this," he demanded.

"Why?"

"Because we're supposed to. That's why." Vladimir did not need any further explanation.

Walking down the street, the boys had to dodge a gauntlet of youngsters darting in and out of the cold spray from the fire hydrant. Anatoly shifted his pack to his right shoulder, away from hydrant, and picked up his pace. Vladimir struggled, but stayed two steps behind until he heard a familiar voice.

"Vlad, Vlad - where are you going?" his ten year old brother, Nikolai, chirped. He was standing in front of the hydrant's stream, soaked and smiling. "You need to cool off," Nikolai said, jamming both hands into the mouth of the hydrant, trying to redirect the gusher to reach his big brother. Vlad jumped away from the curb, crossing his feet and almost tripping over the pack. He had to reach out with his free hand to steady himself on a metal pole bearing a streetlamp and a New York City sign with a red letter warning: No Parking, Tuesday and Friday, 9-11AM.

"Come here," Vladimir squealed once he had regained his balance. Nikolai dutifully trotted over, the water dripping off his clothes and puddling at his feet. Vladimir hugged him. The cold water was refreshing. "Be good," he whispered. "Look after dad." Nikolai just shrugged, pulling away quickly to dunk himself once again in the hydrant spray.

Anatoly surveyed the fraternal scene with an air of indifference. "Let's go," he said impatiently. He had planned their route carefully: the B train to Grand Street in Lower

Manhattan then a transfer to the D express that would take them to the Yankee Stadium stop at 161st Street in the Bronx. The Brighton Beach station was located high above the avenue, suspended just below the elevated tracks. Anatoly ran interference for Vladimir as they climbed the narrow stairway, jostling against the tide of commuters returning from the day's work in the city. He cradled the backpack in both hands, tucked his shoulder, and barged upward. Once through the turnstiles, the boys had to climb another set of stairs to the platform for trains into Manhattan. They were virtually alone here. Vladimir peered down the tracks but could not see a train approaching. He stepped back to sit down on a bench, backpack on his lap. Anatoly remained standing, pacing back and forth. Both were sweating profusely from the heat, the crowd, and their payload. They watched a local pull in on the far track, heading to Coney Island, before their train to the city finally arrived. Since Brighton Beach was the terminus of the B line in Brooklyn, the car was empty. The boys sat next to each other near the center door, staring straight ahead, the seriousness of their mission finally sinking in.

Kings Highway. Newkirk Plaza. Church Avenue. Prospect Park. The train rolled through the various neighborhoods comprising the bulk of Brooklyn. To the outsider, Brooklyn might appear homogeneous, the fourth most populous city in the United States in its own right, but residents knew well that the borough was a polyglot of ethnicities, religions and economics. Russians, Jews, Indians and Chinese; blacks and whites; young families, struggling artists, and wealthy hipsters each had their own territory. Anatoly and Vladimir had ridden the subway to the city many times but had never ventured into the neighborhoods below the elevated tracks. They squeezed closer together as the car steadily filled with passengers. Three thickly bearded Hasidic men, dressed in traditional garb, sweat-stained white shirts open at the collar, grasped the rail above their heads. A black teenager, earbuds firmly in place and head bopping to his own beat, dropped down next to Vladimir, but Vlad's attention was on the two twenty-something women sitting across the aisle. They were obviously dressed for a night out. The blonde wore tight black shorts and matching platform heels, while her dark-haired friend had squeezed into a white jersey that provided little cover for her cupcake-sized breasts. Vladimir stared intently as they jiggled with every lurch of the subway car until Anatoly's sharp elbow broke his reverie. "We change at the next stop," he said. Vladimir's gaze remained on the girls as he followed Anatoly off the train at Grand Street, but they continued to chat away, oblivious to his departure.

"They were hot," Anatoly admitted nodding back towards the train as its doors closed behind them.

"Definitely." Vladimir stammered.

"We will have all the hot girls we want after tonight. They love soldiers."

"Hot girls?"

"They will suck your *chlen* like it was a giant lollipop." Anatoly said playfully. Vlad's eyes widened as he savored the possibility of pleasures that had only existed in his wettest dreams before tonight. Anatoly offered his fist and Vladimir bumped it with his own, sealing their pact for the evening.

The D train arrived quickly and was only half full, so the boys were able to find seats next to each other again. The subway, now submerged beneath the streets of Manhattan, gained passengers at every stop. Business executives and tourists shuffled in and out, while a boisterous coterie of fellow Yankee fans steadily crowded in. By the time the train left the 125th street station, its last stop in Manhattan before heading into the Bronx, it was packed like a giant jigsaw puzzle, arms stretching up to grab handrails, legs staking out territory, and butts bumping against butts. The train's air conditioning, taxed to its limit, kept the temperature in the car bearable, although the air was thick with the dank odor of massed summertime humanity. Anatoly, holding his backpack securely in his lap, motioned for Vlad to do the same. Vladimir obediently followed instructions, lifting his pack from between his legs on the floor. At last, the train arrived at their destination, 161st Street in the Bronx, home of the New York Yankees. Almost the entire train emptied here, its passengers lining up to ascend from the underground station to the streets surrounding the new Yankee Stadium, shimmering in the twilight over the urban landscape.

In 2009, New York City had demolished the original Stadium, built in 1923, replacing it with a modern edifice at a cost of $1.5 billion, the most expensive stadium ever built at the time. Its white facade, encompassing 11,000 pieces of Indiana limestone, towered 140 feet capped by a replica of the original frieze of archways and balustrades encircling the upper levels of the grandstand. The stadium's lights atop the frieze beckoned the boys like candles on a birthday cake.

"How many people will be here tonight?" Vlad asked.

"Fifty thousand - it's a big game," Anatoly replied, steering them towards the park just across the street. His friend, jostled by the surging crowd, could barely keep up.

"One dollar water - one dollar water," the Latino youth with a pock-marked face shouted, holding up a dripping wet Poland Springs bottle that he had just pulled from the ice-filled cooler at his feet. "Five dollars in the stadium," he added.

Anatoly hustled by but Vlad grabbed his shoulder from behind. "They look just like ours," he said.

"Of course, you idiot, Anatoly replied. "That's why I used the Poland Springs bottles. The cops and stadium security guys are so used to seeing these bottles that they will never even notice ours." He sat down on a bench in the park. "Now we have to unpack our toys and ditch the towels." Anatoly opened his pack, gingerly unwound the towel from the first bottle, and placed it on the ground at his feet. He repeated the task with the second bottle and then put both back in his pack. "Slowly. Very slowly," he admonished Vladimir. When Vlad was done, the boys joined the throng heading towards the stadium entrance.

Bill Jones followed the boys with sniper's eyes from his wheelchair a few feet away. Their bright red baseball caps stood out in a sea of Yankee blue and gray. Having grown up ten blocks from the Stadium in an apartment building on the Grand Concourse, Bill had always been a rabid Yankee fan. He could even afford to buy a ticket at the old stadium especially before the team started winning and all the suits and suites took over. The team built the new stadium for them, not the ordinary fan, Bill and his buddies on the Concourse would grumble jealously when they sat on the front stoop of their building, drinking Bud and listening to John Sterling call the game on the radio. Now, Bill often panhandled outside of Yankee Stadium on game days, usually floating in a pleasant fog of painkillers, booze and weed. Bill liked being part of the swelling, boisterous crowd and could always use the extra bucks. He wore his favorite dark blue Yankee T-shirt, sporting Mickey Mantle's name and number 7 on the back, and a traditional Yankee cap, also dark blue with the interlocking NY logo. He would be laughed off the Concourse if he showed up with one of those red ones. Gray shorts and a thin, blue pinstriped blanket covered Bill's midsection and what was left of his legs. A thick beard and weathered black skin camouflaged the jagged scar on his cheek.

Bill had tried a variety of approaches to asking for money, but found that honesty was the most profitable so he had pinned his sniper's medals to a hand-lettered, cardboard sign on his lap, reading "War Vet Needs Beer Money". In fact, he was a veteran of Operation Iraqi Freedom. Watching the boys slip away, Bill's thoughts drifted back to a patrol in Baghdad ten years ago. He was walking down a dusty street when he noticed two teenagers working on the engine of a beat up automobile, a black Mercedes sedan. He was young and stupid then, so he and his partner approached, looking to help. The teens sprinted away into an adjacent building. Bill could still hear the explosion and feel the burning shrapnel bite into his legs. But, as he told himself often, he was the lucky one, returning to the States in the hospital section of the military transport while his partner came back in a body bag. Bill snapped back to reality as he heard the rattle of loose change in his cup.

Anatoly stopped on the fringe of the plaza fronting the stadium. He pulled his phone out of his back pocket and handed it to Vlad. "Take a photo," he said.

"With the stadium in the background?" Vlad asked incredulously.

Anatoly just nodded and smiled while his friend dutifully snapped the picture. He then tapped to send a SnapChat and jammed the phone back into his pocket. Vlad started to move towards the stadium, but Anatoly remained still. He swung his pack around slowly, unzipped a side compartment and pulled out a sealed envelope. Ripping it open, he found another cell phone and a set of instructions, written in Russian. Anatoly read them slowly and then read them a second time while Vlad looked on, unsure of what his friend was doing.

"A clean phone to get instructions from the boss," Anatoly said, as he turned on the new phone and waited for service to connect. Then, he keyed in a ten digit phone number in the address line and the code "2.23.1922" as the body of his text message. It was the date of the first celebration of Defender of the Fatherland Day, honoring veterans of the Red Army. He waited two long minutes, before the reply, "6", came in. Anatoly looked up and saw Gate 6 right ahead of them. He pointed Vlad towards the line heading to the security check there.

Twenty fans were on the queue ahead of them. The boys waited nervously, shuffling their feet and trying to peer ahead to see the nature of the search. They need not have worried much.

"What's in the pack?" the security officer asked.

"Water - it's hot tonight, man" Anatoly replied, taking out a Poland Springs bottle.

"Don't I know it. What about your pockets?"

Anatoly pulled out his keys, wallet and phone, even turning it on to show his lock-screen, the picture Vlad had just taken in front of the stadium. The officer waved him through. Vlad followed quickly behind. They flashed their tickets at the turnstile where an usher scanned the bar codes.

At last, they were inside. The Great Hall, a broad, high ceilinged concourse, beckoned. Vlad looked in awe at its scale, huge photos of past Yankee greats adorning the walls down one side, and banks of escalators, elevators and stairs leading to the seats on the other. Shops hawking expensive Yankee merchandise cluttered the plaza.

"Yankee pigs," Anatoly muttered, as he pulled the secure phone from his pack and texted the next code, "6.12.1990", to the mystery destination. The inaugural Russia Day, June 12, 1990, marked the dissolution of the old Soviet Union and the beginning of the Russian Federation. "100" came the reply. Anatoly scanned the signs in front of them, and pointed Vlad towards the ramp to Section 100.

When the boys passed a men's room, Vlad tugged on Anatoly's arm. "I've got to go," he said, pushing through the door before Anatoly had time to reply. Anatoly waited outside, surveying the crowd and thinking scornfully of his friend's weakness.

"Your buddy's not doing too well," a bald stranger, flab spilling out from both sides of his Yankee tank top, said to Anatoly. Poking Anatoly's pack, he added, "He's puking all over the men's room. Someone's going to have to clean it up."

Anatoly jerked around, knocking the man's hand away from the pack but not even bothering to reply. He half ran into the bathroom. He had to get Vlad out of there before security arrived. A father holding the hand of a small boy pointed him to the second stall, where Vlad was on his knees bent over the toilet bowl. No other men even turned around from the urinals on the opposite wall. Anatoly grimaced as he saw the remnants of his mom's chicken and borscht in the bowl and on the floor. He leaned over his friend's shoulder and said, "We have to go." Vlad just grunted and dry heaved. Anatoly grabbed Vlad's pack off the floor with one hand, and yanked Vlad's shoulder with the other. "Now," he said, dragging Vlad up and towards the door.

"Here, man - clean him up," someone said, handing Anatoly a handful of paper towels. Once out of the men's room, Anatoly pushed Vlad to a corner and handed him the towels. Vlad curled on the floor and Anatoly sat down next to him

"What happened?" he said.

"I can't do it," Vlad sputtered, wiping the dribble from the corner of his mouth. "I can't pull the trigger. I just want to go home." He was almost crying now.

Anatoly wanted to slap his friend, but couldn't attract any more attention from the crowd swirling towards the seats. Fortunately, no one stopped. "We are *not* going to pull any triggers," Anatoly whispered.

"What?"

"I left the detonators home. We are just delivering the bottles - nothing else. I didn't pull the trigger at Sidney's last night either."

"You sure?"

"Yes. Let's go. We're late."

Vladimir shuddered with relief and slowly staggered back to his feet. Anatoly pointed the way towards Section 100. They could see the outfield grass, glowing in the stadium's lights, as they walked. At the top of Section 100 ramp, a vendor with a blue-pinstriped Yankee apron and a red Yankee hat waited, swiveling impatiently to look in both directions. The vendor was tall and stocky with sawdust colored hair, snaking out from underneath his hat in a ponytail, and a square jaw that appeared to sit directly on top of his powerfully muscled shoulders. He held a tray of a dozen Poland Spring bottles.

Anatoly tipped his own red Yankee cap, knelt down to remove the bottles from his pack, and added them to the tray.   He motioned for Vladimir to do the same.   The exchange took only a few seconds. When it was complete, the vendor returned the salute, turned towards home plate and walked away.

"Did you see his right hand. He was missing the last two fingers," Anatoly said.

Vlad just trembled.

"Probably lost them in the struggle. A real *geroy*."

"I want to go home now," Vlad finally replied.

Anatoly nodded, pointing back towards the exit. They tossed their now empty backpacks in a trash bin on the way out.

1

SEVERAL MONTHS EARLIER

The pothole on the West Side Highway shattered the late night stillness as it swallowed the front wheel of the white BMW 3 coupe, biting into its rim and gouging the tire. "Shit," Kris Storm muttered, pumping the brakes as the car lurched to the right bouncing to the thumping beat of a flat. A blue mini-van sped by on the left, while a black Cadillac loomed in the rear view mirror. Tendrils of Kris' long, copper-colored hair tumbled into her eyes. She quickly brushed them away, returning both hands to the wheel, clenching it so tightly that her forearms cramped. A vision flashed of a palomino mare bucking wildly to repel its first ever rider. Kris had spent her high school years helping her parents manage a ranch outside Aspen, Colorado and needed all the strength and reflexes from those days, fortunately not so long ago, to steer the wounded car through the speeding traffic.

The remains of a late March snowstorm had provided Kris and two members from her team at Illuminate, a global giant in search and social media, an excuse to leave the office and the city for the slopes of nearby Mt. Snow in Vermont. Wearing white jeans and a pale green Bogner sweater that swamped her small frame, Mindy Smart jolted up in the passenger seat, scanning the roadside for a shoulder where their listing car could find safe harbor. Mindy was not going to win many beauty pageants, but she did win her state spelling bee in grammar school and was valedictorian of her class at Penn. Boasting more sharp edges than voluptuous curves, Mindy had straight, shoulder length black hair, darting blue eyes, and a small, pug nose that had absorbed its share of blows. Her parents had signed Mindy up for ballet class when she was five, but she had sneaked into the karate studio across the hall and didn't leave until she had claimed a national title. Mindy had grown up in the city, but on the posh Upper East Side, so she was in foreign territory now.

Kris had finally subdued the BMW, now limping slowly in the right hand lane, and switched on its emergency lights. Unfortunately, this section of the highway was elevated above the city streets, so they were hemmed in by a restraining wall which left no safe place to stop. Cars passed by with angry honks, a New York City salute from other drivers impatient with any delays at this hour.

"There's a road sign," Mindy pointed out. "The one hundred and fifty eighth street exit - you can pull over there."

"What's up?" Joe Brady said groggily from the back seat, his nap now interrupted. He leaned his stocky six foot frame forward, grabbing the back of Kris' seat and swiveling his head to take in the surroundings. "Where are we?"

Neither of the women answered. Mindy pointed Kris towards a small deserted parking area just off the exit ramp, dark except for two pools of dull light provided by battle scarred street lamps. It looked out over a path that ran along the Hudson River. Scattered small trees dotted the shoreline, while the apartment buildings on the New Jersey side showed only a few scattered lights at this late hour. The night was cold, but calm, so the river itself barely had any ripples. A lone biker, bundled in yellow fleece, whizzed by, strobe light flickering on the handlebars. He was gone before anyone could open the car window to call out. A baseball field surrounded by a high chain link fence loomed on the downtown side of the lot, while the lights from the George Washington Bridge flickered in the distance uptown. The only sounds were the rumblings of the cars on the highway. Once Kris had shut down the engine, Mindy turned to reply to Joe, "One fifty-eighth, your old stomping grounds, I bet."

"You've got the wrong neighborhood, sister," Joe said, in his best ghetto drawl. His brown eyes danced above a broad, flat nose and open, guileless smile. Tempted to try for a braid, at least on the weekends, Joe had let his thick hair grow out a few inches. "This is Washington Heights, all Dominican and Latino. I grew up in Harlem, thirty blocks south. Us black boys would get our asses kicked up here if we weren't careful." In fact, Joe had left the 'hood six years ago, first for a football scholarship at Yale immediately followed by his job at Illuminate.

"I can't imagine anyone kicking your ass - even when you were in high school," Mindy said.

"Only happened once - on One Hundred Ninetieth Street. Never went that far uptown again. But, it looks like someone kicked your butt," Joe said pointing to a bruise on Mindy's cheek.

"That was the mountain. I face-planted on our last run," Mindy said, looking in the vanity mirror, "I didn't realize it had started to bleed again. Must have been that jolt when we hit the pothole."

"You need ice on that, so we need to get you home, preferably before dawn," Kris said. She was the leader of their team in Illuminate's crack cyber security division. Their job was to foil any bad guys who tried to use Illuminate's information for nefarious purposes. Kris had left the Colorado ranch on a scholarship to Cornell's engineering school, majoring in computer science. Illuminate had recruited her there for their fast track program: two years in Silicon Valley then New York. Tonight, she had packed all that brainpower into a blue and gold checked flannel shirt tucked into faded Levi jeans that highlighted her long, muscular legs. Kris jumped out of the driver's seat, kicking over a half full can of Bud. She stepped around several empties and a crumpled condom to reach the front of the car. At least someone had fun here tonight, Kris thought.

"Where's the spare?" she called out, examining the mutilated tire.

"Spare what?" Mindy replied. Upper East Side girls could take karate lessons but they did not change tires. "Maybe Joe can help."

Joe opened the passenger door and joined Kris in front of the car. He wore loose fitting jeans and a faded blue Yale hoodie. "I never had a car," he said with a shrug. A police siren wailed in the distance.

"You guys are useless," Kris said, moving to the rear of the BMW and opening the trunk. "At least you can help me unload these suitcases. I bet the spare is underneath." Joe complied, moving the three cases on to the tarmac, while Kris hunted for the tire. "Bingo!" she shouted, lifting up the flooring of the trunk to unveil the spare tire, jack and lug wrench. Joe helped carry them to the front of the car.

"Go into the car and set the emergency brake. I need to look underneath to see where the jack goes," Kris said. Joe ambled back to the driver's side, climbed in and hunted for the brake handle to no avail.   Finally, Mindy, exasperated, opened the glove compartment to look for the owner's manual.   "We're like the Three Stooges," she said, flipping the pages.   "I'll set the brake myself.   You go help Kris.   I want to clean up this bruise."

As Joe stepped from the car, kicking the empties out of the way, the headlights of an approaching car snaked into view, framing him.   He tensed, but then exhaled, recognizing the familiar silhouette of a New York City police car.

2

Although he had only graduated from the police academy six weeks ago, Officer Juan Alviro was in familiar territory on 158th Street. He had grown up in this neighborhood and still played softball in the park's A league on summer week-nights. With rust colored skin, jovial brown eyes, and wiry, dark hair barely visible under his blue cap, Juan steered the patrol car through the lot towards the parked vehicle. The lighting here had always been dim. He laughed silently, remembering the search for Maria Gomez's bra under a bench late one summer evening after his junior year in high school, before quickly scanning the bike path and shoreline to look for possible bystanders or troublemakers.

At six feet tall, Juan was once a promising shortstop. He had attended a junior college in Oklahoma to enhance his pro prospects, certainly not for the academics or social life, until a knee injury ended any hopes of a shot with a major league club. Returning to New York, Juan got lucky, landing a sales train-ing internship with a brokerage firm. But two years cold-calling prospects and hand-holding customers with only meager commission checks to show for his efforts convinced Juan that a finance job was not his destiny. When the broker-age firm ran into difficulties, Juan was not that disappointed, deciding to use his tiny severance check to train for the police academy exam. Right now, the job security and health insurance were a necessity, since his first child was on the way, but long-term he hoped to move up to a detective's shield.

Kevin O'Reilly, Juan's partner, fidgeted nervously in the passenger seat, fingering the St. Christopher's medal that he now kept in his left hand pocket. His grandfather had given it to him from his hospital bed before he passed away last month. They had been close. Kevin had inherited his curly red hair, green eyes, and freckles from him. A quick temper too, he always reminded himself. With three years experience on the force downtown, Kevin was technically the senior man in the patrol car but he was new to this beat, transferring to this precinct only two weeks ago. The department needed to fill a vacancy and thought he could use a change in scenery after his partner had been shot.

Kevin picked up the microphone on the dashboard. "Car 1225 - approaching a young black male standing outside a white BMW coupe," he said to the dispatcher, then provided their location. "We'll run the plates as soon as we can see them."

"Anyone else around?"

"No one visible," Kevin said. As Juan pulled their car closer, Kevin added, "Looks like someone's been having a party. Beer cans on the ground."

"Check it out. I'm going to send a back-up unit," the dispatcher said. "It will be there in 10 minutes. Stay safe," the dispatcher signed off.

Stay safe, Kevin thought, the same advice that another dispatcher had offered last fall - thirty seconds before two teens opened fire on him and his partner in Washington Square Park. They had seen the teens loitering on their first rounds of the evening, and knew that they didn't belong. Their jackets were too bulky for the warm evening; and, they were wearing the wrong colors. Two years ago, these suspicions alone would have enabled the cops to stop and frisk the teens, disarming them without any harm. But, under intense pressure from the ACLU and neighborhood activist groups, New York City had changed the rules, so now his partner may never walk again and the two teens were dead. At least, they died with their fourth amendment rights intact, he thought sarcastically. When the patrol car stopped ten feet behind the BMW, Kevin gave St. Christopher one final caress. He then began to type its license plate numbers into the laptop.

Picking up their broadcast mike, Juan announced forcefully, "Stay right there - keep your hands where I can see them." Joe followed directions as Juan stepped out of the patrol car pointing his flashlight, first at Joe, then at the car, and then at the empties.

"What's happening?" Juan asked, his breath leaving trails of smoke in the cold night air.

"We got a flat on the highway. This was the only spot we could pull over."

"We?"

"Two friends," Joe said, pointing to the car.

"Did you call 911?"

"No."

"Looks like you were having a good time," Juan replied spotlighting the beer cans and condom again.

"We found them here. Don't know who they belonged to."

"Let's see your license and registration." Juan said, stepping closer, trying to see if he could smell the beer on Joe's breath. Peppermint, not Budweiser. He shined his light into the vehicle, looking for another beer inside. It was clean.

Mindy stepped into view, "I can explain, officer," she said.

Juan flashed to Mindy's face. "Let's start with your cheek, lady. Looks like you took a beating," he said.

"A bad fall on an icy mountain," Mindy replied, rubbing the blood-crusted bruise gingerly, not wanting to start the bleeding again.

Kris had been crouched down on the far side of the car, jacking it up, when the patrol car approached. She walked quickly around the car, coming up behind Joe and Mindy. Kris's soft red hair had again tumbled into her eyes. She swept it away with her right hand, smearing a streak of black grease across her cheek. "These two work for me at Illuminate. We went to Vermont for the weekend and are heading home. Downtown. Can you help us?" she said.

Juan took three strides towards the back of the car, eyeing the three pieces of luggage on the ground. "I don't see any skis," he said.

"Rentals," Mindy piped in, shivering as a cold blast whipped through the open parking lot. "Can I grab my vest?" she asked.

"In a minute," Juan said, as he tried to decide his next move. He didn't like the beer and the blood, but the car definitely had a flat. It was a close call. He hoped Kevin would decide their next move.

Kevin stepped out of the patrol car, but remain shielded behind his door. "Who's Mike Sheets? White, male, twenty-six years old?" he asked, pointing his flashlight first at Joe and then at the two women.

"That's a friend from work. Lent us his car for the weekend," Kris replied with waning energy, fearing that their cause was heading downhill. She noticed a barge inching up the Hudson River and wished they could climb aboard it. Kris jammed her hands into the pockets of her jeans.

"Sorry, ma'am, hands out," Kevin said, pointing his light at Kris with his left hand while slipping his right hand down to his holster. "Juan, check out the car - inside and out," he ordered, as Kris displayed her empty palms. Kevin took a deep breath. He didn't take chances any more, shifting his light to Mindy and then Joe. Joe grimaced, glancing down at his suitcase. Kevin picked up the tell. "The luggage too," he said to Juan, who sidled towards the trunk.

"Hold on," Kris said defiantly, taking a step towards Juan. "Where's your search warrant? You can't touch anything without a warrant."

"Lady, we have probable cause for suspicion of driving under the influence. We can do this calmly, and, if all is clear, you can go home," Kevin said.

"Or?"

"Our back-up unit will be here in five minutes. With a warrant."

"Why don't you all get in the back now," Juan said, reaching out for Kris' shoulder.

"Get your hands off me," she said, knocking his hand away.

"Be careful, lady, striking a police officer is a felony," Kevin warned.

"Kris, let's get in the car," Mindy said, pulling Kris away. Mindy opened the door, climbing in first, but Kris jerked around to face the officers. She started to speak out again then hesitated. Dejectedly, Joe walked past her. He squeezed into the middle seat, sitting on the hump, head squeezed by the car's low roof. At last, Kris relented, turning around to slide in next to Joe. You've got to like a great looking woman who gets down on her knees to change a flat, Juan thought, as he circled the car, kneeling down to inspect each of the wheel wells. Kevin kept his light trained on the three Illuminators now crammed into the back seat.

"I've got some weed in my bag," Joe whispered.

"Shit. I thought you said that we smoked it all last night," Mindy said.

"I saved a little, just in case, you know," Joe said sheepishly.

"A little pot is not illegal." Mindy said, confidence starting to wane.

"What else do you have in there?" Kris interjected.

"Nothing - what do you mean?"

"What else?" Kris insisted.

"A few tabs of meth. But I hid them real well." Joe admitted at last. "I was planning to head over to the office and pull an all-nighter."

"Just tell the cops that. I'm sure they'll understand," Mindy said, leaning into Joe.

Kris slapped the front seat of the car. "These two cowboys are still violating our privacy. They don't have any real cause to search this car." She twisted towards Mindy, adding, "The government should just stay out of the way."

"Spoken like a true member of the Tea Party," Mindy retorted. "That might work in Colorado where there are more horses than people, but, right here in New York City, I like my government."

"Just not so close," Joe said, craning his head towards the back of the car where Juan was now leaning over the luggage. They heard the wail of a police siren, and then saw the flashing red light as another patrol car entered the dark lot.

"Why don't you call Jim, your FBI friend," Mindy suggested. Kris had helped Jim Bright on two previous cases and he would occasionally stop by the office. "He likes you, and he's hot," Mindy added.

"I know, but it's not a good time for me," Kris said.

"Not a good time? When would be a better time?" Joe piped in.

"OK, OK," Kris relented. "Call Jim Bright," she ordered her Samsung phone. Her crew waited anxiously. No answer. Kris left a message on his voicemail: "Jim, Kris here. I'm in a bit of a scrape. Might need your help. Bye." She took a deep breath, then commanded her phone, "Call Anne Harmony," referring to her boss.

"She knows the mayor, right?" Mindy asked.

3

Anne Harmony had arrived in Illuminate's offices in Lower Manhattan at noon that day. Wearing tailored Versace jeans and a powder blue men's Charvet shirt, she toured her territory, the cavernous ninth floor, checking in on the programmers and data analysts under her command. Although thirty-five as of last week, Anne still boasted the muscular physique of a former heavyweight rower. Her face, framed by shoulder length blond hair tucked under a cardinal red Stanford crew cap, was rugged, forever wind-burned by all the hours on the water. Anne smiled as she greeted several of her people, interrupting their animated discussion of SQL code projected on a 60 inch screen. She was pleased to see so many at work. Anne told her charges that no one had to work weekends, but, of course, she took unwritten attendance every Sunday. In her ten years at Illuminate, Anne had rarely missed a weekend. It was the Illuminate way, Anne thought, enabling her to become a millionaire many times over based on the company's soaring stock price.

Illuminate preached an egalitarian, not hierarchical, organization structure, designing its offices accordingly. The vast, loft-like, open spaces - the building had once been a factory - were separated into workgroup pods by low partitions. Messengers, and other admins, often used GPS-equipped bicycles to navigate the giant labyrinth. Anne strode purposely, devouring real estate with her long strides. She wanted to maintain an element of surprise, knowing full well that the office grapevine would be buzzing with word that she was on the prowl.

Everest, the associates called her on the sly - tall, unforgiving and brutally cold. If that was the price of success, Anne would gladly pay the bill. Finally, Anne reached her destination, the desk flying the blue and white striped Colorado state flag on a tall pole. There was no need to knock.

"Where's Kris?" She asked the sole associate in the vicinity.

"Kris who? I'm new here."

"Never mind," Anne said, stalking back to her corner office, one of the few in the entire building. She slammed the door closed. Anne spent the remainder of the afternoon hunched over her computer, reviewing raw data and editing a presentation for a large client. After five years in the management ranks, she was out of practice. Finally, Anne looked out her window at the West Side cityscape. It was almost dark now. She had dinner plans that evening and had to get home to change.

Anne's home was uptown on Park Avenue. She loved the sturdiness of the squat twelve story, pre-war building, her privacy assured round the clock by two uniformed doormen, and the touches of a gilded age, crown moldings, mahogany paneling and wood-burning fireplace, in her two bedroom apartment. It reminded her of her childhood home outside of Birmingham, Alabama, a giant, rambling house built before the Civil War, surrounded by forty acres of farmland. Anne had excelled in mathematics, so her daddy had sent her to an all girls prep school and then west to Stanford.

After a short soak in the tub, Anne toweled off and strolled naked into her dressing room. Glancing at the full length mirror, she was pleased to see that her stomach remained taut and her breasts firm, although they had always appeared small in comparison to her broad shoulders. She cupped them both, watching her pink nipples darken and swell. Everest, my ass, Anne thought. A text broke her reverie, her driver confirming that he would be in the lobby in thirty minutes. Surveying her closet, Anne selected a black, zip-front wool crepe dress by Chado Ralph Rucci. The halter straps and cut out neckline accentuated her limited cleavage while the braided detail at the waist showcased her legs. She was going to attend a small fund-raising dinner for New York City's popular, young black mayor, Deion Chamberlain reelected by a landslide last November on a wave of anti-Wall Street sentiment. In February, Anne had met the mayor while hosting a tour of Illuminate's New York offices for the city council. The attraction was mutual, immediate and brain-cramping. Anne had visited the mayor in his office at Gracie Mansion twice since then, both times the last appointment of the day. For the record, they discussed Illuminate's expansion plans in the city - before heading upstairs to the mayor's private quarters.

Anne dressed quickly, putting on the finishing touches with her burgundy lipstick five minutes before her car would arrive. She pulled her mobile from her black Chanel clutch, checked her antique gold watch, an heirloom from her grandmother, 4:30 back in San Francisco, and hit a speed-dial. Five rings, but no answer. Voicemail.

"Hi Blake, it's me. Just checking in. How's Sherpa? He looked ragged when I was in town last week. Say hello to William. Bye."

Blake Witherspoon, twenty years her senior, had dazzled Anne five years ago with gourmet dinners, prepared personally in his Pacific Heights apartment overlooking the Golden Gate bridge, midnight sails in the bay, and long walks along the Pacific Coast. Their lovemaking was tepid, but Anne attributed it to Blake's age and the stress they both experienced at work. He was next in line for the chief executive slot at Pan Pacific Bank, while she was rising fast at Illuminate. Their marriage, plastered across society pages worldwide, launched a new power couple. Unfortunately, that power never extended to the bedroom. On their first anniversary, Blake finally explained that he had tried, but his true love was William Randall, a game designer at a Silicon Valley start-up. At least, he had the courage to tell her directly, rather than let her stumble upon his liaisons the hard way. His bank was not ready to accept an openly gay CEO, so Anne had agreed to maintain the charade of their marriage at least for a while. She immediately requested a transfer to Illuminate's then fledgling New York office, throwing herself into her work with renewed zeal.

Anne's driver double-parked outside Marea's discrete powder blue awning on Central Park South and stepped out to open the rear door for her. She was a few minutes early, by design, hoping to catch some time alone with the mayor. The maitre'd ushered her downstairs to the private dining room, the table set with crisp white linen and delicate china surrounded by burnished rosewood panelled walls. Mayor Chamberlain was standing in the corner, scotch in hand, flanked by his top lieutenant, Willis Frazier, a towering black man with a thick, full beard. Chamberlain was imposing in his own right, wearing a custom-tailored gray Ermenegildo Zegna pinstripe suit, that highlighted his broad shoulders and tapered waist. Now forty-two, Chamberlain remained fit playing basketball regularly and publicly, ensuring that his ghetto roots never strayed from the voters' minds. A thin scar running for several inches down his left cheek, rumored to be a vestige of a knife battle in his teenage years, added further street cred.

"Ms. Harmony, what a pleasure," Willis said, stepping forward to intercept Anne. He reached for her right elbow, steering her away from the mayor. "Let me introduce you to Harry Weinstein and Gary Stackman, two of our most ardent supporters in the financial sector." Anne was surprised that Chamberlain had any friends at all left on Wall Street, but she had read that these two had supported Deion for many years. After five minutes of polite conversation, she turned away, sidling towards the mayor, but Willis still tactfully blocked the way. The mayor's wife, Tanya, had just materialized at his side. She was a wide, full-figured woman with a broad smile, perfect white teeth, and a booming voice, which had served her well in the Bedford Stuyvesant church choir where she had met Deion twenty years ago. Her flowing white dress, a trademark of her public persona, highlighted her long straight black hair and coal black skin.

"Don't you go bragging about Deion Junior to these men," Anne overheard her say, loudly as usual.

"But he did score ten points last night. And he's the only a freshman on the College Prep varsity," the mayor countered. "I can be proud of my eldest. But his younger brother may be even better."

"There you go again," Tanya said. "These men want to hear about your policies, not some high school basketball game," she added, pointing to the small crowd that had now assembled around the mayor. Anne turned away.

Not surprisingly, Anne's place card was located at the far end of the table, set for sixteen, while Mayor and Mrs. Chamberlain were seated in the center on the same side. No other women were present. Frank Bromski, an overweight union boss, sat across from Anne, while her shadow, Willis, sat to her right, blocking any eye contact with Deion. Bromski, dressed in his finest Men's Wearhouse wool blend blue pinstripe suit, attacked his food with relish. Anne almost giggled watching his silver tie sink slowly into the sauce of his octopus pasta dish, Marea's signature offering. Mercifully, the waiters finally cleared the table, Deion's cue to rise and address the gathering.

"My friends, we boarded this subway car together four years ago and still have many miles to travel to reach our destination, a safe city that delivers full equality in jobs, housing, education and health care for all its citizens in all five boroughs," he began. With a minister's fervor, Deion pointed directly at Anne to emphasize the booming tech sector, and the opportunities for women, in the city. She smiled demurely, nodding her appreciation. Of course, Deion neglected to mention the huge tax breaks that he had delivered to Illuminate, fueling the expansion of its New York footprint. "We have cracked down on crime, not just on Wall Street but on every street. We are going after the big guys, the insider traders, the corrupt bankers, and the organized crime leaders, who cost our city billions of dollars, but we are making sure that our police respect the rights of the common man," Deion wrapped up.

"You've already thrown all the dirty hedge fund guys in jail. Who's next?," Harry Weinstein asked.

"You're right, Harry. We've cleaned up Wall Street. Now I'm going to focus on the mob, particularly the Russian mob. It's become a menace to this city in the last few years."

"We'll contribute to *that* platform - anything that gives us a break," Gary Stackman joked, pretending to reach into his pocket to retrieve his checkbook. "Seriously, any progress lately?"

"Some. Remember that shoot-out just off Madison Avenue during the holiday season last year?" the Mayor asked. Several heads nodded. "We have reason to believe that the perpetrator was a captain in a Russian credit card gang, the tip of the mob's iceberg, operating out of Brooklyn. The FBI and the NYPD have been working the case hard, but the Russian community is tough to crack. Hopefully, we'll have some arrests soon."

Anne remembered the incident well. Kris' team had helped the FBI track down the scam and were on the sidewalk for the shoot-out. A one minute video, filmed by a pedestrian, went viral on YouTube, showing that Kris and Mindy weren't just bystanders either. It looked like a combination of Annie Oakley and the Karate Kid.

The Mayor answered a few more questions, then sat down as the waiters served dessert, a Ricotta cheesecake garnished with strawberries and blackberries.

Bromski looked ready to pounce, but then glared across the table at Anne, "What about the bike lanes?" he asked.

"What?"

"The bike lanes in midtown. Deion promised me he would get rid of them. They're killing my delivery guys," he grumbled. "They can't park anywhere near the stores. They can't even double-park anymore."

Anne tried to ignore Bromski, ordering another glass of that delicious Tignanello. When he continued his tirade, Anne exploded, "I bike and many of my two thousand employees here in New York bike too. And we all pay taxes." She lifted her napkin off her lap and dropped it down on her dessert plate. "We contribute to campaigns too," she said, rising.

"And we want you all to support this campaign," Mayor Chamberlain said. "With all your energies," he added, sliding his hand onto Anne's knee under the tablecloth, guiding her back down into her seat. Anne had been so angry that she had missed the mayor and his lieutenant's game of musical chairs. Deion was a man of the people, but Anne knew that she turned him on whenever she slapped down one of his sycophantic cronies. Anne sat, separating her knees slightly, encouraging the mayor's fingers to climb an inch higher. Then she picked her napkin off the table and returned it to her lap. She clasped the mayor's wrist underneath as tightly as if it was an oar, pulling it off her thigh.

"Are we done here?" she asked, turning to face Mayor Chamberlain.

"Yes, yes, the party's breaking up," he said, standing and twisting to extricate his wrist. "Busy day tomorrow for everyone. Tanya's already gone home to get the kids settled and check their homework." Mayor Chamberlain moved away to say farewell to his other guests. Anne extended her hand to Bromski, not her cheek, but he still leaned over to look down her dress. She stopped in the ladies room, then headed upstairs and out into the street. Her driver was waiting, holding the rear door open.

"Pull into the spot in front of the hydrant," Anne instructed. "We'll wait there." She texted their location to Mayor Chamberlain. Anne pulled down the armrest in the back seat, making sure that Deion knew that she still wanted to talk business.

"That riff on the Russian mob went over well," she said as soon as he climbed in.

"It works every time. The public loves gang-busters."

"And hates the Russians."

"Damn right."

"If you get the Russians, the next stop could be the White House."

"Damn right there too."

After her driver had turned left off 59th Street, well-lit and still crowded with tourists, onto Park Ave, Anne lifted the armrest and slid close to Deion. "We're going to my place tonight, right?" she asked. Deion nodded. Willis had given him the all clear when he left the restaurant. The paparazzi had gone home. Anne stroked Deion's thigh teasingly on the short ride uptown. The Mayor leaned back, his arm over Anne's shoulder. The car pulled into the building's back entrance, used for deliveries during the day and discreet comings and goings in the evening. Deion cupped Anne's ass in the service elevator, drawing her into him, but she pointed to the tiny security camera in the corner and pushed away.

As soon as they entered her apartment Deion reached for the front zipper on Anne's dress. "You'll break it," she said, "Just wait in the bedroom." Anne unzipped herself, giving Deion a quick glimpse, then turned away. In her bathroom, she quickly stripped off the expensive dress, reached back to unhook her bra, and stepped out of her white thong. She donned a red silk kimono.

Deion had peeled back Anne's cream-colored duvet, scattering the array of colorful pillows, and sat waiting, fully clothed. Anne stopped two steps away, untying the belt on the kimono and dropping it to the floor. Deion's eyes widened, his breath shortened. Anne stepped closer, reaching out to loosen Deion's necktie and unbutton his shirt, then pushing him to his back. Naked, Anne straddled her lover's chest, her hands on the headboard. Deion fumbled with his belt, finally getting his trousers and boxers down to his ankles. Anne wanted to stretch the moment out one more tantalizing second, white hovering over black. The mayor gripped her hips, sliding them down his stomach. He would not wait any longer. But he would have to. Anne's mobile buzzed on the nightstand as Kris Storm's name flashed.

Anne rolled off, grabbing her phone to listen to Kris' plight at the police station. The Mayor tried to wrestle the phone away, but Anne maintained control. She spread her legs, guiding the Mayor's head down between her thighs, while she kept talking to Kris. Concentration was difficult, but she got the basic information before signing off and tossing the phone aside. She reclined on a pink lace pillow, looking down on the Mayor's bobbing head, raking her nails lightly across his muscled, black shoulders.

"I'm going to need a favor," Anne said, when he finally came up for air.

"Then you're going to have to pay for it," Deion replied, flipping Anne over to her knees.

PART 2

"The paths of glory lead but to the grave."

"Elegy Written in a Country Churchyard"
by Thomas Gray

4

After the long dry spell of her married life, the night of lovemaking with Deion energized Anne. An almost forgotten soreness, welcomed back. Still, she waited until ten before rising from her desk at Illuminate and bounding down the long corridor. The sun streamed in through the office's large windows. Anne, hair tied tightly back, wore freshly pressed jeans with crisp seams, a green and white striped collared shirt and navy blue cardigan sweater. She almost bowled over a young associate carrying a tray of coffee and donuts, barely stopping to apologize before heading off again. Anne was pleased to see Kris and crew in full attendance. "Any problems at the police station?" she asked.

"Not after Willis Frazier called," Kris said. She had stopped at her apartment briefly to shower and don a clean blue and orange T-shirt, sporting the Denver Broncos logo. Her hair tumbled loosely over her shoulders.

"They rolled out the red carpet," Mindy chirped, looking up from her screen, thick glasses perched on the bridge of her nose.

"Bad things happen when you stay away from the office on weekends," Anne admonished mockingly. "Now, I need you to get to work. We have a favor to return." She guided the group to a vacant conference room, turning on the laptop and logging in. Joe straggled in last, his trademark khaki cargo shorts sagging below his knees.

Anne called up a map of New York City on the projection screen, then zoomed into the borough of Brooklyn and finally zeroed in on the Brighton Beach neighborhood. It was located on the southernmost tip with beachfront directly on the Atlantic Ocean. Anne then flashed photos of the neighborhood, bustling with its small shops, crowded subway station and boardwalk. "Brighton Beach has a population of 80,000 people, maybe 30,000 households. It used to be predominantly Jewish, but now is home to the largest Russian speaking population in the city."

"Yea - I saw it on Russian Dolls, the reality show on TV," Joe said.

"Tore you away from Jersey Shore, huh?" Mindy cracked. "What's Snooki going to say?"

"We have reason to believe that at least one organized crime ring has roots here," Anne went on, ignoring the banter.

"Any national security threat?" Kris asked.

"Possibly. We need you to find out more," Anne replied.

"How?"

"Turn all our guns loose."

The room went as silent as a morgue. Kris arched her brows and began to twirl a thick strand of hair. "All our guns? On eighty thousand people?" she asked incredulously. Anne just nodded.

"Email, commerce transactions, texts, phone records?" Kris asked again just to be sure. "Tweets?"

"Yes. Top priority. Our advertisers will not stand for any more fraudulent rip-offs."

"Do we even know what we're looking for?"

"Of course, here's some possible selectors." Anne flashed a page of key-words on the screen.

"Wi-Fi intercepts too?" Mindy asked. Again, Anne indicated her assent.

"Wait a second. Are we doing this for our advertisers or the mayor?" Kris queried, a tone of concern readily apparent.

"Both," Anne said.

"Do we have a warrant?"

"Not yet, but we can get one if we need it."

"I thought the rule was to get the warrant *before* you began a search," Kris said. Then she stood, adding, "We don't even have a crime here yet."

"Don't you want to get the guys who shot your FBI friend, Jim, last winter?"

Kris took a deep breath. "Of course, more than anything. But Jim's a lawyer. He wouldn't want us to break the law."

"Look, do a first level scan of the data. Aggregate stuff, no names. Then we'll talk." Anne shut down her laptop and headed towards the door. "In two weeks," she added on the way out.

"Wow," Joe exclaimed with a low whistle, once Anne was safely out of range.

"We better get started," Mindy said.

"Not so fast. This is bullshit." Kris said angrily. "Probably illegal too."

"You heard the lady - two weeks," Joe said.

"I heard the lady, and I'm leaving,"

"Where are you going?" Mindy asked.

"My apartment. I need to get out of here."

Kris stormed back to her desk. She donned a blue sweatshirt, tucking her hair into the hoodie, and then slipped into a burnt orange Patagonia ski shell. The calendar said late March, but the lion was still roaring in the form of a freezing wind whipping off the Hudson. Kris zipped up and headed down Ninth Ave. She loved to walk outside on a cold, bracing day. It reminded her of home. The Aspen foothills could be glorious for a few weeks in the summer, but were bitterly cold for much of the year. Crossing 14th Street, Kris veered left down Hudson Street. She was now in the meat-packing district, only the meat-packers had moved out long ago. They were replaced by trendy restaurants, hotels, and boutiques. The neighborhood buzzed with action from the cocktail hour until dawn, but now was primarily filled with slow-moving tourists headed towards the High Line, the city's latest outdoor attraction. The High Line was a twenty block stretch of elevated train track that had been converted into a public park. Kris climbed the stairs and found an empty seat on a bench overlooking planters of wild grasses, brightly colored flowers and sculptured shrubbery which now overwhelmed the deserted tracks. An elderly couple, sporting black Tyrolean hats and carved wooden walking sticks, sat next to her, speaking German. Kris needed to think, but this was not the place. Too many tourists. She headed back down, turning towards the river.

Kris pulled her hood off to feel the blast of the wind gusting directly into her face. She waited at the light before crossing the six lanes of traffic on West Street, finally reaching the West Side Esplanade, deserted on this cold morning. Like a ten story high spiderweb, the black netting of the golf driving range at the Chelsea Piers athletic complex loomed to her right while the residential towers of Battery Park City beckoned on her left. She headed to the towers, walking slowly. Yielding to the elements at last, Kris thrust her hands into her coat pockets, shivering. She quickened her pace and reached Bank Street in ten minutes. Her apartment was only two blocks away, inland with the wind now at her back. The trees on the narrow street in the West Village were still bare. In a few weeks, this would be the prettiest street in Manhattan, Kris thought. And one of the most expensive. When Illuminate had promoted Kris last year, transferring her to New York, the company had put her up at the Standard Hotel near the office for a month. Kris had spent every one of her few spare minutes searching for an apartment, finally settling on a one bedroom plus den and deck on the third floor of meticulously restored, pre-war brownstone in the Village. Illuminate paid well, very well, but at $6,500 rent per month, the apartment still stretched Kris' budget; nevertheless, she loved the location and character of the brownstone, as well as her private outdoor space. Of course, the building did lack the amenities, doorman and health club, prevalent at many high rises, but, Kris' friends explained, this was New York City. Everyone, or almost everyone, sacrificed something in an apartment.

Walking with her head down, Kris did not see Jim Bright, tall and rangy with closely cropped dark hair, standing next to the black wrought iron gate fronting her building. He wore a gray tweed overcoat, unbuttoned to reveal a midnight blue, three button pinstripe suit. The cold wind had painted his ears a bright red.

"Hey, Kris," he called out when she was just a few steps away.

"Hey," Kris said, still lost in her thoughts.

"I called the office and spoke to Mindy. She gave me some of the details and said that you headed home. Long night, huh?"

"Long night. Long morning."

"I went to bed early so I didn't get your message until I woke up. What happened?"

"Anne got us a pardon from the mayor's office. Now we have to return the favor."

"What?"

"It's cold out here. Come on in. " Kris unlocked the front door. "I'll make some coffee. Better to talk here than in Starbucks."

"How's the shoulder?" she asked, climbing the stairs. She would never forget Jim's blood-soaked shirt on the Madison Avenue side street. Fortunately, he was wearing a bulletproof vest.

"I'll never pitch for the Mets, but it's OK now," he said.

Jim wished that Kris had invited him up under different circumstances, but he wasn't complaining. He knew her story well. They first met when Jim was tailing Ivan MacTavish, a crooked hedge fund manager. Kris almost got caught in the sting, but instead volunteered to turn the tables on Ivan. She daringly ventured onto his private jet, setting him up for Jim to arrest. Then, he had asked her help tracking down a credit card scam. Jim had invited Kris to watch the arrest, wanting to show off, he had to admit. Unfortunately, it had turned into a shoot-out.

"Nice place," Jim said, when Kris opened the door to her living room, revealing a working fireplace and burnished hardwood flooring. Light poured in from two windows, trimmed with thick muslin curtains. A white sofa and loveseat, arranged around a glass coffee table hovering over an oriental rug, faced the fireplace. Several issues of New York, Vanity Fair and Working Ranch magazine were stacked on the table. Kris and her younger sister, Kit, had grown up in a comfortable middle class neighborhood in San Jose, but then her parents, both engineers, had risked everything to start their own company. When the tech bust of 2002 wiped them out, the Storms accepted an offer to manage a ranch in Colorado.

"Grab a seat." Kris said, as she headed into the small kitchen located in the middle of the apartment. Her bedroom, the deck, and the lone bathroom were on the far side. When Kris disappeared, Jim peeked into the cozy den just off the living room. It housed an oak desk and a small sofa, upholstered in a deep forest green and strewn with matching striped pillows. A large screen TV and a Denver Broncos pennant claimed the opposite wall.

Kris returned a few minutes later with two cups of black coffee to find Jim paging through Working Rancher's cover story, "Weaning in Wyoming."

"Fascinating, huh?" she asked.

"Can't say that I ever found this magazine in my family's living room."

"In Brooklyn?"

"Yeah, Canarsie to be precise."

"No ranchers there?"

"None that I know of," Jim laughed, then went on: "Heavily Italian. Teachers, policemen, firemen," He took a sip of his coffee.

"Bright doesn't sound Italian to me."

"My mom's maiden name is Mangano."

"Is Canarsie near Brighton Beach?"

"Not far, but another world. No Russians in Canarsie. Why?"

Kris recounted the events from the previous twelve hours: the flat tire, the cops, the station house, their release and then Anne's request, her order really, this morning. Her words dripped with anger and indignation.

"How long have you been in the cybercrime unit?" Jim asked.

"Just a few months, really. I was a data analyst in marketing before Illuminate moved me," Kris said, modestly not mentioning her raise and promotion. Warming her hands around her coffee cup, she added, "Living in sunny California too."

"Look we're not selling Frosted Flakes here. We're dealing with really bad guys," Jim said, rubbing his sore shoulder.

"Understood. I want to catch them as badly as you do. But..." Kris paused.

"But what," Jim motioned for her to continue

"But, I want to play by the rules. The Constitution of the United States. The Founding Fathers cared about the privacy of ordinary citizens. I do too," Kris concluded, pursing her lips in anger. She pulled out her phone, tapped a few keys, and flipped it towards Jim, "Here, the fourth amendment specifically defends 'the right of the people to be secure in their persons, houses, papers, and effects, against unreasonable searches and seizures.'"

"Look, the technology changes, the rules change," Jim said, standing up. "The Founding Fathers never considered the power of an iPhone and a 4G network. We're not asking you to search anyone's home. We just want you to check into data that people willingly transmitted over public networks."

"But, the data itself could still be considered private," Kris said.

"OK, it's a gray area. We could argue about it all day," Jim said, sitting back down. He stared directly into Kris' bewitching hazel eyes, now boiling with the rage spilling from her overheated conscience. They hypnotized him momentarily, but Jim forged his way back to his argument. "What about 'probable cause'?" He pointed to her phone, "Read the rest of the fourth amendment. It specifically states 'no warrants shall issue, *but* upon probable cause' if I remember correctly."

"Well, is there probable cause here?"

"Yeah. At least I think so. Sergei, the shooter from the credit card ring, definitely had help from the Russian mob."

"Did he tell you that?"

"No. He knows that he'd get a bullet in the head if he did. But, we have other sources."

"Such as?"

Jim shook his head, "Can't go there."

"Well, do you have a warrant for us to sift through all the data that Anne asked us to?"

"No, but I know that there are some Russians who are not going to play by our rules."

"Any terrorist activity?"

"Maybe. We hear rumblings, nothing hard though."

"What about the federal government, the NSA. They listen to everyone. Why do you need Illuminate?"

"The NSA is spending a lot of time in court right now. Look, do what you can. Don't violate anyone's privacy, if that makes you feel better. But we need your help."

"I'll think about it," Kris said putting her mug down on the table and standing. "I'm beat," she said.

Jim took three steps towards the door, then took a deep breath and turned, "Let's go for a walk and check out Brighton Beach this Sunday. I'll buy lunch."

"Can't do. I'm going to be in the office all weekend."

Kris had turned Jim down before, but he was not giving up. "Another time?"

"Call me," Kris said, closing the door.

5

Across town, Deion Chamberlain checked the mirror and straightened the knot on the onyx and gold striped necktie. Tanya always said that this tie amplified the glow of his black skin. He pulled his phone from his suit pocket to check his calendar for the day, and smiled. He had planned well. Two lightweight meetings this morning had provided the excuse for him to stay overnight at Gracie Mansion, while his wife returned to their brownstone in Brooklyn after the dinner at Marea's. He could handle these meetings in his sleep which was just as well since he was beat from the night's exertions at Anne's apartment. Deion had crept out of her warm bed around three AM, meeting Willis downstairs for the short drive from Park to East End Avenue. Willis filled him in on his call to the police station rescuing Kris and her crew. All routine. With five hours sleep, upstairs in the private quarters reserved for the Mayor and his family, Deion was ready to go to work.

Deion could hear the stirrings of the staff preparing Gracie Mansion for the day's visitors. He paused at the top of the curved stairway that led down into the entry foyer. Archibald Gracie, a Scottish merchant, built the original mansion in 1799 as his country escape, overlooking a meandering bend in the East River. It was five miles from the city's center which was downtown encompassing Wall Street and the piers at the time. Deion's ancestors were slaves then on a plantation in Georgia. The Bill of Rights did not apply to them. In fact, the Founding

Fathers specifically avoided any discussion of slavery in the constitution because they knew that such language would doom its ratification. Change had come slowly, and with great bloodshed. Deion could only imagine the face of Thomas Jefferson, the great patriot, patrician and slave owner, if he could see who was the mayor of his nation's largest city today.

"Boss, let's go. Everyone's ready to start," Willis Frazier called gently up the stairs.

■ ■ ■

An arctic gale off the river almost convinced Jim to hop on the subway, but he decided to brave the cold and bike the twenty or so blocks from Kris' apartment down Hudson Street to his office. It would be his workout for the day. He stopped at a Citibike stand on the corner and unlocked one of the bright blue bikes with his membership key. The streetscape was a hodge podge of retail, office, manufacturing and residential buildings. Jim thought that he had made progress with Kris, on both the business and social fronts. He paused for a traffic light across from the soccer field at Walker Park and watched two teenaged girls pass a ball back and forth. They should have been in school, he thought, but they did look talented. Each girl seemed to caress the ball for a split second before flicking it onward. Canal Street was a mess, as usual, as cars vied to enter the Holland Tunnel. Finally, he turned on Worth Street, returned his bike to the Citibike stand there, and entered the FBI's New York Headquarters.

His partner, Glenn Walker, dropped his paperwork and ambled over to Jim's desk. "How did it go with Miss Honey Hair?" he asked playfully. Squat, with a thick chest and a blossoming midsection, Glenn resembled a New York City fire hydrant, if it could be dressed up in a suit and tie. Since he was married with two small children, Glenn savored the voyeur's role in Jim's social life.

"OK, I think," Jim said, sitting down.

"OK what?"

"OK, I think that Kris and her team will finally begin to help us crack this Russian gang."

"We need them. Six months of hanging around Brighton Beach and we have shit to show for it."

"Except a few pounds."

"More than a few," Glenn said, patting his stomach. "And..," he hesitated, "Any sparks?"

"Sparks?" Jim said, playing dumb.

"Are you going to take her out?"

"Maybe."

"Is that a definite maybe, or a possible maybe?" Glenn cracked.

"Forget it. I've got work to do."

Glenn picked up the top two pink message slips from Jim's in-box. "Yeah, real important work. Marcy and Stephanie," he read. "These babes are calling you. Why sweat it with Kris?"

A third pink slip remained in the tray. Jim could see that it only contained a single word. He frowned.

"What's up?" Glenn asked.

"The Pirate. That's his code. He wants to meet."

Glenn knew that the Pirate was Derek Miller, their only source on the inside of the credit card gang. They hadn't heard from him in two months. "Do you think he's in trouble?" he asked.

"There is no 'trouble' with the Russians. You're either in favor or you're dead," Jim said. He checked his watch, "We missed him today. Our plan is to meet on the noon ferry from Staten Island. He lives out there and commutes into the city."

"Plan B?"

"Same time tomorrow."

■ ■ ■

Deion Chamberlain escorted the last of his guests to the door, knowing that his constituents would always remember the personal touch, more than they would the Mansion itself. Few visitors knew that one hundred years ago, Gracie Mansion, a two story, wood framed Federal style home, served as an ice cream parlor and restroom facility for the 11 acre park that surrounded it. Robert Moses, the famed planner of much of New York City's infrastructure, led a major restoration, convincing Mayor Fiorello LaGuardia to take up residence in 1942.

Mayor Robert Wagner further expanded the building in the 1960's and opened it to the public. Still, Deion thought it looked drab until his predecessor, Mike Bloomberg, joined with several of his wealthy friends to rejuvenate it shortly after his election in 2002. Of course, Mayor Bloomberg never actually lived in the Mansion, preferring his own more luxurious accommodations. Now, with a fresh coat of pale yellow paint, black shutters, and wide porches framed in white surrounding both levels, Gracie Mansion would at least fit unassumingly into any of the wealthier suburbs surrounding the city.

The morning meetings had proceeded as smoothly as Deion had hoped. The three chairwomen of the Girls Scouts wanted to solicit funding for their efforts in the city's economically distressed neighborhoods. The president of the New York Philharmonic Orchestra had outlined his plans for concerts in the city's parks during the coming summer. Deion listened attentively and asked a few questions, but generally let his aides run the show. The stress level was low. Much easier than dealing with the teachers' union or the board of JP Morgan, Deion thought. Besides, his mind was already drifting to the next event on his schedule - opening day at Yankee Stadium.

Deion had been an ardent Yankee fan for his entire life. His father had taken him to his first game in 1977; they reveled in the team's World Series win that year and the next. Then came the long dry spell of the 1980's. Still, Deion attended games regularly. It wasn't hard to get good, cheap seats. Finally, the Core Four - Jeter, Rivera, Pettitte and Posada - returned the Yankee franchise to glory in the late 1990's. Deion used his rising political influence to meet them all - and get free tickets to the big games. Now, as mayor, he had the ultimate perk for a true fan, four seats right next to the dugout. Willis was waiting outside with his boys.

"Hurry up, dad, we're going to miss the first pitch," Calvin, 12 years old, wailed as Deion ducked into the black bulletproof Suburban. He checked his watch - 12:20. Calvin was right, but the mayor's office did have some benefits. "Step on it," Deion said. His driver turned on the siren as they headed uptown. Cars parted in front of them as if Moses and the Israelites were crossing the Red Sea.

"Did you guys dress warm? It's going to be cold out there today," Deion, Sr. asked.

Both of his sons nodded, holding up fleece sweatshirts and dark blue Yankee ski caps.

"I've got long johns on under my suit," he replied. The mayor wanted to appear oblivious to the elements when the TV cameras found him.

"Can I see the tickets?" Calvin beseeched. His father reached into his suit jacket and handed them over.

"Section 17B - same as last year, right. I liked those seats."

"If you were any closer, you'd be in the on-deck circle."

"Now batting for the New York Yankees, Calvin Chamberlain," his brother mimicked the Yankees public address announcer.

"Don't bust on your younger brother, Deion. He might play for the Yanks one day," Deion Sr. said.

The boys looked out the window as the Stadium came into view.

"Will we see Mariano today?" Calvin asked.

"He's retired, dufus," his brother replied.

"I know but he stopped by to see us last season."

"I want to see the rookie, Ripcurl Reilly," Deion, Jr. said.

"He had a great spring training," Deion, Sr. agreed. "The most exciting Yankee rookie since Jeter himself - that's what the NY Post said this morning."

"He smashed 10 home runs in spring training," Calvin said.

"And he can run and field. He's a five tool player," his brother added, showing off his baseball knowledge.

"Is he really a surfer, too?" Calvin asked.

"I saw a picture of him on the beach with long blond hair. But the Yanks made him cut it."

"He grew up in San Diego, so I bet he surfs," Deion, Sr. said. "But you never know about rookies. Most of them just flame out. I remember my first season..."

"Oh no, you're not going to tell us about your first game with PopPop again, are you? The grass was so green. The popcorn smelled so sweet."

"You tell us that story every season."

"You boys just don't realize how lucky you are. Going to opening day." Deion, Sr. said, shaking his head, but realizing that he was the lucky one, spending the afternoon with his boys at the ballpark.

■ ■ ■

The limo pulled up to the Mayor's brownstone home in Brooklyn just as darkness was settling in. The three story home sat in the middle of a row of almost identical houses, lights on beckoning families home to dinner. All three Chamberlain boys were still chatting excitedly about the game.

"You wanted to leave early, but I told you the Yankees were going to come back," Calvin said to his older brother.

"Down 6-0, I didn't think they had much chance. And I have a test tomorrow," Deion, Jr. turned to his dad for moral support.

"You didn't count on Ripcurl," Calvin shouted, holding up his #33 Reilly T-shirt. "Walk off home run in the 13th."

"And he knocked in the tying run in the ninth," his father added. "Now, let's go inside. Your mom is waiting."

But Tanya did not meet them at the door. Instead, her older sister, Maya, greeted them sharply, "Where were you boys?"

Calvin started to recount the Ripcurl story again, but his aunt had already spun him around. "Let's go, you're eating at my house tonight." She and her husband lived a block away. Their two children were in college. Maya reached for Deion, Jr.'s shoulder. "Let's go, you too."

"But I have to study," Deion, Jr. replied.

"Grab your books then," Aunt Maya meant business. She glared briefly at Deion, Sr., then frog marched his two sons down the front steps.

"What about Dad," Calvin shouted, but Maya did not reply, or even turn around. Deion, Sr. knew that his evening had taken a marked turn for the worst. He headed past the main stairway, through the dining room, and into the kitchen. Dead man walking. Tanya stood behind the breakfast table, arms crossed. A manila envelope lay flat on the table.

"Where were you?" Tanya fired the first salvo.

"At the ballgame. You can ask the..."

"I know where you were today. Where were you last night?"

"At dinner. At Marea's. With you and my closest friends."

"Don't you be smart with me. Where did you go after dinner?"

"To the Mansion. I told you that I had early meetings this morning."

"Straight to the Mansion? You've got one chance to tell me the truth."

Deion's eyes flashed to the envelope. "All right, I stopped for a drink," he stammered. Taking a deep breath, Deion added, "With a constituent. It's my job, you know that."

"I know that you are full of shit. Right up to your eyeballs."

Tanya picked up the envelope and opened it. "Warren Olsen sent me these," she said, slowly spreading three photographs on the table. Deion silently prayed for a fissure in the earth to swallow him up. Warren Olsen, a reporter for the Daily News, had covered the Gracie Mansion beat for the past ten years. He picked up the nearest photo. It showed him leaning over to enter Anne's car, but she was not visible. Deion's hopes soared momentarily, He started to speak, but then Tanya handed him the second photograph. He was exiting the car at Anne's apartment building, extending his arm to help Anne out. Still some wiggle room here, he thought. But then Tanya pointed to the last one - in the elevator, his hands on Anne's ass. Olsen must have paid off someone in the building to get that one.

"She's a big supporter of my campaign," Deion started to explain, but Tanya cut him off.

"Supporter! Supporter!" she screamed. "The only thing that she is supporting is your big black dick." She put both her hands flat on the table, leaning forward to put her weight on them. Her face grimaced in anger and disgust. "You could have it all - Gracie Mansion, maybe even the White House - and you're throwing it away for that piece of white trash."

"What's Olsen going to do with these pictures?" Deion asked.

"Don't you worry about those pictures," Tanya hissed. "You worry about your family. Me, the boys, do you want to lose us?" She took a deep breath, then pronounced, "because we are not going to stand for this."

Deion staggered as his wife spoke, each of her words stabbing like a knife into his chest. "I don't want to lose you," he said quietly, at last taking a step forward towards Tanya.

"Good," she said, but waved him away. "Now you pack your things, call Willis, and head right back to the Mansion."

"The pictures?" Deion asked again.

"Deion Chamberlain, you start getting your priorities straight. You look after your family, or you won't have a political career left to worry about. I am not going to be like Hillary or Silda and stand behind my man while he makes an ass of himself apologizing to the public." Tanya deflated, like a balloon. "Now get upstairs and then get out. You make me sick right now." She put her head down on the table, sobbing. Deion moved to comfort her, but then thought better of it. He headed upstairs to their bedroom.

Fifteen minutes later, he returned to the kitchen, a blue Yankees' gym bag in hand. Tanya was still sitting at the table, head up, eyes dry now. "I spoke to Warren. I told him that you are a good man who lost his way," she said. Deion put his bag down, looking at his wife pleadingly.

Tanya stood, "He's not going to print the pictures - at least right now. For some crazy reason, he thinks that you can help our city and our country."

"Thank you."

"Don't thank me. Think about your life, our life, our kids. If you ever see her again, it's all over. Understood?"

Deion nodded, and turned to leave.

■ ■ ■

The orange ferry pushed off from the St. George's terminal on Staten Island, crawling towards Manhattan like a giant turtle. The boat, The Spirit of America, could hold 4,400 people and 30 cars on its three decks, but was only half full on its noon voyage. Jim and Glenn wandered forward, carefully checking out the other passengers with the slow eyes of experienced policemen. A family of tourists snapping pictures, a mom with a stroller, two construction workers with hardhats and lunchboxes in hand. Nothing suspicious, but no Derek yet either. Jim, dressed casually in jeans and bright blue Mets jacket, slipped as a wake from a cruise ship departing the harbor caused the ferry to wobble, but quickly steadied himself. When they passed the concession stand, emitting a pungent smell of franks and sauerkraut, Glenn, wearing a business suit and tie, wanted to stop for lunch but thought better of it. Finally, the two FBI men reached the front of the boat and headed outside to the deck, their designated meeting spot. The temperature had warmed into the fifties; the stiff breeze felt refreshing; the city's skyline beckoned in the distance.

Jim gazed forward with his hands on the railing, admiring the Statue of Liberty, while Glenn standing to his right, turned to keep his eyes on the ferry door behind them. Twenty or so other passengers milled around the deck or sat on the benches to enjoy the view. Glenn nudged Jim, who twisted his head around, only to see a tall, thin brunette in black leather pants and tight white V-neck sweater. "Looks like a model," Glenn said admiringly. Jim laughed briefly, shaking his head. Then, he craned his neck to look left and right down the rail. "No sign of Pirate," he replied. The boat plied onward, the Whitehall Street terminal in Manhattan coming into focus.

"What's Plan C?" Glenn asked, now facing forward as well.

"Same time tomorrow."

"Hey," Derek Miller grunted, stepping into the spot next to Jim. He was twenty-two, a former high school football hero, but worry lines were now starting to crease his forehead, the strains of a tough job market and a double life. A beat up gray sweatshirt emblazoned with the Latourette High logo, the Purple Pirates, draped comfortably over Derek's cougar-coiled frame. With the hood pulled up over his brown tousled hair and dark wraparound Oakley sunglasses shielding his eyes, Derek had the appearance of a celebrity rocker going incognito, or an FBI informant.

Jim breathed a sigh of relief, "Hey," he said, "What's up?" Glenn turned around to cover their backs, eyes shifting side to side to monitor the deck behind them. He strained to hear his partner's conversation in the wind.

"Not much," Derek replied.

Jim said nothing, willing Derek to continue. He did.

"Starting to get some action."

"Action?"

"Bill called. Now that Sergei is in the can, he got promoted." Jim just nodded. He knew that Bill Badenov, two years ahead of Derek at Latourette, was the leader of his credit card crew. "He's working on another set of hot cards. Wants *me* to set up the next shopping spree," Derek said.

"A promotion for you too. What did you say?"

"Told him I'm not ready yet. Was that OK?"

"Might help all of us if you took the step up. But it's your call," Jim watched a tug helping a barge navigate the harbor. "Where will Bill get the new cards?" he asked.

"Don't know for sure, but sounds like his old friends. Bill's learning Russian now. Even thinking of getting an apartment in Brighton Beach."

"Is Bill Russian?"

"No - he's Polish. I told him Russians and Poles don't mix, but he told me to fuck off."

"Ask him to Google 'Katyn Forest'" Glenn interjected.

The boat was closing fast on the terminal. They could see the dockworkers preparing for its arrival. "Go shopping then," Jim said. "But stay in touch."

"What about Lynne?" Derek asked.

"You still seeing her?"

Derek nodded.

"She's hot." Jim said, recalling the surveillance photos. Lynne Springer, a lissome Latourette High graduate with spiky blond hair, worked the inside for the crew, getting herself hired as a salesclerk at posh boutiques and then accepting their forged cards for payment.

"Maybe too hot sometimes," Derek said, emitting a soft, low whistle.

"What's that mean?" Jim knew that he had to play the role of lawman, confessor and big brother to the young informant.

Derek shuffled his feet and thrust his hands into the deep pockets of his sweatshirt. "I like to hang with her, you know, but she digs this gig too much. Gets high on it really. Like she's doing coke."

"Danger junkies can be hazardous to your health."

"I should blow her off, but.."

"But what?"

"After a gig, man, it's like the wild side. She could go all night."

To be twenty-two again, Jim thought. "Look, we're not interested in your friends on the crew. We want the guys who steal the credit card numbers and print the cards. The guys in Brighton Beach."

"I got it."

The ferry clanged against the dock. They could see the gates opening on the deck below them, the crowd pressing through to reach Manhattan.

"Stay in touch," Jim said.

"Be careful," Glenn added.

Derek turned to leave, but then swiveled around. "One more thing, almost forgot," he said. "Bill mentioned a guy named Crazy Eight is flying into town in two weeks. Seemed to think it was a big deal."

"Crazy Eight? Never heard that nickname before," Jim said.

"Well, maybe it's nothing, but Bill said that the Russians have set up an apartment for him."

"OK, We'll check it out. Thanks."

Derek slipped into the departing crowd. Glenn turned to Jim and said quietly, "He's a good kid. He doesn't have to do this." He paused while an Asian couple snapped a last picture of the harbor. When they left, Glenn continued, "He was a first time offender. Would have got off with a slap on the wrist."

"I know. He thought the shopping spree was a lark at first, but then realized it was stealing. Now, he has no real way out. The Russians don't offer severance benefits."

Glenn nodded. The two FBI men caught up with the tail end of the crowd at the exit ramp.

6

The weather in New York remained mild all week but Kris and crew rarely ventured outdoors. They battled day and night with their laptops, wrestling with Illuminate's giant databases of information to uncover any clues to criminal activities and homeland security threats emanating from the Russian community in Brighton Beach. Illuminate users generate thousands of data events every minute: location, friends, likes, dislikes, shopping habits, movie reviews, bank withdrawals, photos. From the mundane aspects of daily life to the deepest personal secrets, the information from millions of people is stored on vast farms of computer servers housed in well-protected, well-cooled warehouses around the world.

"Wake up. Go home," Kris tapped Mindy on the shoulder. It was after midnight on Sunday.

"OK, OK, just a few more minutes," Mindy said groggily. "I didn't realize that I sacked out."

"No, now. Joe left a half hour ago. We are going to review everything in the morning."

Mindy stood, stretched her diminutive frame, and removed her glasses to rub the bridge of her nose. Mindy's hair was frazzled, while an unidentifiable brown stain marred her blue cords.

"I'm a wreck," she mumbled.

"Yep."

"You don't look much better yourself." Mindy pointed to the streaks of red ketchup now adorning Kris' white Florida-Georgia Line concert tee shirt.

"Nope. I'm leaving in a few minutes too."

"See you tomorrow," Mindy said, packing up and heading towards the door.

Kris surveyed their bullpen, stacks of print-outs on the floor, a white board cluttered with circles and arrows highlighting promising leads and dead-ends, and waste baskets over-flowing with Diet Coke cans and food wrappers. She shut down her computer, closed up her briefcase and slipped her jacket off its hanger, but then sat back down in her chair. She pulled out her phone from the back pocket of her jeans. Her father, Tom, still woke before dawn to manage ranch chores, but, since her mom, Karen, passed away last year after a long battle with lymphoma, he stayed up much later than he used to.

"Hey dad."

"Hi Kris. What's up?"

"Not much. Just want to see how you're doing."

"I'm fine. But it's really late back East. Something must be up."

"It's been a long week. Nice to hear a friendly voice."

"I hope you're still not at the office."

"Just getting ready to leave."

"What's keeping you there so late?"

"A big project. You know that I can't tell you much more."

"You're doing all that cybersecurity stuff now, right?"

"Yeah."

"Sounds important."

"It is, but tougher than I thought. I can handle the workload, but I'm still not comfortable with the judgment calls."

"Like what?"

"Privacy mostly. We have so much information, on everyone really. How should we use it?"

"Who's we?"

"Illuminate, the government, my boss Anne, me. It seems we reach a new crossroads every day."

"I understand. I just signed up for a new service, SeniorSavers.com. Could save me a lot of money, but I did put some personal information on there. I don't want the government seeing it all."

"Dad, you know that you have to be careful on-line, right?"

"Yes dear. But I have you out there to protect me."

Kris laughed. "Maybe that's the way I have to look at it. Protecting innocent people, not prying into their lives."

"Trust your heart, dear."

"My heart says it's time for me to go home to bed. Love you."

■ ■ ■

The next morning, feeling a renewed zeal after the conversation with her dad, Kris checked out a Citibike from the kiosk on her corner and rode uptown to the office, letting her hair blow freely in the breeze. She wore jeans and a tie-dyed tee shirt under her windproof shell. Kris dodged another biker heading the wrong way on the narrow path, protected from traffic by barricades recently erected by order of Mayor Chamberlain, but kept her bright demeanor. At the office, her team seemed to look fresher too. No food stains at least. They gathered around a conference table to review their progress.

"What've we got?" Kris asked.

Joe fired up his laptop, projecting a table of data on the sixty inch monitor. "OK, our instructions were key words only - no links to individual names or email addresses. First, I narrowed the search down to the last thirty days. With the Brighton Beach population of roughly eighty thousand, I still had a couple of million emails to check. Then, I ran the 250 selectors that Anne gave us and scrubbed down the results to eliminate dupes and misspellings. Here's my top 10," he said, pointing to the screen.

"So the term 'explosive' showed up forty thousand times?" Mindy asked.

"Yep,"

"But we don't know if it referred to 'an explosive temper', 'an explosive athlete', or 'an explosive device that could blow up Brooklyn'" Kris interjected.

"Correct - we would need permission to read the content of each individual email," Joe said.

"We're not there yet," Kris said. She drummed her fingers on the conference table. "Mindy, where are you?"

"I looked at web searches. Pretty much the same thing. Lots of clicks on 'jihad', 'martyr', 'Al Queda', 'ISIS,' but nothing that we can really act on. I called a friend who works at the NSA for help, but she said that her hands were tied too. The government would need a judge to sign a warrant before they could dig any deeper."

"We must have gotten something interesting after all this work," Kris implored.

"We did get a disproportionately large number of clicks to websites that are on Illuminate's official monitor list. Porn, credit card scams, build-a-bomb videos - all kinds of fun stuff," Mindy said.

"Here, look at this," Joe punched a few keys to flip through several screens. "A menu of fraudulent credit card numbers for sale. Visa Signature $24. MasterCard $11. American Express $19."

"Do we know who was shopping here?" Kris asked.

"We can find out."

"OK, go for it - definitely probable cause here. Also, get the info on the websites - who owns them, who operates them, who hosts them. Anything else?"

"A few purchasers of DriveCrypt."

"What's that?" Mindy asked.

"Military grade encryption. You wouldn't buy it just to hide your love letters," Joe replied.

"Speak for yourself," Mindy jabbed.

"Guys take all the shit for talking trash but you girls really are the ones with the slut-mouths."

"Moving right along," Kris said. "Can we follow the money? How do the bad guys buy stuff and pay people? Do they use credit cards and banks, or electronic currencies like E-Gold or Bitcoin?" she asked.

"Good point. E-Gold got shut down a few years ago because of all the illegal activity. BitCoin is getting press now, but the FBI did shut down Silk Road last year. It was a black market, selling dope via Bitcoins," Joe replied.

"I'll work on the money angle," Mindy volunteered.

"OK, back to the salt mines then," Kris wrapped up.

■ ■ ■

The garbage bin overflowed with empty, half-crushed Diet Coke cans by the end of the day. Kris twirled a strand of hair while staring mindlessly at the rows of data on her screen. Finally, she shut down her computer and meandered over to Mindy's desk.

"I'm beat," Kris said. "I'm going to call it an early night."

"No you're not," Mindy replied without even turning around. Kris looked at her quizzically. "You're coming out with me. I need a wingman.

"Huh?"

"I'm meeting Evan for a drink and he just texted that he's got a friend with him from school." Mindy jabbed at several keys, pretending to work.

"Who's Evan?"

"A guy that I met through J-Date. He's the marketing guy at a start-up. We hit it off and he asked me out for tonight."

"Oh, come on. You're too young for an online dating service."

"It's better than Tinder. With all the free time that we have here, a girl's got to do what she can."

"I don't think so."

"Why not? When was the last time that you had a man - I mean a date?" Mindy asked playfully.

Kris stalled, so Mindy pounced. "See, it's been a while for you too. This place can drive you crazy. Just one drink."

"I'm not dressed," Kris said, pointing to her black V-neck tee shirt, now showing traces of sweat stains under both arms. Mindy always dressed a cut above Kris' West Coast casual attire. Today she wore khaki slacks and a pink Brooks Brothers shirt with a button down collar.

"You're fine. We're going out downtown anyway. Anything goes."

"Where?"

"Locande Verde in Tribeca."

"On North Moore. Fun spot. Great food."

"See Evan's got class. Let's get moving." Mindy stood, looking around for her purse.

"We'll stop at my place first so I can clean up," Kris said.

After several seconds of digging, Mindy gave a victory smile, pulling out a small joint. "Maybe this will help us loosen up," she said.

"Unchain our inner slut, you mean."

Both women laughed as they headed to the elevator.

■ ■ ■

Mindy led the way, elbowing past the reservation desk and into the bar, the rich aroma of Italian sauces permeating the air. Kris followed, still wearing jeans but now sporting a blue floral print Etro shirt. Both women had arranged themselves to reveal a glimpse of cleavage, or at least what passed for cleavage on Mindy's bony frame. The crowd was three deep surrounding the mahogany bar which fronted the length of the right wall of the restaurant. The lighting was dim at best, almost dark, but the music, soft rock, was not too loud. John Fogarty's "Centerfield" was the current selection. At last, Mindy waved, then turned to Kris. "There's Evan," she said, pointing towards two young men resting their beers on the low partition that separated the bar from the dining area with its cozy candlelit tables nestled tightly together. Between the darkness and the crowd, Kris could not see much. In fact, Kris noticed a couple, seated at a nearby table, huddled together, shining the flashlight app on a phone to read the menu. Evan stepped forward, kissing Mindy lightly on the cheek. Medium height, softening stomach, wearing khakis and a powder blue polo with a discreet Duke Blue Devil logo, Evan appeared on the pleasant side of ordinary. He turned to introduce his friend. "This is Cameron. We roomed together for a year. He works in LA now but is in town for a few days."

At first glance, much better than expectations, Kris thought as she reached out to shake hands with both men. Standing well over six feet tall with wavy, flaxen hair and pale blue eyes, Cameron could have passed for an actor, model, athlete or just a hunk. When he smiled at the girls, his white bright teeth almost lit up the room. Cameron wore gray twill slacks, a bold blue striped button down shirt, sleeves rolled halfway up his forearms. Kris lingered over the possibilities as Evan and Mindy chattered away, just really getting acquainted themselves.

"What would you like to drink?" Evan asked at last. Mindy ordered a cosmopolitan, while Kris requested a beer, Stella on tap if available. Evan headed to the bar, while Cameron pushed forward to stand next to Kris. He leaned against the railing, and asked "Did you see the markets today?"

Kris shook her head, so Cameron went on. "Crazy day. The EU stepped in. Bonds were up, gold was down, the Euro jumped all over the place."

"I don't follow the markets too closely."

"I thought that the FTSE would tank with the LIBOR scandal breaking."

Cameron was starting to resemble the Titanic, a gorgeous vessel heading for an iceberg, but he refused to change course.

"I tried two currency swaps but got killed on both. Never bet against the dollar, I guess."

"You're a trader, I take it."

Cameron nodded, but his eyes were now glued to the screen of his phone. "Hold on, one sec, the Asian markets are just opening,"

Kris tossed her hair trying to attract Cameron's attention but the Yuan seemed to hold more charm. Fortunately, Evan returned quickly, re-engaging Mindy in an animated conversation. Kris took a deep swallow of her beer. "I work for Illuminate," she said to no one in particular. Cameron looked up briefly, but then a text popped up on his screen.

"I like to run naked in Central Park," she declared.

"Me too. I run after work." Cameron tapped a few more times, then looked up. "What did you say?"

"Gotcha." Kris smiled mischievously.

"OK, OK, I get it." Cameron slipped his phone halfway into his pants pocket, but still within his grasp. "Where are you from?" he asked.

Kris told him a few snippets of her life story, but quickly realized that Cameron was primarily interested in Cameron. His ship was sinking fast. Kris gazed around the restaurant, pondering her exit strategy, finally signaling to Mindy that a trip to the ladies' room was in order.

"He's cute," Mindy said, standing in front of a mirror to freshen up her lipstick.

"With the intellectual depth of a wading pool," Kris replied as she washed her hands. "Is your mind still in the gutter?" she asked mischievously.

Mindy arched her eyebrows, smiling as she nodded yes. "What did you have in mind?"

"Follow me, girl," Kris said, heading for the door.

■ ■ ■

Fifteen minutes later, after brief goodbyes and an even briefer cab ride, Kris and Mindy were standing on Elizabeth Street underneath the kitchy neon palm tree adorning the entrance to Tropical 128.

"My favorite honky tonk," Kris explained as they stepped inside. "This place would work in any ski town."

"Looks more like the beach," Mindy added, as they crossed a wooden footpath bridging a small koi pond bringing them into a lounge area that was much larger than anyone would have expected from the street. Lush foliage, both real and plastic, swayed in the breeze provided by hidden fans. The music was loud - the crowd young and grungy. Six post-frat boys, hard to call them men Kris thought, chugged beers from a four foot high glass tower positioned in the center of their corner table. A waitress ignited a Scorpion, the bar's signature flaming drink, for two women swapping tales of their day at a New York City advertising agency.

Kris and Mindy pushed through to the bar, its neon lights glowing purple, the Yankee game on a large screen overhead. The bartender, sporting shaggy-surfer hair, smiled as he recognized Kris. "Hey there, welcome back," he said, handing her two bottles of Stella. Kris passed one on to Mindy, "No Cosmos here." She pointed towards the wall of faux boulders with a glass tank embedded in the middle. "Let's go watch the fish." For the next thirty minutes, Kris and Mindy checked out the crowd, made small talk between themselves and exchanged a few flirtatious comments with several guys passing through.

When they had finished their beers, Kris tugged on Mindy's sleeve, "Time to go to the back room," she said. They stopped at the bar for another round, then headed through the thick maroon curtains that separated the four pool tables from the lounge area.

"No surprise. All the tables are taken," Kris said.

"Fine with me. I suck at pool anyway," Mindy said cheerfully, turning to head back to the bar.

"I don't," Kris replied walking deeper into the pool hall. Mindy followed reluctantly. Kris quickly passed by the first table occupied by a co-ed group drinking heavily and playing casually. "Office party," she commented dismissively. Kris stopped at the next table, as two single men dressed in tight, skinny jeans appeared to be engaged in a more serious game. "They're cute," Mindy said quietly. Unfortunately, their dates, two even more attractive men, emerged from the restroom a minute later. "Moving right along," Kris said. The next table held even less promise. Three women, chewing gum and playing poorly, circled. Kris cringed as one player almost missed the cue ball completely, her cue stick scraping the felt. "I can do that," Mindy said.

"Tonight is definitely looking bleak," Kris said, as they approached the last table. A hulking-hermit man, wearing overalls and checkered flannel shirt, was practicing. When he stood to chalk his cue, spittle leaked out of the side of his mouth, disappearing into the bushy brown beard that masked his entire face. A red, white and blue trucker cap, emblazoned with "Made in America", perched on his head.

"Yuch," Mindy said, stepping ahead of Kris towards the exit.

"Not so fast."

"Come on."

"He's good," Kris whispered, watching the trucker line up another shot.

"He's a zero."

Just then, another zero, short, stout with large ears sprouting from both sides of his oval-shaped bald head, approached with two bottles of Bud in hand. He placed one on the wood rail behind the shooter and took a swig of the other. Neither man appeared to notice the two spectators as they began to play. Kris stayed rooted in place, watching the action intently; Mindy squirmed at her side. The beard ended the game on a five ball run, claiming a ten dollar bill from his buddy. After they finished racking the balls for the next game, the beard, cue ball in hand, turned towards Kris. "You ladies play?" he asked.

"No," Mindy replied briskly, looking away.

"A little,"Kris said, staying put.

"Well, let's get a little game of 8 ball going then. I'm Joe. Your friend can be on my team," he said placing the cue ball on the table. Mindy looked horrified.

"I'm Steve. You're with me," his bald friend said, handing a cue stick to Kris with a big smile, revealing his jumbled teeth, a dull yellow in color.

"Let's play girls against boys," Kris replied taking a step towards her friend. Mindy breathed easier.

"Any way you want it," Joe said, leaning over his cue to line up the break.

The boys won easily. Mindy really did suck, barely avoiding a scratch whenever it was her turn. Kris pocketed a few balls, but missed a few shots too. A little rusty, she claimed. Joe ended the game, calling the eight ball in the corner pocket and nailing it cleanly. He leaned his cue against the rail and put his arm around Kris' shoulder. "Let's hit the bar, ladies."

Mindy came to her friend's rescue, throwing a $10 bill on the table. "That's your stakes, right?" Steve nodded. "Then let's play another game," she said.

"You're not a hustler are you?" Steve replied, chuckling at his own joke as he racked the balls.

"Not me," Mindy said.

Kris broke this time, with authority, knocking the purple 4 ball into a corner pocket. She proceeded to pocket three more solid colored balls in a row before missing. But she left the cue ball in a difficult spot, deep in the corner and blocked by a solid. Joe didn't have a good shot but he tried anyway, leaving Mindy with a leaner that even she couldn't miss. As the orange 5 ball dropped, Mindy and Kris exchanged high fives. "One in a row," Mindy exclaimed before reverting to form and missing her next shot. Steve, clearly the weaker player among the boys, knocked in the yellow striped 9 ball but couldn't convert his next shot. Kris had the table again, as she had calculated she would. She didn't miss this time, ending the game with a flourish by banking the 8 ball into a side pocket.

"Who taught you to play like that?" Joe said with a touch of admiration. He motioned to his buddy to hand over the wager.

"My dad."

"He taught you well," Joe said stepping closer to Kris. "Let's try again. For a little higher stakes." He pulled a wad of bills from his back pocket, and placed a fifty on the green felt.

Kris ducked around, avoiding Joe's nasty beer breath and reaching for her purse. She pulled out a matching fifty and handed it to her friend. "Mindy can hold the money but she sits this one out."

"Steve needs a rest too," Joe replied, motioning his friend to the sideline. He handed his fifty to Mindy and chalked up his cue.

Kris was warmed up now. She broke, pocketing the blue striped 10 ball, and never looked back. The only solace for Joe was the great view: Kris' ass as she bent over the table, pumping her cue stick, or her breasts tumbling onto the green felt as she stretched for a long shot.

"Nice playing with you gentlemen," Kris said after the eight ball dropped. "We're going to call it a night." She placed her cue in the stand by the side of the table and picked up her purse. Mindy practically jumped to her side. "Good call," she said.

"Not so fast," Joe said, again reaching for his wad of bills. He peeled off five fifties, laying them down on the table. "Steve will match it, right?" His friend nodded meekly, drawing out his own bankroll.

"You don't want to do this, boys," Kris said, taking a step towards Joe. "Let it go."

"Fuck that. Let's see if you have any balls."

Steve was the only one who laughed. Kris fumed, but checked her wallet. "I don't have that much cash," she said.

"Don't look at me," Mindy chirped, jutting out her bony chest. "I don't have any cash - or balls for that matter."

"No tits either," Steve cracked.

Joe reached towards Kris, putting his hand on the small of her back then sliding it slowly down to her ass. "You can wager a little of your sweet loving, if you're up for it."

Kris stepped back, swiping Joe's hand away. She reached into her purse, pulled out her red leather billfold and placed all her cash in front of her on the pool table. "One hundred and thirty two dollars."

Joe picked up two of his fifties. "We're on."

"My choice of game?" Kris asked.

"Your choice now. My choice later," Joe leered in a throaty whisper, as he stepped towards his friend to chalk his cue.

"Mindy will hold the money. We'll play Nine Ball now." Kris picked up the cue ball and handed it to Joe. "Lag for the break."

Joe should have realized right then that he was in over his head. Nine Ball was a pro's game, requiring precision and strategic positioning of the cue ball after every shot. The players only use the number 1-9 balls and must always strike the cue ball into the lowest numbered ball on the table first. The winner is the player who pockets the 9 ball.

Not surprisingly, Joe's lust overcame any reason that he might once have had. He accepted the white ball and lined up his lag. That would be the last time that he would attempt a shot. Kris won the lag, knocked the eight ball into the corner pocket on the break, and ran the table without ever looking up. When the nine ball dropped, Kris breathed a deep sigh, leaned her cue against the rail, and hitched up her jeans. "Game's over," she said.

"And a good night to you gentlemen" Mindy added, opening her purse to deposit the fistful of fifties.

"Not so fast," Steve said. He had moved behind Mindy as Kris lined up her last shot and now reached around her waist to lock onto her wrist. "Kris cheated. Joe never got a turn to shoot," he said.

"I think that was the plan," Mindy said, trying to wriggle free.

"Best of three," Joe snarled, starting to rack the balls again.

"No, we won and we're done," Kris declared as she stepped towards her friend.

Steve wrapped his free hand around Mindy's waist and swung her away. Mindy's parents had taken her to a dance studio on Lexington Avenue when she was five, but Mindy wandered across the hall to a karate dojo and did not leave until she had won a national championship ten years later. The moves now were instinctive. She drove her elbow into Steve's gut, soft as a rotting pumpkin, then spun out of his grasp and drove her knee upward into his groin. The fifties scattered on the floor at her feet. Steve doubled over, puking up a nasty broth of beer and burgers all over his shoes. Mindy jumped back, "Gross," she shuddered, shaking the specks of vomit from her sleeve. Joe dropped his cue and rushed to his friend's rescue. But the curtains to the bar area ripped open as the surfer boy bartender and Tropical 128's steroid-infused bouncer rushed into the pool hall. They obviously had been watching the action unfold on the bar's surveillance cameras.

"Stop right there," the surfer shouted at Joe, as he stepped in front of Kris. "What the fuck is going on?"

"He must have had a bad clam," Mindy said, pointing to Steve, now kneeling in his own putrid puddle, hands on his groin, gasping for breath.

"We were just leaving," Kris said, borrowing a towel from the bartender and calmly picking up the bills.

"Everything square?" the bouncer asked. Joe nodded in defeat.

Kris tossed a dry twenty on the bar for a tip as they left. "There's a soup kitchen in my neighborhood that won't mind cleaning up the rest of these bills," she said.

Once they were outside, the tension cracked like a cheap glass. The girls bent over laughing. Mindy offered a high five, "Nice work, girl."

"I guess I could say the same to you," Kris replied, meeting her friend's hand.

"Where did you learn to hustle like that?" Mindy asked.

"On the ranch. I learned to play pool from my dad in our basement. But, I learned to hustle with the boys in the ranch house."

"You gambled in the ranch house?"

"Not until I was eighteen and home from school. And my dad wasn't around."

"What were the stakes?"

"Tens and twenties, most of the time."

"And the other times?"

"Every once in a while, a brave cowboy would want to play for my pants."

Mindy laughed. "A brave cowboy, or a stupid, fall off his horse drunk cowboy?"

"Hard to remember now."

"Well?" Mindy paused.

"Well what?"

"Did they ever come off?"

"My pants?" Kris asked, wiggling playfully. "Only if I wanted them too."

"Be careful, girl. You keep sticking your ass near the campfire, it's going to get toasted like a marshmallow one night."

7

As the month of April wound down, the weather in New York City warmed up; but, Anne Harmony was frozen in her own private cold spell. The pile of memos and folders on her desk, usually her all-consuming passion, held little interest this morning. She swiveled her chair around to look out the window. Trees were blooming, forming a soft green awning over a nearby park. A small sailboat glided down the Hudson. But these signs of spring did little to brighten her mood. Deion Chamberlain had not returned her calls, texts, tweets or even emails for several weeks. She had tried different pretenses - Illuminate's expansion plans, the need for more bike lanes, the mayor's crusade against the Russian mob - but all had run into a brick wall of silence. At first, she had attributed the lack of response to the mayor's busy schedule; then, she wondered what she had done to upset him; then, she began to fret that he had found a new mistress; finally, she realized that it was none of the above, or maybe all of the above. Regardless, Anne knew that she was now out. But this knowledge only motivated her to renew her efforts, like a wounded lioness trapped in a corner baring her claws. Remembering that the Mayor was a huge Yankee fan, Anne checked the sports section of the New York Times website, picked up the phone in her office and dialed Kris.

"Anything new on the terrorist threat in Brighton Beach?"

"I didn't realize that there was a terrorist threat there."

"Don't fuck with me today," Anne said, standing up and turning on the speaker. "Get me a written summary of your work by 7 tonight."

"Yes, boss," Kris replied, saluting her phone after she had hung up.

"Anne?" Mindy asked. Kris nodded.

"She's been on the rag for a while now," Mindy commented astutely.

"Rag or no rag, we have work to do today." Kris grabbed her laptop and plopped it down on the small table in the center of her team's work area. "Gather round. Let's see what we've got." Mindy topped up her coffee cup before joining her. Joe stayed welded to his screen. "Give me a few more minutes. I am almost in the back door," he said.

"What door?"

"Shit!" Joe shouted, pounding his fist on the desk. "They kicked me out again."

"Where are you going?" Kris asked.

"Nowhere, evidently," Joe said as he shuffled over. "I just emailed my files. Let me walk you guys through them."

Kris opened the attachments, then stepped aside, turning the keyboard over to Joe. He pointed to a spreadsheet of what looked like credit card numbers and expiration dates.

"I bought 50 cards on-line from 10 different websites," he started.

"Stolen cards, right?" Mindy interjected.

"Yeah, it was easy. Like shopping on Amazon."

"You could get yourself arrested," Kris said.

"Arrested again," Mindy piped in. "But, don't worry, we'll visit you in jail. Every other Sunday."

"Thanks for your thoughts, ladies. I ran the plan by our contacts in the fraud prevention units at Visa and MasterCard. They agreed to check out the accounts. No surprise, 90% of the numbers were bad. The accounts were already under surveillance or the holders had closed them down completely. "

"OK, what next?" Kris asked.

"I went back to the website where I bought the good, working cards, and tried to buy more. One hundred numbers this time. Now it gets tricky," Joe tapped a few keys and launched the "www.FreedomFighters.io" site. "The credit card site sent me here to register. At first, I thought that I was supposed to register for the weekly newsletter, but then I found this." Joe scrolled down to a small button, labeled "supplies", on the bottom of the screen. "It's a back-door commerce portal. Requires a user name and password too." Joe pointed to the registration form now showing on Kris' screen. "What's even more interesting is the server address. It re-routed me from the FreedomFighters normal server hosted in Europe, all aboveboard, to a server in Russia. Pretty fishy."

"Agreed," Kris said, twirling a curling strand of hair around her index finger.

"It gets worse," Joe said, tapping a few more keys. "I just tried to register five minutes ago. We are already getting hit with all these pings." He pointed to the graph on the screen showing a sharp spike in attempted intrusions into the Illuminate network. "Someone is trying to break into *our* system now."

"You better let our IT guys know. If these FreedomFighter guys think that we are attacking them, they might very well be counter-attacking us back," Kris said.

Mindy jumped up, skipped over to her desk, and returned with a stack of charts. "I've been tracking searches for websites that the Department of Homeland Security and the National Security Administration have on their watch lists. These sites may just be providing the news to interested American citizens, but they also may be providing operational information to potential terrorists. The big sites, like Al Jazeera, Pravda or even Inspire, show a pretty even dispersion around the city," Mindy said, pointing to a map of New York that looked like it had been attacked by a swarm of red dots. "But when we get to the more specialized Russian sites, like Resrek.com, the Brighton Beach connection becomes apparent." She flipped to a map that showed a swarm of blue dots nestled in southwest Brooklyn. "Now let's check the data on who is logging into the FreedomFighters site." Mindy nudged Joe off the hot seat in front of the computer and began to type furiously. "Look at this," she said, pointing to the screen. It showed only a handful of black dots, but they were all in a three block radius of Brighton Beach Avenue. "Could be where our bad guys live," Mindy said.

"See if you can check those addresses," Kris suggested.

"All apartment buildings," Mindy replied. "Maybe 50-60 apartments in each one."

"Can we find out exactly which ones are surfing the FreedomFighters site?" Joe asked.

"Not unless we have approval to dig into individual IP addresses." Mindy replied.

"We would need a federal warrant for that," Kris said. "And we don't even have a crime yet. We have to respect privacy rights."

Joe leaned over towards Mindy, and whispered, "She needs to get down from her fucking pulpit."

"What's that?" Kris asked, her eyes splitting a crevice in Joe's chest.

"My orange juice has too much pulp in it," Joe replied weakly, pointing to the remnants of his breakfast tray.

"Well, get some prune juice tomorrow. It will flush out all the bullshit," Kris retorted sharply. "Let's write up our progress so I can get a report to Anne by the end of the day."

■ ■ ■

"Good start," Anne said, turning away from her screen after reading the summary that Kris had emailed a few minutes ago. "What's next?"

On the opposite side of Anne's desk, Kris sat anxiously, legs crossed, jeans fashionably frayed at the knees. She wrapped her arms tightly across her chest, "Depends."

"Depends on what?" Anne asked.

"We are at the end of our legal rope right now. We need a government order to go any further."

"Which means that someone in law enforcement needs to take this report to a judge and get a warrant."

"Right. But I don't even know if we're investigating a crime, or a potential crime or whatever." Kris unfurled her arms, but then steepled her hands together in her lap.

"Let's have the mayor decide," Anne said, swiveling her chair around in a semicircle to face her printer. She scooped up three pages, wrote a brief note on the top one, and sealed the report in a legal sized envelope. "I want him to see it tonight," she added, reaching into her drawer for another envelope. "Here are our corporate seats for the Yankee game. They're right behind the Yankee dugout, just over from the Mayor's box. It starts in thirty minutes."

As Anne leaned over her desk to deliver the tickets, Kris noticed the yawning caverns under her eyes, the foundation which had camouflaged them all day now wearing thin. Too much work, too much stress, Kris thought. Anne needs to loosen up, smoke a joint, get laid. Where was her husband when she needed him?

"You can take Mindy with you," Anne said, sitting back down.

"How do you know he'll be there?" Kris asked, recovering the line of their conversation.

"The Red Sox are in town. Deion - Mayor Chamberlain - wouldn't miss it."

"What about Joe? He's the one that really uncovered the FreedomFighters site."

"I have another project lined up. You can send him in on your way out."

Kris rose, both envelopes in hand, and started for the door.

"Don't forget to give the Mayor my regards." Anne said.

■ ■ ■

Kris wanted to take a cab uptown to the Stadium, but Mindy, the true New Yorker, knew that the subway would be much faster. They arrived at the ballpark in the bottom of the first inning, no score, but the hedonistic display of food in the Legends Suite lounge waylaid them. Like a Las Vegas hotel shepherding guests through the casino en route to the registration desk, the Yankees guided their corporate customers past sumptuous tables of food before they could reach the playing field. Boasting quivers overflowing with bright red crab legs, sizzling meats drooling their gravy on platters, and fresh greens sprouting from serving stations, the buffet was the centerpiece of the Yankees' extravagant coddling of their highest paying fans. It anchored an infield sized private dining area, exposed via blue tinted windows to the main spectator concourse, enabling the masses to view the feast from afar. Technically, the buffet was free; but, tickets in the Legends Suite seating sections surrounding home plate started at $750 and topped out at $1,500 each for the front row. For a baseball game. Actually eighty-one of them over the full season.

"Where do we go first?" Kris asked, plate in hand.

"If this is ballpark food, then the Met is just another art gallery," Mindy replied, heading straight for the sirloin carver.

"We need to eat fast. Anne wants me to deliver our report directly to the mayor."

"How can you eat fast here," Mindy said, now piling her plate with crab. "Besides, the mayor is not going anywhere." She pointed to the TV monitor, showing the mayor encamped in his seats right behind the Yankees on-deck circle, empty now because the Red Sox were up.

"Good point," Kris said between bites of a quesadilla. "I'm starved."

The candy display was the final obstacle to reaching their seats. Mindy snatched two packs of M&Ms while Kris opted for Cracker Jacks.

"I could learn to like baseball," Mindy said, as they stepped out into the lights at last. The Yankees were batting again, still no score. The crowd was in full roar, chanting "Boston Sucks" in fine New York fashion. A blue uniformed usher checked their tickets. "Great seats," he said, guiding them towards the field.

"We need to get this to the Mayor," Kris said, pointing to his back, now visible two rows away.

"Sorry, the mayor doesn't sign autographs," the usher replied.

"This is business."

"I'm sure it is, but you will have to check with his security detail," he said, dusting off their two plush seats with a damp white cloth. "Can I bring you a drink?"

At the first break in the action, crowd finally quieting, Mindy stood, waved both hands over her head and yelled to Willis Frazier, who had turned to scan the crowd. He smiled a bit hesitatingly, but urged them forward. The mayor still faced the field, apparently chatting with Ripcurl Reilly who had just kneeled down in the on-deck circle, swiping his bat with a pine tar rag.

"Anne Harmony at Illuminate asked me to deliver this to Mayor. It's important," Kris said.

"I know Ms. Harmony. I'll take it," Willis replied. Kris hesitated.

"I will hand it to the mayor myself. I promise. Right after the inning," Willis added.

"OK. We're sitting right there if he needs us," Kris said passing the envelope to Willis.

"Go Yankees," Mindy piped in before they returned to their nearby seats. "Now let's go back to the buffet."

"Not yet. Let's get a few beers and watch the game."

"I've never been to a baseball game."

"What? You grew up in New York City."

"So did twelve million other people, most of whom have not been to Yankee Stadium."

"On TV?"

"Nope. My folks were into the theater, not sports. My two younger sisters danced, like my parents wanted them to. I did karate."

"And we know the rest of that story."

"Amen."

The public address announcer interrupted the rest of their conversation, booming "Leading off for the New York Yankees, number 33 Matthew Reilly," He slowly enunciated each syllable, stirring the excitement of the crowd. The old Beach Boys' tune, Surfin' USA, blared while an animation of a surfer riding a wave flashed on the giant high def screen out in centerfield, followed by a photo of Ripcurl's smiling, boyish face. The girls didn't need any magnification. They were close enough to the field to see Reilly's pimples pop. The camera then panned around the stadium showing women in various states of hysteria, screaming out his name. "That's my favorite," Mindy said, pointing down the right field line to a twenty-something year old, breasts bursting out of a tight fitting Yankee jersey, brandishing a sign with a color photo of a giant, foaming, curling wave and the block letters: RIDE ME.

"Reilly could take a dip in my ocean anytime," Kris said, absentmindedly fiddling with the top button on her shirt.

"Shit, here we go again," Mindy muttered to herself.

■ ■ ■

Reilly uncoiled his signature swing, heels digging deep into the dirt, bat whipping violently through the strike zone. Unfortunately it whipped well in front of the slow curveball tossed by the Red Sox pitcher. "Strike three," the umpire intoned, contorting his entire body, gleefully it seemed, to point Reilly towards the Yankee dugout. The crowd still cheered in support of the young hero as he slowly ambled back stopping briefly on the top step to remove his batting helmet, shake out his blond locks and put on his cap.

"Next time, amigo," said Curtis Davis, a reserve outfielder and Reilly's only legitimate friend on the team, as Reilly rejoined their perch at the far end of the Yankee bench. Although three years older than Reilly, Davis was the second youngest player on the veteran Yankee squad. Unlike Reilly who was a pure power hitter, Davis relied on speed, bat control and defense to earn his place in the big leagues. He had signed with the Yankees as a twentieth round draft choice after three years of college at Arizona State, no bonus offered, and then worked his way up through two years in the minors. The Yankees had drafted Reilly in the first round right out of high school, paying him a $1.2 million dollar bonus to skip college and leave the beach. The scouts were right as Reilly catapulted through the Yankees' minor league organization in three years, catching up with Davis last year in AAA. The brass would have preferred to give Reilly at least one more year to mature in the minors, but they needed his star power to sell those expensive seats. They promoted Davis too to provide age appropriate moral support. The young outfielders now shared an apartment in Manhattan and a hotel room on the road. Reilly paid almost all the bills.

"How can he throw that chickenshit curve on 3 and 1 *and* 3 and 2? Those are fastball counts, dude," Reilly said plaintively.

"In the minors they are, but you're in the majors now, big boy. Be patient, stop flailing."

"I'd like to flail at that redhead sitting behind the dugout. Great rack."

"Hey, shithead, focus on the game. Watch the pitcher's motion. His delivery point," Davis said, pointedly guiding his young friend's attention back to the field.

Nevertheless, Reilly couldn't resist twisting around for a quick glance at Kris when he climbed the dugout steps to head back into right field for the third inning. The game progressed quickly for a Yankee - Red Sox encounter. Both teams boasted hitters experienced at avoiding bad pitches, fouling good ones off and taking a walk, so games could easily last four hours or more. When Reilly returned to the dugout after the top of the fifth, still no score, he slapped his cap down in disgust.

"What's up?" Davis asked, standing to stretch. He might go in as a pinch runner or defensive replacement in the next few innings, depending on the game situation. "You were in the right position on that liner. It was just hit too hard to make a play."

"I know that, dude. But that red-headed babe is going to leave soon. I can see her pal pulling on her."

"Fuck that, surfer boy. You're in the hole this inning. Hit a bomb now. Chase the pussy later."

Reilly smiled, offering his pal a fist bump. "That's the plan, dude." He watched as the Yanks' lead-off hitter grounded out to short, then put on his batting helmet and headed into the on deck circle. The crowd roared as soon as he appeared. Reilly smiled. He could barely hear the words of encouragement from his new pal Mayor Chamberlain but he didn't turn around. He followed his friend's advice, studying the pitcher carefully. When the next Yankee batter struck out, Reilly decided not to wait for that bullshit curveball again.

Reilly strode slowly into the batter's box, letting the surging cheers propel him. He took two practice swings, loosening up, then anchored his back heel deep in the dirt. One more deliberate arc of the bat before setting his hands high. Mind relaxed, everything moving in slow motion. Eyes lasered on the right hand of the pitcher now midway through his wind-up. If he was right, Ripcurl knew that he would have less than half a second to react. He was ready to ride.

The wall of sound from the fifty thousand Yankee faithful cascaded down as Reilly trotted past first base. He had timed the pitch perfectly, sensed the weightlessness of the bat as its sweet spot launched the ball into the lights, watched the second baseman coil but then relax in defeat as the ball rocketed over his head. A few weeks ago, his first major league home run, he had flipped his bat and stayed in the batter's box to savor the flight of the ball. But he had paid the price for that arrogance. His manager and teammates had lectured Reilly about the ballplayers' code and the opposing pitcher had enforced it by hitting him squarely in the butt with a 98 mile per hour fastball in his next at bat.

Tonight, Reilly acted the role of the humble rookie, head down until he reached third base, finally looking up to shake hands with his coach waiting there. The final stretch was always the best part of the journey, returning to his teammates gathered around the plate to welcome him back home.

Reilly jogged the last few yards to the dugout slowly, reveling in the adulation. The crowd chanted "Rip-Curl, Rip-Curl", emphasis on both syllables. He nodded slightly towards Mayor Chamberlain, now standing along with all the fans in the lower seats. But Reilly quickly shifted his glance to the mayor's right side, just behind the Yankee dugout. Kris and Mindy were standing too, beers in hand, clapping in appreciation of his feat.

"Told you, dude," Reilly said with a huge grin as he returned to his usual perch. Davis could only laugh and shake his head. It all came so easy for his friend, at least right now. The crowd would not relent, its "Rip-Curl" roar pounding down, engulfing the field with its exuberance. The game stopped. Finally, the Yankee manager, Mike Rosetti, walked the length of the bench, rubbing his fingers through his thin crown of prematurely gray hair which had earned him the nickname of "the Caesar" because of the resemblance to the Roman hero and his abilities as a field general. Mike had been a minor league catcher for the Yankees for five years before a torn labrum in his throwing shoulder ended his playing career. The team liked his smarts though, starting him out as a scout, sweating profusely for three summers on hot dusty fields in the deep South, and then promoting him through the managerial ranks. He had skippered the major league team for the past ten years, managing the mostly veteran players with a light hand, and winning two World Series. Mike had no doubt that the adulation would ultimately melt the mind of his young slugger, if his prick didn't fall off first; but he had no choice. The fans had spoken and they paid the bills. He pointed Reilly towards the field. Reilly grinned, then hopped up to the top step of the dugout. He turned to tip his cap, blond hair shining in the lights like a gladiator returning to the arena, the enemy's blood still on his sword. The crowd roared one final time. Kris too.

"Now we reel in the pussy, dude," Reilly said quietly to his buddy making a casting motion while sitting on the bench as the game resumed. "She's got the hook in her mouth and she's twisting on the end of the line. I can feel it." He motioned to one of the bat boys, maybe sixteen, blond, peach fuzz on both cheeks. He promptly trotted over, eager to be of service to the young star. Reilly asked for two baseballs and a sharpie marker. He scrawled *RIPCURL* with his private mobile number on the first one. He passed the second one to Davis along with the marker. "Sign it."

"Why? Who would want my autograph?"

"No one," Reilly laughed. "But it looks better this way. That redhead is going to put her number on the other side and send it back to us."

He handed both balls back to the bat boy and pointed him to the stands. The teenager hesitated, but Reilly reassured him, "Long red hair, two rows back." He cupped an imaginary pair of breasts. "You can't miss her."

"You are going to get me cut, man," Davis wailed.

"No way, you're riding with Ripcurl. It's cool, dude."

The crowd sparked as the next Yankee batter lofted a fly ball to center, but the Red Sox outfielder reeled it in on the warning track, ending the inning. Reilly jogged out to right. The bat boy slipped into the stands. The Caesar caught the exchange, but didn't try to stop it, at least right now. Locker room gossip had already informed him that Reilly swung a big bat off the field as well as on it. He would talk to the youngster after the game, but lecturing hormonal young superstars to keep their zippers up was like convincing an alcoholic to pass up an open bar. The temptations were simply too good-looking and too easy. Reilly might fuck himself out of the spotlight one day, but Rosetti needed him to help the team win at least one more World Series before then.

■ ■ ■

"One more beer?" Kris asked, while signaling the waitress to return to their seats.

"Two is my limit," Mindy replied. "But don't let me stop you," she added, a bit sarcastically.

"Another Stella," Kris ordered. "One of those big pretzels too."

"Sampling all the food groups," Mindy noted, as the waitress headed back up the steps.

The batboy slipped into the empty seat behind them, tapping Kris on the shoulder. "These are from Mr. Reilly," he said, handing down the two balls.

Kris looked at the first, and smiled. She turned over the second with a puzzled look. "Can't read the scrawl here."

"No problem," the young batboy took the ball back and spun it around to the blank side. "You can just sign it here. I'll bring it back to Mr. Reilly."

"He wants *my* autograph?"

"I think that he would prefer your phone number," he said with a surprisingly straight face.

"Oh no," Mindy interjected. "You're not going there."

When Kris hesitated, Mindy grabbed the ball from the batboy's hand, announcing, "I think the Yankees need this one back." She did her best imitation of a wind-up and tossed the ball onto the playing field.

The batboy's eyes shot open as if he had seen Babe Ruth's ghost streak across the diamond. The umpire, mask off standing behind home plate waiting for the inning to start, looked surprised but he calmly picked up the ball and rolled it towards the Yankee dugout. Unfortunately, the security staffer, muscled like a professional athlete himself, who promptly appeared at Mindy's side was not so sanguine.

"M'am, you're going to have to come with me. Your friend too."

Mindy thought for a second about arguing but the sight of two policemen waiting at the top of the aisle changed her mind. "We were just leaving," she said instead, standing. Kris followed, after slipping the Reilly ball into her purse. The fans surrounding them, corporate types, folded away as Mindy and Kris followed the security detail towards the exit.

"Wait, please," Willis Frazier's voice boomed from behind them. "I need to talk to these ladies for a second." The policeman, recognizing Willis, held up his hand to stop the procession. Willis bounded up two steps. "I can't rescue you this time. But the mayor wanted you to tell Anne that he appreciated the report." He hesitated, then added, "He'll call her as soon as he can to follow up."

Kris nodded, turning to rejoin the embarrassing parade.

"What does he mean by that comment?" Mindy asked as they stepped away. Kris just shrugged.

The security supervisor, Kiara Griffin on her nametag, a middle-aged black woman with short, graying curls and commanding green eyes, marched them into her office in the bowels of the stadium, checking their Illuminate IDs and ticket stubs. She had been a math teacher in one of New York City's rougher public middle schools for five years before she realized that she relished supervising the crush in the hallways much more than actually teaching the kids. "I thought that you might have been groupies. The players give them freebies sometimes, you know," she said.

"Not us," Mindy replied. Nevertheless, Ms. Griffin steered them out into the street with a brief schoolmarm-style lecture on ballpark behavior and the admonition that the Yankees expect better from their season ticket holders.

"Upset?" Mindy asked as they trudged back to the subway to return to Manhattan.

"Not really. But, you have to admit, Reilly has style." Kris riposted.

8

Anne Harmony flipped the display on her computer from the YES network feed of the Yankee game to her Illuminate home screen. She had caught a glimpse of Kris and Mindy sitting near the mayor as the camera panned the Yankee dugout. He would get the report. Now, she turned her attention to Joe Brady, slouching on the chair in front of her desk.

"Tough day?" she asked.

"No, ma'am," Joe replied, getting the message, pulling both hands out of his pockets and straightening up.

"You did good work on the FreedomFighters site."

"Thank you."

"I want you to keep digging there, but I have another project for you too."

"OK," Joe said slowly. *In my spare time?* He wanted to ask but thought better of it.

Anne pushed a file folder across her desk. "I need you to do a complete Web check on these guys. They are all in the public eye."

Joe picked up the file and thumbed through the pages. He vaguely recognized the first two, local officials he thought he had seen in the news recently, but the last three were nationally known, two governors from East Coast states and the Democratic senator from New York.

"What am I looking for?"

Anne stood and stepped around her desk. She had client meetings all day so she had worn her power attire, a smoke gray chalk stripe Chanel pants suit and white blouse, open at the throat to reveal a single strand of rotund pearls. Anne strode to the door to her office, closed it, then returned to sit on the edge of her desk. Joe watched in silence.

"Everything. Anything. I want to know where they get the news, where they shop, who they follow on Twitter, if they send photos of their dicks to anyone." Anne folded her hands in her lap, "Understand?"

"Will Kris be in the loop? She's my boss."

"No need to bring Miss Fourth Amendment into this."

"Is it legal?"

Anne leaned forward, placing her hands on her knees. She could see a bead of sweat form on Joe's upper lip.

"Funny question from a guy who got picked up by the cops only a few weeks ago with a couple of tabs of meth and a stash of pot. Seems to me you have a debt to repay."

Joe squirmed, slipping his hands back into his pockets. "I get the point," he said, staring at the floor.

"Report back directly to me in two weeks," she said, standing, breaking the tension.

Joe nodded and sulked to the door.

■ ■ ■

The Yankee bullpen came through, stranding Red Sox runners on third base in the eighth and the ninth to preserve the 1-0 win. Mayor Chamberlain arrived back at his Brooklyn home just before midnight, exhausted but still too wired to go to bed. The Yanks were already five games up in the American League East, but still had two thirds of the season ahead. Nevertheless, Deion lingered over the anticipation of another World Series in the Bronx: he would be in the national spotlight every other night for the entire month of October: a true fan. The electorate would love it. Never too early to begin paving the road to Washington.

Deion poured himself a tumbler of port, Ware's ten year old, not particularly expensive, and sat at his desk in the wood panelled library. A tall grandfather clock cast a patrician's eye over him as it chimed the witching hour, while the gas fireplace provided a warm glow. He could see his two security guards in position on the front stoop, sneaking a cigarette. Deion had moved back into the brownstone after two long weeks in exile. He and Tanya had run out of explanations. One of the boys had the flu; then Tanya caught the mysterious ailment; Deion had to work late; he had to travel to Albany to meet with the governor. The Page Six gossip columnist at the Post was asking too many questions so Tanya relented. She erected a Berlin Wall of pillows down the middle of their bed, her intentions, or lack thereof, perfectly clear, but she appeared with Deion at political events on consecutive nights, quieting the rumors. A night enjoying the wine and jazz at Ginny's in Harlem silenced them completely. The boys, thrilled to have their dad home, broke the frame of Calvin's bed in an exuberant wrestling match. Deion did try to cross the DMZ one night, but Tanya repelled his advance. Then, early last Saturday morning without any warning, she finally warmed, dismantling the barricade before their sons awoke. Tentative at first, they quickly regained a familiar rhythm. A guttural moan from deep inside Tanya's ample, swaying bosom confirmed their reunion. Deion was content; his family life and his career, back on track.

Anne's report was an unwelcome interruption. Deion had observed his agreement with Tanya to the letter, not returning a single call or email from Anne for the past month. At first, flattered, he thought the envelope contained a missive from his jilted lover, but a quick glance while at the Stadium revealed its more serious content. Anne's handwritten note on the top page was brief and all business, but he feared that even her signature would arouse suspicion. Better to deal with it now when Tanya was asleep. He read the memo slowly, then refilled his port and walked over to the fireplace. Deion was torn: he wanted to nail the Russian mob, had spoken out vehemently against it around the city, but Anne was poison, at least in this house. He stood in front of the glowing fire, the light just bright enough, and went through the document point by point. The Freedomfighter site certainly seemed suspicious, but international credit card fraud was not necessarily the bailiwick of the NYPD. There were no names or even any crimes. No terrorist plots in the works. Just suspicions and the desire to dig deeper into the communications of private citizens. He would need to turn the document over to his chief of police who would then have to go to a judge to seek a warrant. They could proceed secretly, but ultimately the news would leak, angering the ACLU and the rest of the fourth amendment crowd, not to mention his wife. He would need more than this to justify stirring up that hornet's nest. Deion tossed the memo into the flames and climbed the stairs to bed.

■ ■ ■

Anne's breakfast meeting the next morning ran late. The head of advertising at a prominent national restaurant chain was angry that Illuminate had just raised prices on its mobile clicks. She had to walk him through the return on investment figures and throw in some prime real estate on their restaurant review pages to calm him. Now, she had a backlog of emails, all marked urgent, to work through. Her voicemail light, flashing red, would have to wait. Finally, an hour later, she listened to the lone message, slamming her phone down in anger afterwards. A deputy assistant, she couldn't even remember his name, had called to say that the mayor had read her report and had decided not to proceed further at this time. He left his number in case Anne had any further questions. She would move to New Jersey before she would ever call him back. Not the Mayor. Not even Willis Frazier. But a deputy assistant fuck off. What a kick in the ass. On a personal level. And a professional level. Anne stalked to her window, staring at the cityscape for ten full minutes, composing herself. Then she strode purposefully down the lonely corridor, report rolled up in her hand and head held high.

Mindy was alone in the bullpen, sipping coffee and pecking on her keyboard, when Anne stormed in. "Where is everyone? We have to talk," she announced, placing both hands on her hips. "Now."

"Joe just texted. He should be here in ten minutes."

Anne made a show of checking her watch. "Pretty late to roll in. Isn't it?"

"He had several projects going on, so he pulled an all-nighter. He just went home to change."

"And Kris?" Anne asked, not relenting, obvious that her patience was being tested.

"She said that she had to pee. I can go and see if she's finished yet."

Even Anne had to laugh. "No, that's OK. I'll wait."

Five minutes later, Kris strolled back into the bullpen, coffee and an apple danish in hand, surprised to see Anne sitting on the side of her desk scanning the report that her team had prepared.

"About time," Anne said. Mindy swiveled her chair and arched her eyebrows, giving Kris a warning signal.

"What's up?" Kris asked.

"The mayor's office shot down your report. All conjecture. No names or hard facts. Not enough to seek a warrant," Anne said, tapping the rolled up report on her thigh and biting her lower lip, barely winning the battle to maintain her composure.

"That's what the mayor said?" Kris asked incredulously. "I thought that he wanted to go after the Russian mob."

"Well, he didn't actually say anything. I got the message from one of the deputy assistants in the office."

Kris started to speak, but then thought better of it. Anne went on in a flat, unemotional tone.

"We have many other projects to work on. Fortress Illuminate is always under siege somewhere. Let's put this one on the back burner for now."

Just then, Joe powered into the bullpen, backpack slung across his shoulders. "Good morning, ladies," he said zestily, before noticing their visitor. He nodded to Anne and slipped over to his desk.

"You have a lot of energy for someone who worked all night," Anne remarked.

"The power of Red Bull," Joe replied.

"Anyway, I just told the team that the FreedomFighter report got nixed. Time to crank up other investigations. You have those spear-fishing emails to Macy's customers and the dummy bids on search terms for women's deodorants, right?"

"Yes, ma'am," Joe said, pulling his laptop from the pack and making a show of getting down to work.

"Wait a second," Kris interjected. "Joe showed me more stuff that he dug up on FreedomFighter last night. He's really making progress."

"I don't want to hear it today," Anne said, eyes down. "Just get to work. I've got some banner ads to sell." She headed back to her office, the aura of defeat apparent in every step.

"Wow. I thought that she was tight with the mayor," Mindy said.

"Obviously, not that tight," Kris said, taking her seat.

"I bet that this is more than just the rejection of an investigation. She's got that jilted lover look."

"Anne's married. Great looking, big shot guy too."

"Who lives in San Francisco. Love the one you're with," Mindy started to sing the opening lines. "I saw Crosby, Stills at the Beacon last week with Evan," she added by way of explanation.

"Spare us," Joe broke into the conversation. "Let's just do what Anne says." Then, looking accusingly at Kris, "Besides, you're always defending everyone's fourth amendment rights anyway."

"But I think that you're onto something right now. We can get to 'probable cause.' I hate to see this dead-ended so quickly."

"Maybe for the wrong reasons, too," Mindy jumped back into the conversation with a slight, knowing nod.

Kris paced in front of her desk for only a minute. "Let's ramp up the other stuff for a few days. Show Anne some progress. I'll take the FreedomFighter analysis over to Jim Bright as soon as I get a break. Let's see the FBI's reaction," she said.

■ ■ ■

"I'm getting a hard-on just looking around," Glenn Walker said drolly, admiring a mannequin dressed in a matching set of electric lime lingerie - bra, navel-highlighting waspie, thong and garter belt. He and Jim Bright had just entered the Agent Boudoir boutique on Madison Avenue. They mingled with the crowd of shoppers, mostly young women. "Surprised more men aren't in here. This is fun."

"Keep it in your pants. We're here on business," Jim Bright replied nodding towards the cash register manned by Lynne Springer, Derek Miller's girlfriend, wearing white pants that spotlighted her lithe, dancer's legs and a pale yellow blouse sheer enough to reveal a low-cut, honey-colored bra underneath. "She just got hired. The scamming crew won't be far behind."

"Her hair is different," Glenn said. Lynne had grown out her short spiky blond hair to shoulder length. And removed the purple streak that she had once dyed in. "I missed her completely the first time through the background check photos. You were right to go through them again."

"She doesn't want to be recognized, obviously. That's why we had to check her out in person," Jim said.

"Not exactly hardship duty."

Jim strolled to the back of the store, stopping at another mannequin in a lacy red outfit.

"Think about Marcy or Stephanie prancing around your apartment in that," Glenn said, sidling up behind him. "Or maybe Kris," he wisecracked.

Just then, a stiletto-thin saleswoman with light coffee colored skin, approached.

"Can I help you gentlemen?" she asked.

"Just looking," Glenn offered. "My wife's birthday is coming up."

Jim smothered a laugh. "We need to head back to the office."

They walked over to Lexington Avenue to catch the subway downtown. When they arrived back, Glenn started preparing the report of their day's activities, deciding not to mention the fact that they had drooled over the lingerie. Jim scanned two message slips on his desk and headed off to the men's room. He returned with tie straightened, hair combed and a trace of cologne.

"Did you clean up just for me?" Glenn asked when he returned.

"Kris is going to stop by soon. She has a report that she wants to show us," he said, embarrassed that his partner had noticed.

"I don't want you to think about that Agent Boudoir get-up now. It will cloud your brain," Glenn said before returning to his typing. Jim took the ribbing in stride, but the image of Kris in the red underwear lingered as he scanned another batch of ID photos on his screen.

Fifteen minutes later, Jim's phone rang. "A Kris Storm here to see you," the receptionist droned.

"Send her back."

"Hey, guys," Kris trilled as she stepped towards Jim. "I want to get your thoughts on this." She dropped her leather satchel on the floor and bent over to remove two copies. Her black jeans, embroidered with small, diamond-shaped sequins on both back pockets, tapered into well-worn black, calf-length boots. She had set her hair up in a bun for the day in the office. Jim and Glenn took the reports and began to read. Kris sat down in the chair between their desks, vaguely noticing the scent of cologne but not quite sure who was wearing it.

Jim finished first. "Great work. It gives us some clues to the source of the hot credit cards. What do you want us to do now?"

"I'm not sure. Anne Harmony, my boss, sent this report over to the Mayor's office. She thought that he would get a warrant to dig deeper."

"But?"

"He shot her down."

"Doesn't leave us that many options then."

"Can't you link the Russian card connection to the Russian mob guy that almost killed you?"

"It's not that easy. Russia's a big country," Jim said, then added, "Remember the fourth amendment, too?"

"I know, I know," Kris said, now twirling a loose tendril of red hair around her index finger.

"What about Crazy 8?" Glenn piped in.

Jim flashed a warning look to his partner, but Glenn went on. "We have reason to believe that an operative, nicknamed Crazy 8, recently entered the United States. We know that the Russian mob welcomed him but we haven't been able to find out anything else. No name, no photo, no address."

"You've got a source inside the Russian mob?" Kris asked.

"We didn't say that," Jim said hurriedly.

Kris stopped twirling and jumped up. "OK, OK. But we have identified a prominent source of hot credit cards, hosted in Russia, accessible only through a back-door, password-protected commerce portal on a website that spouts jihadi news, and we know the addresses in New York City, primarily in Brighton Beach, that are searching for this website. Now we add in this big-time operator, who just arrived in the same neighborhood. Isn't that enough to get a warrant to dig deeper?"

"When you put it all together like that, you may be right," Glenn said.

"We'll start working on the paperwork tonight," Jim said, turning his attention to his computer screen. "I just sent an email to our lawyers and Homeland Security to get the ball rolling on their end. We should be able to get the warrant in two or three days at most."

"Potential terrorist threats usually get everyone's attention," Glenn said, handing Jim a thick binder. "Here are our surveillance reports to get you started."

"Once we get the warrant, we can head back to Brighton Beach and start scouting around. We need to set our locations for the communications intercepts."

"I think I could use a little sun this weekend," Kris declared, peering out the window at the steel-gray cityscape.

"A trip to Brighton Beach might be just what the doctor ordered then," Jim replied, flipping through the reports to hide his smile.

"We're visiting the in-laws in Jersey this weekend, so you two will have to go without me," Glenn chipped in, a bit hurriedly.

9

Jim Bright sprinted the final quarter mile along the waterfront before turning inland to return to his apartment on Bridge Street in one Brooklyn's now trendy neighborhoods, Downtown Under the Manhattan Bridge Overpass, DUMBO for short. Normally, the reflection of the rising sun on the skyline of Lower Manhattan, just across the East River, occupied his attention for most of the five mile run, but this morning Jim hardly noticed. His thoughts were focused on Kris Storm and their upcoming afternoon together. He climbed the stairs to his apartment slowly, savoring his surroundings. Jim had just moved in three months ago. His first solo apartment. Big shot lawman now, his friends back in Canarsie had jibed. He was still in Brooklyn, Jim countered. Not too far from home. In fact, Jim had lived at home during his terms at City College and Brooklyn College law school, then shared an apartment with friends during his first years with the Bureau. While Jim would admit that he occasionally longed for the camaraderie of his old roommates, particularly on weeknights after a long day, he certainly did not miss their detritus: stacked pizza boxes, stuffed up toilets, unknown women mumbling an embarrassed morning greeting. The new apartment, at $3,000 per month, stretched his budget but it did come fully furnished. Jim was twenty-eight now, time to step up in the world.

After a long shower, Jim agonized for the third time over his choice of attire before deciding to go totally casual, khaki shorts and a mango/

gray checked Island Hopper short sleeve shirt, purchased yesterday at the Patagonia store downtown. The clerk had assured him that the moisture wicking fabric would not show any sweat stains under his arms. As a side benefit to his new digs, Jim could commute to the office on foot or on his bike, a short hop over the bridge, or by subway. He had considered selling his car, but his attachment to his wheels, an eight year old silver Audi A4 convertible, was too strong. And he could park it at his parents for free. Jim had returned to Canarsie last night, ostensibly for dinner, but actually to pick up the car. He drove in this morning, arriving around 9, parking right outside the FBI building, an almost impossible feat during the week. Jim had to review the file for a new case, an attempted bank robbery on the East Side, before picking Kris up at noon, but his concentration was sketchy at best. The warm, stale air in the office didn't help. He had forgotten that the FBI shut down the AC on Sundays to save money.

Jim picked up the new file but put it back down unopened. Instead, he scanned the top page of the warrant application on his desk, asking the court to authorize the FBI to tap into electronic communications from the IP addresses in Brighton Beach that regularly accessed the FreedomFighters site. He thought that approval would be a lay-up but the judge from the federal government's secretive Foreign Intelligence Surveillance Court, established in 1978 specifically for this purpose, had rejected it yesterday, citing the new regulations that the President had recently put in place. From 2008 to 2012, the FISC had only declined two of over 8,000 warrant requests from the FBI and NSA combined. But, after ex-government contractor Edward Snowden had leaked thousands of pages of classified documents revealing the US government's spying programs and tactics, the rules of counter-terrorism had changed. The wheels grinded much more deliberately now, the FBI lawyers had explained, unless Jim and Glenn could demonstrate a "fast-moving exigency", their words exactly. How could they discover a "fast-moving exigency" if they couldn't tap into communications? The lawyers believed that they would get the warrant eventually, but would need to provide a much more detailed rationale. It could take another two weeks. Might be too late then, who knows. Jim had not told Kris the bad news yet.

At last, time for the rendezvous. He texted that he was on his way. Kris replied that she would meet him outside her office in 10 minutes. Fortunately, the weather report looked great, sunny and seventy-five, as the popular country song went.   In the elevator, he visualized Kris in a string bikini, a pleasant diversion. Jim tapped the remote control in his pocket as soon as he reached the street. The navy blue ragtop peeled slowly back finally descending into the trunk. Jim ran through his checklist one more time. He had packed for every possibility: beach blanket, cooler, umbrella, portable Wi-Fi interceptor, holster, gun. Reflexively, he checked the small of his back. His weapon was there, hidden by his floppy, untucked shirt. Jim settled his wraparound Oakley sunglasses on the bridge of his nose and climbed in.

Kris was waiting on the sidewalk chatting with a gawkily tall young man who had his brown hair tied back in a ponytail. She sported an orange Denver Broncos jersey, number 18 of course, draped over white denim shorts with matching open toed sandals on her feet. The white straps of a bow-tied halter top dangled at the back of her neck. Jim felt a brief stab of jealousy, but then relaxed as Kris said a quick good-bye and stepped around to the passenger side of the Audi, pulling a Broncos cap out of her multi-colored beach bag before tossing the bag into the back seat.

"Nice wheels," she said, fixing the cap over her own ponytail.

"Thanks. Get a lot of work done this morning?."

"Met with one of our techies. The guy I was talking to," Kris said.

"Is he a Broncos fan?"

"Yeah, how did you know?"

Duh. I could become a Broncos fan too, Jim thought, noting how Kris' full breasts levitated beneath the oversized blue numerals on the jersey.

"Just a guess," he said instead. Pulling away from the curb, he added, "Too early for football for me. I'm a baseball guy. My Mets are right in the middle of the race."

"Mindy and I went to the Yankee game last week. We had a blast."

"Did you see that Ripcurl Reilly? What a jerk for a rookie."

"He looked OK to me."

A city bus pulled away from the curb and cut in front of the Audi. Jim had to jam on the breaks, cursing. "Bus drivers think they own the damn street." He decided to take the short way, through the Battery Tunnel, and pay the $7.50 toll. No commuter buses in the tunnel on Sunday.

"Fresh Brooklyn air," Jim exclaimed as the Audi emerged into the sunlight. They zipped through the E-Z Pass lane onto the Brooklyn-Queens Expressway heading towards the Verrazano Bridge and Staten Island. The highway soared above the industrial Sunset Park neighborhood and the warehouses and lofts of the Brooklyn waterfront. Fifty years ago the piers would have been active, the embarkation point for goods and tourists heading to Europe, but they were deserted now. Jim turned the radio up, Sirius XM's Alternative Rock channel, as Cage the Elephant's "Ain't No Rest for the Wicked" came on. Jim sneaked a glance at Kris, tossing her ponytail back and forth as she hummed along. No traffic on Sunday so they quickly reached the fork for the Belt Parkway headed towards Long Island. The Audi took the long curved ramp gracefully. Jim stepped on the gas as the highway flattened out, stretching along the shoreline and passing under the Verrazano Bridge. A mammoth cruise ship, departing from Manhattan now, headed out into the Atlantic. Five minutes later, he pulled off the highway at the Ocean Parkway exit, swept through the intersection with Brighton Beach Avenue, and emerged onto Surf Avenue heading into Coney Island.

"Wasn't that the way to Brighton Beach?" Kris asked.

"Yea, but we're going to park in Coney Island, grab something to eat, and then walk on the boardwalk over to Brighton Beach. You ever been to Nathan's?"

"Sure, at the ballpark."

"Well, this is the original one. Opened in 1916." Jim said, backing the car into a parking spot nearby. The ragtop on the Audi rose slowly and locked into place. "Never take chances on the street," Jim said as he grabbed his beach bag from the trunk. Kris slung her tote across one shoulder as she followed Jim down the bustling street. "We're the minority here," he said, alluding to the sea of black and brown faces that engulfed them.

"Feels like we're in the Caribbean," Kris said

"That's a good way to look at it."

"And how does the lawman look at things?"

"Very carefully," Jim said, swiveling his head to check out the crowd. "When I was growing up this was considered a tough neighborhood. Low income housing projects. We didn't come down here very often. But it's much safer now."

Nathan's Famous hot dog stand squatted over half a block at the corner of Surf and Stillwell, a block from the Atlantic Ocean. Jim led the way to the counter. "What'll you have?"

"Two franks, fries and a beer," Kris ordered.

"Same for me. But lemonade, not beer. I'm working," Jim said.

"Really?" Kris asked, smiling. Jim fumbled with his wallet, pulling out the cash to pay the bill.

They loaded up on mustard, ketchup and sauerkraut and were in the right spot when a family of four vacated one of the concrete slabs masquerading as a picnic table just outside.

"Did you know that FDR served Nathan's franks to the Queen of England?" Jim asked between bites. Kris shook her head. "And had them shipped to Yalta for Stalin and Churchill?" She shook her head again, laughing. Jim wolfed down the rest of his lunch, suppressing a belch when he finished the last bite. Kris wasn't far behind. After tossing the trash, they headed down Surf Avenue. Kris spun around to take in the sights, some of the world's most famous amusement park rides - the Wonder Wheel, the Parachute Jump and the Cyclone, as well as one of the newest, the Thunderbolt roller coaster. Its bright orange steel track corkscrewed in dives, loops and rolls.

"Want to try?" she asked.

"Maybe later," Jim said, without much conviction. He eyed the one hundred foot high monstrosity with great suspicion as squeals of delight and horror cascaded down.

"Come on. It looks like fun," Kris dared, tugging Jim towards the ride.

"Let's head over to the boardwalk," Jim replied, steering Kris in the other direction. "It will take us right into Brighton Beach."

The boardwalk overlooked the sandy beach and the Atlantic Ocean. The day wasn't too hot, but it was certainly warm and sunny enough to bring plenty of Brooklynites out of hibernation. They strolled past elderly couples, dodged around mothers pushing strollers, and caught a stray frisbee. After three blocks, Kris grabbed Jim's elbow to lead him onto the sand. The beach, roughly as wide as a football field, was a checkerboard of blankets, coolers and umbrellas. Cocoa butter, baby oil and sweat combined into the distinctive fragrance of summer. She picked their way around, through and over the mass of bodies until they got down to the ocean. The waves rolled in but they were small ones. Kris kicked off her sandals and waded in up to her knees. Jim followed.

"The water is cold," she said, splashing Jim playfully. Kris almost tripped into the surf, but Jim caught her. She draped her arms around his back, holding on, faces close. A second longer than needed for balance? Then, Kris stepped away, her fingers, tipped with orange nail polish, lingering on Jim's arm for another moment. Jim savored the scent of her hair, the touch of her hand. While he definitely savored the contact, it reminded Jim that he had his automatic tucked into the small of his back, still hidden by his shirt tail. He reached to make sure that it was still secure. They would be headed into enemy territory shortly.

Back on the boardwalk, they passed the entranceway leading to the New York Aquarium, its tired facade adorned with carvings of swimming dolphins and schools of fish, before reaching Brighton Beach. Jim had planned their approach carefully, preferring to mingle with the beach crowd rather than risk being recognized immediately on the avenue. He was sure that he and Glenn were known to the Russian mob from their hours on the street tracking the credit card crew. The change in the streetscape was immediate: pale faces, signage in Russian, a gruff Slavic rhythm to the language. Kris slipped her hand onto Jim's elbow as they walked.

"We're in Indian country now," she said, tension creeping into her voice.

"Correct, Kemosabe," Jim was pleased that she recognized that the game had changed. "But you're safe with the Lone Ranger." He guided them towards a bench near the Brighton playground. "Let's get our bearings for a second." They watched the young children soaring on the swings, swishing down the slide, and sifting through the sand. Kris tapped her phone, calling up a local map.

"No need, I've been here many times. We're going to walk along Brightwater Court, then head up and down Fourth Street, and then over to Sixth. Most of the addresses that we want are on those blocks."

"What about the ones on Brighton Beach Avenue? Isn't that the main drag?"

"Yes but I want to avoid it as long as we can."

They chatted idly for fifteen minutes. Jim recounted tales of growing up in Brooklyn. He got mugged in the subway when he was fourteen, surrounded by three black teenagers, baggy jeans sagging down to their balls he remembered, on his way home from a Knick game at the Garden. He surrendered his wallet and his Walkman without a fight, avoiding a beating, but vowed never again. Right then and there, he committed himself to a career in law enforcement. Kris listened with interest. She had spent her elementary and middle school days near San Jose, not quite the melting pot of Brooklyn, but a city neverthe- less. Life changed dramatically when her family's financial fortune cratered and they moved to Colorado. She would tell Jim about it another time. Nature called now. She looked around for a public restroom, finally finding one across the boardwalk.

When Kris stepped away, Jim pulled the portable Wi-Fi interceptor out of his pack. It had the same dimensions as a large screen smart phone or an iPad mini. He switched it on, checked the settings, and returned it to his pack. He saw Kris heading back and met her halfway. A young girl, maybe ten, long blond hair, wobbled by on a scooter, determined but precariously unsteady, like a foal taking her first steps. Dmitri Remko, her older brother, tossed his cigarette and jumped up off his perch to intercept her just before she crashed into a startled elderly woman. The woman, wispy gray hair bundled underneath a faded shawl, berated the pair in Russian. Dmitri's obsidian eyes betrayed his penchant for violence, but he remained silent, fists clenched at his side. He turned to his baby sister, scolded her briefly and pushed her along. When Kris and Jim passed, Dmitri pulled his phone out of the back pocket of his jeans.

"Hey, Rock, check out the couple coming off the boardwalk now. They look familiar?"

"Got'em. He's one of the FBI guys. I've seen him here before." Leonard Boykin rubbed his prodigious stomach, a roll of jelly seeping over the belt buckle on his jeans, never failing to appreciate the irony of his nickname. Lenny had studied accounting at Brooklyn College. He would have been a CPA by now if he hadn't failed intermediate and mauled the professor at the bus stop that night.

"And the *pizda?*"

"Don't make her."

"She's the one that pulled the gun on Sergei on Madison Avenue. On that YouTube video, remember?" Dmitri asked as he followed Jim and Kris out of the playground.

"Just enjoying a day at the beach together. Maybe the FBI guy's fucking her now, eh?" Lenny said, stroking his goatee which resembled a tuft of unruly pubic hair.

"Nice *sis'ki*, huh."

"Or maybe they're here on business," Lenny said. "Hold on a sec," he interrupted the conversation to hand over a dollar bill to a street vendor for a can of Diet Coke.

"Police business?"

"What else?" Lenny replied. Dmitri had never been a rocket scientist.

"Should we call Mr. Nakitov?"

"Not yet. Let's just keep an eye on them. We'll call later." Lenny pondered their options as he slowly sipped his soda.

Jim and Kris turned on Brightwater Court. A municipal parking lot and the beach stretched to their right, while a row of apartment buildings, six floors high with weathered brick facades, sat across the street to their left. A copse of trees reached the second floor windows. Jim maneuvered Kris to his right side, pointing out a freighter just visible on the horizon. His interceptor needed a clear line of sight. Jim knew that his chances of garnering any real intelligence were slim, but he hoped to at least test the strength of the signals from the buildings. The interceptor was relatively new and he wanted to make sure he set it up right when the warrant came through. He slowed their pace and then stopped, leaning on the low fence guarding the parked cars and staring out into the ocean. Kris stood close, a cluster of pinpoint freckles visible on her nose. She tracked the freighter for a minute or two, but then swiveled around to check out the buildings. Jim sensed her impatience and resumed their casual stroll. They made a left on Brighton Fourth, heading towards the Avenue.

Dmitri was fifty yards behind them. He kept walking straight along Brightwater Court, signaling to Lenny, across the street, that he should pick up the surveillance now. Lenny huffed into position, relieved that his targets were keeping a leisurely pace. He snapped a photo with his phone, then turned to snap another one of the beach, trying to look disinterested.

Glenn Walker wasn't fooled. He had been tailing Jim and Kris all afternoon. Jim had tried to dissuade him at first, but Glenn wouldn't give in, refusing to let Jim take Kris into Brighton Beach without a back-up. He texted:

Fat guy is the tail now

Kris and Jim headed deeper into the neighborhood, stepping around three young boys kicking a soccer ball on the sidewalk. Drab, but neatly maintained, apartment buildings stood sentinel on both sides of Fourth Street. Fire escapes, a series of metal terraces and connecting ladders, zig-zagged up from the second floor to the rooftop of each building. Air conditioning units sprouted from many windows. Two elderly men sat in folding chairs, concentrating on a chessboard set up on a folding table between them. Jim stopped midway up the block, pulling the interceptor out his pack. He checked briefly to make sure that it was still working.

"What's that?" Kris asked.

"My new iPad. Thought I'd snap a few photos."

"Really?" Kris leaned over, trying to see the screen. Jim stepped back to shield it.

"It's a portable Wi-Fi interceptor. It seeks out Wi-Fi signals and stores communications traffic."

"I know what they do. We're not standing still long enough to capture much though, are we?"

"No, you're right. But I will get some data. Just enough to check it out."

"I thought that you and Glenn would park in a van and sit out here all night."

"We may do that, or just drive around the neighborhood for a few hours."

"When?"

"When the warrant comes through."

"*When* the warrant comes through? I thought that you had it already."

"Almost. The judge wants some more background information."

"What does that mean?" Kris was starting to boil, again.

"New rules now, I guess."

"To protect the rights of our fellow citizens."

"That's one way to look at it."

"Is there another way?"

"Don't you think that our citizens would sacrifice a small bit of privacy in exchange for their safety?"

"Yes, I do. But what's a 'small bit" of privacy? Who draws the line? You? Me?"

"Look, we're going to get the warrant soon - two weeks at most. I just want to be ready to go."

"So you're going to break the law today? Correction, we're going to break the law today?"

"Crazy 8 may not wait." Jim said, reaching out for Kris' arm.

"That's bullshit, and you know it. There will always be a threat." Kris pulled away, the anger in her voice readily apparent.

"You're exactly right. There will always be a threat. And it's our job, our duty, to defend against it. 24/7." Jim stood his ground, hands on hips.

"But you can't break the law. Does the end justify the means?" Kris returned for one last salvo.

"Yes, sometimes it does."

"Well, I'm done for the day." Kris spun around, spotting the elevated subway tracks hovering over the street on the block ahead of them. "I can catch the subway back to Manhattan," she said, stomping off.

"Kris, wait."

"No, I'm leaving. You do what you have to do."

Jim watched in dismay as Kris walked away, at last slipping from view in the crowd on Brighton Beach Avenue. I'm right. I'm not going to chase her and apologize, he thought. Jim turned quickly, catching Lenny off guard with his stare. Lenny froze, like when his mom had caught him surfing porno websites. But, this was his neighborhood. He could stand here all day if he wanted to. Lenny took his phone out, pretending to resume his game of Candy Crush. Who should he follow now? He picked Jim and texted Dmitri. More determined than ever to finish his testing, Jim followed Kris' path to the top of Fourth Street, then crossed over to head back down the other side.

Confused by the confrontation, Glenn backed away, keeping his partner in sight but giving him a wide berth. If Jim needed help, Glenn was sure that he would text. Jim stopped at the chess game, pretending to study the board, but just wanting the wi-fi interceptor to have more time to lock in on a signal. "No kibbitzing," one of the players murmured as he leaned over to move his knight. Jim laughed. He barely knew how to play. He headed back towards the beach and then over to Sixth Street.

Dmitri was confused too, but Lenny had said not to bother Mr. Nakitov. Instead, he texted the new man in town, Crazy 8. Nakitov had introduced him as a seasoned field operative, whatever that meant, and they had shared a few beers together. Crazy 8 met him five minutes later at the bottom of Sixth Street. Lenny caught up with them as well, using his shirtsleeve to wipe the sweat dripping from his nose.

"He's FBI. We can't touch him," Lenny declared, finally catching his breath.

"But he's here alone. No flashing lights, no back-up," Dmitri said, as he scanned the street.

"Maybe he's not supposed to be here," Lenny replied.

Crazy 8 remained silent, just staring up the street. When Jim pulled an about-face again, heading back towards them, Crazy 8 stepped forward. Dmitri and Lenny scrambled to flank him, walking three abreast like Russia's new Terminator tanks moving through Chechnya. The sidewalk in front of the trio cleared rapidly. Two young girls in pigtails packed up their jump rope and moved inside. A middle-aged woman dropped a shopping bag, spilling a handful of oranges, and ran across the street. Jim was lost in thought, rehashing the conversation with Kris in his mind, not focused on his surroundings. A rookie mistake. When he looked up, the wall of Russian thuggery was only five car lengths away. Jim reached back to check his firearm and dried his sweaty palms on his shorts. Crazy 8 strode purposely forward, arms hanging loosely at his side. Dmitri slipped his right hand into the pocket of his jeans, eyes flaring in anticipation of a fight. Where was Glenn? Jim knew that he could not call in any other support, given his previous activities today with the Wi-Fi interceptor. No way out now unless he wanted to try to climb up the fire escape. The three Russians were less than ten feet away, closing fast. What the fuck, I'm FBI. Jim picked the sliver of daylight between Crazy 8 and Lenny, and barged through. Crazy 8 did not budge, bumping Jim's shoulder, but Lenny did, sliding just enough to allow Jim to pass.

"Be careful, FBI man. You don't have your girlfriend to protect you this time," Dmitri hissed.

Jim kept walking, eyes straight ahead, head high.

"I had you covered," Glenn said when he caught up to Jim on the next block.

"Yeah, thanks."

"What are friends for?"

Glenn clapped Jim on the shoulder as they headed back to the safety of Coney Island.

10

Kris climbed the stairs to the Brighton Beach subway station. She had to wait at the turnstile as a smattering of passengers exiting a train from the city filtered through from the other side. She noticed a young father with dreadlocks and his son, maybe seven or eight, with a burgeoning Afro walking together. They were both in Yankee gear, matching caps and pinstriped Ripcurl jerseys.

"Did the Yanks play today?" she asked.

"Yep, won 5-2." the dad answered, resting a hand on his son's head.

"We went to the game," the boy added, taking a swing with an imaginary bat. "Ripcurl hit another homer."

"Really?"

"Let's go," the father directed his son towards the street. "I'm sure the lady doesn't care about Ripcurl. It's almost dinner time. You're mom is waiting." They headed off, the youngster taking one more mighty swat.

Kris thought back on the day with Jim and the disappointing turn of events. She definitely had snapped, but he had not been straight with her on the warrant. The battles with cybercrooks, with her boss, with Jim, and even with her own conscience had battered Kris' usually indestructible self-confidence over the past months, leaving it raw and bleeding. She needed a balm, even if it was just for one night. Kris fished around in her purse and found the baseball with Reilly's phone number. She twirled it in her hand for a second. Would he even remember her? Only one way to find out. Kris texted him:

Got kicked out of the stadium last week. Want to get back in the game. Dinner tonight??? Kris

She peered down the track. Her train was rolling into the station. How would Reilly know her name? She sent him another text.

The redhead

The doors to the subway car split open and Kris stepped in. The train was almost empty. No trouble finding a seat. The train was running local, so progress to the city was slow, peppered with frequent stops. Kris watched the borough of Brooklyn pass by, fidgeting impatiently. At last, a response from Reilly:

Thought you tossed my ball back onto the field

Kris did not hesitate:

That was my girlfriend

Nice arm

She throws like a girl

What about you

I throw better

Want to show me??

Kris wasn't sure how long the train would stay on the elevated tracks before entering the tunnels to Manhattan and killing her phone signal. It *was* Sunday. Pretty early in the evening too. She thought about going back to the office. Always work to do. Decision time. I'm twenty-four. No attachments. If not now, when?

Sure

Cool. Come on over

No way, Ripcurl. The subway swooped down into the darkness. The bars on Kris' phone disappeared, replaced by the always frustrating "No Service" message. Shit. The train pulled into the Barclays Center stop. Still "No Service". Same result at DeKalb Avenue, the last stop in Brooklyn. Maybe Reilly would think she had changed her mind. Did he have a pinch hitter waiting in the dugout. Another woman with a signed baseball? Finally daylight appeared as the train headed over the Manhattan Bridge. Five bars! Kris quickly punched in her reply.

U come over to my apartment. I'll make dinner
Where?

Wow, this was going to happen. Reilly really was available tonight. Right now actually. Was that good or bad? She tugged on her Broncos jersey, smoothing it down over her shorts.

Bank Street. West Village
When?

Kris checked her watch. Waited thirty seconds.

Two hours

K

The subway descended underground again. Kris began planning her meal, not a particularly difficult task since her cooking repertoire was extremely limited. Pasta with meatballs. A salad would work too. Beer or wine? Both. She checked the subway map app on her phone. No easy way to get close to her apartment on this train. She decided to get off at West 4th and walk ten blocks. The stop came up quickly, so quickly that she almost missed it, jumping out of her seat just before the subway doors closed. Kris was pleased to be back above ground. The sun had just set, lighting up the western sky with a soft, golden glow as it sunk into New Jersey. Kris passed a newsstand on West 4th Street. Matt Reilly's picture, in mid-swing, forearms bulging, was plastered across half the back page of the Post. RIPCURL RIDES TO THE RESCUE the headline shouted. Kris couldn't resist. She bought the paper and a pack of spearmint gum. Seems Reilly had homered in the game on Saturday night as well. Kris tried to scan the article while she walked but a near collision crossing Grove Street with a pizza delivery man, biking hurriedly in the wrong direction on the one way street, convinced her to save the reading for later.

Kris approached visits to the D'Agostino's supermarket, just around the corner from her apartment, with as much enthusiasm as a visit to the dentist. She generally got lost in the aisles, run over by the shopping carts of young mothers distracted by their whining toddlers, or waited impatiently in the express checkout line behind someone with twice as many items as permitted. The store could use a map app like the subway one, she thought. But, tonight, she was on a mission. She enlisted the help of a chatty assistant manager, broad smile peeking out from a bushy, handlebar mustache, to guide her around. He convinced her to buy Rao's marinara sauce, a New York favorite, and fusilli for a first date, no sense twirling linguini and splashing the red sauce all over, he explained. The only hard decision was the alcoholic beverages. She settled on a six pack of Stella, her favorite, and two bottles of chianti, a good match for the pasta and not particularly intimidating for her guest. Kris was in and out of the supermarket in twenty minutes.

When she arrived back at her apartment, Kris parked the groceries on the kitchen table and put the beer in the fridge. A solitary carton of orange juice would finally have some companionship. She pulled out the Post, scanning it while standing at the counter. Reilly was definitely pin-up material even in black and white, but Kris lingered on his eyes, pupils expanded, completely locked on the task at hand. Did she project the same intensity at her computer screen? She admired his concentration, but really envied his opportunity to demonstrate it in the public spotlight. It must be a better high than any hallucinogenic drug could produce. Kris opened the paper to the Reilly article, skimming the baseball stuff but searching for any details on her dinner companion's personal life. Not much there. Reilly was approaching his twenty-second birthday, single, and devoured a chocolate milkshake after each game. Too late to buy ice cream now. Then Kris noticed a small picture in the bottom corner of the page. Reilly was on one knee with each arm around the shoulder of a young boy standing by his side, one in a Yankee cap while the other's bald head reflected the sunlight. The caption read: Matt Reilly fulfills the Make-A-Wish requests of New York City kids every homestand. Reilly either has a big heart or a great PR agent. Hopefully both, Kris thought.

Kris checked her watch as she stepped into her bedroom. She had never found the time for much decorating. A four posted, king sized bed adorned with a powder blue and white striped down comforter dominated the space. Matching curtains outlined the windows. A framed Van Gogh print, Starry Night, centered above the bed. Three decorative pillows were strewn by the headboard. They always got in the way during her usual half-hearted attempt to clean up in the morning. Kris peeled off her Broncos jersey and tossed it on the wing chair, upholstered in a midnight blue floral, in the corner of the room, her favorite reading spot. She stepped out of her shorts in the bathroom as she turned on the shower hovering over the tub. An hour till his scheduled arrival. Would Reilly be on time? Probably not. Was he exhausted from the game this afternoon? Did he have a game tomorrow? A team curfew? What about her own schedule? Kris tapped on her phone on the bathroom counter. Her Monday morning calendar was empty. She quickly checked herself in the mirror, confirmed that no sunburn splotches appeared in contrast to her white bathing suit, then stripped.

Kris loved her shower. The water got scorchingly hot; the throbbing pressure cleansed away her cares. As the streams coursed through her hair, Kris slid her hands down her flanks, finding loose granules of sand clinging to her hips, remnants of the day at the beach. She pried the shower head from its perch, guiding the spray to the nape of her neck, underneath her breasts, and into her navel, slowly washing the sand away. The powerful waves set her thoughts adrift. But not to Reilly, or to Jim. Kris imagined the Yankee Stadium crowd roaring *her* name. Fans standing, enveloping her with cheers as she brought a terrorist to justice. Why not? The shower head glided downward, circling her pubic mound, seemingly on its own volition. Kris savored a ripple of arousal from the pulsing spray. It could easily turn into an unstoppable tidal wave. But, not now. She regained control, directing the jets down to her knees, then between her toes. A final, teasing trip all the way back to her neck. At last, Kris stepped out of the bath, wrapping a towel around her wet hair. Still naked, she dried it vigorously, then ran her drier quickly through, its blast of hot air disrupted her reverie. Kris thought briefly about a pony tail but decided to arrange the ginger strands loosely around her face. At last, Kris dressed in faded jeans and a gray "Ski Aspen" T-shirt. Reilly's ego was undoubtedly big enough: she did not want to overdress for him. A dab of perfume, a beguiling, musky fragrance, added the final touch.

Kris returned to her kitchen with little time to waste. She set her phone to Pandora's mellow country channel, organized the ingredients to prepare dinner, and then set the table for two, a rare event. Her mother would have wanted her to take out the fancy dishes for company, but she only had one set with a mundane floral trim. Kris set a large pot of water to boil, hacked up the lettuce, and spread the chopped sirloin on the cutting board. She sprinkled seasoning on the meat, then kneaded it with both hands, her fingers sinking into the loamy softness. While her fingers worked the meat, molding it into eight large, round balls, Kris thought about the crowd at the Stadium. It would never shout her name. A more private fulfillment would have to be her measure of success. Enough deep thinking! Kris rolled two of the balls together and caressed them mischievously. Smiling, she separated the meatballs and stepped away from the kitchen counter. The meal was prepped and ready to cook, whenever Reilly arrived. She sat down on the couch in her snug den and punched out ESPN on the TV remote. The Rockies-Dodger game at Coors Field had just started. At least, she had a rooting interest. The Rockies had a runner on second in the bottom of the first inning when the intercom shrilled. Kris looked out the front window. A uniformed driver was nursing a black sedan into a parking space in front of the fire hydrant across the street. Kris buzzed Reilly in.

Kris was surprised by Reilly's height and bulk. She had always thought of baseball players as wiry, finesse athletes, but the behemoth filling her doorway could easily have played linebacker for the Broncos. His barrel chest was sharply defined even underneath a black San Diego State windbreaker and loose fitting button down denim shirt. His thighs threatened to bust out from his tight, tailored jeans. Reilly brushed a lock of blond hair off his forehead, flashed a toothy grin and extended his hand, "Matthew Reilly at your service." He handed her a Baskin Robbins paper bag with two quarts of ice cream. Kris firmly gripped Reilly's hand, looked directly into his beaming blue eyes, and introduced herself. She guided her guest to a chair in front of the fireplace while she stepped into the kitchen to put the dessert in the freezer, pleasantly surprised by Reilly's thoughtfulness. Kris grabbed two beer bottles and then paused for a deep breath. The dinner plans had unfolded so quickly and unexpectedly that she did not have any time for first date jitters. Would Reilly have anything interesting to say?

Reilly surprised her again by breaking the ice before she could even sit down. "You ski?", he asked, pointing to her shirt.

"I snowboard mostly."

"Dude! That's surfing on snow." Reilly swilled his Stella.

"You ever tried it?" Kris asked.

"Snowboard? Yeah, we went up to Mammoth every winter until my junior year in high school."

"Then?"

"My dad passed away suddenly, a heart attack, so my baseball coach squashed any more riding. Didn't want me to get hurt and risk my bonus money. He knew that I would have to look after my mom and brother."

"That's tough. He didn't stop you from surfing though."

"Nothing would stop me from surfing. I even got the Yankees to agree to let me surf for five days every winter. You ever ride a wave?"

Kris crossed her legs, her orange painted toenails flexing in her sandals. "Yep. Before high school though. We lived in San Jose then, so we would head down to Santa Cruz."

"There's some wicked waves in that ocean."

"I stayed away from them. We just rode the ankle-snappers close to shore." Kris stood, pointing to the kitchen. "You hungry?"

"Always."

Kris laughed. "Well come on in here and keep me company while I finish preparing dinner. It's almost all ready."

Reilly followed. No offer of a pre-dinner blow job? Did his hostess know that she was entertaining Ripcurl? This one definitely had balls.

"Grab another beer," Kris said, pointing to the refrigerator while she tended to the stove.

Reilly obliged, wisecracking, "Pretty lonely in there," as he pulled out two more Stellas.

He sidled over to the stove, slipping his pinkie into the pot of red sauce on the burner. "Tastes just like Rao's." Reilly rested his hand on Kris' lower back. "You ever eat there? It's not far from the Stadium," he asked, his hand drifting down to her ass. She did not move away.

Kris shook her head. "I hear that it's impossible to get a reservation."

"Not if you're with Ripcurl."

"I guess that fame has its advantages." Now she was getting the picture, he thought.

Kris leaned over to reach the pepper shaker. "I like it spicy. How about you?"

Reilly admired the feline curve of her hips. "Spicy is fine with me."

Dinner went smoothly. Kris thought that she had made enough food for at least four people, but there were no leftovers and only a sprinkling of conversation between mouthfuls. Reilly was surprisingly well-read for a baseball player. Lots of time on buses and planes, he explained. Kris was surprisingly earthy for an Ivy League computer geek. Lots of time on the ranch, she explained. Before clearing the table, Kris offered to refill Reilly's wine glass, but he refused.

"Two beers and a glass of wine. Three strike limit during the season."

Reilly brought his plate over to Kris at the sink, his hand reclaiming its former perch on her ass. She seemed to move closer this time as she rinsed the dishes. When Kris bent to put the plates in the dishwasher, Reilly moved right behind her, his hands now resting on both her hips. No questioning his intentions. Kris lingered, arranging the utensils in the tray. But then she suddenly stood and twirled around. "Dessert?" she asked stepping toward the fridge.

Reilly laughed to himself. She was definitely going to make him work for it. "Of course. Chocolate for me."

Kris handed him a spoon and the container of ice cream. No bowls. "Let's go to the den," she said pointing the way with her own spoon. Reilly was hoping to go the other direction into her bedroom, but he followed again. Kris parted the curtain on the window in her living room and looked out into the street.

"Your getaway car is still there."

Now, Reilly laughed out loud. "Caught me."

"Well, I hope that you're going to stay awhile," Kris said, curling her legs up on the small sofa.

"I'll tell the driver to turn the engine off."

Reilly sat down next to Kris, draping his arm over her shoulders to draw her close. Kris dipped her spoon into the shared ice cream carton and greedily licked it clean. With his free hand, Reilly pressed the remote, turning the TV on and switching the channel. Now it was his turn to tease. "Let's watch a little SportsCenter."

Kris sighed, playfully running a hand along Reilly's leg as a commercial for an erectile dysfunction drug aired. He turned to nuzzle her hair, but then the SportsCenter anchor intoned: "Ripcurl Reilly rescued the Yankees again this afternoon with his fifteenth home run of the season." Reilly snapped his gaze back to the screen. The highlight clip zoomed in on home plate as his bat connected with the ball to launch it over the wall in left center field. Kris watched too, again focusing on Reilly's eyes, locked in ferocious concentration at the moment of contact.

"What do you see when you hit the ball?" she asked.

"See? See? I don't see anything. I don't hear anything. I just swing, dude."

The announcer continued, "Reilly really stayed back and waited on that curveball."

His color man added, "The rookie is learning. He's finally hitting the ball to the opposite field."

Reilly shouted, "Yeah dude! I've been working in the cage on that all month."

"Smooth swing. Incredible bat speed," the anchor concluded.

Kris had had enough. She crossed her arms, reached down to her waist, and lifted her T-shirt over her head. She paused, making sure she had recaptured Reilly's full attention. When he finally put the remote on the floor, Kris unsnapped her black lace bra and tossed it towards the TV. Her breasts surged from captivity, bouncing freely, mesmerizing her young lover. He pawed them with both hands but Kris placed her fingers on top of his to slow down his enthusiasm. "They're not baseballs." She guided his hands down to the top of her jeans. While Reilly fumbled with her belt buckle, Kris unbuttoned his shirt and massaged his cinder block shoulders. As soon as she heard the crisp click of her jeans unsnapping, Kris kicked both legs up in the air, lifting her ass off the sofa. Reilly swept off her pants and black thong in one motion, tossing them aside. Kris draped one leg over the back of the sofa, orange toenails dangling, and reclined against a green striped pillow. Reilly gaped, his breaths now in short bursts. Kris licked the last bit of chocolate ice cream from her lips, beckoning him forward with a centerfold smile. He stood, unbuckling his own jeans and dropping them to the floor. No underwear to encumber him. Kris studied his eyes, locked in concentration on her wantonness. "Just swing dude," she gasped.

11

"See ya," Reilly murmured, lacing up his sneakers as the first rays of light seeped into Kris' bedroom. "We're leaving town tonight for a road trip. Cleveland and Chicago."

"Bye." Kris pulled the comforter over her shoulders as the door closed. She rolled over languidly, felt the wetness under her bare bottom, and curled back onto her side. The first time had been on the sofa in the den. The second in the kitchen. She had stopped there, naked, on the way back to her bedroom. Reilly had taken her from behind as she reached to put the dishes away. Kris stretched an arm out from the warmth of her bed for her phone on the nightstand, confirming that her morning was free. She slipped back under the weight of the comforter, savoring his masculine scent on the sheets. The third time had been here: Kris bull-rode Reilly, pinching his nipples until they poked through the wisps of blond hair that straggled across his chest. She thought that they were done after that but Reilly had woken her just before dawn, coaxing her with whispered intimacies.

Kris' phone vibrated. It was Mindy. Kris had turned her ring tone off but Illuminate had still found her.

"Yes?" Kris asked, the drowsiness readily apparent.

"Anne wants to see you."

"On my way."

■ ■ ■

Kris sauntered into the office at ten thirty, slung her satchel over the back of her chair as she sat, and flipped on her computer.

"Good morning, boys and girls," she announced breezily to Joe and Mindy, lost in their computer screens.

"You seem pretty cheery this morning," Joe replied, swiveling in his chair.

"You'd be cheery too, if you rolled in at lunchtime," Mindy said sarcastically without looking up.

"You're all sweetness and light today."

"Since when did you become a candy striper in the cancer ward?" Mindy asked finally looking at Kris. She studied her boss for several seconds, as Kris settled in at her desk, a smile creasing the corners of her lips. Mindy thought that Kris was actually humming a song. That was too much. She ambled over to Kris' desk.

"OK. What's up?"

"What do you mean?"

"No sane person is that happy on a Monday." Mindy plopped down in an Aeron chair wheeling it right next to Kris. "And you never come in this late. Something's up."

"Nothing's up," Kris reassured her, pretending to turn her attention to her computer.

"Wait a second. Didn't you go to the beach yesterday with Jim?"

Kris had almost forgotten that. "Yes," she said meekly.

Mindy seized upon Kris' recalcitrance, leaning over to whisper, "You got laid last night, didn't you? That explains everything."

"You've got it wrong."

Mindy gave her a knowing look just as Anne wheeled into view.

The meeting with Anne was brief. She wanted them to forget Brighton Beach and devote their full attention to other projects. Macy's was not pleased that their customers' email accounts had been hacked. They needed to know the extent of the breach. The women's deodorant fiasco needed attention too. Kris and her crew accepted their marching orders and returned to their desks. They ordered lunch in.

"You didn't? You didn't?" Mindy's wail shattered the afternoon calmness of the office. Fortunately, Joe had stepped away so she was alone with Kris.

"What are you screeching about?" Kris asked, annoyed at Mindy for breaking her concentration.

Mindy bustled over to Kris's desk, breathlessly tossing the afternoon edition of the Post, opened to its Page 6 gossip column. Kris scanned the article and photo spread, seemingly focused on a society ball at the Met last night. "What?" she asked confused. "I wasn't there."

"Down here. The last blurb." Mindy pointed to the headline below the fold of the newspaper, RIPCURL ROAMS, and began to read: *Yankee heartthrob Ripcurl Reilly spent last night, yes all night ladies, in the West Village across town from his own apartment on the Upper East Side. The Post tracked his car and driver to a Bank Street address where it remained parked outside until dawn. Who is the mystery woman? What is her relationship with Ripcurl?*

"You called him, didn't you?" Mindy sat on the edge of Kris' desk. "I bet that you slept with Ripcurl. I suppose your following him on Twitter now too." She spit out the last few words as if they were rotten fruit.

Kris just smiled, an image of Ripcurl in her den flashing through her mind, and turned away. When Mindy seemed settled again, Kris stepped away. Out of sight, she texted Reilly. She wanted to catch him before he got on the team plane.

Did u c the Post?
Yeah. No big deal.
K
Comes with the territory. Later dude

■ ■ ■

By Monday evening, Kris had returned to full on work mode, blocking out all distractions. She and her team traced the attacks at Macy's to a recently fired employee, the most frequent source of security breaches, turning their findings over to local law enforcement. By Friday afternoon, they had identified an offshore competitor, probably in China, as the source of the dummy bids on women's deodorant search terms. Not much they could do there though. Mindy had skipped out of the office for a meeting, but she had left the Post on her desk. Kris couldn't resist. The Yankees' loss last night dominated the back page. Reilly had struck out four times, the golden sombrero the reporter had called it. Kris wondered who, if anyone, he had turned to for solace. Not her. She hadn't heard from Reilly all week. Not that she expected to anyway. She flipped to Page 6. More coverage of the Manhattan social scene, but no mention of Reilly or her apartment. Yesterday's news. The front page featured a story on Mayor Chamberlain and his war on crime. He had decided to visit Brighton Beach, facing a more hostile audience than he had anticipated. Kris realized that she had not heard from Jim all week. She had called him but he had not gotten back. Kris had wanted to apologize for leaving him alone on the street, but not for her stand on the fourth amendment. Jim should have gotten the warrant by now, so his silence was even more bizarre. Kris called again. No answer. Was he avoiding her? Kris decided to stop by the FBI office.

The FBI office was usually vibrant with activity, but Kris sensed it grind to a halt when she walked in. The receptionist rang Glenn, not Jim, and then quickly cast her eyes downward. An agent, Kris had forgotten his name, almost bumped into her shoulder as she approached Jim's desk. His chair was empty and his desktop was bare of all papers. It did not look as if Jim Bright was not coming back here anytime soon.

"Well, if it isn't Mata Hari herself," Glenn said disgustedly, barely looking up from the neighboring desk.

Kris's frown displayed her bewilderment. "Who?" She walked over to Glenn. "Where's Jim?"

"Don't you know? He's suspended. Somehow the boss found out that he conducted an illegal search on Sunday." Glenn stood to face Kris. "The shit really hit the fan."

"And you think that I turned him in?"

"Who else even knew about it?"

"Look, I *was* pissed off. But Jim's a good friend. I would never rat him out like that."

"Well, somebody certainly did." Glenn reached out, tapping Kris' shoulder and pointing her towards the door. "I think that you should leave now."

Kris slumped dejectedly. "OK, I'll give Jim a call tonight to straighten things out. It wasn't me."

As Kris spun around, she noticed four photos pinned up behind Jim's desk. The first showed the three Russians marching up Sixth Street in formation. The other three were blow-ups of each individual. "Who are the three stooges?" she asked Glenn.

"They were tailing you and Jim in Brighton Beach on Sunday. There was a little showdown after you left."

"Who took the pictures?" Kris leaned closer to examine the faces more carefully.

"I did," Glenn said, now standing just behind Kris.

"You were there? I never saw you."

"Jim didn't want me there. But he's my partner. I always have his back."

"Do you know these guys?"

"The two wingmen are local thugs. We don't have anything on the one in the middle. Yet."

Kris stared at the photos for a full five seconds. Glenn shuffled his feet impatiently, waiting for her to leave. Kris pointed to the middle one. "Look at his right hand." It was swinging freely at his side.

"What?" Glenn asked, leaning over.

"Can you blow that up? The guy with the ponytail - looks to me like he is missing the last two fingers."

"So?"

"I majored in computer science, not math, but I am pretty sure that only leaves eight."

"Crazy 8?"

"That's our man."

Glenn unpinned the photo and placed it flat on his desk, squinting down to see if he could confirm Kris' observation. Kris aimed her phone at the photo. "Here, we can use my magnifying glass app." They both counted eight fingers.

Glenn bounded up. "I need to call Jim right away."

"Are you going to arrest Crazy 8?" Kris asked.

"For what? Walking down the street?" Glenn sat at his desk. "With Jim's suspension, we can't even go near him now."

THE FOURTH AMENDMENT 111

Kris sat down in front of Glenn's desk. "Seems like Crazy 8 has some friends in the right places." She pointed right at Glenn's face. "They're the ones that got Jim suspended, not me."

"OK, OK. I apologize," Glenn said, smiling. "You are officially removed from my Leading Bitches of the World list."

"That's a relief. But how are you going to get Crazy 8 if he has protection?"

"Well, now that we have a photo, we can run it through all the facial recognition databases - immigration, NYPD, Homeland Security, CIA, NSA. If we get any matches, then we have a good chance to get that warrant."

"And get Jim reinstated," Kris said as she stood up to leave. "Thanks."

■ ■ ■

While Kris was counting fingers at the FBI office, Joe Brady was combing the Illuminate databases to count the number of times that Warren Hoover, the forty six year old borough president of the Bronx, had searched on-line for a "spit roast" in the past month. At first, Joe had thought that Mr. Hoover was planning a family barbecue, but when a should-have-been-forgotten friend from high school sent around a link to photos on a swingers' porn site, Joe realized that Mr. Hoover was not so well-intentioned. Joe hated this secret project, digging up dirt for Anne, but, with the dope charges hanging over his head, he had little choice. She had made that point abundantly clear on Monday night, when he had dropped off a two page summary of his preliminary research on her desk. Anne's words still echoed darkly: "Nice work - for a high school civics project. Now get me something I can use."

Joe would have preferred to devote these extra hours to researching the FreedomFighters' site, but, here he was on a Friday night, hacking away, turning over every on-line stone that he could find to uncover information that might satisfy his boss' personal quest. He had realized several weeks ago that Anne's targets were all potential political opponents for Mayor Chamberlain. The Mayor had always appeared to be a straight shooter. Did he even know what Anne was up to? Why was she trying so hard to play Lady MacBeth? Joe was actually relieved that he couldn't find much that would help her Machiavellian plans. Warren Hoover might be a swinger, but that wasn't illegal or even that startling today. Governor Sharon Proctor's son had gotten expelled from boarding school. A local newspaper had hinted about a drug bust. Senator Stevens' young wife was an avid Rolling Stones fan. Joe found a clandestine photo of her backstage during a break at a recent concert, sitting on the lap of the lead singer. New York City's Public Advocate Harold Klotz had a taste for "fact-finding" trips abroad: Paris, Rome and Moscow in the past year alone. Governor Swenson had served in the military for two years as his bio ostentatiously highlighted, but in fact he had only left his desk job in Washington for four days to accompany a UFO tour to Iraq. Joe would have to keep digging.

12

The menacing dark clouds rolled quickly into the sky over Brighton Beach late on Saturday afternoon. The rumble of thunder, the flash of lightning over the Atlantic, and the driving pelt of raindrops quickly cleared the crescent of sand leading down to the ocean. Hastily packing towels, closing coolers, stuffing young children into strollers, the beach crowd scurried towards shelter. The black Mercedes sedan rolled down 6th street, fighting the human tide escaping from the beach. It pulled up in front of the entrance to Galina's, a dining establishment and night club renown in the Russian community and Brooklyn social scene. Dmitri Remko hopped out of the driver's seat, the driving rain soaking his dark suit and tie in the three seconds that he required to unfurl an umbrella broad enough to shield a royal procession. Unfazed by the water dripping into his eyes, Dmitri hastened to the rear passenger door to shepherd his boss on the brief crossing into the restaurant.

"Your table is waiting, sir," the maitr'd bowed obsequiously as he ushered Ilya Nakitov towards the covered veranda fronting directly on the boardwalk. Tall, broad-shouldered, sporting a full head of aristocratically gray hair, Ilya was the embodiment of a life well-lived, Russian style. His face was weathered, the furrows of years spent outdoors clearly visible. Unusually prominent brows jutted out over alert brown eyes that seemed to capture every movement in the room. Ilya wore an impeccably tailored Zegna navy blazer, gold buttons gleaming, over a white linen shirt open at the collar to reveal a chain of gold bullets circling his neck. He did little to discourage the notion that each bullet represented a mujahideen that he had killed in Afghanistan a lifetime ago in the service of the Soviet Union. A gold Rolex watch, the size of a small manhole cover, adorned his right wrist.

Ilya Nakitov was a businessman and the corner table in Galina's was his office, particularly in the warmer months. A bottle of Stolichnaya Elit and a platter of caviar awaited him. Nakitov had risen steadily in the military until the mid-90's when the financial spoils of the disintegrating Russian empire proved too great a temptation. Realizing the burgeoning potential of cyber activities, Nakitov established a consulting company that would protect, disguise and distort the breathtakingly enormous pool of assets amassed by the cadre of Russian oligarchs. Demand for these services skyrocketed, enabling Nakitov to employ hundreds of the best and brightest technical minds in Eastern Europe. With this success came the jealousy of his powerful customers who realized that Nakitov ultimately sat on a treasure trove of information that should never see the light of day. The government's income tax inquiry was the first warning that Nakitov's days of freedom in Moscow were dwindling. He did not wait for the midnight knock on the door signaling his arrest, but instead quickly negotiated a settlement, turning over both the complete records of his business and his own sizeable personal fortune to the state in exchange for a life in America, a much better alternative than a prison cell in Siberia. Nakitov had wisely maintained his contacts in the cyber underground, recognizing that they would serve him well in his new home.

Nakitov poured a shot of vodka and tasted the caviar, nodding his approval to the hovering waiter. Ten minutes later, Dmitri, his dark suit thoroughly soaked, entered the veranda and assumed a sentinel post, hands clasped behind his back, careful not to drip on his boss' table. The restaurant filled steadily with the casual early dinner crowd, not to be confused with the more fashionable late dinner crowd which gathered at Galina's every weekend to enjoy the sumptuous menu of Russian delicacies, the cabaret show and the all night revelry. The maitre'd approached Nakitov tentatively, pointing to the drenched guest trailing him and inquiring with his eyes whether he should be welcomed or dismissed. Ilya pointed to an empty chair, "Ah, Bill, please sit down." The waiter immediately bustled over with a towel for the now approved visitor.

Bill Badenov, proud of his recent promotion into Nakitov's circle of top lieutenants, had planned to make a more auspicious entrance to the scene at Galina's. Instead, he felt like a nearly drowned mutt that had slipped in through the kitchen door. Bill delivered a crisp 'thank you' to the waiter in Russian and dried off his face. He hoped his boss would notice his language study. Bill was stocky, a few pounds shy of fat, as his once muscular football player's upper body melted into his gut. The salesman at the Men's Wearhouse had assured him that the navy blue pinstripe suit would slim his silhouette, but the torrential rain had left it clinging to his rotund frame. He nodded slightly towards Dmitri, standing behind Ilya, who returned a grimace of disgust. Bill would deal with him later.

"Eat. Drink." Ilya, speaking English, motioned Bill to partake in the bounties of his table. Both men downed a shot of vodka in a demonstration of camaraderie.

"How is business this month?" Ilya asked.

"Excellent, sir," Bill replied, noticeably relieved to converse in his mother tongue. "My team is in position for another big payday on Madison Avenue."

"America is truly a wonderful country. All these luxury goods available in stores right on the street in every city. No cash needed. Anyone with a credit card can walk out with thousands of dollars of merchandise."

"Yes, sir," Bill said, boldly deciding to sample the caviar. He wasn't quite sure of the etiquette but guessed that the small spoon in front of him should have a role. He dipped it into the black mass and ladled the fish eggs onto a piece of white toast. Not bad, but he doubted that his friends in Staten Island would think that the delicacy was worth the fuss or the price. Fuck them. "And your contacts back in Russia are wizards at obtaining the information to make the credit cards for us."

"Yes, my friends are good. The best actually. But the American retailers make it so easy." Ilya reached into his jacket pocket for his wallet, pulling out two cards and laying them down on the table. "In Europe, every card has an encrypted chip. Much more difficult for us to counterfeit." Ilya pointed to the back of a Visa card issued by JP Morgan New York. "In America, still magnetic stripes. Virtually no encryption here. It is child's play for us to steal the data and print our own credit cards."

"When will the Americans switch to the chips?"

"Soon. Next year, maybe. They are finally losing so much money that they will have to change over."

"All the press on the data heist hurts them too."

Ilya smiled, recalling a personal triumph. "Yes, we have been too successful. And too greedy."

"So what are we going to do next?"

"Smart question. We are diversifying, starting up new businesses, almost legitimate, to capture consumer data, so we won't have to rely on obtaining it the old-fashioned way. Then we will have to find new ways to use it."

Ilya withdrew a gold pen and wrote on the napkin, handing it over to Bill.

"www.seniorsavers.com" Bill read. "I'll check it out."

"Good. I may need your help there soon."

A small commotion at the back of the room interrupted their conversation. Ilya looked up and beamed. He pushed back his chair to stand, spreading his arms wide. "Natasha, my dear."

An olive-skinned Eurasian woman dressed in fire engine red shorts, matching platform heels and a diaphanous white blouse swept ostentatiously through the room. Her lustrous black hair, falling like a waterfall down to her ass, fluttered as she walked. She stopped in front of Ilya placing her hands on his hips. He kissed her on both cheeks, beckoning her to sit. "Our business is over. My associate was just leaving." Bill stood, nodded a polite greeting, and turned towards the exit, not waiting to be introduced. Dmitri flashed a wry grin at his superior's dismissal. He recognized Natasha Bubka as the lead dancer in the cabaret show.

Natasha made a show of checking her watch, her petite breasts bouncing with the rise and fall of her wrist. "I can't. I'm already late. You know how Galina gets." She offered her cheek for another kiss from Ilya. "Are you staying for the show?"

"No. I have another meeting. Dmitri will pick you up outside afterwards. We'll head into the city for a nightcap." He was not asking.

"Sounds wonderful," Natasha said, attracting the gawking attention of neighboring diners as she sallied off to the stage door.

Ilya lingered over the last of his caviar, savoring the envy of every man in the room. He washed it down with a final shot of vodka and then stalked towards the boardwalk. Dmitri scrambled to keep two steps behind. The rain had stopped but a thick cloud cover obscured the moon and stars. The air smelled clean and fresh. The storm had erased the heavy aromas of sweat and sunblock from the afternoon. Ilya checked both directions before approaching a hulking figure with a ponytail looking out over the railing at the turbulent sea. He reached out and they embraced briefly but warmly.

"Comrade, it has been too long," Ilya said stepping back to view his companion.

"I was a boy then," Gregor Trotiak replied, slipping the 3 fingers on his right hand into the pocket of his jeans.

"And how is your father?"

"As angry as ever."

"Thirty years in a wheelchair will do that to any man. He will always be a brave *voin*. And very proud of you."

"He was a foolish warrior and paid the price. The bullet that shattered my father's spine came from an American rifle, not the mujahideen. The Americans have always hated us."

"Feared us." Ilya corrected. "Come, let's walk."

"We should not be seen together," Gregor said, following along nevertheless.

"No, you are right. This will be the only time. Is your plan set?"

"Yes. I was at Yankee Stadium last week. Amateurs at the gate. No metal detectors. I will not have any problems."

"Are you sure? Ilya persisted.

Gregor nodded, "Americans love their freedom - they just don't want to wait in line for it."

"What will you need?" Ilya asked, stopping his stroll at last. Gregor placed a handwritten shopping list in his hand. Ilya gave the list a cursory glance then slipped it into his pocket. "Not much here," he said.

"I am not looking to take down the whole Stadium," Trotiak replied.

"A young man who works for me will help you. Anatoly Turken."

"Why?"

"Why what?"

"Why will Anatoly Turken help me?"

"Because he believes that he is a patriot serving Mother Russia."

"Stupid boy."

"Yes, you are right," Ilya replied, shaking his head sadly. "The old Mother Russia no longer exists. The country is all business now."

"That is true. So you will transfer one million dollars to my account in Namibia?" Gregor asked.

"A capitalist too, eh?"

"An entrepreneur is the proper term, no?"

"Very good." Ilya said. "I will deliver the money." He stopped walking, once again looking out at the waves, listening to them crash against the sand. Gregor joined him, placing both hands on the boardwalk rail. He looked up as a commotion rattled overhead, but could see nothing in the ink black sky. A second later, a loud splat resounded between the two men. Gregor jumped backward, left hand reaching for his weapon.

Ilya laughed heartily, pointing to the gooey mess of seagull droppings on the railing. "You were wise to keep your mouth closed," he said merrily, pounding Gregor on the shoulder.

Gregor took a deep breath, calming himself. "When?" he asked.

"Soon. I want to give our ambitious mayor one last chance to back off his Russian crusade. If he does not, then we will send a message to the entire city."

"The fucking FBI, the fucking cops. They are all over the neighborhood." Gregor shook his head in disgust.

"I sent some photos of their *illegal* surveillance activities to a friend in the district attorney's office." Ilya said, turning again towards the restaurant. He added, "That should slow the FBI down for a few weeks."

"But they will be back, eh?" Gregor said, kicking at the sand.

"Yes, that is true. I believe that our mayor has set his sights on the White House. And we are his launching pad, so he will be relentless."

"Not good for you, is it?"

"No it is not. I did not go to jail in Moscow. I am not going to jail here in America." Ilya faced the son of his old compatriot, reached into the side pocket of his blazer and handed an ancient black flip-phone to Gregor. "Please stay out of sight and wait for my signal. I will send one of Natasha's friends to keep you company. A redhead maybe?" Ilya extended his hand, "Nothing crazy right?"

Gregor's three fingers gripped Ilya tightly. "Nothing crazy," he replied.

13

"Whadda we doin' here?" Joe Brock asked no one in particular as he shuffled along in the picket line outside of City Hall in downtown Manhattan. He wore a beat up pair of cargo shorts that once were khaki and the plain white Hanes T-shirt that he had been issued. Joe hadn't showered or shaved yet this week, it was only Wednesday, so he was not surprised that no other marcher was too close. "It's too fucking hot for June," he said wiping the sweat from his bald, black head, then scratching the open sore on his nose. Despite the distractions, Joe kept his sign, tacked to the top of a three foot plywood shaft, aloft. It read: BED STUY SUPPORTS BRIGHTON BEACH on one side and RUSSIANS HAVE RIGHTS on the other.

"Keep walkin', if you want to get paid," ordered Shirley Jones, a round woman whose thick, fleshy thighs threatened to burst from her shorts as she tried to maintain some semblance of order on the line. She was the daytime supervisor at the soup kitchen where the ten marchers had been recruited that morning.

"Who payin' us? I don't got no money yet," another man on the line complained.

"I heard some rich Russian is puttin' up the cash," Joe answered.

"Stop complaining, gentlemen, and just follow that group of students," Shirley bellowed. She pointed to a gaggle of long haired youths, hard to tell the boys from the girls she thought, traipsing around the flagpole and up the steps of the imposing limestone building, constructed in 1812 and now the oldest city hall in the country that still houses its original governmental functions.   ACLU DEFENDS BRIGHTON BEACH and THE FOURTH AMENDMENT IS RIGHT FOR EVERYONE read their placards.

"Who they?"

"Don't ask so many questions, man. We in good company. They rich college kids."

The rich college kids mingled with the marchers from the Russian Anti-Defamation League, a mixture of elderly men and women, between the tall white pillars supporting a portico that provided shelter from the broiling sun. Two of the women, gray hair swept back babushka style under red plaid kerchiefs, opened folding chairs and sat down to rest.

An imposingly tall woman with tightly cropped blond hair, her long, pinched face dominated by a beak-like nose, walked up and down the line, handing out a sheet of slogans and lyrics. "Listen," she shouted. "When the TV cameras start filming, we will start the chant on the front page: *Mayor D go home - leave our Russian friends alone.* Keep your signs up high so the cameras can see them. Everybody got it?" She walked down the steps to greet a famously liberal reporter from CNBC News. The camera crew settled into position, framing the reporter in front of the protesters on the steps and under the portico. The red light flashed and the crowd began its rhythmic chorus.

■ ■ ■

"What the hell is going on out there?" Mayor Chamberlain asked, looking up from his desk as the cacophony of the protest breached the thick windows of his first floor office.

"The Russians are at it again, sir. Seems they have some company this time," Willis Frazier replied.

"Turn on the TV - let's see the coverage."

Willis punched the remote just in time to see a picture of Jim Bright flash onto the screen.

"Our sources inform us that FBI field agent James Bright has been suspended indefinitely for conducting illegal surveillance operations in the Brighton

Beach neighborhood of Brooklyn, home to a large enclave of Russian-American citizens," the reporter intoned. The camera then panned to the protesters on the steps who had just launched into a rendition of "America the Beautiful," surprisingly on key.

"Shit, that FBI agent has gotten his ass in the wringer," the mayor said, standing up to get a better view of the TV screen. "How did we ever find out what he was doing?"

"One of the assistant DA's had some photos of Bright using a Wi-Fi interceptor in Brighton Beach. He had applied for a surveillance warrant but it hadn't been approved yet."

"Bright couldn't wait another week?"

Willis shook his head. "I heard that he had that redhead from Illuminate with him. The one that delivered Ms. Harmony's report at the Stadium."

"Never fails. You always get in trouble when you start thinking with your cock."

"I'll remember that, sir." Willis deadpanned as he sat down in the armchair in front of the Mayor's desk. "What are you going to do now?"

"About Bright? I can't do much to help him, can I?"

"No sir. Not with Illuminate involved. The press will crucify you over all their other privacy issues." Willis didn't want to even mention the mayor's wife's reaction to any signs of support for an Anne Harmony project. "But what about Monday? You have that speech scheduled in the Bronx."

The mayor pointed to the TV screen. "Look at that rabble. I'll get more votes for blasting the Russian mobsters than I will for caving in to them."

14

The aircraft carrier USS Enterprise, now a museum, loomed on Joe Brady's left as he pedaled slowly uptown on the bike path that encircled almost the entire island of Manhattan. Joe craned his helmeted head to admire the sleek, silver fighter jets on its deck. While they were, in fact, relics of past wars, they appeared poised to take off at a moment's notice. The crowd of tourists leaving the museum clogged the path, forcing Joe to slow down and then stop completely, unclipping his right foot from the pedal for balance. The twilight sky over the Hudson was a magnificent melange of orange, red and pink rays glimmering through an armada of white puffy clouds drifting towards Manhattan. The light breeze off the water provided a small measure of relief from the June heat wave. Dressed in tight black biking shorts and a white tank unzipped to his navel, Joe gathered speed as he left midtown planning to cross the George Washington Bridge for a thirty mile loop along the quieter coastal roads in New Jersey. The mouth watering aroma of burgers on the grill wafted from a riverfront restaurant. Joe reveled in the responsiveness of his white SPCarbon road bike as he shifted gears to accelerate. Joe pulled behind a long-limbed female biker, purple spandex shorts clinging to her toned flanks, blond hair billowing in the breeze like a spinnaker. While he couldn't see her face, Joe decided that the rear view wasn't too bad, so he slowed, content to follow for a few minutes at least. Joe willed the pressures of the office to fade away, but they refused, overwhelming his otherwise pleasant thoughts. Women's deodorant ads and Macy's email scams were not the problem. He had handled those type of issues every day for the past year; but, Anne's "secret" project gnawed at his conscience every day.

Joe switched on the headlamp attached to the fork of his bike as he saw the lights of the bridge sparkling in the distance. The path narrowed as it traced the riverbank. Joe accelerated past the blonde, but then had to dodge two teenage rollerbladers, lost in the beat of their headphones, heading the opposite way. He heard an outburst of Spanish profanity from the right fielder at a softball game on the field just below 158th Street. Joe recognized the parking lot where he, Kris and Mindy had pulled over to check their flat tire what seemed like a lifetime ago. He grimaced as he recalled his brush with the NYPD on that harrowing night. The GW was almost upon Joe now as he passed a set of tennis courts, emptying in the fading light. Suddenly, he stopped completely, unclipping from both pedals, and walked his bike off the path. He was in deep shit on two separate accounts. Maybe the only way out was the FreedomFighters' site. Despite the leads that he and Mindy had uncovered, he had stopped his research here as ordered. But, Joe had not stopped believing that they had uncovered a window into the netherworld. If he was going to break the law, it might as well be in pursuit of possible terrorists, not in pursuit of Anne's personal agenda. His bike light cast its narrow beam on the Hudson River as it tumbled under the bridge towards Lower Manhattan. The two hijacked airliners that crashed into the World Trade Center towers had followed this same route in 2001. Joe spun his bike around to head back to the office, the image of a fighter jet racing off to defend its country flashing through his mind.

■ ■ ■

As Joe popped off the elevator at Illuminate, he bumped into Kris, her head down on the way out.

"Hey," she said, stepping back. "I thought that you were going for a long ride."

"I was, but I realized that there are some loose ends here that I need to tie up." Joe held the elevator door so that Kris could enter.

"Tough luck. See you tomorrow," Kris said breezily as the door closed.

Joe strode down the corridor to his desk, passing several bullpens that were still half full of Illuminators despite the late hour. His biking attire generated one or two brief looks, but everyone seemed preoccupied with their own work. Kris looked more put together than usual after a long day, Joe thought. Fancy print button down tucked into her jeans; no tee shirt. A whiff of perfume, definitely not normal for his boss. Joe was relieved to find that Mindy had left for the night as well, so he had their team's space all to himself. He sat down, fired up his computer, and checked his old notes.

Several weeks ago, Mindy had unearthed the IP addresses of the few regular visitors to the FreedomFighters website. Now Joe needed to discover the real identity of these guys and what else they might be up to. He could use his own security clearance to get the inquiry started, but, if he tried to dig too deep, Illuminate's compliance department would get suspicious. He typed in his password and the job code for his Macy's work. Since that project involved email attacks, his investigations tonight would seem normal. An hour later, Joe had fifteen email names and the metadata, headers and recipient addresses, of three thousand most recent messages. Obviously some of the computers were shared by family members or one computer was used for multiple email accounts. Pretty normal. He spent the next hour manually scanning the database that he had assembled but it was simply too large and too vague. And it was only for the past thirty days. He really should go back at least ninety days, maybe even longer. Joe knew that he really needed to access Illuminate's highly secret Deep Dive technology developed to help its largest advertisers. It scanned the content of individual emails, social media posts and web searches for key words and then placed ads accordingly. Joe remembered discussing a trip to Spain with a friend after college graduation and then seeing ads for airlines and hotels in Madrid pop up on his screen for weeks afterward. He had wondered how the advertisers knew his plans until he had started working at Illuminate. Joe had used Deep Dive a few months ago on an email related review for another e-retailer but he had needed Anne's written approval. Joe rummaged through his file cabinet, finally finding the right folder. He had written down three passwords associated with this project. Definitely against the rules, but he had kept forgetting them. He typed in the first one - access denied. Same result for the second password. Joe took a stroll to the men's room before trying the third one. Three strikes on old passwords would definitely arouse the interest of the compliance department. Joe returned to his seat, crossing his fingers as the logon screen popped up. It flashed the time. Almost midnight. Joe decided to wait and try his luck again tomorrow night.

15

The bright morning sun streamed through Illuminate's giant windows. Mindy, usually the first one on the team to arrive, was surprised to see Kris already typing away on her computer.

"Hey."

Kris nodded hello, barely looking up.

"What are you doing in so early?"

"Work to do."

"I thought you had a date last night. With Ripcurl," Mindy slowly spit out the name.

"I did. Went well," Kris clearly was preoccupied, but Mindy was not deterred.

"Then why are you here so early?"

Kris chuckled and finally looked up.

"The Yankees had the night off, so Matt took me to Rao's for dinner. We met his roommate there. Nice guy."

"And then? No clubs? No parties?"

"You are really in a nosy mood. No, we just went back to my place."

"A real meeting of the minds, huh," Mindy said scornfully as she sat down at her desk.

"OK. A meeting of the bodies too," Kris replied playfully standing to stretch. "But Matthew left early. They have a big series with the Orioles starting tonight. He wanted to get his rest."

"I think I'm going to puke," Mindy said, pretending to gag.

"Don't you have a report to prepare? Anne is waiting for it."

The rest of the morning passed uneventfully, the clicking of fingers on keyboards marking off the time. Kris left at noon for a client lunch uptown, and did not get back to the office until after two.

Mindy was waiting with a triumphant expression plastered across her face when Kris returned. She let her boss settle in before pouncing. Mindy slapped the Post down on Kris's desk and slowly opened it to the Page Six gossip column.

"Looks like your favorite Yankee played a doubleheader last night," she snickered, pointing to a picture of Ripcurl, his arm flung across the shoulder of a dark-haired beauty, his nose nuzzling her ear. The caption read: ABOUT LAST NIGHT - *Yankee star canoodles with dancer Natasha Bubka at after hours party in Chelsea. Bubka was rumored to be the steady squeeze of Russian businessman Ilya Nakitov but she appears to be playing with a new teammate now.*

Kris stared at the page for several long seconds, willing its message to change but to no avail. Finally, she slowly folded the paper and tossed it in the trash. "That jerk. Looks like he really played me."

"It could happen to anyone. Ripcurl Reilly is a hot number," Mindy said.

"I should have known better," Kris said sadly, shaking her head in disgust. "It's not like we were going steady or anything, but he didn't have to outright lie."

Mindy returned to her desk without offering a reply. Kris stared at her screen for five full minutes, regaining her composure. She realized that she was more upset about her embarrassment in front of Mindy than anything else. Finally, she took out her phone and tapped out a succinct text message to Reilly: **ASSHOLE**

■ ■ ■

Across town, Ilya Nakitov had an even more vehement reaction to the Post's revelation. He had caught a matinee showing of "Lone Survivor" in nearby

Sheepshead Bay. The movie's setting in the hills of Afghanistan brought back many memories. Lenny Boykin, the Rock, had picked him up outside the theater, silently handing Ilya the newspaper as he climbed into the back seat of the black Mercedes. Nakitov slammed his fist into the armrest when he read the front page headline, Mayor Rips Russians Again, but exploded into a long stream of Russian profanity when he came across the Page Six photo.

"Take me home," Ilya ordered.

As the Mercedes crossed Ocean Parkway, Ilya changed his mind.

"I want to walk by the ocean," he announced.

"Yes sir." Lenny parked the car and followed three steps behind his boss as he stormed down the boardwalk. The late afternoon sun was still strong, enticing a throng of beach goers to linger on the sand. A bright red umbrella wobbled in the breeze. Two teenagers, done with school for the day, zipped by on skateboards veering perilously close to Nakitov. Lenny tried to chase them but he was woefully slow. Ilya just waved Lenny back to his post. Finally Ilya sat down on an empty bench, staring blankly at the waves, his anger barely contained. At last, he reached into the side pocket of his sport jacket and pulled out a battered phone. He hesitated for only a second, then tapped in a number from memory.

"Yes," Gregor answered on the third ring.

"The mission is on," Ilay stated.

"Confirmed. But first I will need a test run tonight."

"That is fine. But I have an additional request."

Gregor listened quietly for the next minute. "Ah, two birds with one stone," he replied.

"Yes." Ilya said, pausing for a second before adding, "Your country will be proud of you."

"Save the bullshit for Turken. I am doing this for my father."

And the money, Nakitov wanted to add, but thought better of it. "Your father will be proud," he said.

"See you on the other side."

"Be safe, my friend." Ilya signed off, then beckoned Lenny forward and handed him the phone.

"Please toss this into the ocean."

■ ■ ■

At 7PM, Mindy enticed Kris to head out for a cocktail to drown away her memories of Ripcurl, but Joe remained at his desk. He worked on a routine project for another thirty minutes, then pulled up the FreedomFighters file. Fifteen email addresses but, if there was a bad guy in the bunch, he needed to find a real name and identity. Joe reminded himself that this quest might just be a wild goose chase. All the effort, all the risk, might only uncover some ordinary and legitimate web surfing. But his gut told him otherwise; and, he would have to get into the Deep Dive analytics to find out. Joe slowly typed in the last of his old passwords. ACCESS DENIED again. Shit. Joe banged his palm on the screen. He was not ready to give up yet. One last try. Joe changed the last digit on the password. It was a flyer but it was his last hope. Bingo! He was in to Deep Dive. But he couldn't stay long.

Joe typed furiously for thirty minutes checking key words, search terms, browsing history and email content. One name kept popping to the top of the list. Heavy minutes on the FreedomFighters site, a subscription to the on-line jihadi publication Inspire, a query on pipe bombs, another on explosives, read every article on the Boston Marathon bombing, a download of an anti-American treatise by an ultra right wing Russian politician, three radical posts by Turken himself, Death to America. All legal, no single action damning by itself, but Joe realized that he was assembling the portrait of a potential terrorist on American soil. Joe needed to be off Deep Dive in five more minutes so he launched a final scan - looking for any international commerce transactions. Holy shit! Joe could not believe that he had missed this one the first time through. An order of mining supplies from the FreedomFighters site. What was Turken going to do with mining supplies? And how did he pay for them? MasterCard? Visa? Paypal? No - Bitcoin. No one conducts a legitimate transaction in Bitcoin, Joe thought as he signed off Deep Dive. He could return to normal channels now. Facebook, Twitter, Instagram, Snapchat - if Turken was posting on any of these media, Joe could track him down. He vowed to stay all night if necessary.

16

Determined not to languish over Ripcurl, Kris dressed as smartly as practical in this June heat wave, olive cargo pants, navy polo, hair tightly tied into a ponytail, and was again the first one of her team to arrive at the office. She was surprised to find a sealed legal sized envelope, marked CONFIDENTIAL - REQUIRES IMMEDIATE ATTENTION and signed by Joe, commanding the middle of her desk. Intrigued, Kris resisted the tempting aroma of freshly brewed coffee and began to read. She immediately recognized that Joe had put himself at risk. At minimum, he had broken corporate rules. At worst, he had broken the law. Why? Joe was already in hot water over the drug bust. As she read on, Kris could see the evidence mount. The radical fervor percolating, then exploding in the anti-American blog posts. But, everything that Joe documented was all circumstantial. America respected freedom of speech. Nothing illegal here, at least not yet. But the last point, the order of mining supplies paid in Bitcoin was definitely alarming. Kris thought back on her conversation with her dad. She was supposed to be protecting the innocent, not waiting for them to be attacked. Anatoly Turken required her immediate attention. She dialed Jim Bright.

The phone rang and rang. No answer. It was still early in the morning, just about 8. Government employees worked better hours than Illuminators.

Kris shuffled the other papers on her desk, but could not focus on them. She gave into temptation, pouring a mug of coffee and munching on a glazed donut. Mindy arrived a few minutes before nine, but no sign of Joe yet. Kris debated for just a few seconds before deciding to bring Mindy over the line, handing her the envelope. She watched as Mindy read, lines of consternation creasing her forehead. No wisecracks this morning.

"Wow," Mindy finally commented, looking around for the still absent Joe. "What are we going to do?"

"I tried Jim, but he wasn't in yet. I want him to read it before I show it to Anne. Joe violated almost every privacy protection that we have in the department."

"Anne won't care. She's been pushing us to dig up this kind of stuff for weeks. I bet she takes it right to the mayor." Mindy stood, returning the report to Kris.

Kris put the envelope in the top drawer of her desk. "Maybe, but Anne's been a loose cannon lately. I can't figure out what's bugging her. Besides, the mayor shot down our last proposal."

"You're right. Let's try Jim again."

Five rings. No answer. Finally, the receptionist picked up.

"Jim Bright's line."

"Is he in?"

A hesitation. "No, I'm sorry. He is out...for a while."

Doesn't sound good, Kris thought. "Is Glenn Walker in?"

"Yes," a noticeable sigh of relief, "I'll transfer you."

After three rings, the receptionist jumped back on the line. "I'm sorry, he's out this morning. Can I take a message?"

Kris left her callback information, turning to Mindy with a shrug. "We'll have to sit tight."

When Joe came in, a few minutes before ten, Kris let him know that she had read his report and was trying her best to follow up today if possible. The rest of the morning crawled along. Finally just after one, Glenn called.

"Sorry, I've been tied up in meetings."

"Where's Jim?" Kris asked.

"Still suspended. The Russian protests, the ACLU, all the news coverage. It's spooked the DA. He's up for reelection, so he can't take any chances. I think that he's going to try to fry Jim's ass."

"No help from the Mayor's office? He keeps bashing the Russian mob in every speech."

"Not a fucking peep. The word around here is the mayor doesn't want to take on the DA on this one. Everyone seems to have discovered the fourth amendment. You too, if I remember correctly."

"Yes, you remember correctly." Kris hesitated. "But I've got some new information. Maybe a real lead. We need to talk as soon as possible."

"Can you give me a clue?"

"Not over the phone. I need Jim's opinion. Yours too. Something may be up."

"Something?"

"Something bad."

"Ok, I've got some news for you too. Jim's probably home. He can meet us here at the coffee shop downstairs."

"Somewhere more private would be better."

Glenn thought for a second. "What about Jim's apartment in an hour. It's not far."

"Doesn't he live in Brooklyn?"

"Yeah, just over the bridge. I thought you might have …" Glenn coughed, slowing down the conversation. "Never mind. Here's his address. I'll give him a call."

"See you there."

■ ■ ■

Jim's apartment in DUMBO was less than five miles from the Illuminate office, but getting there in the afternoon crush of a hot summer day in New York City would be like crossing the Sahara. Kris checked the queue of traffic backing up on the West Side Highway. She looked at the subway map but dreaded going into the underground sauna. Finally, she tapped on the CitiBike app on her phone. Two bikes were still available on her corner and there were plenty of open spots to dock at the kiosk near Jim. The map app plotted her route across the Manhattan Bridge. Riding at ten miles per hour, she could be at Jim's apartment in thirty minutes. Probably a great view crossing the East River. Why not?

An hour later, Kris climbed the last of the three flights of stairs leading to Jim's apartment on Bridge Street, sweat streaking her shirt and dripping into her right eye, but otherwise no worse for wear. The pedestrian traffic on the streets and the bridge had slowed her pace.

"Did you walk here?" Glenn asked sarcastically.

"Biked." Kris said, wiping away the moisture on her face.

"Really? Brave girl."

Jim sat at the kitchen table, studying a stack of photos. Kris looked around the apartment. Not bad, but sterile, she thought. Barren walls, few bright colors or soft textures anywhere. A bachelor pad that needed a personal touch.

"Look at this," Jim said, pulling the top photo off the stack.

"Crazy 8?" Kris said tenuously.

"Yep, Independence Square in Kiev." He pulled another picture from the pile. "Here's our man in the crowd in Benghazi two years ago." Jim flashed one more snapshot, "And in Kabul the year before that."

"A world traveler," Kris said.

"Probably a hired gun, or an Al Qaeda instigator," Glenn interjected.

"How did you get these pictures anyway?" Kris asked.

"They are NSA and CIA surveillance photos. They just sent them over this morning. Their facial recognition software picked out Crazy 8 based on the photo that I snapped in Brighton Beach," Glenn said. "I was working with Homeland Security this morning, trying to develop a plan."

"And?" Jim asked.

"First we need to find him. DHS has access to cameras all over the city. Streets, subways, stadiums - almost every public venue has a closed circuit hook-up now. They'll run the same facial rec program to scan every face."

"Any luck yet?" Kris asked, taking the seat next to Jim.

"No." Glenn shook his head. "But they just started the process. It will take a few hours to get cranking."

"Do they have an ID?" Jim asked.

"They think his real name is Gregor Trotiak, but they're not 100% sure yet," Glenn said, pulling two Diet Cokes from the refrigerator and handing one to Kris. "He's never been on any of our official watch lists, but the CIA guy thinks he's dangerous. A Russian Army brat. Born with a gun in his crib. CIA can't understand how DHS let him into the country."

"Finger-pointing is not going to help right now," Jim said.

"We need to find Mr.Trotiak," Kris interjected before taking a long draught of the cold drink.

Jim pushed his chair back from the table. "Glenn said that you had something important."

Kris handed him the envelope with Joe's report. "I'm going to wash up while you read it. Where's the loo?" she asked. Jim pointed to the back of the small apartment without even looking up from his reading.

"This looks nasty," he said when Kris returned. "The pros need operational support. Someone with local knowledge. Turken could be the guy."

"Or one of the guys," Glenn chipped in. Jim handed him Joe's report as soon as he had finished it.

"We're going to need to move quickly," Jim said, standing to take command.

"You're suspended, remember," Glenn said.

"That's right, so you're going to have to be the front man. Take Joe's report and retype the high points. Say that you searched the web and found all this stuff."

"But how did I get Turken's name in the first place?"

"Our guy inside the credit card crew gave it to us. If that doesn't work, make something up. We need to get a warrant tonight."

"Jim, your name, our name, is mud right now. Nothing is going to happen that fast."

"We've got to try."

Glenn nodded, and left to return to the office.

"What do you want me to do?" Kris asked.

"Let's go over Joe's report line by line. Maybe we can turn up some clues." Jim sat down again, pulling his chair up next to Kris.

■ ■ ■

"Turn on the six o'clock news, Channel 5," Glenn said breathlessly over the phone.

Jim fumbled for the remote. "What's up?" he asked, but then quickly shifted his attention to the screen.

The local reporter, the hot one with the curly blond hair who looked like she just graduated from high school, stood in front of a burnt out storefront. "I am here at Sidney's Cleaners, or what used to be Sidney's Cleaners, in Brighton Beach, Brooklyn. Sidney's was devastated by an explosion and fire late last night. Firefighters finally got the blaze under control this morning. Fortunately, no injuries were reported. Police investigators are searching for clues in the rubble, but no official report has been released yet. Back to the studio for our weather report. The heat is…"

Jim shut off the television.

"What do you think?" Kris asked.

"I don't know. It could be Crazy 8. Or it could have nothing to do with him at all." He picked up the phone and hit the speaker button, "Glenn, what's happening downtown?"

"It's like a fire drill here right now. The CIA guy just called in from Brooklyn. Said the bomb signature looks like the IED's on the roads in Afghanistan. They won't release any of this to the public, but the DHS people are scared shitless. They practically ran our warrant request over to the judge. It got approved in thirty minutes."

"What's next?" Jim asked.

"We're going to send an NYPD anti-terrorist team to Turken's apartment in Brooklyn. Also, the FBI will send a formal request to Illuminate and the other email providers to start checking their databases."

Mindy and Joe would have a long night, Kris thought. But at least Joe would be off the hook. "You need to check all the social media sites too," she almost shouted into the speaker.

"We've got Facebook and Twitter covered," Glenn replied.

"Instagram and Snapchat too. Young guys like to send photos," Kris railed.

"What about Crazy 8?" Jim asked.

"Still looking at all the camera footage, but no sightings yet."

"OK, we've got work to do here. Keep me in the loop."

"Yes boss," Glenn signed off.

17

"You hungry?" Jim asked. "We could be here for a while."

Kris looked up from the photos on the table. "Yeah, the only thing that I've eaten today was a glazed donut. Want to order a pizza?"

"How about some pasta? I have time on my hands these days, so I made a fresh batch of marinara sauce yesterday. All I have to do is boil water."

"Sounds like a plan," Kris said, returning to work while Jim busied himself at the stove. The buzz of Jim's phone interrupted the peaceful scene.

"The NYPD squad just got through interviewing Turken's mom," Glenn said.

"And?" Jim said, pacing around the small apartment.

"Turken had dinner with his mom tonight but then went out with a friend, Vladimir Unchkin, but she didn't know where they were going. The cops think that she's lying but there's not much they can do right now."

"OK, what next?"

"They're going to search the beach and the boardwalk. The streets are packed so its tough to find anybody out there. Remember, Turken's an American citizen and he hasn't committed any crime so there's really not much that they can do."

"Has not committed any crime yet," Jim said, signing off and returning to the kitchen. Ten minutes later, he wheeled out with a heaping bowl of linguine. "Help yourself."

Kris attacked the pasta with relish. Jim, the proud chef, ate a bit more slowly. Kris had just twirled the last strands on her plate when Jim's phone buzzed again. "What's up?" Glenn, he mouthed to Kris.

Jim remained rooted in his chair but Kris could sense the urgency in his voice steadily increase. Finally, he slapped the phone down on the dining table and jumped up. "Let's go," he snapped.

"Where?"

"Yankee Stadium. You were right. DHS just intercepted a Snapchat of Anatoly and his buddy on on the concourse out in front of the ballpark. There's a big game tonight."

"Holy shit. What's DHS going to do?"

"Contact stadium security and the mayor. See if he wants to evacuate."

"Do you think that we have enough to evacuate 50,000 people?"

"Not even close. That's why I want to go there myself." Kris stood, plate in hand. "Leave it. I just need to grab something from the bedroom," Jim said. His gun, Kris realized as they hurtled down the steps and out into the street.

Jim led the way to his car. He opened the door for Kris, then swung around to jump into the driver's seat. Kris buckled in, ready to go, but Jim had paused to look directly at her.

"If you're going to recite the fourth amendment to me, you can just get out now," he said.

"No lectures. We have to find Turken. Tonight."

Jim nodded and pulled away from the curb.

"Don't you have a flasher and siren?" Kris asked, as they waited at a red light.

"Yeah, but I'm still suspended, remember. I know a back way to the Stadium so we should be able to avoid most of the traffic."

Jim steered the car up the ramp onto the Manhattan Bridge. Cars were backed up leaving the city, but the traffic moved briskly in their direction. The FDR Drive northbound also flowed smoothly until 96th Street, then it ground to a halt.

"Shit, we're almost there," Jim said, reaching into the back seat to grab his flashing light and affix it to the dash. The cars in front slowly peeled to each side, creating a lane for Jim to inch through. He headed up onto the First Avenue Bridge, crossing the East River, then headed onto Morris Avenue.

"Almost there," he said as they passed 145th Street. Jim's mobile rang, so he hit the speaker button. Glenn's voice boomed, "What the fuck are you doing?"

"Going to the ballgame," Jim replied jauntily. "With my friend Kris."

"Yeah, well a patrol car just called in to inform the FBI that a suspended agent is disrupting traffic on the FDR in a rush to get somewhere. The boss went apeshit. He said to tell you that he will shove your badge so far up your ass that you will need a proctologist to ever get it back."

"Understood. Ask him to trust me here. What did the mayor say about the possibility of evacuation?"

"No way."

"No surprise." Jim made a hard left turn onto 161st Street, the Stadium almost in sight. Kris had to hang on to the safety handle above her head to stay planted in her seat. Jim finally turned off the flashing light, slowing down to show his badge to a cop checking credentials at the tunnel that ran under the Grand Concourse. "Almost there," he said. Glenn's voice broke up as they blitzed through the two blocks underground.

"Lost you," Jim said as they emerged at the elevated subway tracks for the #4 train from Manhattan. The Stadium, now visible, electrified the night sky. "Repeat that last bit."

"Mayor Chamberlain is at the game himself. He is not going to panic just because of a quote 'Illuminate inspired wild goose chase' end of quote."

"What's with the Illuminate shit?" Jim asked.

"Rumor is Mayor Chamberlain and Kris' boss, Anne Harmony, had a falling out. No one knows why. He thinks that she's drumming up this idea of a terrorist plot to get back in his good graces." Kris shrugged her shoulders to indicate that she knew nothing here.

"Doesn't matter now anyway. We're here. Pulling into one of the designated security parking spots on 161st right now. Right across the street from the Stadium."

"Well, partner, I hope you enjoy the game," Glenn said.

"Later," Jim said, jumping out of his seat and beckoning Kris to follow.

"The game's in the third inning already," Kris shouted as she chased Jim across 161st street. Jim climbed the steps to the plaza fronting the Stadium.

Now that he was here, he wasn't really sure what to do next. He looked around at the ragtag collection of panhandlers, limo drivers, ticket scalpers and neighborhood kids.

"You need tickets man? I got Field MVP," A stout Hispanic with a pitted face grunted, pulling two from his back pocket. Jim flashed his badge and the enterprising salesman melted away. Finally Jim noticed the medals pinned to the handmade sign on the lap of a grizzled black man sitting in his wheelchair, head down, eyes buried in the sports page.

"You really a war vet?" Jim asked, gently shaking his shoulder.

"Operation Iraqi Freedom," Bill Jones mumbled distractedly, holding his cup up for a contribution.

"Have you been out here all game?" Jim asked, showing his badge.

Jones snapped to attention. "I didn't do nothing. Just another Yankee fan who can't afford to get into the Stadium."

"Don't worry, don't worry. You're not in trouble." Jim stuffed his badge back in his pocket, replacing it with his phone. He tapped three times and leaned over to show it to Bill. "You see this guy tonight? Maybe with a buddy?"

"Yeah man, they were here."

"You sure?"

"Definitely. They looked like two flaming peacocks with those red Yankee caps."

"You said 'were' here?" Kris interjected.

Bill squinted at the attractive redhead. "She your partner?" he asked Jim.

Jim smiled. "Yeah - for tonight at least."

Bill appraised Kris one more time and nodded his head to Jim in approval. "I'd tap that too man."

"What about the two peacocks?" Kris asked, unfazed by the unwanted attention.

"They left about ten minutes ago. Headed back towards the subway."

"You sure?" Jim demanded.

"Damn sure. Like I said, can't miss those red hats. They were acting strange too."

"Strange?" Jim asked.

"I was in Iraq, man, a sniper, you know, so I learned to watch people. Study their faces. Figure out where they going. What they doing. Only made one mistake in two years and it cost me both legs."

Jim wanted to offer his sympathy, but he had no time. "So what about these two?"

"They were up to no good, I'll bet my whole cup here." Bill said, rattling the coins around. "Wait a second, just wait one sec. They came in carrying backpacks but they left without them. I'm sure of that."

Kris and Jim shared a frightened glance. The buzz of Jim's phone jolted the already turbo-charged air.

"Glenn, you must be reading my mind. We…" Jim stopped talking suddenly as Glenn cut him off. Kris waited nervously while Jim listened for an interminably long ten seconds. Then he hung up, wild-eyed.

"Crazy 8 is here too. The facial rec software picked him out a few minutes ago."

"Shit," Kris exclaimed. "What took so long?"

"He was one of the first to arrive. They checked that tape last."

"What now?"

"Stadium security is on full alert. They'll search every aisle. The SWAT team and the snipers have their orders too."

"Snipers?" Bill asked.

"They're up in the rafters for every game."

"Lemme see that guy," Bill demanded, now part of the team. Jim complied, showing him a photo of Crazy 8 on his phone. Bill just whistled, pantomiming a sight down the barrel of a rifle, and pulled the imaginary trigger. "Good-bye asshole," he exclaimed, exploding his hands.

Kris looked frantically up at the lights and then around the bustling plaza. "I'm going to the subway," she announced determinedly.

"Be careful," Jim said, grabbing Kris by the shoulder. "Turken and his pal could be armed."

"You look out too." Kris said, then she sprinted towards the elevated tracks, while Jim turned in the opposite direction to head into the Stadium. Bill Jones raised his right hand, delivering a crisp military salute from his wheelchair. The screech of sirens shocked the crowd lingering on the plaza as five police vans and two ambulances wheeled into position.

18

Kris raced down the Stadium plaza, passing by the revelers downing beers on the patio of the Hard Rock Cafe in the sticky night air, then crossed River Avenue under the elevated subway tracks. She could see the puzzled looks on two uniformed cops on the corner, wondering where she was going so fast and this early in the game; but they did not move to stop her. Kris reached the steps to the platform for the 4 train but then froze as she heard a roar swelling from deep inside the Stadium, the banks of bright lights on its roof casting a warm glow on the Bronx skyline. Kris laughed, almost maniacally. The game was going on. Life was still normal. She pulled out her phone to check ESPN. The Yankees were batting: Ripcurl Reilly in the on deck circle. The fans exuberantly anticipating his turn at the plate. A train rumbled overhead, burrowing deeper into the Bronx. No big deal. Kris wanted to head in the other direction, towards Manhattan. Then, she stopped. Turken lived in Brighton Beach. She remembered her subway ride home from there a few weeks ago. Turken and his accomplice would likely head back home on the D or B train, not the 4. These trains ran underground, not above ground, so she spun around. The stairs descending to the underground station were right in front of her. Kris cast one last glance at the gleaming edifice across the street before beginning her descent. She had just reached the fifth step when another wave of sound rose from the Stadium. But this time it was a wail of shock and anger and fear. Like molten lava spilling from a volcano, it erupted from the grandstands, tumbled across the plaza and smoldered through the surrounding streets. Kris bolted back up to River Avenue in time to see a plume of dark smoke streaming through the Stadium lights. Police and ambulance sirens filled the air. Kris realized immediately what had happened. Fighting back the impulse to return to the Stadium, she could do nothing to help there now anyway, Kris hurtled underground to pursue the terrorists.

■ ■ ■

Jim was twenty five yards from the Gate 4 entrance behind home plate when the bomb went off, its blast goring the dulcet buzz of the ballgame. Screams of hysteria soon followed as the crowd swarmed out of the Stadium in a mass panic. The police formed a cordon around the plaza, helping people along and triaging the walking wounded. A SWAT team, weapons at the ready, burst through the crowd and into the Stadium. Firemen and paramedics followed close behind, wheeling in two stretchers. The pungent mixture of explosives, smoke and burning flesh overpowered the more familiar ballpark aromas of hot dogs, beer and popcorn.

Jim tried to dodge his way through the frantic crowd, but quickly realized that he was swimming upstream against an overwhelming current. The first responder teams would know what to do inside; he might be able to help more out here. Jim anchored himself against a now deserted souvenir stand, allowing the crowd to flow by. He could hear the whir of helicopters overhead and the amplified voice of a police captain trying in vain to instill order. Did Gregor Trotiak blow himself up in an act of martyrdom? Not likely, Jim thought. He was a professional soldier, not a deluded suicide bomber. In that case, he would need to exit the Stadium at some point. Jim decided to wait here and scan the runaway horde. A father carrying a bleeding child in one arm while steering another youngster by the neck to safety. Twentysomething lovers, holding hands, eyes plastered wide open with disbelief. An elderly man staggering, trying in vain to keep pace with the flow of humanity, supported by helping hands from behind. The brawny figure walking alone, picking his way through the throng with a steady, purposeful gait, stood out like a ballet dancer in a mosh pit. The red Yankee cap perched on his head confirmed his identity. In the heat of the moment, Trotiak had not tossed his telltale hat. Jim fell in behind, waiting for the crowd to thin enough to provide a path of attack.

Lurking in the shadow of the Stadium's limestone wall, Bill Jones could not demonstrate such restraint. He had spotted the blasphemous red cap at fifty paces, compared Trotiak's visage to the image that he had committed to memory at twenty-five paces, and lined up his assault vector at ten. Even in his most booze-addled dreams, Bill never imagined that he would have the opportunity to strike back against the unseen bombers that had crippled him a decade ago. When the terrorist reached five paces, Bill launched his wheelchair with every ounce of force that his forearms could deliver, bursting right between two long-bearded Hasidic men, a black hat spinning to the ground. An atavistic wail exploded from the depths of Bill's diaphragm as he crashed into Trotiak's knees. With the surging crowd behind him, Trotiak had nowhere to go. He tried to push away, but Bill had catapulted himself from his wheelchair to clasp Trotiak's waist with both hands, screaming "MOTHERFUCKER, MOTHERFUCKING BOMBER" at maximum volume, his lifeless lower body dragging on the ground. The quilt of spectators, already dazed by the night's gruesome events, unraveled, leaving the combatants alone on center stage. Gregor took a step backwards to brace himself, flinging his hands in the air, as if to say who is this crazed beggar. But a quick survey of nearby faces revealed a rapidly dawning recognition of the truth. Gregor knew that he would be at the mercy of a bloodthirsty crowd in a few seconds at most. He smashed his fist into Bill's face, trying to tear away. But Bill's grip, forged by years in his wheelchair, would not yield. Two Latinos, sweat glowing on their bronze skin, stepped forward. Cooly, Gregor reached behind his back and pulled his knife from its sheath. The blade gleamed as he pointed it menacingly at the pack. Bill still hung on tenaciously, but he had slipped down to Gregor's right knee. Gregor tried to kick free, but Bill summoned one final surge, rearing up to clamp his teeth into Gregor's thigh. The terrorist screamed in pain and in defeat as he thrust his knife downward. Bill's blood spurted up, splashing his chest. Gregor raised his knife to strike again, humiliated that his life was going to end this way, brought down by a crippled American. A millisecond later a fusillade of bullets smashed into his brain.

■ ■ ■

Mindy Smart was at her desk in Illuminate's offices, complying with the government's urgent request to review all of Anatoly Turken's electronic communications, when the first tweets crossed her screen.

just saw a huge blast in the lower deck #yankeestadium a bomb????
#yankeestadium

will the stadium fall??? I am in the upper deck section 416 HELP
#nycbombing

don't panic firemen coming now hear the sirens #nycbombing

Another shortly followed with a photo taken from an upper deck seat. It showed the field area behind home plate in disarray, two bodies, one in black and one in a Yankee uniform, sprawled lifeless on the ground. Mindy screamed. An Illuminator at a distant pod echoed her cry. Joe Brady was absorbed in the data on his screen and the music pumping through his headphones when he felt Mindy's fists pounding his back. The tears on her face signaled a catastrophe in the making. She shakily pointed to the Twitter icon on his dashboard and they read the string of tweets together.

yankee dugout destroyed #yankeestadium

body parts scattered over box seats #nycbombing

first rows of section 17B hit hardest #yankeestadium

on deck circle is gone #yankeestadium

paramedics working frantically on Ripcurl Reilly #yankeestadium

where is the mayor??? He was here. I saw him on the big screen
#nycbombing

Joe stood and hugged Mindy tightly. They drifted towards the main aisle, joining the handful of other Illuminators still at the office. Disbelief, desolation and fear were apparent on each face, as eyes boomeranged from Twitter feed to friend then hurriedly back to Twitter feed again. Someone switched on one of the large screens, tuning it to a TV stream. The group congregated around it, unsure what to do next. Suddenly the boom of gunfire exploded from the monitor. The camera jerked, but then flashed to a chaotic scene on the Stadium plaza, the crowd diving for cover, someone obviously shot in the center of the pack.

"They got him. They got him. The cops just shot the bomber," a voice in the background yelled to the TV anchor.

Anne Harmony emerged from her office, striding purposefully down the corridor towards the group. She projected a commanding presence, but Mindy could see a trail of dried tears on one cheek and a smudge of mascara on the bridge of her nose. Anne stood in front of the TV screen.

"Back to work everyone," she ordered. "Our country needs us tonight."

19

Anatoly Turken lunged for the closing doors of the subway, getting half his torso in just before they closed. When the doors backtracked, he pulled Vladimir on board. They stumbled to seats by the window and stared at the smoke rising from the Stadium as the train pulled away from the 161st station.

"What happened?" Vlad asked.

Anatoly clamped his hand on his friend's shoulder and pulled him close. "Shut up and keep your head down," he ordered.

"Why are we on the 4 train? It's the wrong one. Where are we going?" Vladimir whispered, the panic now obvious in his plaintive tone.

"I'm following instructions," Anatoly replied, trying to calm his friend down. "If we made the hand-off, we're supposed to take this train."

Vlad still looked confused. "Well, where do we get off?"

"125th. Three stops. Someone will meet us there."

As the train dove into the tunnel heading towards Manhattan, Vlad buried his face in his hands.

"Don't cry. You did well. Everything's going to be OK." Anatoly said.

When the two young men slinked off the train, they could see the increased police presence on the platform. Blue uniforms every fifty paces. They seemed to be guarding the station, not searching for anyone in particular, Anatoly thought, as he climbed the steps to exit to the street. Relieved to be back above ground, he gulped the night air still thick with the residue of the day's heat. Anatoly surveyed the streetscape: a neon sign advertised check cashing services, a city bus rumbled by, a group of black teens jammed in front of a storefront with a TV in its window. Harlem was not his home turf.

Rough hands latched onto Anatoly's shoulders, steering him towards the open door of a black Escalade double-parked in the street. "Heads down lads. Get in," an unknown voice ordered in a thick Irish brogue, pushing him into the back seat. Vladimir was shoved in right behind. One of their greeters wedged into the back with them. The other opened the front door and climbed into the passenger seat.

Sean O'Keele swept a mop of wheat brown hair out of his eyes and powered the SUV into the flow of traffic. He was the eldest, and in command of his beefy brothers, Padraig, Rory and Ian, dressed identically in blue jeans and tight fitting black T-shirts. They were a family of warriors going back several generations now. His dad, god rest his soul, had died in Maze prison but not before teaching his sons the arts of battle. Bedtime stories were tales of Sparta, the great warrior state of ancient Greece. With peace prevailing at home now, the O'Keeles had turned to the export market. It paid much better than driving a lorry in Belfast, even if they could find the work. Sean thought that he would pass on the skills to his own two young boys in a few years. He drove slowly, obeying the speed limit and stopping purposefully as the traffic light on Madison Avenue switched from green to yellow. A police cruiser pulled alongside but paid them no attention.

"Who are you?" Anatoly asked, trying to regain his composure.

"Mr. Nakitov sent us to look after you," Rory replied from the passenger seat. Anatoly brightened.

"But you don't sound Russian," Vladimir chirped.

"Smart friend," Padraig commented, poking Anatoly in the ribs.

Rory pointed Sean to the GPS map on the dashboard. "Roadblocks at every bridge and tunnel." He then lowered his voice to a whisper, holding up his phone, tuned to the police frequency. "They have the lads' names and photos circulating everywhere now."

"We'll be fine," Sean loudly assured everyone. They had worked for Nakitov several times over many years, but never in America. The old general was ruthless, but meticulous, sparing no expense to get the job done properly.

Anatoly overheard bits of the brief conversation up front. "Where are we going?" he asked.

"Moscow - a little vacation till things cool down here," Padraig said, rummaging in the gym bag resting on his lap for two plane tickets. He waved them in front of Anatoly. "Here."

Anatoly could see his name on one ticket and Vladimir's on the other. Aeroflot flight 101, leaving from Newark Airport in two hours. He breathed a sigh of relief, but then a concerned expression creased his face. "Will we get to the airport in time?"

"No worries," Padraig said, slipping the tickets back into his bag. "We've arranged special transportation."

The Escalade rumbled down 125th Street towards the Hudson River. Sean looked into the faces of the pedestrians milling on every street corner. The same blank, scared looks that he had seen back home during the Troubles. Of course, New Yorkers had been down this road before too, when the Twin Towers fell in 2001. They were a tough lot. He would be relieved to return home.

Vladimir pointed to a McDonald's on the left hand side of the street. "Can we stop? I'm starved?"

Padraig and Rory exchanged glances. "Not a good idea right now, lads," Rory said. "Besides, there'll be a big meal on the plane. All first class."

Sean accelerated onto the ramp leading to the West Side Highway, traffic extremely light for the early evening hours in Manhattan.

"Can I call my mother?" Anatoly asked, reaching for his phone.

Padraig snatched it quickly from his hand. "No," he hissed menacingly. "The police could be monitoring your calls now."

"You can ring her from New Jersey. I'll give you a clean phone," Rory said reassuringly. "You can make a call there too," he added, pointing to Vladimir. That seemed to quiet the back seat duo down at least for a few seconds.

After a little more than a mile on the highway, Sean flipped his right hand turn signal, maneuvering the Escalade to exit for the West 79th Street boat basin. He entered the small traffic circle at the end of the ramp, but then diverted only a quarter way around to a maintenance road. He stopped in the dark under a thick curtain of trees. Rory checked his own phone, relieved to see a text from his brother waiting. "Ian's docked and ready," he announced, as he opened the front door.

"Let's go gents," Padraig ordered, prodding Anatoly and Vladimir to exit. "We're taking a little boat ride across the river."

Rory led the way through the brush, a gym bag slung across his shoulder. The boys followed docilely while Padraig brought up the rear. Sean stayed in the car with the headlights out, watching the procession thread its way down to the dock. He texted Ian their codeword, Dieneces - one of the brave Spartans who died at the battle of Thermopylae. Mr. Nakitov did not want any loose ends. The motorboat had barely swung into the current when Sean saw the muzzle flashes of the silenced pistols. The vessel did not slow, but continued on its journey towards the Statue of Liberty and then out into deep water.

■ ■ ■

Just before ten, Kris stepped off the elevator at Illuminate. She started walking towards her desk but stopped at the big screen TV where a newscaster appeared to be reading a press release from Moscow: *The Russian people extend their deepest sympathy to the victims at Yankee Stadium. Terrorists destroy the lives of innocent people all over the globe. If the American government did not meddle in disputes beyond its borders, it would be better able to protect its own citizens at home.* Some condolence message, Kris thought, as she turned away. The floor was humming with activity as many Illuminators had returned to work looking to contribute in any way possible to the pursuit of the bombers. Mindy and Joe looked like virtuoso pianists performing at Carnegie Hall as they pounded away on their keyboards.

Kris tapped Mindy on the shoulder. "Hey," she said quietly.

Mindy banged a few more keys, still lost in concentration. Then she sensed the presence behind her and turned. Seeing Kris, at last, she stood and wrapped her arms around her. "Where were you?"

"Riding the subway. To Brighton Beach and back." Kris flopped down, exhausted, at her desk. "Twice."

"No luck?"

Kris shook her head. "The cops were all over the trains too. Turken and Unchkin had to have escaped another way."

"Yeah, they booked a flight to Moscow."

"What?"

"We tried to call but you must have been underground. DHS found the reservations, but they never showed up for the flight."

"Where did they go?" Kris asked, sitting down at her desk.

"No one knows."

"Is Jim OK?"

"He's fine. He called looking for you too. Said he had Crazy 8 in his sights but the SWAT guys pulled the trigger first."

"What about casualties inside the Stadium?" Kris asked, checking her Twitter feed for updates.

"Ten spectators confirmed dead so far, including two kids at their first baseball game. Another fifteen people wounded."

Kris dejectedly cast her eyes to the floor. Mindy took a deep breath. "Mayor Chamberlain and Matt Reilly are in intensive care. It looks bad. The doctors don't know if they'll make it."

Kris finally cracked, tears streaming down her cheeks.

"One hour, one day, one week earlier. We had the information. We could have stopped it."

For once, Mindy had nothing to say.

PART 3

"Screw your courage to the sticking place,
And we'll not fail."

Macbeth
by William Shakespeare

20

"Fuck the fourth amendment," Kris thought bitterly, still blaming herself for not derailing the carnage at Yankee Stadium. Wedged into a pew at the back of New York's massive St. Patrick's cathedral, she craned to see the President of the United States tread slowly to the altar to deliver the eulogy for both his good friend, Mayor Deion Chamberlain, and the heroic Iraqi war veteran, Bill Jones. Of course, Kris understood that as of a week ago she had been the amendment's staunchest supporter. She twisted uncomfortably on the wooden bench, not knowing what to think anymore.

The days since the bombing had been a blur of black and blue. Manhattan and the Bronx were in a virtual state of siege: uniformed police checkpoints at every bridge and tunnel, bomb squads and detection dogs patrolling the major tourist centers, helicopters overhead, patrol boats in the water. When Anne heard that whispers of her past affair with the mayor had started to circulate, she decided to refrain from any public appearances, asking Kris to take her place. Kris had been in the small entourage that accompanied the President as he toured Yankee Stadium two days after the bombing and met with first responders, survivors and grieving families. The next day, she represented Illuminate at the mayor's funeral in Bedford Stuyvesant, an invitation only, standing room event. On the fourth day, Kris had attended the funeral for Bill Jones at the Bronx Baptist Church and then bid a last farewell outside Penn Station as the train bearing his flag-draped casket began its journey to Arlington National Cemetery. The newspapers estimated that over a million thankful Americans lined the hero's route. After today's mass, Kris planned to permanently retire both of the black Chanel dresses that Anne had authorized her to charge to Illuminate.

A gentle light permeated the cathedral as the morning sun filtered through the stained glass windows set high in the arches. The marble cathedral, originally dedicated in 1879, consumed an entire city block in midtown Manhattan with its front steps opening onto Fifth Avenue between 50th and 51st Streets. Its twin Gothic spires soared over 300 feet, a reminder of a heavenly presence in the commercial heart of the city. The 10AM start to the memorial was designed to capture the coolest part of the June day, but there was no way to escape the urban oven. Attendees had to navigate police checkpoints a block away from the cathedral and then wait on line to pass through the metal detectors at the main entrance. Not surprisingly, semicircles of perspiration already ringed both sides of Kris' dress. Scanning the crowd, Kris could see the famous, the powerful and the beautiful all suffering in the New York heat: the dank, locker room stink from two thousand sweaty bodies mingling with the heavy incense of the church ceremony.

Mount Rushmore solid, the President gripped the podium set at the center of the altar. He wore a tapered black suit, white shirt and pinstriped navy blue tie. The fluted marble columns running down both sides of the cathedral funneled all eyes towards him. Classroom-sized American flags, discreetly positioned on each wing of the broad stage, rested limply in the still air. The President paused briefly, making eye contact with Tanya Chamberlain, before commencing his speech. Kris' eyes moistened as he offered personal words of condolence to Tanya and to Bill Jones' mother, both sitting in the first row with their closest family members. The President invited the Chamberlain boys to visit the White House for a basketball game in honor of their dad. He added a personal anecdote about watching the Final Four with Deion and cited several of the Mayor's accomplishments, particularly related to housing and education. The President moved on to recount the valorous acts of Bill Jones, both in Iraq and outside Yankee Stadium. Steeling himself for the emotional climax, the President paused and squared his jaw.

"Deion Chamberlain and William Jones were born and raised in New York City. They lived here, loved here, worked here and rooted passionately for their baseball team, the New York Yankees. Tragically, they both made the ultimate sacrifice at Yankee Stadium for their city and their country. It is only fitting that we remember them both this morning here at St. Patrick's. New Yorkers have also gathered at this great cathedral to celebrate the lives of Babe Ruth and Joe DiMaggio with memorial masses. We are honored today to add the names, Chamberlain and Jones, to this pantheon of heroes."

A faint smile creased Tanya Chamberlain's full face. She glanced at her boys, and then briefly cast her eyes heavenward. She remembered her husband warmly: he had lived his life to the fullest. He would be pleased with this tribute.

The President launched into his final proclamation, his baritone voice blasting across the giant cathedral like the sonic boom of a fighter jet:

"Bill Jones and Deion Chamberlain will be Yankees forever.

The Bronx will remember her brave.

New Yorkers will again rebuild from the ashes of a terrorist attack.

The citizens of the United States will never yield to terrorism. We will never retreat from our stadiums or our cities or our countryside. Our nation will always shine as a beacon of hope and freedom in a darkening world. God bless you all. God bless America."

The President stepped down from the altar, stopping to add a parting word to the Chamberlain and Jones families. Kris could just about see the top of his head as he bowed to talk to Deion's sons. The Secret Service detail then guided the President to a side door. As soon as he had exited, the crowd slowly filled the cathedral's main aisle to file out.

Kris scrutinized Arnold Klotz, the former Public Advocate, as he led his stubby, over-coiffured wife past the last pew. A draft from the open doorway tented her black dress around her ample waist. A week ago, few people even knew Klotz's name, let alone that he was next in line for the city's highest office. Now, he would hold the mayorship for the remainder of the year at least, probably longer. According to Section 10.c.1 of the city charter, Klotz had called for a special election this fall to select a new mayor to fulfill Deion Chamberlain's term. The political pundits expected Klotz to run, and win. Klotz was much slimmer than his wife, but not much taller. He would fit comfortably in the middle seat of a tightly packed commuter jet. Underneath a helmet of black hair jelled into place, Klotz set his lips in a grimace befitting the occasion; but, his hazel-gray eyes, spinning like bicycle wheels, betrayed his enthusiasm for his newfound prominence. He shook hands with several well-wishers as he descended the steps to Fifth Avenue.

After the crowd had departed, Kris remained anchored in place, a solitary tombstone in an empty field. She reflected on the President's speech - what he said, and, more importantly, what he didn't say. There was no mention of Mayor Chamberlain's campaign against crime or the Russian mob. No mention of the search for the real masterminds of the attack on the Stadium. Did the government think that it was the work of a lone terrorist, aided by two local nitwits? Where were Anatoly Turken and Vladimir Unchkin anyway? She hoped to get some answers tonight when she met Jim Bright at Yankee Stadium for the reopening ceremonies and ballgame. But first, Kris had to pay a visit to a friend in the hospital.

■ ■ ■

Actually, Kris first had to return to her apartment and focus on the work that she had neglected all week. She was tempted to walk downtown after the memorial, but the furnace blast that greeted her on Fifth Avenue convinced her to take advantage of the car and driver that Illuminate had put at her disposal. Once home, Kris refreshed in the shower, donned a T-shirt and shorts, and sat at her desk. Her family did not even have air conditioning on the ranch in Colorado, but it was clearly a necessity in New York City. She was exhausted, but the icy drafts kept her awake. Kris knew that she should be wrestling with the security problems of Illuminate's advertisers but she couldn't resist calling up the files of Turken and Unchkin one more time. She checked every email account, tracked past correspondence, looked for new Instagram and Twitter posts, and even peeked into the archives of their parents, but could not find a single trace of activity since the bombing. The two accomplices to murder had vanished. Kris finally succumbed to the weight of her drooping eyelids, the stress of the past week draining the last of her energy reserves. She closed down her computer, flopped down on the sofa in her den and switched on the television to ESPN.

But Kris still couldn't escape the coverage of the aftermath of the bombing. A video of Matt Reilly's last home run swept across the screen. Then a reporter standing in front of Columbia Presbyterian hospital provided an update: "Doctors here are pleased to report that they have moved the young Yankee slugger out of intensive care. He is showing the first signs of recovery after the amputation of his right leg and a long week of surgery to remove shards of metal from other areas of his body. They believe that he will be able to walk again with the aid of a prosthesis. No word on when he will meet with fans or the media." Nothing new here. Curtis Davis, Reilly's roommate, had called her the night before to deliver the good news and convey Matt's request for her to visit him at the hospital. The ESPN telecast then switched back to the studio where the anchors discussed the plans to reopen Yankee Stadium. Kris had heard this discussion before as well. She fell asleep to the sight of the Stadium flag at half mast.

Kris awoke two hours later. With only fifteen minutes before the Illuminate car was scheduled to pick her up for the ride to the hospital, Kris did not have much time to ponder her wardrobe. It would be a relief not to wear black tonight, but it was definitely not a festive occasion. She selected white Capri pants and a navy blue Etro button down shirt. Kris had been surprised when Curtis' name had flashed on her phone. Now, sitting alone in the back seat, she was apprehensive. What do you say to a friend who is so lucky to be alive, but whose life is shattered nevertheless? Words of encouragement and cheer would sound hollow. Matt's road forward, physically and mentally, would be long and hard. Kris realized that she didn't even know Matt well enough to know where he would want to go or what he would want to do when he left the hospital. Prior to the bombing, Matt had led a gilded existence: the team set his schedule, he played ball, and the public adored him. He would, deservedly, be a media magnet for a few more weeks, but soon, the spotlight and roar of the crowd would be gone, probably forever.

The sedan whisked up the West Side Highway, traffic still light as the city gradually returned to normal. Columbia Presbyterian was located in the northernmost quarter of Manhattan in the shadow of the George Washington Bridge. The driver estimated that they would only need twenty minutes to reach the Stadium after her visit. Kris checked her watch as the car pulled into the hospital entrance. A yellow taxi depositing a young Hispanic woman, bursting out of outrageously snug white shorts, and her grandmother blocked their way. Kris waited patiently while the elderly woman settled into a wheelchair. It was 5:30 - Kris would have an hour with Matt. Would it be long enough, or too long? Camera crews from ESPN and the local channels lounged on the street, but Kris did not attract their attention as she stepped from the car. Kris picked her way through the crowded lobby to the registration desk where a policewoman waited to escort her upstairs. Two male orderlies, dressed in powder blue scrubs, shared the elevator. Kris sensed their knowing smiles when the policewoman pressed the button for Matt's floor. They walked down a long corridor past a bustling nurses' station, several more heads turning, before reaching Matt's room. Another uniformed officer sat outside on a gray metal folding chair. He nodded curtly towards the closed door but made no effort to greet her. Kris murmured a brief thank you to her escort before she knocked.

Matt's mother, obviously the source of his height and good looks, greeted Kris with a harried smile. "Hi, I'm Mary Kate," she said, extending a hand to welcome Kris. Matt was the sole occupant of a room clearly designed to hold at least 2 patients. The far half resembled a traditional hospital but the near side looked like the ring toss prize table at a church carnival. It was littered with bouquets of colorful flowers and balloons, stuffed animals of all shapes and sizes, and stacks of get well cards. A baseball bat wrapped in red, white and blue thong underwear leaned against the bathroom door.

"I thought that one might cheer Matt up," Mary Kate said, almost apologetically.

"Very creative," Kris replied.

"I know that Matt has lots of, um, friends, but you are the only one that he asked to see."

"That's nice to hear. I wanted to see him too."

"He's sleeping now," Mary Kate said, pointing to the bed against the far wall near the lone window, curtains drawn to shield the setting sun. A vase of blue and white tulips stood sentinel on a nightstand on the far side of the bed, while a Yankee batting helmet and baseball glove rested on the near side table. "He dozes off and on, so he should wake up soon," she added hopefully.

Kris took two more steps into the room but stayed a respectable distance from Matt's bed. He was lying on his back, a picture of winsome innocence if not good health. Matt's left eye was bandaged pirate-style and his left arm was elevated in a thick sling. Kris studied Matt's sleeping face: the deep ballplayer's tan was gone, but not as pale as she had feared. Tinges of color had seeped back into Matt's cheeks now that he was out of the ICU. Kris couldn't resist surveying the length of Matt's body, thickly swathed in hospital issue blankets to camouflage the amputation.

"Have you and Matt been friends for a long time?" Mary Kate asked, interrupting Kris' inspection. She bustled past Kris to take a vigilant position at her son's bedside.

"No, just a few weeks actually," Kris replied, then blushed as she realized what Matt's mother must be thinking. "I cooked dinner for him a few times. At my apartment," she stammered, unsure if she was heading in the right direction. "He was a real gentleman."

"No need to explain. He's my angel," Mary Kate said, rearranging the blankets covering her son.

"Well, I'm glad that he's still on this side of heaven."

Kris sat down in the empty chair next to the bed, unsure what to do next. Fortunately, Matt stirred awake, smiling when he saw Kris.

"Hey," he murmured groggily.

"Hey," Kris replied softly, stepping closer to the bed. "How are you feeling?"

"OK, I guess."

"Must have been a horrible week."

"I don't remember much, actually. I was in the on deck circle checking out the pitcher, Gonzalez. He had a nasty cutter. Next thing I remember was being wheeled into the operating room. Now, I'm here," Matt said first looking around the room and then down at the lower half of his body. "With only one leg."

"Well, the doctors say that you will be walking again soon. Everyone in New York is rooting for you," Kris said, trying not to sound like a cheerleader for a losing team.

Mary Kate fussed with her son's blankets, but he brushed her hands away. "I think that I'll go for a fresh cup of coffee," she said, closing the door as she left.

"Mom's been great. This has to be so hard for her," Matt said, spreading his good arm wide to encompass the entire scene. "Curtis has been here every day, too."

"What about your other teammates?" Kris asked, taking a step closer to Matt's bed.

"Yeah, they all stopped by, even the Caesar. The dugout protected everyone except me."

"The home plate ump got wounded pretty bad."

"He's going to walk out of here, though."

"You'll walk again. Surf too, I bet."

Reilly cast his eyes downward and shrugged his shoulders, "We'll see."

"I have faith in you," Kris said, placing a hand on Matt's stovepipe thick left forearm.

"Mom said that you were in the paper, that you were helping the FBI."

Kris nodded.

"Just do me one favor," Matt asked, pushing himself to sit upright. "Get the fuckers who did this. Show them that they can't mess with America."

"The SWAT guys shot the bomber right outside the Stadium."

"A Russian, right?"

"Yes."

Matt shook his head slowly, his one good eye blinking. "It goes deeper than that."

"What do you mean?"

"Look, I don't want to piss you off - again, but that Russian dancer, Natasha, told me that her boyfriend was the jealous type and could get real violent."

Kris remained silent, contemplating the possibility that Matt was actually the target of the attack.

"I told her that I'd kick that old fart's ass all the way back to Moscow, but she said no fucking way: he had the entire Red army behind him."

"The Russian army?"

"That's what she said."

Mary Kate rapped once on the door, but didn't wait for a reply before whirling back into the room. Her eyes immediately swept to Kris' hand resting on her son's arm, but she held back any comment. Instead, she fluffed up Matt's pillows to his obvious displeasure. "You're sitting up, that's real progress. The docs want to get you out of this bed for a few minutes as soon as you feel up to it."

"In a wheelchair?"

His mother nodded, "It's the first step."

Matt stared glumly out the window for a few seconds. The sunlight seemed to revive his spirits. He turned to Kris. "I'm going to fly back to San Diego soon. Do my rehab close to home."

"That's a great move," Kris enthusiastically replied.

"The Yanks are going to open a youth academy there for kids from Mexico. They said that I'm going to be the hitting coach, as soon as I can get around."

"Fantastic," she said, slicing the air with an imaginary bat. "Just swing dude."

Matt had to chuckle at their private joke, but then winced. "The ribs are still a little too sore for swinging."

"Something else to look forward to," Kris said, but noticed that Matt was dozing off again.

"He needs to rest for later," Mary Kate said, turning off the lamp on the nightstand.

Sensing Mary Kate's construction of a motherly barricade around her son, Kris leaned over and kissed Matt on the forehead. "I'll call soon."

■ ■ ■

"We only got a few mediums left," Eric Martinez, a recent graduate of Stuyvesant High, apologized to the Santa Claus sized prospect on the plaza outside Yankee Stadium. He had watched the President's address on TV this morning, and convinced his uncle to advance him the cash to rush print the dark blue tee shirts: BRONX BRAVE in big white letters on the front and CHAMBERLAIN and JONES on the back. They had cost him $20 each but he was selling them for $40. Not quite the iPhone app business that his best friend had started, Eric thought, but, at least he would have some spending money when he went to Amherst College in the fall.

"I'll take one," Kris said, handing over two twenties. She wriggled the tee over her dress shirt and headed towards the entrance to the Legends Suite behind home plate. Jim Bright was waiting, dressed in khaki slacks and red golf shirt with the FBI logo. As Kris had expected, security measures were much tighter than before. Fans had to pass through metal detectors; they were only allowed one small handheld bag; and all pockets had to be emptied. Squads of uniformed soldiers, as well as police, manned every portal. All day long, the media had admonished ticket holders to arrive early but the lines still stretched out onto 161st Street. Fortunately the wait at the suites' gate was not nearly as long. Kris was relieved that none of the security staff remembered her ignominious departure with Mindy a few weeks ago.

"Amazing," Jim gaped, ogling the display of food at the sumptuous buffet in the Legends' dining room. "Clearly above my government pay grade," he whined, grabbing two shrimp. "Not much of an appetite tonight though."

"Maybe later. It's open all game," Kris said, pointing them to the stairway to the playing field, dressed in mourning for the occasion. A black tarp covered the lower seats in Section 17B, site of the bomb blast; the chalk lines marking the home plate area and extending down the first and third base lines were black, not the usual white; and black bunting hung from the grandstands. The usher, wearing a black armband, guided them to their seats, just a few rows away from ground zero, and informed them that no alcoholic beverages would be served until the first inning.

After the long week, the pre-game ceremony was anti-climactic for Kris. The players from the Yankees and the visiting Detroit Tigers stood outside their respective dugouts with their caps off while the West Point band played the national anthem. The minister from the Bronx Baptist Church delivered the invocation, followed by brief remarks from Mayor Klotz. He tried valiantly to invoke the themes of patriotism and resolve, but his delivery fizzled like a faulty firecracker. Kris looked around at the nearby fans, clearly fidgeting. "Public speaking just might be above his pay grade," she whispered when Klotz mercifully stepped down from the podium.

Suddenly, a roar erupted from the grandstand as the giant video screen in centerfield projected footage of Matt Reilly smashing a home run. The crowd launched into its Ripcurl chant as he rounded the bases. Reilly's image, live from his hospital room, captured the screen next. He was sitting up in bed wearing a Yankee jersey and cap. Kris did not think that Reilly was remotely ready for prime time when she left the hospital, but her friend had clearly rallied. He waved with his good arm before speaking slowly, "I want to thank all the fans from around the world for their cards, emails and tweets. They really mean a lot to me and my mom. I am truly blessed to be alive today and promise to work my butt off to get back to Yankee Stadium. Now, let's play ball!" With that, the Yankees sprinted out to their positions on the field as the crowd bellowed its approval. All heads then turned to the Yankee dugout as Tanya Chamberlain, flanked by her sons, stepped onto the playing field. A photo montage of Deion's first term in office played on the centerfield screen as his family marched slowly to the mound. The Yankee pitcher handed each boy a baseball for the ceremonial first pitch. First, Deion, Jr and then Calvin wound up and completed the toss to the Yankee catcher. The crowd stood to deliver an ovation. The Tiger batter stepped into the box, the beer started to flow, and New York City took a step closer to recovery.

"I want to get an update on the investigation," Kris said after the third inning.

"Not here," Jim said, eyeing the packed seats.

"Let's go back inside," Kris suggested.

"Sure," Jim said with a faint smile. "Hate to see all that roast beef go to waste."

The dining room was virtually deserted as most of the fans were outside at the game. Nevertheless, after they completed a tour of the buffet, Jim steered Kris to a corner table well away from any potential eavesdropper.

"The investigation is winding down," he announced before punching his fork into a prime cut of beef.

"What?" Kris asked, incredulous. "We haven't found..."

"We probably never will." Jim chewed for a few seconds to let his words sink in. "It's been a week and we have no credible leads."

"Where could they be?"

Jim shrugged. "Their photos were at every airport, train station and bus depot within an hour of the bombing. We're still checking every car heading into Canada and even Mexico."

"Could they have escaped by sea?"

"The Coast Guard had patrol boats in the water pretty quickly but there is too much open sea to cover it all, so I guess that's a possibility. The boat would have had to dock somewhere though."

"It could have hooked up with a submarine."

Jim put his fork down and looked at Kris quizzically. "You're watching way too many movies."

"Do you think that they are still in the country then?"

"The truth is they could be anywhere in the world by now. Or dead, which I think is the most likely scenario."

"What about the parents?"

"Turken's mother is sticking by her story that she knew nothing. The father didn't come home from work until after the boys left. Unchkin's mother is dead and his father is a drunk. I think that they want to believe that their sons escaped. Maybe caught another flight to Russia. We're monitoring all of the parents' communications but not a peep from their sons so far. The only items of interest are the anonymous death threats."

Kris nodded. "Not really a surprise."

"NYPD offered to post officers outside the building but the parents refused. They said that their neighbors will protect them. Now, the mayor is afraid of a vigilante war breaking out in the streets so he's asked us to quote 'be respectful of Russian rights' end quote."

"Whose side is he on?"

"Good question. It gets worse. He's starting to pull manpower off the bombing investigation."

"But didn't he just try to fire up the crowd out there about justice."

"That's the public posture. But I'm telling you, privately, he's going to put less resources behind it. We got the bomber, and no other group has stepped up to claim responsibility."

"What about the two thugs marching down the street with Crazy 8 that day in Brighton Beach? The guys in the picture in your office."

"Dmitri Remko and Lenny Boykin. We grilled them for hours but their alibis were airtight. They were hanging out with friends on the boardwalk till well past midnight. Plenty of witnesses."

"So we're back to Turken and Unchkin, right? They didn't just vanish by themselves. Either someone helped them escape or someone killed them."

"Smart lady, now tell that to the new mayor." Jim cracked open a crab leg and focused his attention on extricating the juicy white meat with his fork.

Kris picked at her own food for a few seconds, contemplating her next step. "Before I came to the Stadium, I visited Matt Reilly in the hospital."

Jim put down the crab and dried his hands on the cloth napkin resting on his knees. "I didn't know that you and Ripcurl were close."

"We're friends," she replied curtly and then related Matt's words of warning from the Russian dancer.

"Ilya Nakitov is the boyfriend, right?"

"That's what the New York Post said."

"He had quite a career in the Russian military but then became a persona non grata over there. We keep a loose eye on him but really thought that he had retired."

"To play bocce?"

Jim laughed. "Maybe not. I'll look into him again. If I still have clearance."

"Are they going to keep you on the Stadium case?"

"I really don't know. But Glenn and I will keep tracking the credit card scammers. I bet that the money trail leads us back to Brighton Beach."

"Good luck."

"We're going to need your help."

"I thought you'd never ask."

21

The roiling waters of New York Harbor spit white foam against the hull of the Staten Island ferry as it plowed towards Manhattan. Leaden storm clouds building over New Jersey promised a downpour later in the day, hopefully delivering the end of the heat wave that had roasted New York City for the past two weeks. Jim braced himself in a wide stance on the top deck, holding fast to the rail. A gust of wind blew his Mets' cap off, forcing him to stumble along the deck in pursuit. Fortunately, the cap pinwheeled into the cabin door, providing a brief window of opportunity. With the cap secure in his back pocket, Jim returned to his former perch, looking both ways to spot the approach of his informant, Derek Miller. Jim's stomach was in knots, but not because of the bouncing boat. Jim was the one who had signalled for this meeting, even though it posed additional risks. He insisted that Glenn case all decks looking for their Russian "friends", keeping his eyes off the pretty ladies. Jim breathed easier when Glenn gave him the all clear sign before assuming a sentry post a few steps away. Derek's shopping crew had not hit the Agent Boudoir shop as expected. Jim needed to know why. He didn't have long to wait.

"Hey," Derek mumbled, arriving a few minutes after one. "What up?" He offered a handshake which turned into a bro hug. Derek was wearing khaki slacks and a bright red golf shirt with the Verizon logo.

THE FOURTH AMENDMENT 167

"That's what I'm trying to find out," Jim said when they disengaged. "You're looking sharp. Heading into the city for work?"

"Yeah, I need some bucks so I got a sales job downtown. Working two till closing today."

"Your shopping crew has been on the sidelines for too long. I was beginning to worry about you."

"Yeah, it's cool. The big boss insisted that everyone stay off the streets. We're going back to business this weekend."

"Who's the big boss?"

"Don't know," Derek said shrugging his shoulders. The wind tossed his wavy hair, but Derek comfortably maintained his balance on the shifting deck. "All I know is that I take orders from Bill, my high school bud."

"When did he get the command to go underground?" Jim asked.

Derek looked at Jim like he had just asked one of the seagulls flying overhead to deliver a pizza. "Who knows. Maybe two weeks ago."

"Right before the bombing at Yankee Stadium?"

"Yeah, sounds right."

Jim paused for a few seconds, staring ahead at the Manhattan shoreline. "What's the plan now?"

"We hit the underwear store on Saturday. I'm in charge of the crew now."

"So you accepted the promotion. Congratulations."

"Yeah, well, moving up in the world, I guess." Derek said, putting on his wraparound sunglasses despite the darkening sky. "That's what you wanted me to do, right?"

"Yes, that could help us," Jim said, marveling at Derek's balance. Jim released the rail, turning to face his agent. "What's Bill doing now?"

"He's still my boss, but he told me that he's broadening his horizons now," Derek said, rolling his eyes. "He's managing two other shopping crews and a bunch of cashers."

"Cashers?"

"Yeah, they use phony debit cards to rip off banks. They'll hit an ATM a hundred times in a few hours. Get all the cash they can carry."

"Do you know what bank is next?" Jim asked, regripping the rail.

"Chinese bank, somewhere in Chinatown. I'm pretty sure the hit's going down tonight. Bill was complaining all week about working with Chinks. He thinks that he's a fucking Russian now."

"Did you ever meet any of the Russian guys that he works for?"

Derek shook his head, turning around to survey the deck. It was practically empty except for Glenn whom he acknowledged with a slight nod.

"What's your friend Lynne up to?" Jim wanted to recapture Derek's attention.

"Not much. Working the register. Being a good girl."

Jim looked up sharply at the last remark. "Until this weekend," he said.

"Yeah, then she opens the gates for us. You going to be there?"

"We'll be around. You just do your business. But keep your eyes open. We need to get to those Russians."

"I'll do my best."

Glenn gave Jim the two minute signal as the boat slowed to approach the dock.

"You're doing a great job. Now get moving."

Derek nodded and headed for the door. Glenn followed a few steps behind, allowing two young couples laden with cameras to slip between them, while Jim lingered on the top deck as long as he could. Finally, he headed towards the exit, the last of the departing passengers, but a scream from the ladies' room stopped him short. Jim looked around in vain for a ferry worker.

"Oh my god," a woman's voice squealed from inside.

Jim knocked sharply as he opened the door with one hand and checked for his gun with the other. "Police. Coming in now," he announced.

A thirty-something brunette, hair tied back in a ponytail, was wrestling with an infant on the changing table. Jim could see a brown smear across her pink blouse and the mother of all diamond rings on her finger. An empty stroller stood a few feet away.

"It's the nanny's day off," the woman said, her lips puckered in disgust at the mess in front of her.

"Yeah, well, diapers can be tricky," Jim replied quickly closing the ladies' room door before the stench could escape. He shook his head as he turned again towards the ramp just in time to see Glenn charging back towards the boat. A Port Authority officer in the terminal tried to stop him but Glenn flashed his FBI badge and hustled across the ramp.

"The two Russian thug, Remko, was waiting for Derek," he told Jim breathlessly.

"Did he talk to him?"

"No, he stayed away. I watched to make sure that Derek left the terminal alone. Looks like he's tailing him though."

"Do you think that Remko saw you?'

"No, it was pretty busy inside."

"And you're sure that he wasn't on the boat?"

Glenn shook his head vigorously, "No way." He stuffed a handful of sunflower seeds into his mouth.

Jim hesitated before replying, "Then, I bet the mob is just vetting their new shopping crew chief. Checking out his daily routine."

"Making sure that he doesn't talk to guys like us you mean?"

"Yeah," Jim said with a wry chuckle.

"You're the one who said that the Russians don't have any severance plan."

"I know, but from your description, I don't see any urgency on their part."

"At least not yet. Don't you think that we should warn Derek?"

"No. It might throw him off his game. If he starts turning around to see who's tailing him, the Russians will know something is wrong."

"We could be putting him at risk."

"He's at risk one way or another now," Jim said, gulping in fresh air in a lame effort to quiet the nauseous grumblings in his stomach as the ferry rocked again. "Derek's our only link to the Russians. We have to let it play out. Derek will be in touch if he needs help."

"I don't like it." Glenn said, spitting the sunflower seeds over the rail into the frothy sea.

"That's OK. We don't have to like everything we do." Jim said. "Now, let's get off this damn boat before I puke."

■ ■ ■

"I know the Chinese government doesn't trust us, and I am sure that we don't trust them, but we are trying to help here," Jim said into the phone, the exasperation evident in his voice. He listened for several seconds before breaking in,

"Look, we have information from a credible source that one of their banks with at least one branch in Chinatown has had a data breach and is going to get hit by a criminal gang. Maybe *tonight*. We're trying to protect *their* money." He put his feet up on his desk and looked over towards Glenn, miming the string of bullshit coming from the voice on the other end of the line. "Yeah, yeah, yeah, I know that you are looking at the global picture. I'm just trying to catch the bad guys here in New York. I guess we'll just sit tight and wait for the diplomats to figure things out. Bye." Jim pounded the phone back into its cradle.

"Our cyber-security geeks and their cyber security geeks are not exactly the best of friends," Jim said to Glenn by way of explanation.

"Sounds like the Yankees and Red Sox."

"Not even that friendly," Jim said snapping upright in his chair. "Like hell we'll wait though." Glenn followed his partner out the door.

The storm had blown violently through the city that afternoon, dropping the temperature into the seventies and leaving a refreshingly clean scent in its wake that would take at least an hour to dissipate. Jim and Glenn stepped around a Great Lakes sized puddle on Canal Street and turned right down Mott, the heart of Chinatown. Jim led the way down a short flight of stairs into Wong Fat, a basement hovel that also served great food.

"My family's been coming here for years," Jim said. "Can't beat the shrimp fried rice or the prices." He pulled out a city map while they waited for their order. "Chinatown's only a few square blocks and there are only three Chinese banks that have branches here. Five branches in total," he said, pointing to the large X's that he had marked.

"Do you have any idea which one will get hit?" Glenn asked.

"Not really but I did a little research. The Bank of Beijing is the largest and has the most ATMs in both of its branches. We'll split up and cover them first."

"We're looking for repeat customers, right?" Glenn said before shoveling another spoonful of rice into his mouth.

"Yeah, very frequent flyers." Jim nimbly picked up a shrimp with his chopsticks. "If we don't get any sightings by midnight, we'll switch to the other banks."

"What do you want me to do if I see something?"

"Nothing. Just call me. I've got the camera here," Jim said, patting his backpack.

"I thought we take pictures in the station *after* the arrest," Glenn said smartly.

"No arrests tonight. Just photos."

"We're going to let them steal the money?"

"Yep, if we bust anyone tonight, it could implicate Derek. We can't let that happen."

Jim paid the bill and then donned a gray Jets hoodie and his Mets cap. "Let's go to work."

Jim hastened back uptown on Mott Street while Glenn turned towards Mulberry Street. He walked slowly past the Bank of Beijing branch on the corner. All quiet inside. Even though it was eleven PM, pedestrian traffic in Chinatown was still brisk. Jim meandered among the tourists, college kids, and revelers from the outer boroughs for fifteen minutes. For his second pass, he stuffed his hoodie in his pack and switched to a white cap with the NY Fire Department logo. This time, the brightly lit lobby holding three ATM kiosks was full: a short black man with his hair braided into cornrows, a dumpling shaped teenaged girl snapping a selfie while her buddy withdrew cash for their evening activities, and a tall, willowy woman with long straight black hair that almost reached her barely there butt. Jim took up a position across the street in front of a now shuttered discount clothing store. The woman left the bank first. She was younger than Jim had thought, attractive Asian features, but flat-chested, wearing an NYU tee shirt and jeans ripped at the knee. The teens followed shortly, while Mr. Cornrows lingered, fussing with his wallet. Maybe he was looking for another fake ATM card. But then he jammed his wallet into the back pocket of his shorts and marched out the door.

Jim waited another five minutes. He was just about to circle the block again when Miss China appeared again, this time with a scarlet satchel slung over her shoulder. She hesitated at the bank door when a NYC cop in his blue uniform turned the corner. The cop seemed to stare at her for a second but then shook his head and kept on walking. As soon as he was three stores away, Miss China inserted her key card into the reader and was buzzed inside. Jim reached for his camera.

Rachel Ko, named in honor of the matriarch of a Jewish family that had helped her great grandparents settle in New York City, had never snorted coke until her boyfriend turned her on to it a few months ago. She grew up in Chinatown. Her parents owned two laundries on the Upper East Side and worked seven days a week. Rachel helped out in the stores whenever she wasn't studying. She wanted to be a doctor. Her middle school science teacher urged her to apply for a scholarship to the prestigious Stoke School in rural Connecticut. The day the acceptance letter arrived Rachel burned her hand on a hot iron jumping in celebration. At Stoke, Rachel graduated Cum Laude, just missing out on valedictorian. She wanted to go to Stanford, to see California, but instead accepted a full ride to NYU when her mom was diagnosed with lung cancer. She met Karl in the hospital cafeteria while she was keeping her mom company during chemo treatments. With wavy, black shoulder length hair and a thin wisp of a mustache, he looked like a rock and roller. In fact, Karl only bussed tables at the hospital during the day. Most nights, he played drums in an indie band that worked a few of the grungier clubs around the East Village. The coke helped him stay up all night, Karl said. Rachel started using to keep up with him; then, to pull an all nighter studying for a chemistry exam; then, when some friends from boarding school came down to the Village to party. It was getting expensive. Fortunately, Karl had a friend, Bill, who was willing to pay well, really well, for a night's work withdrawing cash from an ATM. Rachel balked at first, but then Bill explained that the depositors were insured. They wouldn't lose any money. Only the bank was liable, and it had been ripping off people in Chinatown for years, right? Karl accompanied Rachel on her first cashing night. He even taught her to slip a few twenties in her back pocket. Bill would never notice, he said. Tonight, Rachel was on her own for the first time. She wanted to finish up in time to catch Karl's last set.

Jim stayed in the shadows, surreptitiously snapping photos when the street was clear. He needed less than thirty minutes to confirm his suspicions. He watched Rachel work steadily, alternating machines and cards. She appeared to have a list of PINs that she consulted for each new card. After each successful withdrawal, she would stuff the bills into her satchel. Jim texted Glenn to head over and provide backup. Five minutes later, another young Chinese woman appeared at the bank's door. Rachel stopped when she heard the buzzer and applied some lipstick while eyeing the newcomer. Jim thought that he might have another member of the cashing crew, but she left quickly after only one withdrawal. Rachel returned to her task. Around 2 AM, her stack of cards exhausted, she zipped up the scarlet satchel, and left the bank.

Jim texted a photo to Glenn who had stationed himself a block away. Glenn, now wearing a white Bronx Brave cap and blue Yankee T-shirt, let Rachel pass by and then turned to follow. The street was virtually deserted so it was easy to keep her in view. Rachel stayed on Mott until it dead-ended at Worth Street. A police car slowly cruised by, but then stopped.

"Rachel, Rachel Ko," a voice called out. A uniformed cop hopped from the passenger door. He was tall and gangly, resembling an airplane, two wings protruding from a narrow tubular frame. He flapped one arm, "Hi, I thought that was you down by the bank a few hours ago. I haven't seen you around here in years."

Rachel jumped back, her face blanched with fear at the sight of the uniform, but she quickly composed herself. The satchel slipped from her shoulder but she caught it before it could hit the sidewalk. Rachel recognized the patrolman's face, and the physique, but couldn't recall his name.

"Er, hi, I went away to boarding school. Haven't been around much since then."

"Wow, you look great. Charles Chung, remember me."

"Charles, of course I remember. From eighth grade." Rachel fidgeted in place. "Mmm, I've got to meet some friends. Is that OK?"

"Of course, you're not under arrest or anything. I just wanted to say hi."

"Well, hi then." Rachel turned to leave.

"It's pretty late to be walking on the street by yourself. Are you heading home? Do you want some company?"

"I'm meeting a friend, actually, so that might be a little awkward."

"Oh, I understand, sorry. Well, here's my patrolman's card. It could come in handy if you ever get a parking ticket or something."

Jim had caught up to Glenn. They couldn't hear the conversation but watched from across the street, terrified that the cop would interrupt Rachel before she could reach her handlers. Jim breathed an audible sigh of relief when Officer Chung returned to his car.

Rachel had only taken a few steps before Chung rolled down his window. "Can I call you sometime? For a cup of coffee?"

"Sure, I live over in the NYU dorms now. I'll text you the phone number." Rachel replied, holding up his card.

"Fantastic," Chung said before his partner peeled the patrol car away from the curb. Rachel checked her watch. She was late now and walked hurriedly down Worth Street towards Columbus Park. Jim and Glenn followed. Rachel barely walked two blocks before turning right into the playground area. It was a new facility, featuring a sprawling red jungle gym and twisting slide surrounded by benches and tall trees. A streetlight shining through the branches cast an eerie shadow. The cool night breeze whipped a discarded yellow candy wrapper in front of Rachel, startling her. It brought a waft of cigarette smoke as well.

"Hey, over here," a gruff Slavic voice grunted from a dark corner of the playground. Rachel turned to locate its source.

"You got something for me?"

Rachel finally discerned Dmitri Remko sitting on a bench, puffing away. "Yes, right here," she said, swinging the satchel off her shoulder as she approached. "Who are you? Where's Bill?"

"He'll be here in a few minutes. We work together." Dmitri's eyes roamed up and down Rachel's body. A little scrawny, but not bad, he thought. For a Chink. "Let me see it," he said, motioning to the bag.

"When do I get my cut? I've got to meet someone." Rachel unzipped the satchel and showed the contents to Dmitri.

"What's the rush?" he leered, motioning for Rachel to come closer. "I've got to count it first."

Rachel looked around but didn't see that she had much choice. She kneeled to place the bag in front of Dmitri and then stepped back. Dmitri dug both hands into the cash, like a baker kneading a buttery dough. He pulled back swiftly though when he saw Bill Badenov approach.

"Just checking out the take, boss," he said.

Bill briefly nodded to Rachel in recognition, then handed a printout to Dmitri. "Here's what it should total out to: $9,970."

Rachel's gut clenched in fear. No one had a print-out to reconcile the withdrawals the first time that she and Karl had cashed out. Dmitri started pulling the bills out, counting them and stacking them in a black doctor's bag on the bench. Math was obviously not his strongest subject: he had to restart twice. Rachel snickered; Dmitri cast her a chilling glance. Bill finally grew frustrated with his henchman, pushing him away from the stash. "Let me count it," he commanded.

Bill did not appear to have the same mathematical deficiencies. He methodically fingered every bill, totaling $9,870. Bill looked at his printout again and then at Rachel. "Maybe I made a mistake," he said, starting the count all over again. Rachel squeezed her thighs together to avoid peeing in her jeans. She heard the mew of an alley cat in a far corner of the playground. Dmitri took a step closer to her, while watching Bill closely. Rachel could smell the pungent sweat from his body. Bill finished his work and looked up, "Still $9,870. A hundred short."

Rachel wanted to run but realized that she wouldn't get far. Dmitri ended any thought of escape when he wrapped his fingers around her wrist in an iron grip, yanking her towards Bill.

"Where's the money?" Bill demanded.

"I don't know," Rachel stuttered, wriggling in Dmitri's grasp.

"Search her."

Dmitri pulled her towards him, a mixture of lust and greed in his eyes.

"Wait, wait, it's in my back pocket, Karl said..." Rachel's confession was interrupted by the back of Bill's hand stinging her across the face. She drew back, a ripple of blood seeping from the corner of her lip. Bill nodded to Dmitri, then slowly packed up the bag of cash and strode towards the street.

Rachel started to sob, but Dmitri had no pity. His fist crashed into her taut stomach. When Rachel doubled over, he drove his knee into her startled face. She staggered backwards, flailing to grab hold of the sliding pole on the jungle gym before falling to the ground. Rachel curled in a fetal position, blood gushing from her now broken nose, as Dmitri straddled her, unzipping the fly on his blue jeans. He slowly pissed up and down Rachel's huddled form, shaking one final squirt into her long black hair. "Fucking Chinese cunt. Next time, you won't be this lucky," he hissed. As Dmitri stomped away towards Baxter Street, Rachel shut her eyes tightly, willing out the world that had washed over her, knowing that she would never be clean again.

Glenn jumped out from behind the bench across the playground, but Jim wrapped his arms around his partner before he moved two steps. "We'll settle the score with our friend Dmitri later," he whispered. "Right now, I need you to stick to Bill. Follow the money." He pointed Glenn towards the playground's exit on Mulberry Street. Bill had lingered there, watching his henchman's retribution, before stalking away. Glenn picked up the tail.

Jim called 911 as he watched Dmitri step into a taxi. Then, he sprinted over to the fallen girl, checking her pulse and wiping her face with his handkerchief. Jim mumbled trite words of comfort, but Rachel was sobbing uncontrollably. He waited until first a patrol car and then an ambulance pulled up to the entrance to the park. There was little else that he could do to help Rachel now. She would have to explain herself to the cops. Jim just hoped that it wasn't Rachel's friend in the police car, but that was not his problem now. He hastened to catch up with Glenn.

22

Kris, Mindy and Joe shuffled into a drab, windowless conference room littered with empty coffee cups and crumpled napkins from the previous occupants. Jim had invited them to the FBI office to help plan the next phase of the investigation. After he and Glenn cleared away the debris, Jim placed a white Agent Boudoir gift box on the table. All eyes widened in anticipation.

"No PowerPoint presentations today," Jim announced, briskly opening the box to reveal an embroidered cream silk set of bridal undergarments, including bra, suspenders and thong.

"Oh my god!" Mindy shrieked, looking directly at Kris. "Who is the lucky girl?"

"That's what we want you to find out," Glenn said, barely suppressing a laugh.

"Seriously," Jim said, taking the underwear out of the box and passing the items around the table. "This stuff is expensive. We've been tracking a shopping crew for months now. They're all set to hit the Agent Boudoir shop on Madison Avenue and probably several other women's clothiers nearby."

"How do they operate?" Kris asked.

"The shoppers are just the head of the snake. In all likelihood, they're part of a multi-level, multi-location gang. Hackers - they could be anywhere in the world - break into networks and steal card numbers or even entire identities. These hackers are good. Once they infiltrate a network, they may be able to access every account and see every transaction. The hackers sell the card information to middlemen who work for months to create phony credit histories or just inflate the histories that already exist. When the histories are ripe, the gang brings in a forger, a manufacturer really, who prints the credit cards. The last phase is the shopping crew. They use the phony cards to purchase high end consumer goods."

"Then they sell the goods on-line to cash out," Glenn interjected.

"That's where we come in, I bet," Joe piped up.

"Exactly," Jim said. "We need you to do the research. Who's searching for AB underwear, who's buying it, who's selling it?"

Mindy opened her laptop and began typing. "There are seventy-four sellers on EBAY right now. How do we know which one is moving the hot goods?"

"We don't, at least right now. But AB is cooperating with us. They've put tags in all their high end inventory in the Madison Avenue store so that we can track it on the streets," Jim said.

"So, we've got to buy a lot of underwear and check the labels," Kris said.

"Then we can trace the money flow from the seller back to the source of the goods, and then to the source of the cards," Glenn said.

"I think that I know an app for that," Joe said, smiling.

"What do you mean?" Jim asked.

"Well, I've got a friend…" Joe hesitated.

"Go on, we're not interested in your friend," Jim said brusquely.

"OK, a guy from my old neighborhood, he never did much in school but he took a few on-line courses in programming. He developed a game - a Candy Crush knock-off - for the iPhone. Calls it Sweet Things. It's a free download in the App Store. But what's really sweet about the game is that it captures every click that a player makes."

"Even when they're not playing the game?" Kris questioned.

After a second's delay, Joe nodded his head. "Once the code gets into a phone it never quits. And it transmits the data back to the server. My friend says that the data helps him improve the game. Let's him know what players like so that he can create more wizards that they will buy."

"Sounds like you've got a pretty smart friend," Glenn climbed back into the conversation.

"A real smart-ass," Jim added.

"Yea, probably," Joe said.

"But, if we can get the Russians to start playing Sweet Things..." Glenn wondered aloud.

Kris looked around the table, recognizing that all eyes had turned towards her, expecting a diatribe on the fourth amendment. Not this time, she thought, staying silent.

Jim broke the tension. "It would be the equivalent of a wiretap on their phones. I bet that our cyber guys can add some bells and whistles too. We'll get the warrant. No problems this time," he declared forcefully, sneaking a glance Kris, pleased to see her smile.

"Let's do it!" Glenn declared, ending the conversation.

■ ■ ■

Lynne Springer, dressed gaily in white capri pants decorated with fire engine red balloons and a matching Motherwell tee shirt, turned the key and pushed opened the door to the pop up shop on East 64th Street. No need to remove the "Closed" sign, she thought. The store had no merchandise and the public was not welcome. Lynne, sipping her morning Starbucks, stepped around the clutter of folding tables, plastic chairs, and wastepaper baskets stuffed with crumpled papers that the shop's previous occupant, H&R Block, had left behind after moving out in April, right after tax preparation season had ended. The old signage still hung in the window, while the musty scent of dust and neglect still hung in the air. Lynne, Derek and Bill had moved in last week, largely ignoring the debris, but setting up a computer, phone system, WiFi router, and credit card verification terminal in the back room out of sight from the street. The next morning, they carted in the crown jewels: two low filing cabinets containing brightly colored Pendaflex files of data on several hundred "customers" and "prospects". Boardwalk Trading, Inc. had a new headquarters.

Lynne pulled a blue file, indicating an untried account, and sat down in front of the computer, scraping her chair along the cracked linoleum floor. She brushed away loose strands of her blond hair, remembering why she had always preferred to cut it short, as she examined the information - Alison Rose, 67, re-tired, widow, two children, four grandkids, an IRA at Fidelity and an account at First Indianapolis Bank. Lynne scanned down the page, circling Alison's social security number, date of birth, and the name of her first pet with a red Sharpie marker. Then, she dialed the bank's toll free number.

"Bill Belter, please," she asked. "Hi. This is Alison Rose. I have an account at your branch but I don't believe that we've met." Lynne breathed easier when Bill indicated that they hadn't met, but he would be glad to help out, if at all possible.

"I'm going to be visiting New York City soon - yes, first time - and plan to do some shopping. I just want to check the balance in my account." Lynne patiently answered the banker's questions to verify her identity.

"Twenty six thousand two hundred and twenty six dollars, let me write that down," she repeated. "Now there's one more thing that you can help me with." The banker seemed eager to please.

"I want to apply for a credit card."

After hanging up with Mr. Belter, Lynne transferred Alison Rose's paper-work to a gold folder, highlighting that she was now a qualified, prime prospect. With that much cash in the bank, Ms. Rose could easily qualify for a loan. Of course, Ms. Rose would probably never even know that she applied for the loan as Boardwalk would fill out the paperwork and pocket the cash.

For the next two hours, Lynne worked through the same dialog for ten more blue files, only once running into a roadblock that forced her to hang up abruptly. She shifted the paperwork for this account into a red folder, placing it in a wire basket on the tabletop which held a stack of a dozen or so other reds. Lynne stood and stretched her dancers' legs, relieved that her backlog of blue files was now empty. She knew that real people on the other end of these files would suffer the consequences of Boardwalk's scams, but what did they expect when they stupidly registered all their personal information on SeniorSavers. com in search of deals and discounts. They needed to learn a hard lesson - don't trust the Internet.

Lynne walked to the front window, watching the pedestrian traffic flow by. She laughed at the irony of the old H&R Block sign, promising rapid refunds, that Bill had decided to let hang even after Boardwalk had moved in. Lynne turned and disgustedly looked at the mess in the front room of the shop for several seconds. Finally, she decided that she had had enough. Lynne propped open the door to let some fresh air inside, and retrieved the cleaning supplies that the Block people had left in the back closet. She wiped down the tables, arranging them neatly in a classroom formation facing the door, and mopped the floor. Pleased at the rejuvenation of the shop, Lynne closed the front door and returned to work.

The green files were Lynne's favorite. They represented people that, in fact, did not exist. Boardwalk had painstakingly created these identities over the past few months by combining phony social security numbers and drivers' licenses that they had purchased on-line with local addresses, and then had applied for credit cards in their names. Lynne liked to imagine that these creations were her friends, and often daydreamed about their life stories. A handsome fireman to rescue her from a burning skyscraper; a kindly physician to care for her wheelchair bound grandmother; a rich husband for her older sister. Last week, Lynne "helped" her friends by recording purchases for them on Boardwalk's own credit card terminal. Today, she had to pay off the balance of each card from a Boardwalk account. Of course, no goods ever changed hands but the transactions enabled Boardwalk to establish a credit history for each account that helped pump up its line of credit. By this evening, Derek's crew would be armed with a thick stack of fraudulent, but verified, credit cards ripe for shopping.

A sharp knock on the glass of the front door interrupted Lynne's good deeds. Right on time, she thought. Derek was standing outside with a shopping bag overflowing with mail in each hand. He had made the rounds of all their boxes this morning. She let him in, turning her head up for a kiss. But Derek stormed past, dumping the contents of his bags on the nearest table. Lynne was doubly disappointed: Derek did not even notice her cleaning spree.

"One of the Russian assholes beat the shit out of a guy on my crew's girlfriend last night," he said angrily. "Now the guy's afraid the crazy Russian will come after him. He's heading out of town tonight."

"What happened?"

"She was a casher. Hitting some ATMs in Chinatown. The Russian thought she shorted him, so he whacked her around."

"Did she?"

"My guy - Karl - wasn't sure."

"Probably means she did."

"But you don't beat up a girl," Derek said, flopping down on a chair.

"Why not? Don't you read the news. Guys fuck women over all the time even when they're not stealing. Sounds like this chick got what she deserved."

Derek just shook his head. Lynne sat down on his lap, looping one arm behind his head.

"So you're one shopper short now for tomorrow. I'll go."

Derek looked at her like she had just escaped from the asylum.

"No fucking way. Bill pulled you out of that store for your own good. He wants you to lay low this weekend."

"I can shop other stores," Lynne purred, stroking Derek's hair.

Derek shook his head. "We need you here. We're going to be in and out all day. Bill will be stopping by too. He's got a fence that wants to inspect the merchandise before he buys it."

"I met him last week. Creepy Russian guy," Lynne said, hopping to her feet. "Looked like he couldn't wait to bury his nose in all that fancy ladies underwear."

"He probably wanted to bury his nose in your underwear."

"And what would you like to do?" Lynne asked, flipping her head back towards Derek as she pranced over to her computer.

Derek was sorely tempted, but tomorrow would be his first time as crew leader. Lynne would wait. He drove both hands into the mountain of mail.

23

Facing his shopping crew in their pop-up store at noon on Saturday, Derek felt like a high school football coach. He stood in the center of the room while everyone else - 4 women, 3 men, all twenty-something - lounged against the tables. They were dressed in a potpourri of different colors and styles, but all neat and modest. Nothing that would stand out. First, Derek passed out envelopes containing the fake credit cards to each crew member, then he launched into the briefing that he had rehearsed several times last night:

"Ok guys, we've worked together before so it's the same plan. Team up and shop as couples. Hit Madison Avenue from 57th to 72nd. Everyone stops at Agent Boudoir because Lynne has set it up." Lynne, still pissed that she would be stuck in the store all day by herself, broke the conservative dress code, wearing a white mini-skirt, showcasing her long legs, and a lime green scooped top. She waved sheepishly from the back.

"Look like a shopper. Try stuff on. Show it to your partner. Make one big purchase at each store, shoot for a thousand dollars, but never hit the same store twice. Drop the merchandise off back here every two hours. Lynne will check it in. We'll settle up at 5 sharp."

"Shall we gather in prayer now?" Karim Marwan asked mockingly as he stood and clapped his hands. "Coach B would be proud of that pep talk."

Karim had played football with Derek at Latourette High, so he had heard it before.

Derek laughed. "Let's be smart and stay safe. Any questions?" he concluded.

"What about me?" Annette Doume pouted, looking around the room. "Karl's not here. Who am I going to work with?" Boasting shoulder length raven hair, an alluring smile and breasts that even a navy crew neck tee could not camouflage, Annette was not accustomed to solitude.

"I'll go with you," Derek volunteered, ignoring Lynne's stern look. He brought up the rear as the crew bounded out of the store.

The day was gray and unsettled. The cloud cover kept the summer temperature comfortable, but Derek feared that rain, or even worse a thunderstorm, could develop at any time, crimping his crew's plans for the day. As he walked uptown with Annette, Derek's thoughts drifted back to Coach B, actually Bill Badenov's dad. He had passed away last year, a sudden heart attack, after coaching football at Latourette for thirty years. A rhinoceros of a man, Coach B was an intimidating force, his voice bellowing across the field. He was tough but fair, and prided himself on looking after his players even after graduation. Bill, the team captain, knew that he had gored his dad by partying away his senior year, rather than cementing his college scholarship. They had grown further apart as Bill descended into a life on the wrong side of the law.

Derek, two years younger than Bill, was disappointed in himself for following Bill's path off the gridiron. After high school, Derek had enrolled in community college, but then dropped out to take a course in computer repair. It led to a job with the Best Buy store in downtown Manhattan. He had worked there for 2 years, earning several raises, but then the store closed. His boss blamed the recession. Bill had read a few of his despairing tweets and offered Derek a position on his shopping crew, making the job sound legitimate, some sort of freelance work with good pay. Too good, Derek had thought at the time. Unfortunately, he realized that he was right when Bill provided the details. But, Derek had plowed ahead, rationalizing that he needed the money, until it was too late to retreat. Helping the FBI was his only way out now, or at least he hoped that was where it would lead.

"Here we are," Annette announced, pulling to a stop in front of the Etro boutique. She slipped her hand inside the crook of Derek's elbow. He flashed a puzzled look. "Ready, partner?" she asked, squeezing his forearm like a ripe melon as she guided him to the door.

The sky never brightened, but the rain held off. Derek's crew worked methodically up and down Madison Avenue: four happy couples out for a day of shopping in the big city. Lynne neatly stacked their purchases, some gift-wrapped, some not, on the tables in the front room of the pop-up store. All it needed now was a pine tree and Santa Claus to resemble Christmas morning. An occasional passer-by would knock on the front door, but Lynne shooed them away. As of 4PM Bill, and his fence, had yet to make an appearance.

Lynne gave Annette a nasty grimace as Derek handed over two boxes with the Judith Ripka logo. Annette retaliated by brushing close to Derek, her hand lingering on his shoulder. "Are we finished now?" she asked. Derek shook his head, "One last stop. Agent Boudoir." This time, Derek bore the brunt of Lynné's glare as he guided Annette towards the door. On the way out, Annette, clearly reveling in her co-worker's envy, leaned into Derek again. "Fucking A! I really need a new bathing suit anyway," she whispered.

While watching Annette model bikinis would be easy on his eyes, Derek wanted to go to Agent Boudoir to see Jim and Glenn. They had not crossed paths all day, so he had assumed that they had camped out at the store. Derek wasn't expecting a welcome hug, but the sight of his FBI handlers would be reassuring after the full day as a double agent. Now emboldened, Annette clasped Derek's hand, yanking him towards the swimwear. Derek swiveled his head in all directions as they walked, narrowly missing a crash with a mannequin, but could not find Glenn or Jim. Glenn had always blended into the background, but Jim was usually front and center, he thought worriedly.

Annette was determined. She displayed several hangers holding bikinis, tough to call them swimsuits Derek thought, each with less material than the previous one. Exasperated with Derek's wandering attention, Annette finally fixed on a bright pastel by Stone Fox, "Kate Upton wore this in Sports Illustrated," she said. "I want to try it on. Come on." When Annette entered a dressing room, Derek turned to scan the store again. Still no luck.

"Hey, Derek," Annette called from inside. He ignored her for a few seconds, still hoping for an FBI sighting, but Annette did not give up. Finally, he stepped towards the back. "No one else is here," she whispered, opening her door by a few inches to make sure that Derek could see inside. Wearing only khaki shorts, top button undone, zipper at half mast, Annette thrust her chest forward. She held the Stone Fox top loosely in front of her with one hand, but it did not conceal much. Her bare breasts looked as firm as a pair of barbells.

"What do you think?"

"Hmm," Derek mumbled, taken completely by surprise.

"Come on in," Annette beckoned with a crooked index finger.

Derek stepped forward to the threshold of the room, placing his hand on the curved, silver handle of the half open door. Confident of her pulchritude, Annette curved her lips in a victory smile. She dropped the bathing suit top from her grip, watching Derek watch it float to the floor. She reached for Derek's wrist to pull him inside.

"Get dressed. We have work to do," he commanded, stepping back and closing the door.

Flabbergasted, Annette switched fingers, flipping off the closed door. "Fuck you," she shouted.

Derek shrugged his shoulders as a grandmotherly woman, Mary O'Donnell, appeared, clearly the warden of the dressing salons. "Can I be of assistance?" she asked with a trace of a British accent.

"No, I think we'll be fine now," Derek replied chastely.

"Young lady, please remember to keep your knickers on," Ms. O'Donnell said, rapping a knuckle on the closed door, then added, "when you try on any swimwear, of course."

"Fuck you too," Annette muttered under breath as she zipped up her shorts, pulled on her tee shirt, and brushed out her hair. Satisfied that all the pieces were back in place, Annette finally marched out, undaunted and defiant despite the stern glare from the matron. "We'll take these," she said, handing two bikinis to Derek and leading the way to the register.

The check-out line was short, but it stopped completely as a new cashier appeared and settled in. The two women ahead of Derek and Annette chatted too loudly. The one on the left, the older one, was obviously the nervous bride to be, while her younger friend, the wingman, assured her that their purchase would be perfect for her third wedding night. Derek shuffled his feet impatiently, holding Annette's swimsuit as if they were radioactive. He looked longingly outside.

The rain had held off all day. Annette, exasperated, wanted no part of Derek. "I'm going to the ladies room. Then I'll meet you outside," she said curtly. Derek nodded, relieved both to watch Annette leave and the new cashier signal for the next customer.

When Derek finally reached the register, he handed over the swimsuits and a credit card. Annette's seduction scheme had distracted him sufficiently to forget that he was going to be using a fraudulent card. He reached into his back pocket to reassure himself that he had the appropriate driver's license as well. "Presents for Labor Day weekend," he said feigning embarrassment. "I'm sure that she'll look great in them," the cashier replied, not even bothering to ask for identification as she swiped the card. Derek hastened away, feeling the tension in his neck ease as he headed for the exit. He glanced around the store one last time for Jim and Glenn. Nothing. Derek stayed calm: they were pros and would contact him soon enough. All he wanted now was to get out of Agent Boudoir. Lynne would be waiting back at their makeshift headquarters. Five more steps to the street.

Before Derek reached the door, a piercing siren suddenly wailed. He stopped mid-stride and spun around. A fire drill now? Two burly plainclothes security men, looking like defensive tackles pouncing on the quarterback, appeared at his side. They latched firmly onto Derek's arms, steering him towards a corner of the store. The other shoppers standing nearby faded away.

"What's in the shopping bag?" The one wearing khakis and a tightly fitting red polo asked.

"Bathing suits, I just paid for them at that register," Derek stammered, reminding himself to stay calm. He pointed back to the check out station.

"Let's take a look," the other one, clad in jeans and a purple Brooks Brothers striped button down, demanded.

Derek opened the bag, relieved that the cops were checking the goods, not his credit cards.

"Nice," red polo said, examining both of the skimpy bathing suits. "But look at this. The security tags are still attached."

"What? I paid …"

"Sure you did," his partner said mockingly. He turned the now empty shopping bag upside down. "Where's the receipt?"

Derek searched through his pockets, trying to remember if the cashier had even handed him one. Annette joined the fringe of onlookers, her head visible through a gap. Derek briefly wondered if he saw a faint smile of revenge.

"Well?" purple stripe asked.

Derek just shrugged, recognizing that there was nothing that he could say that would help his cause. He couldn't demand a return to the register because of the phony card, and couldn't reveal his FBI connection in public. The store cops took his silence as an admission of guilt. Red polo spoke tersely into his phone. Within seconds, two uniformed police officers appeared, almost as if they were waiting right outside the door, Derek thought.

"We'll take it from here," Officer Shanahan, a wiry woman with a witch's' nose that dominated an otherwise pleasant face. She took up position slightly behind Derek while her partner, Sergeant Kendrick, a thick, muscular man with a marine crew cut, conferred with the store security men in front of him. Derek could feel the angry stares from the spectators, mostly young women who appeared to resent the intrusion of reality into their shopping fantasies. He felt like a gladiator in an old movie awaiting the thumbs up or down signal from the blood thirsty rabble. Finally, Kendrick turned to him and removed a set of handcuffs from his belt.

"We're going to take you to the station. Our car is parked in front," he said, motioning for Derek to put his hands forward. When Derek hesitated, he said smoothly, "Don't make this hard. Right now, we just have you for shoplifting. Probably a misdemeanor."

Shanahan gently pushed him forward. Derek locked eyes with Annette, seeing her wince as Kendrick snapped on the cuffs. The two cops and Derek formed a conga line to march out to Madison Avenue. A patrol car was idling in front of a fire hydrant. Another cop, a black guy was all Derek could see, sat behind the wheel. Monahan climbed into the passenger seat, while Kendrick helped Derek into the back and then followed him in, wedging closer than Derek thought necessary. The driver turned on the siren and flashing light as he peeled away from the curb.

"Not bad, huh? Kendrick asked. His breath smelled of garlic.

"What?" Derek replied, incredulous.

"Your FBI buddies wanted us to put on a show. Make sure that everyone saw you get arrested."

Derek swiveled around, trying to look out the rear window. Monahan turned but Kendrick motioned to keep her eyes forward. He placed a hand on Derek's handcuffed wrists, and said in a measured tone, "We're taking you to the 19th precinct house. It's just a few blocks away. When we arrive, we're going to follow normal procedures and book you. Bright and Walker will meet you there later tonight."

■ ■ ■

Parked in a gray Chevy on the far side of Madison Avenue, Jim and Glenn stayed in place as the patrol car pulled away. Jim sipped coffee, while Glenn munched on a chicken parm sub. "There's Annette. She's probably headed back to the store," Glenn pointed with his elbow, a dab of red sauce dripping onto his tie. Jim nodded. "I want to stay here for another ten minutes. I didn't see anyone tailing Derek today but I want to be sure that none of those Russian slimeballs surface now," he said.

"They're going to find out about his arrest soon enough."

"I certainly hope so. It's the best life insurance policy that we can give him."

"Are you sure that Badenov and the Russians still trust him?"

"He ran the whole show today, didn't he?"

This time it was Glenn's turn to nod. "Do you think that we can still trust him?" he asked.

"Derek?"

Glenn nodded, swallowing the last of his sandwich.

"Yeah, I do. He's managing pretty well. You watched him on the store video - pretty impressive to turn down Annette in that dressing room."

Glenn laughed. "She did look fetching."

"Yeah, but he punted her. I think he stays loyal to us too."

Jim surveyed the sidewalk in front of Agent Boudoir one last time, then shifted the car into gear, "All clear. Let's get over to the station. We're going to have to spend some time training Derek on the Sweet Things app."

"I've been practicing," Glenn said, holding up his phone. "Getting pretty good at it too."

■ ■ ■

After five hours in the police station, Derek returned to the pop-up store just in time to see Lynne slap Bill Badenov's favorite fence across the face. They were alone in the back of the store when Derek walked in. The fence, a fleshy Russian in tight jeans, looked similar to his jovial family butcher on Staten Island. The one that got arrested for selling horse meat. The Russian had made the mistake of reaching for Lynne's ass. Her blow spun his head around so fast that Derek thought that his switchblade thin mustache might slide off. Before the fence could recover, Derek jolted between them.

"That asshole tried to feel me up," Lynne shouted over Derek's shoulder.

"Hey man, I just lifted her skirt to see if she was wearing those lace panties. I didn't touch her twat. Bill said that I could check out the goods before I buy, you know."

"Get the fuck out," Derek said with quiet determination.

The fence reached into his back pocket. Derek feared he might be going for a weapon, and stepped forward to keep the initiative. But the fence just pulled out a handkerchief and dabbed a few specks of blood from his nose.

"OK, OK. I'll come back tomorrow morning, man. Tell Bill to meet me here. Not that crazy bitch."

"Out," Derek pointed to the door. When the fence had slinked away, Lynne wrapped her arms around Derek's neck. "You OK," he asked, burying his head in her blond curls.

"Yeah, yeah," she mumbled. "How about you?"

"I'm good," Derek said as they separated. He leaned against the back table, still holding Lynne's hand.

"Where's Bill?"

"He left a few hours ago right after Annette came back screaming that you got arrested. He said that he was going to get a lawyer to bail you out."

"I should call him."

"We were all worried, you know," Lynne said, running a hand through Derek's hair.

"Where did everyone else go?"

"Home, I guess. They were spooked."

"So you stayed alone?"

Lynne nodded, pointing at the boxes piled up on the folding tables in the storefront. "Bill wanted all the merchandise out of here by tomorrow anyway, so I said that I would wait around for Andrei. I knew he was a douchebag but..."

"Somebody should have stayed with you," Derek cut her off.

"I can take care of myself," Lynne said, straightening up. "Did Bill's lawyer every show up?"

Derek fumbled in his pocket for a business card. "Yeah, Benjamin Mintz. He blasted into the station right after they booked me. The cops said they kept me locked up for an extra two hours because he was such a dick."

Lynne stifled a laugh. "Did he put up the money for bail?"

"There was no bail. First offense, shoplifting. Steinberg said that the store might not even press charges."

"That's great news." Lynne said, pulling Derek up to his feet. "Let's go celebrate."

Derek checked his watch. "How about we do our celebrating back in Staten Island. We can catch the midnight ferry and get to Hobnail's before last call."

■ ■ ■

"Why wait for Staten Island?" Lynne asked, pointing towards the concession stand which doubled as the bar for the late night crowd. Although the ferry was still docked, it was already surrounded by several young people intent on keeping the party going on the way home.

"Five minutes," Derek said distractedly. He sat down on one of the dark wood, high backed benches on the main deck, near a couple that had clearly partied too much already, and pulled out his phone. The horn sounded, signaling that the boat was pulling away.

"What are you doing?" Lynne asked, sitting down next to Derek, her annoyance evident. "You were banging away on your phone for the whole subway ride down here."

"Playing a new game, Sweet Things."

Lynne displayed her best are-you-kidding-me look. "When did you get it?"

"At the police station. A guy there, Jim, showed it to me. Check it out." He flipped his phone around so that Lynne could see the explosion of a chocolate duck fill the screen. "Great graphics, huh?"

"You're kidding, right? You're playing a game that you got from some guy in jail?"

"Well, um, yeah, I guess."

"You can blast another duck later, OK. It's Saturday night. Let's have some fun," she said, looking again towards the revelry. "And the bar is open."

Derek put the phone face down on his knee. "You call what we're doing fun. Stealing identities. Ripping people off," he said in a low voice, visibly upset.

"So that's what's bothering you. Forget it. It's too late to go back and play the white knight now."

"I don't know about that."

"I do. What's Plan B? You already tried community college. How'd that work out?"

"I could try something else."

"Yeah? Computer programming? Rocket science? Brain surgery? Tell me. What are the golden opportunities for two kids like us that barely graduated high school?" Lynne stood and turned away.

"I've got a friend who might be able to help us." Derek said hopefully.

"If I want a savior, I'll go to church on Sunday, OK?" Lynne snapped.

"Ok, Ok. What's your plan then?"

Lynne didn't hesitate. "My plan is to get a Bud Lite, go to the top deck and check out the stars."

Derek watched Lynne stomp away. She lingered at the bar, chatting, for a few minutes more than was necessary before taking her beer upstairs. He tried Sweet Things again, but couldn't make it past the first level. He'd practice more tomorrow. He would have to get good enough to entice Bill, and maybe even some of his Russian buddies, to challenge him at the game. Derek looked at his watch. Still fifteen minutes left before Staten Island. Maybe he would check out the stars too.

Derek scanned the upper deck. The clouds had broken, exposing a crescent moon smiling over the harbor, but there was no sign of Lynne. Four young men, obviously drunk, grasped the rail, hoisting cans of beer and singing in German. A couple, leaning against the cabin door, was in full steam make out mode, their face-sucking sounds audible across the deck.   But, as the ferry trolled by the Statue of Liberty, all the passengers gravitated to get the best view. Finally, Derek sighted her, alone in a dark nook on the far side of the boat, away from the commotion, staring out into the sea.

"Hey," he said, wrapping his arms around Lynne's waist.

"Hey," she said, turning her head slightly and burrowing her mini-skirted butt back into him.

They stayed locked together for several seconds, rocking with the gentle motion of the boat.   Almost imperceptibly at first, their rhythm gained a beat. Derek leaned over and nuzzled Lynne's ear, the floral scent of her hair arousing him further. Lynne responded by rotating her hips, still pressed tightly against her lover's loins. She teased him with several more gyrations, relishing the return to familiar ground in their relationship. The feeling of control whetted her desire, but Lynne was careful not to push Derek too far or too fast. At last, she twisted her head, flashing a biker babe smile.

"Fuck me," Lynne commanded.

"Here?" Derek hurriedly surveyed the deck. The few passengers that were topside remained enthralled by Lady Liberty. He returned his attention to Lynne, rejoining their private waltz.

"Now," Lynne urged, reaching back to lift her skirt. Derek watched, mesmerized, as she gathered the thin white material in her hand revealing her taut, tanned cheeks split by just a wisp of a scarlet thong. Lynne reared her hips, beckoning him to enter.

Twice in one day, Derek thought. This time, though, he plunged ahead.

24

"What the hell is going on here?" Anne Harmony exclaimed, bounding into the bullpen housing Kris and her crew. Separated by a low fabric covered partition from neighboring teams, the space contained three desks surrounding a rectangular white table. The table was usually littered with reams of print-outs from the team's database scans, but, today, several open shipping boxes, contents clearly visible, replaced the paper trail. Anne, dressed in a summer-weight gray suit and prim white blouse, displayed a black lace teddy with the look of a surprised parent expecting an explanation from a wayward child.

"We're doing some undercover work for Jim Bright and the FBI," Kris volunteered.

"Well, put this back under the covers then," Anne said, wrapping the teddy in tissue paper, placing it back in the box, and folding up the lids. She then proceeded to close the other two boxes as well.

"They weren't my size anyway," Mindy piped in to break the tension.

"Why did you get the boxes delivered here?" Anne asked Kris, obviously ignoring Mindy.

"I live in a walk up. No doorman," Kris said.

"Same here," Joe added, while Mindy just nodded in agreement.

"Are you expecting more shipments?"

"We've already ordered another dozen, maybe more," Kris said, looking around the bullpen at her team.

"What are you going to do with them?"

Kris began to explain the tagging scheme to track the credit card scammers, but Anne cut her off. "Keep me in the loop but I don't need to know all the details. Just tell the mailroom to keep the packages downstairs. I don't want this floor to look like a brothel."

Mindy jumped up, placing the three boxes in a stack on the floor. She searched through the print-outs for a few seconds before finally settling on one set of figures. "Let me show you the data from the..."

"Not now. I want you guys to work on another project," Anne interrupted, reaching into her briefcase. She spread out a map highlighting Illuminate's expansion in the downtown area.

Kris and Joe wheeled their chairs around the table while Mindy remained standing.

"Illuminate's going to need some zoning changes from the city to facilitate our plans. From what I can tell, the new mayor, Klotz, is not necessarily sympathetic to our needs or the needs of New York City businesses in general."

"He seems pretty sympathetic to the needs of the Russian community though," Kris said sarcastically. She opened the New York Times, pointing to a photo of Mayor Klotz on the boardwalk in Brighton Beach. "He's calling for the city to heal and move forward. Jim says that behind the scenes he's winding down the investigation of the Stadium bombing - even though we still haven't found Turken or his buddy."

"I bet we never will," Mindy interjected, regaining her confidence.

"Mayor Chamberlain believed strongly that the Russian mobsters were a blight on the city. I think that he would have handled things differently," Anne said, clearly choosing each word carefully. "But we all have to move forward now," she added, standing to make her point. "And that means preparing for our negotiations with the new mayor."

"Klotz doesn't have much of a track record on anything," Kris said.

"Correct. But Klotz just got reelected last fall along with Mayor Chamberlain, so he has to have campaign speeches on record somewhere. I need your team to dig into them, as well as his actions during his last term in office."

"Klotz is clearly in campaign mode now too," Kris said, pointing again to the newspaper.

"What did Klotz do before he got elected as Public Advocate?" Mindy asked

"He was a lawyer and a community activist, I believe," Anne replied.

"What's that?"

Anne shrugged. "I'm not sure. But I want to know anything that Klotz did, or didn't do, to see if we have any ammunition for the negotiations."

"We can check his tax returns too. I'm pretty sure all city officials make them public," Mindy said.

"Great idea," Anne replied. Mindy beamed, while Joe sat silently, fingers steepled in his lap. He had pulled the returns a few weeks ago in his private assignment for Anne, but had let the project fizzle out in the aftermath of the bombing.

"Joe, you've been pretty quiet. Anything to add?" Kris asked.

"Klotz likes to travel abroad," Joe chipped in, but Anne shot him a nasty glare.

"I read it in the Times," he explained meekly.

■ ■ ■

Even at four in the afternoon, the sight of bundles of cash intoxicated Ilya Nakitov. He leaned forward in his seat at the corner table of Galina's empty dining room as Bill Badenov deposited a red nylon gym bag in front of him and briskly unzipped it. The bag was overflowing with rubber-banded stacks of twenty dollar bills. Cyber money was no substitute for the real thing, Nakitov thought. Lenny Boykin and Dmitri Remko, standing guard behind him, could not help shuffling a foot forward to glimpse the stash.

"How much?" Ilya demanded.

"Fifty thousand, plus loose change," Bill answered without hesitation.

"Count it," Nakitov ordered, nodding towards Lenny. The big man stepped to the table, making a small show of peeling back the flap of the gym bag. He pulled out the first bundle, held it in the light and nimbly fanned through the bills. Then he removed the rest of the bundles, one at a time, stacking them in groups of ten. Bill crossed his hands nervously behind his back, waiting for Lenny's proclamation of approval. He did not have to wait long.

"All there," Lenny said, stepping back to his sentry position.

"Good work," Ilya announced, fondling a bundle of cash from the top of the nearest stack. He gently placed the bundle down, spinning it three times on the tabletop. "But there is one problem." On cue, Lenny handed a print-out to Nakitov.

A young busboy, wheeling a tower of trays of clattering stemware, burst through the kitchen door interrupting the conversation. He appeared oblivious to the meeting as he started to set out the glasses on an adjacent table. Bill hastily reached out to close the gym bag, while Dmitri hastened over to roughly prod the busboy back into the kitchen. Recognizing Mr. Nakitov, the boy's eyes widened in fear. He cowered behind his tower as he pushed it away. Ilya's eyes, or more accurately, his nose followed the busboy. "Almost dinnertime, eh?" he asked the table, reacting to the tantalizing aroma from the back room. The crew nodded obediently.

"But business first," Nakitov said, returning his attention to the print-out. "I see ten deliveries of ladies' undergarments to one address on Ninth Avenue."

"Maybe someone's having a fuckerware party," Bill replied, forcing a laugh. No one else followed suit.

"Probably not," Nakitov said, glaring at Bill. "This address is the New York headquarters of Illuminate."

"So, even those geeks like to fuck." Bill clearly had not made the connection.

"I don't think that is the case here. Illuminate is the employer of Kris Storm, associate of FBI agent Jim Bright. You remember the photo of Ms. Storm holding a gun on our friend Sergei when he was arrested last year, don't you?" Nakitov did not wait for a reply. "Dmitri and Lenny chased them out of Brighton Beach a few weeks ago." He placed the print-out down and took a sip of water. "I believe they are tracking our activities."

"I never saw them," Bill said, frowning. "I was with the guys shopping on Madison Avenue all day," he added.

"Bright and Storm were there, I'm sure."

Bill squirmed in his chair. He could see the flicker of a smile on Dmitri's face, relishing in his superior's discomfort.

Ilya Nakitov continued," I will deal with Mr. Bright through my own channels, but we are going to have to send Ms. Storm a more visible warning. Dmitri,
I understand that you have a way with troublesome women?"

Dmitri nodded. He could not contain a dungeon master's grin. "Any sug-
gestions, sir?"

"I will leave it to your imagination."

■ ■ ■

Thwack!

Kris slammed a forehand. Unfortunately, the ball soared over Joe Brady's
head, clanging against the green chain link fence on the fly. "Shit," she cursed
quietly as Joe turned to retrieve it. They had taken a break from the office and
walked over to the three public tennis courts just below Houston Street. The
courts were wedged single file into a narrow ribbon of the Hudson River Park,
bordered by a promenade overlooking the river on one side and the traffic-
clogged West Street on the other. The late summer sun hung languidly over the
still waters, baking the players like cookies in the oven. Joe set up to serve. He
held two balls in his left hand, bouncing one slowly before tossing it skyward to
begin his motion. He purposely hit a soft shot but it had enough spin to induce
a futile flail from Kris. His next serve was flat without spin. This time, Kris
connected, sending a bullet down the sideline. Joe sprinted but couldn't reach it
in time. With his back to the net, Joe held out his palm parallel to the ground,
indicating that the ball had landed inside the baseline. "Great shot," he called
over his shoulder.

Kris loved the outdoors even when it was hot and sticky. She had spent
her high school years, and every break during college, helping her folks out
on the ranch. Money was always tight, but it didn't matter much. The Rocky
Mountains were right outside the door. In the summers, Kris would get up
before dawn to wrangle the horses and remain in the saddle all day. When the
snow fell, she would hike or board, or sometimes both, in the backcountry.
While her computer science studies kept her indoors at Cornell, she conscien-
tiously snagged some time for long walks or runs. Kris thought of trying out
for the polo team there, but didn't have the time, or really the inclination, to ride

inside an arena. The work days at Illuminate were even longer than the ones at school. Fortunately, New York City had significantly expanded its recreational opportunities in recent years, particularly on the west side which now enjoyed bike paths, ball fields, and playgrounds. Tennis was not quite the same thrill as riding, but it was convenient and beat sitting at her desk.

Kris tried a few serves herself, but couldn't seem to get much pace on the ball. Beads of sweat bubbled on her forehead, dripping into her eyes. Joe suggested that she come to net. He lofted a short lob which Kris smashed to Joe's backhand. That was fun, she thought, watching Joe lunge fruitlessly as the ball bounded past. Kris had at last shed the cumbrous cloak of guilt that had shrouded her since the Stadium bombing. She had tried her best within the constraints of the law, and would continue to do so, although she was secretly pleased that Jim had been the one to assume the mantle of the fourth amendment at their last meeting. Joe hit another lob, but this one was much deeper in the court. Kris backed up but could only manage a feeble overhead into the net. "Step into the shot," Joe urged from across the court. Kris trotted back to the baseline, her most comfortable position on the court. Joe alternated shots to her forehand and backhand, and Kris returned most of them successfully. As she got into a rhythm, Kris' mind wandered. After Matt Reilly had moved back to San Diego, she had almost become a social recluse, throwing all her energy into work. Mindy had finally convinced her to try another date with one of Evan's friends. The first one hadn't gone too well, but Kris had to admit that she was looking forward to getting out again and meeting someone new. Tonight! Distracted now, she hit three consecutive balls into the net. "Let's switch sides," Joe offered. "There's a little more breeze on this end."

As they crossed paths at mid-court, Joe rested his racket and the balls on the bench, reaching into his gym bag for a dry tee shirt. The orange Mets' one that he had on was soaked completely through with perspiration. Kris, white shirt and clammy sports bra plastered against her torso, dried her face off with a towel and sucked greedily from her water bottle. She was just about to head back onto the court when her phone buzzed. She didn't want to answer but saw that it was Mindy calling from work.

"What's up? Joe's giving me a tennis lesson."

"You'd better come back here. We may have a problem with the, um, underwear."

"On my way."

"Game over?" Joe asked. Kris nodded, bending over to pack up her gear.

On the other side of the fence, Dmitri Remko leaned against the river rail, admiring the view. Like the gangsters in his favorite TV drama, CSI Miami, he wore a white linen shirt, dark sunglasses and a checkered fedora. Dmitri had spent most of the last hour watching the boats in the Hudson River. A cruise ship, as big as one of the apartment buildings on Brighton Beach Avenue, had just powered by, heading out to the Atlantic. He wondered what people did on a cruise. Dmitri realized that he had never been on a boat, let alone a huge ship, even though he lived near the ocean. Never been on an airplane either, he thought, scanning the sky overhead. Mostly, he looked after his baby sister. His mom worked all the time cleaning the fancy houses in Manhattan Beach and his dad had moved out long ago. Other times, he did what Mr. Nakitov, or that Polish asshole Bill Badenov, told him to do. Remko relished his role as the primary muscle for Mr. Nakitov. People in the neighborhood, particularly the kids, respected him, or at least feared him. Either way was OK. The pay was good too, better than he could get working construction or driving a cab, if he could even get a job. Dmitri had spent the last few days dreaming up the appropriate warning for Kris, but still hadn't settled on anything definite. Mr. Nakitov had never given Remko the opportunity to plan before, so it was a stressful experience. Much easier simply to follow orders. He had bought Lenny a few shots at Galina's last night to get his opinion. Lenny was a thinker, but he didn't have much to say. When Kris and Joe left the tennis court, Dmitri tossed his cigarette into the Hudson and followed.

25

Kris braced for the bad news. Hair still wet from a quick shower in the Illuminate locker room, she tried to peer over Mindy's shoulder without dripping all over the desk. Mindy fluttered her hand over three open shipping boxes, mimicking the host on Let's Make a Deal. "Two Stone Harbor bathing suits and a bridal set," she explained. "All contain the FBI marker."

"That's good for us, right? Bingo."

"Yes, and we've got more downstairs by the loading dock. But look here," Mindy said, slowly scrolling her finger across her computer screen. "We set up a little spreadsheet. Here's the item and the price. We paid with Paypal. Now check out the names of the sellers."

"Boardwalk Trading. Boardwalk Trading. Boardwalk Trading. It's the same for every item."

"Right," Mindy said, sliding her finger further across the spreadsheet. "So, we sent this information over to Jim Bright. He contacted Agent Boudoir's security people. They checked the cash register receipts for the names of the purchasers who originally bought the items in the store."

"Thomas A. Storm, Sally B. Cudlow, Thomas A. Storm," Kris read aloud, then stopped suddenly. "Whoa, that's my dad's name," she exclaimed.

"That's what I thought," Mindy said. She spun her chair around to face Kris. "Look at the address listed for him."

"It's somewhere in New Jersey. Maybe it's another Tom Storm then. My dad lives in Colorado."

Mindy shook her head. "I spoke to Jim Bright and asked him to check. He called back a little while ago. Said that the social security number and bank reference on the credit card matches your dad's."

"Shit. I bet that someone stole his ID and is using it on-line," Kris said, slipping both hands into the back pockets of her jeans.

"He's definitely been hacked." Mindy said, standing up to put a hand on Kris' shoulder. "What if they start drawing money out of your dad's real accounts now?" she asked.

"Maybe they already have." Kris replied, spinning around to return to her desk. She sat down and banged on a speed dial button.

"Dad?"

"Kris, how are you?"

"I'm fine, Dad. But you, I mean we, have a big problem." Kris recounted the details of the fraudulent transactions. "So either you traveled to New York to buy some presents or you're the victim of identity theft," she concluded.

"Are you sure? I mean, I didn't go shopping in New York. You know that."

"We're sure, dad. Now we have to stop it. Immediately." Kris tried to keep her voice calm, but firm, like the doctor telling her dad to leave the bronco busting to the younger hands.

"OK. OK. Let me go over to the computer."

"Dad, you need to check your credit card bills and bank statements. Can you access them on-line?"

"You know that mom handled all our financial stuff. Since she passed, I haven't ..."

"Well, you're going to have to look at it. I've got a friend from school who's a CPA. I bet that he can help you out."

"All right, all right, I'll call him." Kris could still hear the grief in her dad's voice. "But, I didn't do anything wrong." he asserted.

"Let's take a look at your computer," Kris said, pulling out a pad to take notes. "Have you downloaded anything new lately? Games, photos, docs?"

"No."

"Have you replied to any emails asking you for personal information, like your address or social security number?"

"No."

"Sometimes they look official. Lots of people get fooled."

"No."

"OK, good. I hate to ask, dad, but do you ever look at porn online?"

"No, dear." Tom Storm's irritation practically burst through the phone.

You're probably lying dad, Kris thought. She knew the statistics on Illuminate searches, but decided not to challenge him now.

"Wait, wait," Mr. Storm said, breaking the silence. Kris recoiled. She really didn't want to know.

"A few months ago, I signed up for this new website. I told you about it. Remember."

"Which one?" Kris asked, unsure where her dad was headed.

"SeniorSavers.com. I installed their toolbar on our Mac. It's great. It's got one-click buttons for great deals on shopping and travel. It's got weather reports too." Mr. Storm tapped a few keys. "I saved over one hundred dollars on a new TV for the bedroom," he said proudly.

"Dad, did you have to provide any financial information when you signed up?"

"A few things. But they said that it was all encrypted and secure."

Dad, how can you be so stupid, Kris wanted to scream, but held it in. She remembered her first, and last, tattoo. Freshman year in high school. Kris was so upset that their family had pulled her out of school in California and moved to Colorado that she had their old zip code, 95125, tattooed in the middle of a broken heart above her right ankle. Her mom had freaked out, but her dad had stayed cool, explaining that she might seek other ways to express herself in the future.

Joe had wandered over, standing behind Kris and listening to the last few snippets of conversation. Sensing Kris' frustration, he tapped her shoulder and indicated that he could help out. Kris stood, surrendering her seat to Joe.

"Hi, Mr. Storm. It's Joe Brady. I work with Kris. It's not your fault, Ok. That toolbar that you downloaded is probably crimeware - the virus is called

GameOver Zeus. It tracks everything that you do on-line and sends the in-formation to a server that the bad guys operate. It would have discovered your financial info even if you didn't give it to them. "

"The toolbar tracks everything that my dad does?" Kris asked. Joe nodded. "Dad, do you access the ranch's system from that computer?"

"Yes."

"Do you have a password?"

"Yes. I keep it on the desk right here."

"Shit," Kris and Joe cursed in unison.

"Dad, we're going to have to tell Mr. Doren. You might have opened the door for the hackers to get into his network."

"What?" Mr. Storm's fear was tangible. "The ranch is just a hobby for Mr. Doren. He's chairman of the board of Transactions Worldwide. It does the back office processing for credit cards for retail merchants. Links them to all the banks. I'm sure the company has millions of financial records stored in its data centers. He's involved in a few e-commerce companies too.

"Anything else?" Kris asked.

"I'm pretty sure that he owns a big piece of the Boston Red Sox."

"Well, I'm confident that his companies have strong cybersecurity protec-tion," Joe said reassuringly.

"What do I do now?" Mr. Storm pleaded.

"Go to another computer and change your password. Then call Mr. Doren. Immediately. But stay away from your computer. Do not use it again."

"OK."

"I'm going to call a friend in our Denver office. He'll come out and check it carefully. We'll identify all the crimeware and then figure out where to go next." Joe said.

"We're going to have to tell the FBI too," Kris chimed in. "Just sit tight, and wait for us to get back to you."

"Got it."

"Bye dad. Love you."

After the call, Kris turned to Joe. "I'm going to find the location of that server and who's controlling it," she said determinedly.

"That won't be easy," Joe replied. "If the bad guys are any good, they will have covered up their network tracks by now."

Kris thought for a second. "My old comp sci professor at Cornell is a cyber-crime guru. Maybe he can help."

"It's worth a shot."

Kris checked her watch. "It's only 7:30. The night is still young at Gates Hall," she said, looking up the phone number in her contacts' directory. Fifteen minutes later, Kris had set up a meeting in Ithaca for the next morning, reserved a rental car and hotel room, and bustled out of the building. Her double date with Mindy would have to wait.

Dmitri had just topped his hot dog with sauerkraut and onions when Kris burst onto the street, clearly agitated. He made a quick phone call, then hurried off in the opposite direction.

■ ■ ■

An hour later, overnight bag slung across her shoulder, Kris waited impatiently outside her apartment in the West Village. She wore faded shorts and a red "Cornell Wrestling - NCAA Champions" tee shirt, recalling memories of the good friends and good times of her college days. At last, a gray minivan pulled up. "This is the only vehicle available on such short notice," the rental car company employee apologized, as he handed over the keys. "There's a big jam at the Lincoln, so I would avoid it," he added. Kris thanked him and tapped on her phone to scout an alternate route to Cornell. She had at least a four hour drive ahead.

Dmitri, sitting across in the street in his red Camaro, smiled. Lenny was right. Kris was going away for the weekend, probably driving out to the Hamptons. He would send him some pictures, he thought, as he followed Kris onto West Street, packed with cars but moving. Dmitri did not have much trouble keeping the minivan in sight. He expected Kris to cut across 23rd Street to get to the Midtown Tunnel on the east side which would lead them towards Long Island, but she kept heading north. They stopped frequently as cars backed up approaching the entrance to the Lincoln Tunnel, burrowing west to New Jersey.

The tightly spaced traffic signals slowed the pace even further, but finally by 42nd Street they passed the mess. After 57th, West Street turned into highway. Kris pulled into the left lane, accelerating smoothly. The minivan has some pep, Dmitri thought, staying two cars behind in the middle lane. The twinkling lights of the George Washington Bridge quickly came into sight. Kris cut across Dmitri to pull into the exit lanes. She chose the upper level of the bridge, westbound. Definitely not going to the Hamptons, Dmitri thought. Crossing the span, Kris drifted into the right hand lane and then exited onto the Palisades Parkway, northbound again. The Parkway quickly reentered New York State. Thirty minutes later, Kris wheeled onto the New York State Thruway, destination Albany. Traffic was light; the surrounding countryside dark. Kris ramped the minivan up to 80 miles per hour. Dmitri looked at the GPS on the dashboard. The Thruway cut a glowing ribbon through an otherwise caliginous map. In foreign territory now, Dmitri considered turning back, but he had already texted Lenny about his plan to ambush Kris. He cranked up the volume on the Heavy Metal station on his satellite radio and followed Kris into the blackness.

Oblivious to her pursuer, Kris kept a heavy foot on the gas pedal while listening to CNN handicap the upcoming Congressional debate about the fourth amendment, or more specifically, the impending expiration of Section 215 of the Patriot Act. Motivated by the World Trade Center disaster in 2001, Section 215 enabled the federal government to secretly collect personal, "tangible things" relevant to an authorized international terrorism investigation. When Edward Snowden, a former CIA employee and consultant, leaked thousands of classified documents revealing that the United States had extended this collection process to telephone metadata, a record of who called whom but not the content of the call, for millions of people, a global outroar erupted.

At Exit 16, Kris turned off the Thruway onto Route 17 west, two lanes in each direction, climbing into the Catskill Mountains towards Binghamton. The Catskills, featuring more than thirty peaks above 3,500 feet, preside over the Hudson River valley. Slide Mountain is the tallest at almost 4,200 feet, not much of a mountain by Colorado standards, Kris thought. She remembered studying the tranquil landscapes of the famous Hudson River school painters of the nineteenth century, Frederic Church, John Kensett, and Albert Bierstadt, in an art history elective, but could only see a mind-numbing mass in her headlights tonight. When Kris darted around a tiring truck on an uphill stretch, Dmitri stayed in formation, keeping the taillights of the van in view at all times.

With the drone of CNN heightening the monotony, Kris opened the window to stay awake and scarfed down two chocolate chip cookies. A man's home is his castle - that was the English precedent dating back to to the early seventeenth century for the fourth amendment. Kris had researched its history to help assuage her guilt after the Stadium bombing. Colonists in Massachusetts took up the privacy battle in a landmark lawsuit in 1761, arguing, in vain, to prevent the King's customs officials from physically entering their homes to search for smuggled goods without a specific warrant. The colonists' defeat in this trial, and subsequent actions by the British government, effectively ignited the Revolutionary War, according to John Adams, who went on to write the fourth amendment itself along with help from James Madison. The founding fathers added the amendment to the Constitution as part of the Bill of Rights in 1791. The gut-wrenching angst of the privacy debate had not abated yet, Kris thought wryly.

Needing a break, Kris switched the radio over to a local station. Its ramble about tomorrow's river conditions, the approaching town of Roscoe apparently was the trout fishing capital of the east, reminded Kris of her dad. He loved to fish. More determined than ever to protect him, Kris turned her thoughts back to the fourth amendment. The most recent Supreme Court decision had actually extended privacy protection to mobile phones, recognizing that they now contained more information than might be found in a home. OK, that made sense. But what about information that was *sent* from a mobile phone, or a web browser. Why should a visit to jihadist website be any more protected than a visit to a jihadist storefront? Email, like a phone call, was more complicated, but as Jim had pointed out at the beginning of their investigation, the parties had willingly transmitted their messages over a public communications network, giving up their right to privacy at least in the FBI's opinion. Furthermore, as Kris knew well from her work at Illuminate, a large database was necessary to scan for patterns and connections. In this light, was a warrantless collection of email and telephone metadata really "unreasonable"? The right hand side of

Kris' brain still said yes, she had to admit, but it provided only a cold comfort now. Her emotional side wanted to power the van right over the bastards who orchestrated the bombing at Yankee Stadium, and then back up and do it again. More important, she wanted to insure that they did not strike another target. A snippet of privacy seemed like a small price to pay.

The roadside billboard proclaimed Roscoe as the home of a famous diner. Even if the food did not live up to its billing, the diner would have a much-needed restroom. Kris veered off the highway. Dmitri followed, now directly behind Kris. He had figured that she would have to stop sooner or later. He steered into the parking spot next to Kris, the diner looming in front of them. She would have to pass him to reach its entrance. The Camaro and the minivan were the only two cars in the dimly lit lot. Dmitri grabbed the lug wrench that he had kept within easy reach on the passenger seat and stepped out of the car. He could hear the cars passing by on Route 17 but no one was in sight. He swatted away a mosquito that buzzed his face, attracted by the fleeting glow of his car's interior light. The gas station across the street had already closed, now just a deserted silhouette. Dmitri bolted towards the front of his car, hoping to catch Kris before she climbed out. Maybe she'd piss her pants, he thought, picturing the wetness seeping through her jeans.

Kris was pleased to see the sports car pull in next to her. The empty parking lot, a ghost town, was spooky at this late hour. She looked up at the diner as she reached to unclip her seat belt. No signs of life or light. Shit, it's closed. Kris swiveled her head around to check out the gas station. Closed too. She remembered a sign for a rest stop a few miles ahead, a Text Stop the sign had actually announced in an attempt to highlight the hipness of upstate New York. She couldn't wait much longer, Kris thought, squeezing her thighs together. She shifted into reverse and peeled out. Dmitri pounded the wrench into his open palm. Despite his frustration, Dmitri knew that he couldn't follow immediately. After one more quick survey of his surroundings, Dmitri unzipped his fly and splashed a golden stream against the diner wall.

Dmitri did not have any trouble catching up to Kris on the climbing curves of Route 17, but he stayed several car lengths behind to be safe. Even if Kris had seen his car in the parking lot, she would not be able to distinguish it on the open road at night. They stayed in tandem for five more miles. Up in the mountains, the exits were spaced far apart with nothing but fir trees, boulders and an occasional creek between them. At last, Dmitri's headlights played over the blue sign for the upcoming stop. He bet himself a bottle of Stoli that Kris would break there, smiling when her brake lights pumped up ahead.

The deserted diner back in Roscoe looked like Times Square at noon compared to the isolation of the Text Stop, Kris thought. The driveway passed a row of empty picnic tables that stood as silent sentinels standing vigil over the dense forest that lay just beyond. Kris parked as close as possible to the comfort station and skipped out, afraid that her teeth would start floating if she had to wait any longer.

"Hoot! Hoot!"

She spun her head to the woods at the sound of the owl's call. Kris imagined the headless horseman bursting from the tall trees at any moment as the semi-darkness crawled up her skin like a lizard. She pushed the door to the Ladies Room tentatively, her mood brightening to find it unlocked. The white tile floor was cracked but clean. The smell of disinfectant filled the room; could be worse, Kris thought. Both toilet stalls were empty. No surprise. Toilet paper rack full. A good sign. In her haste to seek relief, Kris did not bother to close the latch.

Dmitri shut down his headlights as he cruised into the Text Stop. He stayed in the car until Kris entered the bathroom, reveling in the remoteness. No witnesses, no way out, he thought, his right hand gripping the lug wrench as he stalked to the comfort station, growling like a pit bull. Kris heard the ladies room door open and checked her watch, wondering what had propelled another female traveler here at this late hour. Dmitri's tongue darted over his lips when he saw Kris' sneakers flat on the floor in the first stall, her shorts bunched around them. Kris felt a jolt of concern when the other woman stopped in front of her stall. She reached for her coiled underwear. Dmitri almost laughed when he saw the unlatched door. This was going to be even easier than he thought.

Dmitri slammed the lug wrench against the loose door, sending it clanging against the side of the metal enclosure. The sight of Kris, still sitting on the toilet, fed his frenzy. She looked up, stunned, vaguely recognizing Dmitri, noticing a beaver chipped tooth in his grim smile. He grabbed at her red hair, ripping her off the seat and halfway out of the stall. Kris tried to pull away, but her half-mast shorts betrayed her, sending her slumping to the floor. Dmitri crashed the wrench next to Kris' feet, a deafening boom filling the small room.

"Go ahead, crawl, *suka*," he hissed, as Kris tried to slither away. "There's nowhere to go."

He slashed the wrench down again a few inches from Kris' head sending a shower of tile chips into her neck and hair. "Stay away from the credit cards. Stay away from the underwear sales." He spit out the words in staccato bursts, like a cog wheel train chugging up a steep hill.

Kris fumbled in her purse, trapped underneath her curled body, for her keys. She clasped the chain in her fist, exposing one jagged key between her knuckles. Dmitri's exposed ankle was within reach now. She could stab it and try to scramble away. But Dmitri stepped over Kris' head, taking two long strides towards the exit door. Turning one last time, he reached into his back pocket and pulled out his phone to snap a photo of Kris bare-assed for Lenny. He got off on women with tattoos, although Kris' broken heart was pretty small.

"Am I clear?" Dmitri asked, his voice returning to a more normal cadence. Mr. Nakitov had said to warn Kris, not beat her up. He had delivered the message. Time to return to Brooklyn.

Kris nodded slowly, releasing her key chain. She waited in the fetal position until she heard the door close and could not see Dmitri's feet on the tiles. At last, Kris stood, wobbling, clasped her shorts and brushed off the tile debris. She remembered Dmitri from the photos in Jim's office. He was one of the thugs that had tried to scare Jim in Brighton Beach. Fuck you, she proclaimed, her voice echoing in the empty bathroom. And your constitutional rights, she added silently. The rest of the drive to Ithaca was uneventful.

■ ■ ■

"Ahh, Miss Storm, truly a pleasure to see you again," Professor Hayden drawled in a mellifluous Southern accent as he leaned back in his cracked leather chair. His attire, a gray poplin suit and thin black tie, was Georgia peach, not Cornell academic. "You have not graced our halls of learning here in quite some time." Hayden's craggy face beamed with enthusiasm but his pasty, miner's complexion and shoulder-length, scraggly white hair testified to the many hours in front of a computer screen.

"No sir. I mean, thank you, sir." Kris had always mumbled like a starstruck schoolgirl in the presence of the revered Harold "Hal" Hayden. For his day job, Hayden taught the intro computer science course in the engineering school, weeding out the wanna-be programmers from the truly gifted. No freshman ever missed his theatrical 8AM lectures. Hayden's public questioning, needle-sharp but cloaked in Southern charm, snapped the most hungover to attention, while his exams and homework assignments required even his brightest pupils to pull the occasional all-nighter. Away from the light, Hayden was rumored to be the batman of the cyberworld, leading top secret projects for the government and publishing a blog under a pseudonym that unmasked the technical tricks of cybercrooks worldwide. An unmarked private jet was always on standby at the Ithaca airport.

"What can I do for you?" the first person pronoun stretched for three beats.

Kris provided the details on her dad's foibles.

"Yes, yes, SeniorSavers.com has been on our watch list for several months now. Some of the best hacking work that I have seen. Probably generating millions, possibly tens of millions, of dollars in illicit gains."

"At least my dad's not the only one duped, I guess."

"No, your father is in good company."

"How do they do it?" Kris asked.

Hayden stood and ambled over to his white board. With a red marker, he drew several X's in a circle. "The hackers plant their crimeware, like the toolbar on your dad's machine, on as many computers as possible. They use sites like SeniorSavers, phishing emails, offers of free porn, anything that can entice an innocent person to connect and download. Then they watch and wait."

"That's all?"

"Sounds simple, right? But the genius is in the crimeware. It leaches on to any computer that the original host connects to. Not that hard to do, right?" He drew another circle of X's surrounding the original ones and connected them. "But this crimeware is programmed to identify and capture only financial related information - passwords, personal data, credit card records, bank accounts. It leaves everything else on the computer alone, so it's almost impossible to detect."

"How many X's are on the network?"

"Good question. Thousands? Tens of thousands? We really don't know. What's worse, a single X," he said, tapping one on the whiteboard, then continuing," can actually be a corporation or a bank that has millions of financial records. All feeding data to the cybercrooks." Hayden grasped a green marker and drew a box in the middle of all the X's. "Sometime between 3 and 6 AM local time, the crimeware ships the stolen data to a central server here in the States. Hiding in plain sight, if you pardon the cliche." He linked the inner ring of red X's to the green central box. "The data just sits there for several days. The bad guys watch to see if anyone, like us, is looking for it, or even knows the data's missing."

"Then?"

"The data disappears, unfortunately." Hayden pointed to the central green server. "Software here creates an, um, onion, if you will. The real data lies at its center encased by several layers of protective skin. Each layer contains instructions to ship the data to another server which in turn peels the layer of encryption off and ships the rest of the onion onward. All the relay points are random, so we can't establish a pattern." Hayden picked up a black marker, and zigzagged it from the central green box through several of the red X's and then off the edge of the white board. "We think that financial data ultimately ends up on a server in Eastern Europe but we can't be sure."

"Why don't you just shut the SeniorSavers site down?"

"We don't want to shut it down. It's just a pawn in the game anyway. They would just start up a new scam in a matter of weeks. We want to identify the brains behind the entire network and take him, or her, out of circulation. Completely." Hayden trailed his index finger across his throat, emphasizing the final point.

"Are you sure that it's just an individual, not a gang, or even a government?" Hayden shrugged.

"How do we break up the network?" Kris asked, standing up at last.

"We have to go back to square one, I think," Hayden said, again tapping a solitary red X.

"My dad?"

"Yes, he's vetted and trusted already. We can set up a honey trap that starts on his computer, and hope that it attracts the queen bee."

"Then what?

"What do you mean?" Hayden asked, sitting back down behind his desk.

"What do we do if we find the queen bee? Suppose she's sitting in some big dacha outside Moscow protected by the KGB?"

"You know that the KGB does not exist anymore and that the Russian Federation is now our ally in the war against terrorism," Hayden declared with all due bombast. Kris did not reply, but her expression conveyed the skepticism usually reserved for an infomercial on late night TV.

"Yes, my sentiments exactly. But, rest assured, if there is truly a link to the bombing at Yankee Stadium, then we will flush her out of the hive."

"I'd like to help."

"I'm not so sure that's a grand idea. They play rough."

No kidding, Kris thought.

26

"To the loss of your virginity," Bill Badenov solemnly proclaimed, tossing back a shot of vodka at the bar at Galina's.

"To virgins everywhere," Lenny added, saluting Derek with his glass.

"Your first arrest," Dmitri toasted.

The vodka burned his throat, but this was not the first time that Derek had done shots. He slammed his empty glass down on the bar, and looked into the eyes of his new band of brothers for their approval. Bill had picked him up at the Verizon store after work today and drove him to Brooklyn, proud of his protege's performance and eager to introduce him to the inner circle, at long last.

"Another round," Bill ordered. The bartender, a slim blonde with a nose ring, poured four more drinks. She turned to help another patron waving a fifty in her direction, but left the bottle behind. The bar was starting to fill, a boisterous exuberance building. Lenny pointed to an empty table, a "Reserved for Bottle Service" sign warding off the riff raff. Dmitri grabbed the vodka bottle and led the way.

"Nice spot," Derek remarked as they sat down to the envious looks of several bystanders.

"This is our place," Bill asserted. Dmitri filled the four glasses again. The musketeers clinked, glasses meeting high in the center of the table, and slugged down the round. But the pace slowed as no one seemed to know what to say next.

"Great legs," Dmitri proclaimed, breaking the stalemate by pointing his glass at a basketball tall brunette in a willowy white skirt that tickled her ankles. The others followed his gaze, silently agreeing with Dmitri's astute observation. Five minutes of quiet meditation followed. Lenny cleaned his fingernails with a toothpick. Dmitri belched loudly.

"Smartest thing that you've said in weeks," Bill commented dryly. He filled everyone's glasses one more time, noting Derek's discomfort in his new surroundings. "We need a drinking game," he announced, signaling for the mini-skirted waitress to bring over another bottle. "Sweet Things. Derek showed it to me last week. It's got more action than Candy Crush, and they don't charge you for power-ups." Bill passed his phone around so his associates could see the opening sequence. "I'll buy the caviar for anyone who can beat him."

"I'm pretty good at Candy Crush," Lenny said, holding on to Bill's phone and starting to play the game. The waitress poured another round, leaning over Lenny's shoulder to check out the game, her breasts on full display. "Looks cool. I'll give it a try too," she said.

"Sit right here. We can play together," Dmitri said, pointing to his lap. The waitress smiled indulgently as she spun away. Bill let Lenny struggle with Sweet Things for a few minutes before signaling for him to pass the phone to Derek. "Let the champ show us how it's done."

Derek survived the first two levels of the game on muscle memory, but he was swallowed by a bottomless pit of molasses in the third level. The vodka was taking its toll. Bill swept his phone away and handed it to Dmitri.

"I'm no good at this *der'mo*," Dmitri carped as he died three quick deaths in the first level.

"Derek will teach you some tricks," Bill said, as he passed the phone onward. Lenny's Candy Crush skills got him through the first level, an impressive feat for a rookie Bill remarked, but the strawberry patch in level two nailed him.

"Let me try again," Lenny said determinedly, hitting the reset button to launch a new game. The waitress poured another round. The crowd, now filling the bar, surged around their table. A glittering disco ball and flashing strobe lights inspired four women in stiletto heels to start swaying to the pounding techno beat.

Natasha, trailed by two other dancers, knifed through the mass like the Praetorian Guard. She tapped Lenny on the shoulder, and cupped her hand to his ear, "All work and no play is not good," she admonished, breaking Lenny's concentration. He jumped up, bobbling Bill's phone before finally corralling it into his pocket, "Ms. Bubka," he mumbled, but realized that she could barely hear him over the din. Natasha motioned for Lenny to sit, and nodded a greeting to the rest of the crew, now all standing as well. "Ilya wanted you to celebrate. He will pay," she almost shouted, pointing to the bottle of vodka in the center of the table. Bill signaled for more glasses which appeared immediately. Everyone downed a shot in a single, celebratory gulp. "My friends want to dance," Natasha mimed this time, looking towards the center of the room. Bill pushed Derek forward. "Have some fun," he said.

As the first rays of sunlight peeked over the boardwalk, Bill bundled Derek into an Uber car for the ride back to Staten Island. The vodka high had worn off, replaced by the hangover regrets. He had betrayed his friends, no question there. Where would it lead? For them, he could guess. For himself, redemption? Hopefully. Where else he had no clue. Derek pulled on his sunglasses and dozed off.

■ ■ ■

"Where do you want to go for lunch?" Kris called out.

"Is it lunch time already?" Mindy asked, looking up from her screen to check her watch.

"No, but it will be in an hour or so," Kris said, munching on a Hershey bar.

"Can't wait that long, huh?"

"I wish I could, but I'm trying to fatten up. Hayden and the FBI guys are afraid that someone might recognize me if I have to go out there, so we are making a few changes."

"The Little Miss Piggy look?"

"Probably a little of everything, they said. Weight, hair color, eyeglasses, boobs." Kris flattened her breasts against her chest. "I'm not really sure how it will end up, but this is the hardest part," she said, holding up the candy. "All I do is eat. I've put on almost thirty pounds in the last month. I'm going to pop like a balloon if something doesn't happen soon."

"You know that Joe and I will do anything that we can to help."

"I know, but right now all we can do is wait. In the meantime, this work is driving me nuts. It's so...pedestrian," she said, finally finding the right word. Since she had returned from Cornell, Kris had to force herself to focus on the routine security work at Illuminate. Last week, she had helped a high fashion shoe store in Chelsea, a small client, defend itself against a denial of service attack. It turned out that the owner's recently dumped mistress had hired a high school hacker to bombard the shoe store's ads and website with traffic, effectively shutting them down until the owner paid the $5,000 rent that he owed on her apartment. This week, she was compiling data on attempted intrusions into Illuminate's network hub in Thailand. At this level, the hacking was pretty simple, often utilizing outdated approaches that the Illuminate team had little trouble countering. But the Russian credit card crew would be another ballgame. Kris checked her email every thirty minutes to see if Professor Hayden had any news on the honeypot that they had dangled.

"You're becoming a cybersecurity snob," Mindy countered.

"I'm trying to become a competent hacker," Kris said modestly. She was confident in her coding skills, but hacking was different. It required taking systems apart, bit by bit, not building them up. Joe, their resident hacking whiz, was teaching her the latest tools in late night sessions in the small den at her apartment. The FBI had installed a dedicated server there that Kris could practice on. It contained virtual machines that replicated the IT defenses and databases of some of the largest institutions in the country. Using Metasploit, an open source database of known exploit codes, Kris could now routinely penetrate them, at least in her living room.

"Well, Superwoman, are we still going out tonight?" Mindy asked, purposely changing the subject.

"Shit, I'm a blob. No one is going to want to look at me."

"You're not that big - yet," Mindy joked. "Evan's friend, Andy, is a really good guy. And cute. I met him that night that you stood us up to go to Cornell."

Kris wheeled her chair closer to Mindy. "You really like Evan, don't you?" she asked in a lower voice, not really necessary since Joe, working at the next desk, had his headphones on anyway.

"Yea," Mindy admitted, "We've been seeing a lot of each other lately."

"That's cool. Is it going anywhere?"

Mindy shrugged. "Maybe. He sort of hinted that we should move in together."

"I bet that he just likes your apartment," Kris kidded.

"He shares a two bedroom with three other guys in Queens," Mindy admitted. "But it's so much easier for him to get to work from my place. Come out with us tonight. You have to eat dinner anyway."

"OK, OK, but it can't be too late."

Kris changed after work into her new fat girl jeans paired with a pink button down shirt, untucked in an attempt at camouflage. She met Mindy and friends at the North End Grill, down in Battery Park City. One dollar oysters after eight on weeknights. Andy had a toothy, winsome smile and tried hard to be funny, but Kris did not laugh much. She begged off around ten and headed home.

"You look all spiffy. Hot date?" Joe greeted Kris in front of her building in an obvious attempt to boost her spirits.

"Funny guy," Kris said sarcastically as she led the way into the small lobby. "How did you guess?"

"Mindy's been trying to fix you up for weeks. She was preening at her desk all afternoon, so I guessed that tonight was the big night," Joe said following her up the stairs.

"Moving right along," Kris replied, opening the door to her apartment and closing the subject. She brought out a six pack of beers, a bowl of chips, guacamole dip and Oreos from the kitchen for nourishment. They spent the next ninety minutes hacking away in silence before the intercom jangled loudly. Kris didn't budge from her seat in front of the computer. When it sounded again, Joe tapped her on the shoulder. "I think that's your doorbell."

"What?" Kris replied, obviously in a fog.

"Your doorbell, right?"

"Oh yeah. Who could it be now?" Kris walked over to the panel by the door to find out. "Jim? Come on up," she squawked, buzzing him up. Jim Bright bounded up the steps, pizza box in hand. Gray suit rumpled and tie loosened, Jim had come over straight from the office.

"We got word from Professor Hayden a few hours ago," he explained. "They're starting to pick up some chatter in the hacker forums about a big new potato field that needs farming."

"Potatoes? "I'll have two," she joked, picking up a slice of pizza and pointing Jim to the beer.

"Hacker slang for credit cards," Joe chimed in.

"Hayden's people worked with your dad's boss - Doren, right?" Kris nodded between bites. "Well, they upgraded your dad's access into his company's network and then created a little maze there, some false files and encrypted data that should keep the hackers busy for a while at least. We thought that if it was too easy to get the financial data, they would get suspicious," Jim went on. "Now, they're stuck."

"They'll probably try to brute force it," Joe said.

"Exactly right. The head hackers, we think that they're two women actually from their online posts, are looking for help. They've put out a call to arms."

"A hackathon?" Kris asked. "We have them here at Illuminate sometimes to tackle really tough technical problems. The coders get all pumped up."

"They'll probably use Burp Suite. It's like a Swiss Army knife of tools to attack any web app," Joe interrupted. "I know it pretty well. You won't have any trouble picking it up."

Jim looked longingly at the pizza. "OK if I take a slice? I haven't eaten dinner yet," he apologized before scarfing down several large bites.

"Where? When?" Kris asked.

"Moscow. Next weekend."

"What a surprise." Kris said. "I always wanted to go to Russia."

"No way." Jim said, coughing up a wad of cheese. "We couldn't protect you there."

"I'm a big girl."

"Bullshit. Even if you connected with the hackers, the Russian government would never let us even talk to them, let alone prosecute them."

"So, we're fucked," Kris said.

"Maybe not," Jim replied. "Hayden thinks that the hackers are antsy, maybe feeling some pressure from Nakitov. He thinks that they might be willing to travel to get the keys to unlock the data before the hackathon."

"We're going to invite the Russian hackers to New York?" Joe asked incredulously. "Maybe they'll want to take in a Broadway show too."

"No. Hayden's cousin owns a small hotel on Hvar. It's an island in the Adriatic Sea, belongs to Croatia. Not too far from Moscow, but there is no love lost between the governments. He thought that Kris might want to visit."

"Isn't Hvar a big party town?" Kris asked.

"Just like the Hamptons. Evidently, the hackers party hard."

"I guess I'll need a new bathing suit," Kris said, looking down at her thickening middle.

"Not so fast."

"This is a lot more complicated than learning a new hacking tool, or putting on a few pounds," Jim protested. "We're going to have to build you a whole new identity too." He wanted to tell her how dangerous it would be, but Joe cut him off again.

"Kris is also going to need street cred with the black hat community. Some accomplishments to show that she's one of them."

"Professor Hayden's already started," Jim admitted. "I think that he knew where Kris was headed all along." Jim took a long draught of his beer and pointed at Kris' computer. "He asked Doren's guys to put his system on Kris' server. It should be up by now."

"Let's take a look," Kris said, sitting back down at her desk.

The trio hunched over the computer screen in Kris' den for the next hour: Kris in the hot seat, Joe sitting to her right, and Jim standing behind, hand resting lightly on the back of Kris's chair, occasionally grazing her hair and neck. Noticing Jim's fingers stray again, Joe stood. "I'm beat," he said. "You guys can finish up without me."

"We'll see you here tomorrow too, right?" Kris asked. Joe nodded, then left. Kris rubbed her eyes and clambered up to stretch. "Let's take a break," she said, stifling a yawn.

"We can all call it a night," Jim replied.

"You go. I want to take one last crack at Doren's system." This time the yawn won. "Right after I take a break." Kris opened the last beer and flopped down on the sofa. Specks of tomato sauce and guac drizzled her date night shirt. She picked up the remote, cycling through several channels before settling on a rerun of Friends. Jim hesitated, taking off his suit jacket at last, before joining her. He clasped Kris' wrists together in his hands. "You don't have to do this," he implored. Kris put down the beer, turning up towards Jim. For the first time, he could see the strains in her face: a new pudginess in her cheeks, the droop of a second chin, a picket line of perspiration above her lips.

"I do. It's my dad. It's my country," Kris declared quietly. She snuggled under Jim's outstretched arm. "It's me," she whispered before resting her head on his shoulder. Jim inched closer, savoring the warmth of Kris' body and its tangy fragrance. He could feel her chest rise and fall with each rhythmic breath as she fell asleep.

27

Brighton Beach lolled in a late summer stupor. Sun worshippers packed the sand like a rush hour subway car, but no one seemed to have much energy left. A volleyball lay untouched under the net; the surf washed over a neglected boogie board; a sandcastle crumbled from neglect. Bill Badenov stomped across the boardwalk, the only one in a hurry.

"Sorry, I'm late," he apologized as soon as he reached the bench where Ilya Nakitov held court, Lenny Boykin standing behind him. Nakitov gazed out into the ocean for several seconds as if he were searching for Moby Dick.

"Sit," he said, giving up his quest at last and patting the place at his side. Bill obeyed obsequiously. "You need to get your shopping crews ready to go," Ilya went on.

"Yes, sir."

"We have the lead on a new haul of card numbers. Possibly a big one."

"Yes sir. When?"

"Soon. There are still some technical difficulties but we expect a resolution shortly. My best people are working on it. I will be in touch."

Nakitov stood and strolled leisurely away. Bill sat for a few more seconds to make sure that the interview was definitely over.

"Hey, tell your man Derek that I'm ready for him," Lenny said, his head half-turned towards Nakitov.

"What?"

"Sweet Things." Lenny pointed to his phone. "I've been practicing," he said before striding off to catch up with Nakitov. Lenny stayed three steps behind his boss for the next fifty yards. Nakitov stopped at a vendor's stand to buy a bottle of water, then resumed his stroll. A toddler's wail distracted Lenny. The boy, wearing only a diaper, crashed into his leg and fell on the wooden planks. His mother, pushing a stroller, rushed to pick him up, apologizing profusely in Russian. "He hates the suntan protection," she explained, holding up a spray can. Lenny turned quickly to locate Nakitov, relieved to find him again sitting on a bench.

Lenny resumed his sentry position. "Can I make a suggestion, Mr. Nakitov?" he asked. Ilya nodded. "We need to raise our prices, sir. Our cards are the best on the market. Everyone recognizes that."

"How do you know?"

"I track the chat rooms - online sir. Our clients are lining up to buy our merchandise whenever it will be ready."

"The next few days, I hope."

Lenny shook his head. "Ten days at least. The girls texted yesterday. They are calling in a few of their friends to help them solve the problem."

"That is not good. They have never needed help before. Perhaps I should enlist another one of our teams as well." Nakitov shifted on the bench. "A little *konkurentsiya*, eh?"

"The task is getting more difficult. Another reason to raise prices," Lenny said.

"I will give them one more week," Nakitov said, then his attention drifted back out to sea.

Lenny tapped his phone. "I thought you might enjoy this photo of your computer whizzes. They sent it yesterday," he said, displaying a snap of two young women, topless, arms around each other's waist, a beer held aloft in a mock salute.

Nakitov grimaced. "Stupid girls. Where are they?" he asked.

"Looks like Serebryany Bor park in Moscow from the location data," Lenny replied, fiddling with his phone. "Great tits, huh?" he commented, taking a long, leering glance at the photo.

"They are lovers," Nakitov said, pouring cold water on Lenny's enthusiasm. "Those *sis'ki* can only get us in trouble now. Who knows who is monitoring our communications?"

"That is why they communicate through me, sir."

"Please let the girls know that if they persist in these dangerous activities, the consequences could be dire. Very dire."

"Yes sir." Lenny said somberly.

Nakitov stood abruptly, motioning for Lenny to come closer as he grasped the rail of the boardwalk. "Can you deliver the photo, discretely of course, to our favorite civil servant - an addition to his collection. It will bring back pleasant memories for him, eh?"

■ ■ ■

Lynne tumbled off, spent at last, rivulets of sweat sluicing between her breasts. Derek, flat on his back, rolled his eyes and wiped his forehead. He had finished first, easy to do, but always a mistake, especially with Lynne.

"You need to crank up the AC. It's a fucking sauna in here," he said.

"My dad gets really pissed off when I leave it on when he's at work. Really pissed. I opened all the windows this morning," Lynne replied, sitting up to reach for a handful of tissues. Her family lived in a two bedroom ranch-style house in a working class neighborhood near the ferry terminal on Staten Island. Her older sister had just moved out so Lynne had her own room at last. "Are you complaining?"

"No, just fucking hot." Lynne's father was a large man. Almost played linebacker in the NFL, he had said. Maybe the AC wasn't such a big deal.

"That's good," Lynne laughed, patting his thigh. "Hungry?" Derek nodded. "What a surprise. I'll see what's in the fridge." Lynne picked up a black Cage the Elephant tee shirt from the floor and padded out. Derek's eyes followed. Unbelievable body, he thought, anticipation starting to build for the next round. He pulled the thin sheet up to his midsection and turned on the television to the midday edition of SportsCenter. Lynne returned shortly, tee shirt on now but barely covering her ass. She put a tray down next to Derek with three sandwiches and two beers and climbed back into bed. Leaning against the headboard, Lynne popped open a can and sipped. "Figured you might want seconds," she said, pointing to the extra sandwich.

"Good call," Derek said, smiling as he reached for lunch.

ESPN had been showing highlights from last night's MLB games, but the anchor interrupted, announcing a flash to the White House for an historic ceremony. The President stood in the Rose Garden, flanked by Bill Jones' mother, two generals in full dress uniform and the Congressional leaders of both parties. "We are here today to award the Medal of Honor posthumously to retired Private First Class William Jones in recognition of his gallantry and valor well beyond the call of duty on the plaza outside of Yankee Stadium two months ago. The people of the United States of America will be forever grateful for his heroism and sacrifice."

Derek put his beer on the nightstand and turned up the volume, captivated by the proceedings. The President went on to detail Jones' actions from his wheelchair that brought down the enemy combatant before he could murder more innocent spectators. He noted that Jones would be the first, and hopefully last, recipient of the Medal of Honor for action on American soil in the war on terrorism. The commentators later explained that the previous recipient for action in the United States was Lieutenant Commander William Corry, Jr., a passenger in a Navy airplane that crashed outside of Hartford, Connecticut in 1920. Although tossed from the plane and seriously injured himself, Corry returned to rescue the pilot from the flames. Corry died four days later. In 1963, Congress prohibited the award in non-combat situations. William Jones would be the sixteenth recipient of the Medal of Honor in the twenty-first century. Wiping the tears from her eyes, Mrs. Jones accepted the medal and hugged the president. ESPN switched back to baseball.

"Wow," Derek said, almost crying himself. "Did you see that?"

"What? Huh?" Lynne replied, barely looking up from her phone.

"What are you doing?"

"Playing Sweet Things."

"What?

"The game you told me about. It's pretty cool. And it's free."

"You can't play that," Derek said, wresting Lynne's phone from her hand.

"What are you doing? You're acting like a douchebag."

Derek took a deep breath. "That game is an FBI plant."

"An FBI what? How do you know?" Lynne screeched, sitting up abruptly, breasts bouncing.

"Because I planted it." He started to explain, but Lynne looked at him like he had just defecated on her sheets. "Get out. Get the fuck out of my house," she commanded.

Derek stood, pulling on his shorts. Scrambling to her knees, Lynne threw the remains of his sandwich at him. A beer can followed, narrowly missing his head. Derek ducked, fearing that the other can was coming next. But Lynne just curled up and started crying. Her tee shirt bunched up, revealing her nakedness. Derek returned to the bed, sitting by Lynne's side. He reached for her shoulder. "I had to do it," he said. "They're pigs. They're murderers. It's our only way out."

"Your only way out. I've got nowhere else to go." Lynne buried her face in her hands, refusing to look at him. "Leave!" she ordered.

"You can't tell anyone. They'll kill me," Derek pleaded.

"Don't worry. I'm not a rat like you," Lynne snarled, then pulled the sheet over her head.

28

Elena Smokina sat still, staring at her computer screen, the only light in the dark room, struggling to decipher the puzzle that it presented. An empty bottle of vodka, a chipped plate with remnants of a sausage, and an overflowing silver ash tray rested on the blonde wood of the desk, an IKEA original. Stale cigarette smoke circled her head stirred by a breeze, surprisingly cool even for a summer night in Moscow, that fluttered through the open window. In the distance, the klaxon siren of a police car wailed, then faded away. Elena wore a checkerboard flannel nightshirt, nothing else. Absentmindedly scratching her crotch, she tried to remember when she had showered last. Two days ago, she decided, right before they had started to attack this system. Doren Enterprises, fuck you. The penetration had started easily enough, a password swiped from one of the geriatrics who had signed up for the SeniorSavers scam site. Her partner, Yana Lykin, sleeping now in the king sized bed that dominated their studio apartment, had discovered it, diligently combing through the trove of data that they had collected. Yana had the patience for the digging; Elena didn't. She lived for the thrill of the chase: burrowing through a complex corporate information system to find the mother lode. Only now, she had crashed into another dead end.

Orphaned at thirteen by a car accident that claimed both her parents, Elena had grown up in foster care. Only her studies, computer science in particular, had kept her sane, earning her a spot at Moscow State University. She excelled there too, graduating to a job in the Ministry of Economic Development where she met Yana, three years her senior, in the next cubicle. After Elena's first year, her boss, married with three sons, called her into his office. She had expected praise and a promotion, and was partly right. Her boss did compliment her work, but noted sadly that the government did not approve of lesbian activities. He unzipped his pants, offering Elena the opportunity to prove her heterosexual proclivity. Elena kneeled down and hawked a gob of spit on his cock. She was moved to the secretarial pool the next day. Two weeks later, Ilya Nakitov contacted her. She eagerly signed up to work for his company. Despite stern warnings from her solidly middle class parents, Yana elected to follow her impetuous and voluptuous lover out the door. They had worked for Nakitov for three years now. The pay was slightly better than government grade and the job was much more challenging.

"Mr. Ruth, you are a cocksucking cunt," Elena shouted, banging the heel of her palm on the screen. Yana stirred, then sat up, the down comforter sliding off to uncover her naked torso. Yana had a labrys, a double-bladed battle axe, an ancient symbol of feminine strength, tattooed on her right breast and an intricate chain encircling her left. "What's wrong, my sweet?" she asked.

"I'm fucked again."

"Show me," Yana said, climbing out of bed and wrapping herself in a thin cotton robe. She looked over Elena's shoulder, gently massaging her neck with her right hand.

"We broke in with the Thomas Storm credentials. But they didn't get us too far."

"But they did get us into an employee database."

"Yes, we spent an entire day digging through it looking for someone with access to the credit card files. Then you found Mr. Russell Dent, a systems administrator."

"In account verification. He looked promising."

"He looked fucking gorgeous."

"But..."

"But, I can't crack his password."

"Even with Hydra?"

"Yes, and every other power tool that we have."

"It's high grade encryption."

"Hashed and salted."

"Let me see." Yana reached around Elena to tap on the keyboard.

"Someone else is here too."

"What?"

"There's someone else trying to hack in. I can see the tracks."

"Fuck." Elena reclaimed the keyboard, pounding away again.

Yana stroked her partner's stringy black hair, ignoring its oiliness. Then, she unfastened the top two buttons of Elena's nightshirt and slipped her hand inside. Elena ignored the advances, concentration locked on the screen, frustration building. Yana was not deterred, opening the rest of Elena's buttons and sweeping back her shirt. Yana cupped both of her lover's breasts, kneading them, savoring their succulent weight. Elena's nipples puckered in her grasp. ""Mr. Dent can wait till morning," Yana purred. Elena bit her lip, a soft moan escaping anyway, and pushed away the keyboard.

■ ■ ■

"She's not James Bond," Jim protested into the speakerphone. Glenn sat on the edge of his desk, hands wedged into his pants' pockets.

"She doesn't have to be," Professor Hayden replied, sitting behind his desk at his Washington office, buried in a nondescript office building a few blocks from the Pentagon. The CIA did not spend much of its black operations budget on office space. "The hackers should know by now that they have company in Doren's system. I bet they will reach out to Kris in the next twenty-four hours and suggest teaming up."

"But then she has to lure them out of Russia. To Hvar."

"That won't be hard. Nakitov is pressing for the card data, so they don't have much time and they can't afford to come in second place. Besides, from what I understand, those girls don't need much prodding to enjoy themselves."

"OK. Let's say they do meet up with Kris. What happens next?" Jim pressed.

"That's above your pay grade," Hayden said.   "What you need to know is that Kris will be in our safe house in Hvar. We will take good care of her - as long as she follows directions." Sitting across the room, Lieutenant Bill Rawlings, a Navy SEAL, nodded in agreement. Although only thirty, Rawlings had already commanded combat missions on three continents, documented by the ribbons and warfare insignia above the left pocket of his service khaki uniform. A trace of gray in his crew cut belied Rawlings' youth, but his bulldog body looked primed to explode into action.

"In fact, my associate, Lieutenant Rawlings, and his team will be heading to Hvar tomorrow to begin preparations," Hayden went on. Rawlings smiled. He couldn't wait to leave town. His wife of eight years - no kids fortunately - had booted him out last week after finding him in bed with a Congressional intern. Those Washington newbies got all wet just looking at the uniform, and he could never resist the temptation. Better to be in the field and out of trouble. His SEALs had been training in a mock-up of the hotel for the past week. They were ready to go.

"I'd like to go too, sir," Jim offered.

"That's a grand gesture," Hayden replied. "But, unfortunately, the Russians know your face. Why don't you come down here and help me coordinate the operation."

"With all due respect, the FBI needs to be on the ground in Croatia. We owe it to Kris. My partner, Glenn Walker, can go." Glenn stood at the mention of his name.

Back in Washington, Rawlings shook his head. Rescuing a damsel in distress was his job. His boys didn't need any help from the FBI.

"That's a fine idea. I will have Lieutenant Rawlings contact him," Hayden said. "Now let's all get to work," he concluded, hanging up the phone.

"I bet that Bright is banging that Storm girl," Rawlings declared after he was sure the line was dead.

"You have a devious mind, young man," Hayden said knowingly.

"I'm not the only one, sir. Pardon my language, but you can fuck someone without pulling out your dick."

"Whatever do you mean?"

"You certainly downplayed the risks of this mission. Nakitov is a tough nut. He won't let us snatch two of his top hackers without a fight."

"I doubt that he will even know that they are in Hvar."

"But, if he does, Storm could easily wind up dead or in a Croatian jail for the rest of her life."

"Don't you create a foofaraw now. Ms. Storm is an extremely resourceful young lady going to vacation on the beach in a friendly country - as plain as vanilla ice cream." Hayden stood, signaling the end of the discussion.

"Understood sir," Rawlings said, putting on his hat. "You've been chasing Nakitov for years. You want him bad, don't you?" he asked as he reached for the door.

Hayden did not reply, but the gleam in his eyes answered the question completely.

■ ■ ■

Sitting in her den, the entire team crammed into the apartment, Kris scanned the script one more time. Her makeover was complete now: boyishly short brunette hair, thick framed glasses, and a heftier physique. Stretching out the quiet moment, Kris looked out the small window, admiring the glimmer of the sunlight through the treetops of her block. "Ready," she announced at last.

"Name?" Mindy fired.

"Karen Starr." An easy first name to remember, Kris thought sadly. Her mom would be pleased though. She had wanted Kris to look after her dad. Mindy rolled through a dozen biographical questions. Kris answered each one flawlessly.

"Your Facebook page and Twitter account are all set," Mindy concluded.

"I saw that you set up a few locations on Foursquare too. Good job," Kris said.

"How long have you worked in IT for Doren Enterprises?" Joe's turn now.

"Three years."

"What's your beef?"

"My boss kept hitting on me. When I wouldn't go out with him, he started giving me the worst jobs in the department. Real low level programming stuff. He said that I didn't have the skill set that he needed."

"Why didn't you just report him to HR and sue the company?"

"Hacking their system is much more fun."

"How did you get in?"

"I'm in IT, remember, so I have access. I created a new account, pretty low level so no one would notice. Then I hacked into the employee database with an SQL injection, looking for admin credentials for customers' financial data. That's the crown jewels," Kris said.

"But Doren Enterprises locks that data up tight."

"Yea, lots of false leads, firewalls and high level encryption. I took some vacation days and beat against it until I created a small crack."

"Go on," Joe said.

"Well, I knew that John Doren owns the Red Sox. He grew up in Boston and is fanatical about the team actually. So when I saw administrators named George Ruth, Russell Dent and Aaron Boone, I knew that they must be false flags. On the other hand, I guessed that the files for Ted Williams, Jim Rice, and my favorite, Dora Ortiz, led to the good stuff."

"Not bad," Joe laughed.

"It's just a start actually. I still need to crack the passwords - which won't be easy - but I think that I'm ahead of the Russians."

"They're not big baseball fans over there," Mindy cracked.

"No. I posted on DarkLife 2.0, a hacker forum, yesterday as Cursed Bambino, and got an inquiry back late last night. Sounds like the Russian girls."

"Are they interested?" Jim asked.

"Definitely. I hinted that I might be taking a trip to Croatia to visit friends."

"And?"

""Nothing yet."

"Let's get back to the hacking," Joe suggested. For the next two hours, he and Kris batted around strategies to attack the passwords. Mindy helped a little, while Jim and Glenn were as useless as traffic cops at the Indianapolis 500. Glenn made a run to the grocery store, while Jim paced back and forth, occasionally peering over Kris' shoulder. Concentration interrupted, Kris looked up and smiled at Jim. She was nervous too, even fearful, about the days ahead, but Jim's concern made her feel safer. He would sweat every last detail to protect her - that was his job. But Jim cared much more than that. Kris had no doubts there. But did she want him that way? The answer would have to wait until she got home. A beep from Kris' computer interrupted her rhapsody.

"They're in," she announced. "They'll meet me in Hvar."

"Wow, I guess this is for real now," Mindy said.

"You know these girls are gay, right?" Glenn asked.

"Yes," Kris replied condescendingly. "I've met gay people before."

"OK, OK. Just wanted to be sure."

Jim looked at his watch. "We've got a car on standby. You can catch the last flight tonight to Frankfurt, then transfer tomorrow morning to Split for the ferry to Hvar."

Kris nodded. "I'm packed and ready to go," she said pointing to a tan valise by the couch.

"OK then. Can you guys clear the room? I want a few minutes to talk to Kris. Alone," Jim requested.

Mindy hugged Kris and led the way out. "I just hope this doesn't turn into a Red Wedding," she said to Joe while they were clambering down the stairs.

"You're watching too much Game of Thrones," he replied. "Kris will be fine."

Kris fiddled with the papers on her desk until she heard Jim click the door closed. Looking out the window, she could see three teens shambling home from school, backpacks on their shoulders, chatting away, oblivious to the world. Kris wheeled her suitcase towards the center of the living room, pausing there for a long second. Finally, Jim reached out and drew her close. "I'll be in Washington with Hayden. We'll be monitoring everything. You'll have plenty of protect..." Kris cut him off by touching her index finger to his lips. She dawdled in Jim's arms, a safe haven to gather her courage. At last, Kris lifted her face and kissed Jim firmly but chastely on his lips, then pulled away before he could try to coax more. "Time to go," she said, opening the door.

29

The Judita, a 40 meter catamaran, chugged into the crowded horseshoe of Hvar Town harbor, plowing through a clutter of yachts, sailboats, and dinghies. Just past 4 PM, the sun still blazed in a pristine sky broken only by a scattering of puffy white clouds. Clad in the jeans, stained with a red wine spill from the overnight flight, Kris stood outside on the top deck. A gentle breeze jostled the straw hat that she had purchased at the terminal in Split earlier in the day. At 42 miles between its tips, Hvar is the longest of the Croatian islands in the Adriatic Sea, featuring thick pine forests that rise steeply from the sea culminating in stark limestone cliffs. Its east coast faces the Croatian mainland, while its west coast fronts open waters. A terraced field displayed a shock of lavender on the hillside above the harbor. Kris could easily see why the Greeks had chosen to settle here in the fourth century BC. She pictured an ancient trireme sprinting along the shoreline, the muscled backs of its crew straining at the oars.

With the high season racing to conclusion, the Judita was almost completely full, three hundred passengers, all eagerly anticipating their arrival in paradise. Kris jostled her way down the stairs and over the ramp to the dock. She wasn't quite sure which way to turn when a sprite, silver-haired woman with sun-dappled cheeks appeared at her side. "Hello, Ms. Storm. I'm Inga Lucic, the concierge from the Pharos Apartments. Please follow me," she said in English tinged with a Slavic accent, while reaching for the handle of Kris' suitcase. "It's not far to walk." Kris had little choice. The pair made their way along the broad sidewalk of sun-baked stones that encircled the harbor. They passed festively-awninged food stands, shops offering an array of trinkets and beach goods that would be familiar at any tourist location, and the parasols of beach cafes, still half full. The late lunch crowd, chiseled, tan, and barely clothed, lounged with cocktails in hand. Kris could pick out a smattering of languages - Croatian, Italian, German, and English. Inga entered the town square, dominated by the colonnaded bell tower of St. Stephen's Cathedral, built on the site of a sixth century Christian church, then quickly turned left, away from the water. She climbed a flight of stairs, checking frequently to be certain that Kris was in tow, to reach Petra Hektorovica Street. "Here we are," she announced, pointing to the entrance to the Pharos, a sand-colored stone building streaked by the rust iron railings of terraces on all three of its floors and topped with a Venetian style terracotta roof, common to many dwellings in Hvar. "We are small - only 6 rooms, but yours is on top. You can almost see the harbor from there." They squeezed into the tiny lift, so close that Kris had to flatten against the back wall. The car creaked slowly upward. Inga opened the door to Kris' room, simply furnished with a queen bed sporting a faded pastel spread, a nightstand and a desk with a wicker basket of fruit, crackers and cheese resting on top. After a quick tour of the bath and terrace, Inga fussed about. For a second, Kris thought that she expected a tip and reached for her purse, but Inga waved her off. "Good luck," she said before leaving.

Kris didn't have much to unpack: her laptop was her top priority. She set it up on the desk, surprised at first to see that the WiFi strength was excellent. Then she remembered who owned the hotel. A private message awaited her on the Dark Life forum. The girls wanted to meet at 7 on the roof deck at the Hotel Adriana. They would each wear a flower in their hair. Kris confirmed, checked a map to see that the Adriana was only a five minute walk, and then scanned several Trip Advisor reviews praising the hotel as one of the hot spots in Hvar. She set her alarm for 6:15 before crashing for an hour power nap. Deep asleep, Kris first thought that the chimes from her phone were wedding bells. She fought back to the surface, fumbled for her phone and turned them off. In her dream, two of her Cornell roommates were bridesmaids with white flowers perched in their long blond hair, but Kris, walking down the aisle, couldn't picture the face of the groom waiting at the altar. She struggled for a few seconds to bring the image into focus but finally gave up and tossed off the coverlet. Kris showered quickly, cold water first to wake up, and then dressed in a royal blue halter sundress, its billowing skirt camouflaging her new figure. Kris devoured an apple before walking down the Pharos stairs, not risking the elevator again. She didn't see any of the hotel's other guests.

Too early for the dinner crowd, the burnished wood deck at the Adriana was almost empty when Kris arrived. She ordered a Stella and looked out to the sea. The sky was a palette of sapphire, auburn and gold as the sun set over the Pakleni Islands that guarded the entrance to the harbor. Gleaming white yachts and powerboats were packed tightly together at their moorings. Kris could only find one empty slip along the length of the promenade. She turned just in time to see the arrival of her fellow hackers, yellow sunflowers nestled neatly into their braids. Kris watched them sit at a table towards the back of the deck away from the rail. Yana's hand rested leisurely over Elena's as the waitress approached for their order. Pivoting back towards the harbor, Kris waited five minutes, gathering her courage for the night ahead. Ready at last, she took a long swig of her beer then approached. "Hey," Kris said placing her bottle down on their table. "Welcome," Elena replied, motioning for Kris to sit down and join them. She pushed their bottle of vodka across the table. Kris poured herself a shot and introduced herself, remembering that she was Karen Starr now.

While the Russians' command of English was modest, the trio quickly grew comfortable in their conversation. "I'm starving," Kris said after about thirty minutes. She pointed to her stomach, then waved the waitress to come over. She ordered a platter of steak frites, but the Russians just shook their heads. Combining words and gestures, the girls shared stories of life, programming, abusive bosses, and true love.

Looking down at Kris' tattoo, Elena asked, "You have a boyfriend in prison, yes?"

"What? No," Kris declared.

"The numbers? I thought they were his prisoner number."

"No, no," Kris laughed, explaining her anger at her family's move from California.

"I would be angry too if my family moved away from California," Yana said. "Do you have a real boyfriend?" she went on slipping her vodka slowly.

"Not a quick fuck," Elena joked.

"Not now. Not for a long time actually," Kris said ruefully, thinking back to her college days, her last true beau. Matt Reilly was a fling, she had accepted that at last, and Jim Bright was only a possibility.

"Well, you need a lover, a true soulmate," Elena declared, taking Yana's hand. "Like us," they said almost in unison, and laughed.

Kris raised her glass and toasted, "To love." The girls heartily joined her. At last, Kris' food arrived.

"You rich, eh?" Yana asked, watching Kris devour her dinner.

"No, why?"

"Food here at the Adriana is expensive. Too many kunas," Yana said, pulling some bills from her purse to make her point. "We eat in our room down the street," she added, pointing away from the harbor.

"We save our kunas to drink and have fun," Elena declared, raising her glass in a toast.

"Much fun," Yana said, her right arm now wrapped around Elena's shoulders.

"To fun - and profit," Kris returned the toast, downing the vodka in one gulp.

"Profit yes," Yana said. "We will share the profits, OK?"

"That is the Russian way," Elena mocked.

"But how will we get paid?" Kris asked.

The Russians looked at each other. Yana shrugged, then explained, "Our boss, Mr. Nakitov, he lives in New York. He pays us for each financial record that we download."

"He doesn't pay us enough," Elena burst out. But Yana shushed her, stating calmly: "Nakitov has the organization to use the data. We don't."

"That is child's play. We are doing the hard work," Elena protested.

"And Nakitov has other hacking teams if we fail," Yana said.

"The women get fucked again," Elena declared loudly, turning heads at the next table. She poured the last of the vodka into her glass and pounded it down.

Yana stroked Elena's forearm soothingly, then looked at Kris. "We should get to work when you are finished eating. It is not too late to start. We can go to our apartment."

Elena started to protest, but Kris interrupted. "Let's go," she said, pushing the last of her french fries across the table to her new friends who gobbled them hungrily. Despite her nap, Kris was still beat from the overnight flight. But the sooner they went to work, the sooner she could go home.

Yana signaled for the check and carefully divided the bill. When they stood, Elena, still pouting, pulled out her phone from the back pocket of her jeans and handed it to the waitress. "A photo, please - the three of us - before our big night," she said sarcastically.

"You are like a teenager," Yana scolded.

"Let's get the harbor in the background," the waitress suggested helpfully.

Elena posed between Kris and Yana. After the photo session, the girls trudged out into the street. Kris stopped abruptly a few paces up the hill. "Shit, I don't have my laptop," she said, turning around.

Yana reached for her shoulder, "Where are you going?"

"Back to my hotel. Come with me. It's not far."

"I think that we will wait here," Yana replied cautiously.

"Your choice. I have some munchies there too," Kris said starting to walk away.

"Let's go," Elena broke in.

"No, we should stay."

"I want to see how the rich American lives. Not like our shitty apartment, I bet." Kris linked arms with Elena as they strolled together back down the street. Yana hesitated for a second, then hastened off after them. She quickly reclaimed her lover's attention.

Smart girl, Lieutenant Rawlings thought, tucked into a doorway across the street. His small team had fanned out around the Adriana futilely trying to cover all directions. Heading back to their command post at the Pharos, Rawlings figured that this job might even go smoother than he had expected.

■ ■ ■

"I can't believe that they're fucking lesbians," Lenny said aloud, looking at the latest photo of Elena, Yana and their new friend on his phone.

"What?" Dmitri mumbled, half asleep and half drunk. With little to do this afternoon, they had taken a cooler of beer down to the beach.

"They're so hot, but Mr. Nakitov said that they're fucking queer. Looks like they're going to have a threesome tonight." Croatian time was six hours ahead of Brooklyn.

"Why don't you ask them to come down here? One night with me will straighten them all out," Dmitri joked, sitting up to check out the picture.

"Good thought, but they're in Croatia. On some island. Hvar."

"How do you know that?"

"The location data is embedded in the photo file. I have an app that can place it right on a map," Lenny said, showing Dmitri.

"Cool boats," Dmitri replied, looking at the background of the photo. "We should go there."

"Shit, I'm going to have to tell Nakitov."

"That I want to go to Croatia?"

"No, asshole, that the girls are still sending photos. And that they have left Russia. He'll be really pissed off."

Lenny was right. Nakitov had just dozed off sweating after a midday dalliance with Natasha, now lounging next to him, still naked, watching TV. "Fuck," Nakitov shouted into the phone as Lenny's information registered. Natasha bolted up, breasts jiggling before she pulled the sheet over them. "Bring the photo over here. Now." Nakitov commanded Lenny before turning to his companion. "Get dressed. I have work to do."

Lenny and Natasha crossed paths in the hallway outside of Nakitov's penthouse apartment in Brighton Beach. Ilya, now swathed in a thick terrycloth robe, studied the photo carefully on Lenny's phone.

"Are you sure they are in Croatia?"

"Yes sir, I have the exact GPS coordinates here if you want to see them."

"Not now. Who is their new friend?"

"Their new partner, according to the text. She is probably going to help them crack the credit card files."

"Didn't you order them not to send any more photos?" Nakitov paced over to his living room window, looking out over the ocean.

"Yes, sir," Lenny replied, trailing his boss. Nakitov snapped around violently almost knocking Lenny off balance.

"Let me see that photo again." This time he focused on the third girl, swiping his thumb and forefinger to enlarge the image, then handing the phone back to Lenny. "She looks familiar."

"I don't recognize her."

"I think that's Kris Storm, the young lady who has been helping the FBI."

"Are you sure? Storm has long red hair and a great body. This girl has short dark hair." Lenny scrutinized the photo again. "And, she looks like she needs to lose a few pounds before she goes to the beach," he added trying to lighten the mood.

Ilya didn't laugh. He walked into his dressing room and parted a row of neatly hangared blazers to reach a safe. He twirled the dial three times, opened the heavy steel door, and withdrew a weathered black address book. "Send the photo to this number," he ordered, displaying only a single page of the book to Lenny. "Request a facial recognition test. Immediately. Use this codeword." While Lenny did his bidding, Nakitov stomped into his study and poured two shots of vodka. "We will wait," he said. Thirty minutes later, Lenny confirmed his boss' fears. "It is Kris Storm," he said. "Who..."

"Do not ask questions," Nakitov cut him off. "Please write down the exact location of the photograph for me," he said, handing Lenny a notepad and pen. When he had finished, Nakitov delivered another order: "Tell the girls that I enjoyed the photos. Ask them to send more." Lenny nodded. He wanted to ask why, but held his tongue.

"Now, it is time for you to go." Nakitov said, walking Lenny to the door. Nakitov returned to his bedroom, drawing back the drapes to brighten the room. He stared at the waves rolling onto the beach for five full minutes debating his next step. At last, he decided. Ilya genuinely liked the girls and had tried to help them, but they threatened his entire operation now. He did not have any other options. Nakitov retrieved a mobile phone from the still open safe. He again consulted his address book before punching in a number. After a short delay, the phone rang in Belfast, Ireland. Sean O'Keele answered on the third ring.

30

Elena crunched on an apple while she cut a thick wedge from the circle of brie. "Not bad," she said, surveying Kris' room at the Pharos, "but I was expecting more."

"Champagne and caviar, maybe?" Yana asked sarcastically.

Ignoring the banter, Kris sat down at the small desk, popped open her laptop and started typing. "Let me show you something," she said.

Elena wandered over, but Yana remained rooted near the door. "I thought we were going to pick up the computer and go back to our place."

"No rush. Besides I'm hungry," Elena replied, gobbling the cheese.

"We should head back now," Yana declared.

"Here's where you guys got trapped," Kris said, pointing to the screen.

Reluctantly, Yana joined the group, listening closely to Kris' brief lesson on the history of the rivalry between the Yankees and Red Sox. "That's bullshit," she said. "I've never seen an American company set up their system based on sport."

"Let her explain," Elena said, sidling closer to Kris. "She has gotten much further inside than we have."

"But she still doesn't have the data. We have a lot of work ahead of us."

"So let's get started," Kris said. "Why waste time changing rooms?"

"OK with me," Elena replied.

"Something smells here, *podozritel'no*," Yana said, struggling to explain her fears in English. She paced around the room, picking up lamps, running her hand around the perimeter of the bed, and examining the room phone on the nightstand.

"Maybe Karen farted," Elena joked, now resting her hand on Kris' shoulder.

"What if she's police, FBI, Interpol?" Yana scanned the ceiling of the room for any signs of a video camera.

Elena pulled back her hand. "No way."

"Ladies, do we want to crack this system? Or sit here and squabble like old women?" Kris retorted, continuing to type away.

"I want you to take off your clothes," Yana requested, now standing directly behind Kris.

"What?" Kris and Elena replied, almost in unison.

"Strip off your dress. Show us that you are not wearing a wire." Yana explained.

"You think that she's recording us?" Elena asked incredulously.

"Possibly, my sweet. If Karen is working for the US government, she will need to gather evidence."

Kris reached back and undid the knot on her halter. She stood, letting the blue dress fall to the floor. Now wearing only a white thong, Kris pirouetted once. "Ok? Or do I need to take my underwear off too?" She asked brazenly, hooking her thumbs under the slim waistband of the thong. Kris had waxed bare before the trip, painful as the process was, to be certain that she would not have any trace of red hair.

"OK for me," Elena volunteered.

"OK," Yana said grudgingly.

"Now, your turn," Kris demanded. "How do I know that you're not working for the cops and taping me?"

Yana and Elena looked at each other, shocked by Kris' suggestion. "She's right," Elena said, tugging her peach blouse over her head. She wriggled out of her bra, unzipped her white jeans, and clasped her hands over her head. Yana followed suit, a dark haired beauty in her own right but of more modest proportions. Kris could not help but admire Elena's blue ribbon boobs, definitely a cut above her own not inconsequential rack, she grudgingly admitted. Yana thought that Karen could be attractive, if she lost a few pounds. Elena was oblivious, accustomed to the attention that her body always received.

Dragging her gaze towards Yana, Kris asked, "The battle axe and the chain - great looking ink. What do they mean?"

"They reflect my wish that the gay community in our country will break free one day," Yana replied earnestly.

"A worthy thought. Now can we all get dressed and get to work?" Kris implored, hanging her dress in the closet and grabbing a tee shirt and shorts from her suitcase. The Russians put their clothes back on as well.

■ ■ ■

"Looks like they're hacking away," Rawlings said over the secure phone connection to Washington. "We've tracked their movements in Doren's system for the past two hours."

"We can see them here too," Harold Hayden replied. "Do you have audio or visual contact?"

"No, the FBI thought that might compromise Ms. Storm's safety and privacy. But we are set up in the rooms next door and down below. She's fine for now at least. But I think that we should pick up all three girls immediately. It's almost midnight here. We can be off this island in an hour and no one will even know that we were here."

Jim fidgeted in his seat, clearly eager to get Kris back home, while Hayden took a deep puff on his pipe. "Not yet," Hayden declared at last. "I want to see how they operate. I think that we can learn enough now to help prevent the next cyberattack."

"But the goal of the mission was to lure the two women out of Moscow and take them into custody," Rawlings protested.

"That is true, and we will do so, in the morning. Let's give them a few more hours to play their cards."

■ ■ ■

Kris let the Russians lead the wild goose chase. Elena downloaded a Hashcat password cracker, bragging that it could generate and test 8 million passwords per second. Just what they needed for a brute force assault. Yana used her tablet to access a database of known passwords that she kept stored in a secure cloud environment and emailed the link over to the laptop. The girls cheered on each other like Kris' high school ski team. Kris took her turn in the hot seat but she knew that the entire network was a sham. Doren's staff had set up a shadow infrastructure, running real applications and simulating high volumes, but completely obfuscating the valid data. The "Red Sox" files, administered by Williams, Rice and Ortiz, were decoys too. They looked unpatched and vulnerable, but, in reality, they quarantined the crimeware that the Russians used in their attack.

By three AM, Kris could not keep her eyes open. She pulled a spare blanket down from the shelf in the closet and rolled it over the floor. "You guys can have the bed," she said, "I'll crash on the floor." As Kris curled up, she watched Yana knead Elena's shoulders while her partner sat hunched over the keyboard.

"I need a break," Elena declared an hour later, standing to stretch. "Otherwise, I'll be out like her soon," she added, pointing to Kris' sleeping form.

""I'll take over," Yana said, taking the hot seat. She swiveled sharply when she noticed Elena heading for the door. "Where are you going?"

"Out for some air," Elena whispered.

"There is the terrace."

"I need to walk."

"And find a drink?"

"Vodka would help, yes."

"It is very late. Be careful."

"You worry too much."

Yana returned to work, but her concentration was ragged. She didn't like to be the mother hen, but Elena could be impetuous and foolish. She seemed to attract trouble. Yana leapt up when she heard a soft knock on the door, but then relaxed when she heard Elena's muffled voice, "It's me."

Elena had a bounce in her step, a big smile, and a half bottle of vodka. "The bartender across the street gave it to me," she explained.

"And what did you give him in return?"

"I just told him that we would meet for breakfast. We need to eat, right?"

"Yes, yes," Yana replied wearily, returning to the computer. Kris snored loudly. Both Russians smothered a giggle. Elena took a nip of vodka, then pulled out her phone. "Smile," she said, framing Yana in the screen.

"What are you doing?" Yana asked, obviously annoyed.

"Snapping pictures of my love. Why are you upset?"

Yana shook her head. "Sorry, my sweet, I must be getting tired."

"Besides, Mr. Nakitov wants to see them." Elena replied, head down tapping her phone.

"What?" Yana gasped, corkscrewing her face in confusion.

"Mr. Lenny texted a little while ago. He said that Mr. Nakitov enjoyed our pictures and asked me to send more." Elena looked up, surprised at her partner's reaction. "I sent him a selfie from outside the hotel a little while ago."

"You just sent him a photo?"

"Yes, maybe ten minutes ago."

Yana stood up, her chair scraping noisily, not worrying about Kris any more. "Let me see your phone," she demanded, pulling it away from Elena and searching the settings.

"Stupid girl, your photos have GPS locators attached. Nakitov wants you to send photos so he can track us."

"I will turn them off," Elena said.

"It is too late," Yana replied, searching for her purse. "I do not trust Nakitov. We need to go."

Elena knelt by Kris, then turned towards Yana for approval. When Yana nodded, Elena nudged the sleeping form. Kris didn't stir, so Elena shook her gently. After two more progressively rougher shakes, Kris finally opened her eyes. "Wake up. We're leaving," Elena urged. Kris slowly looked around the room, her disorientation fading gradually. "Get up. Right now, please," Yana commanded, opening the door a few inches and peering into the hall.

"What happened?" Kris asked.

"I made a mistake. Our boss is tracking us now," Elena explained.

Kris shivered and wrapped the blanket around her shoulders. She needed to get her wits quickly. They would be safer here, or at least she certainly would be. Could she convince the Russians to stay without revealing her true identity? Probably not. Who cared? Hayden wanted to arrest the hackers and interrogate them anyway. But Kris' evening with Elena and Yana had softened her view. Could she get the information that Hayden needed without committing her new friends to a life in prison? Only if she went with them. Kris got to her feet, shakily at first, and stuffed a clean tee and underwear into her purse. "Ready," she said.

Yana was out on terrace. She beckoned the others to come outside. "There are lights on in the room next door. Let's climb down from here."

"Wait," Elena hastened back to the computer, then returned to the terrace. "I set the password cracker to automatic. If anyone is tracking us on-line, it will look like we are still working."

"Let's go," Yana said, throwing her right leg over the railing. Elena followed, while Kris brought up the rear. After Elena's head disappeared, Kris hesitated for a brief moment, a last chance to change her mind, then scrambled to follow. Yana must have had some rock climbing experience in her youth, Kris thought, as she found nooks, cracks, windowsills, and vines to aid their descent. A stray branch whipped into Kris' cheek just before she hit the ground. Wiping away a smear of blood, she trailed the couple down the street.

Giddy from their escape, the girls broke down laughing when they reached the apartment. Elena had been right: it was shabbier than Kris' room. The threadbare carpet sported a pizza-sized stain, the bedspread frayed, and the lone window looked out over an alley. Nevertheless, a celebration was in order. Elena opened a new bottle of vodka and three glasses were raised to the budding partnership. Alcohol, adrenaline and exhaustion now combined to reduce everyone to a sloppy state. Elena and Yana slipped off their jeans and sat cross-legged in their underwear.

"Do you remember the last time that Mr. Nakitov wanted our photographs?" Elena asked.

"Shush," Yana cautioned, but Elena was not deterred. "When he paid us to fuck little Mister Klutz in Moscow," she slurred.

"Mister Klutz?" Kris asked, perking up but forcing herself to lean back against a pillow on the floor. The sour stench of the three sweaty women was almost overpowering.

"Now he is the great mayor of New York City. Last year, he was just a little *chlen*." Elena took a long swig of vodka. "A very little *chlen*, actually," she said, holding her thumb and forefinger about two inches apart.

"We don't sleep around," Yana said defensively, "but Nakitov threatened to cut us off if we didn't help him." She signaled for Elena to pass the bottle. Kris stayed silent, watching the first gray streaks of dawn climb up the window shade. "We met Klutz in the bar and pretended to be impressed by his fancy title," Yana explained, then tilted her head back to pour down the vodka.

"Now, Mister Klutz works for Nakitov." Elena spit out derisively before she belched, not bothering to cover her mouth.

"And we know too much," Yana concluded. A ferry horn sounded in the distance.

31

While the girls were hustling between hotels in the middle of the night, Glenn Walker was sleeping fitfully, ensconced in his quarters on Wild Horses, a 15 meter boat, tough to call it a yacht here in the Adriatic, that the Special Forces team had chartered to serve as their floating communications center in Hvar harbor. Although FBI, Glenn was the lone civilian onboard, and, as such, merited his own room. He appreciated this privacy even more when he awoke with a raging hard-on to several loud raps on his door. Glenn slowly shook off the cobwebs, not really wanting to leave the dream of the girl with the red string bikini that he had seen on his walk along the shore yesterday afternoon. He had just rescued her from the clutches of a Soviet army squadron, dressed in black ninja commando gear, and brought her back to the boat. She was topless, as most women were on the Croatian coast, and was just about to show her gratitude. The knock on the door persisted, preventing Glenn's dream girl from going any further.

"Coming, coming," he called, standing in his tented boxers and looking around, unsuccessfully, for a robe. On to plan B: Glenn forced himself to think of his two young children back home. Manhood quickly receding - plan B had never failed - he opened the door.

"Sir, I think that you need to see this right away," the young intel analyst said, handing him a legal-sized envelope. She wore crisp whites that accented her mocha skin. Glenn had forgotten that the boat was staffed by a team of four, two men and two women, all dressed in the uniform that would be typical of the crew on a luxury vessel.

"Wait here, I'll put some clothes on," Glenn mumbled, taking the envelope and closing the door halfway.

"Yes, sir."

He put the envelope down on the gleaming mahogany table, the boat was richly appointed, and grabbed a pair of khaki shorts from his suitcase open on the floor. He broke the seal, intending to skim its contents while buttoning his Hawaiian sunrise shirt, but it contained only three photos, heisted by the Sweet Things app on Lenny Boykin's phone. Glenn never made it past the first button.

"Shit! Why didn't I see these earlier?" he demanded, ripping open the door.

"The last two just came in, sir."

"We need to contact Washington immediately."

■ ■ ■

The chain of command on a Special Forces mission was short. Lieutenant Rawlings received his orders to evacuate Kris roughly ten minutes after Glenn's call. Hayden, Jim Bright at his side, had recoiled at the photo of the three women on the deck of the Adriana that now resided in the hands of the gangsters in Brighton Beach. He had known all along that Kris' disguise, while sturdy enough to stand up to a casual comparison to newspaper or Facebook photos, would not fool a rigorous professional review, let alone sophisticated facial recognition software. The next photos, Elena's self portrait outside the Pharos and Yana at the keyboard, triggered his worst fears. Hayden checked his computer screen, relieved to see that the girls were still hacking away and awaited Rawlings message that they were in friendly hands.

"They're gone," Rawlings shouted into the mike clipped to the shoulder harness of his ammo belt.

"Please repeat," Hayden replied, struggling to maintain calm. Jim gripped the damning photo in both hands, almost tearing it in half.

"The room is vacant," Rawlings said, directing his two teammates with hand signals to inspect the room. The fourth operative stood guard outside the door, while two more were hastening to the street below. Rawlings did not inform Hayden that he had instructed the pair to catch some rest two hours ago because he thought that the situation in Kris' room was well under control.

"I can see them typing here - trying more password combinations - on my screen," Hayden said.

"Looks like they set the cracking tool to auto. We've been right outside all night. They must have climbed down from the terrace."

"Are you certain?"

"As certain as I can be, sir. The room is completely empty. Remember we were not allowed to set up audio or video surveillance inside the room." FBI orders, Rawlings wanted to add. Probably some fourth amendment shit. Or, maybe Agent Bright was just afraid that the feeds would show the Russian dykes going down on his honey pie, he thought. Now, they were all fucked.

"Any signs of force? Did the Russians kidnap her?" Jim broke in.

"Nothing broken or unduly disheveled."

"It's not relevant now. The women could not have gone far. Please find them immediately," Hayden ordered.

■ ■ ■

Kris rolled over on the floor around ten, head aching from the night before. While only a slice of blue sky was visible through the small window, she could tell that it was a sunny day. Not really a surprise in Hvar. Kris sat up, noting Elena still sound asleep, blanket drawn over her shoulders. Kris didn't see Yana - her side of the bed was empty and the bathroom was dark. Maybe she went out for some breakfast. Perfect. Kris crawled quietly on hands and knees to her purse lying open on the floor a few feet away. In the morning light, Kris realized that she should text her location to the support team. Rawlings, or any of his operatives, had never met Kris face-to-face for fear that a glance of recognition in a chance encounter on the street might jeopardize the mission, but he had provided her with a contact number and a set of coded messages for a variety of circumstances. Kris reached into her purse, rummaging through her clean clothes, but couldn't find the phone. She scouted the floor but no luck. Elena tossed, but remained sleeping. Fighting to remain calm, Kris reviewed the sequence of events the previous evening. The last time that she had used her phone was right before heading out to the Adriana. Then she put it in her purse. The phone could easily have fallen out while she climbed down from the terrace. Or anywhere along the route of their mad dash between apartments. Did she put it on the TV? The nightstand? The table near the small refrigerator? Kris stood gingerly and padded around the room, careful not to disturb the sleeping beauty. She had just reached the windowsill when Yana opened the door.

"Morning," Kris chirped, trying to disguise her surprise.

"Hey," Yana replied, putting down a plastic bag of groceries. "I bought some fruit and yogurt for breakfast." She started to unpack, then turned and asked casually, "Are you looking for something?"

"Yes, my phone," Kris had no choice but to own up. "I thought that it was in my purse but it's not there," she said, pointing to the array of her personal items now strewn on the floor.

"I have it," Yana announced.

"Fantastic!" Kris couldn't keep her voice down.

Elena sat up at the shout, tossing the cover off the upper half of her frame. "What is the matter?" she mumbled groggily, rubbing the sleep out of her eyes.

"I have our friend's telephone," Yana replied. "Yours too."

"No, mine is right here," Elena said, leaning over the nightstand, its dark wood scarred from wear and age. "At least it was here last night."

Yana stepped into the bathroom, pushed back the shower curtain, and reached into the tub filled halfway with water. "They are right here," she declared, shaking droplets of water off the two dripping phones. "They have been soaking for a few hours. I do not want them to get us into any trouble today."

"What the fuck?" Kris exploded. She grabbed her phone from Yana and tried to turn it on. Nothing. She held down the reset keys for ten seconds, then twenty, then thirty, but still a black screen. Yana watched stoically. Finally, completely exasperated, Kris slammed her phone against the porcelain toilet bowl, watching the screen shatter.

"There. Are you happy now?"

"Yes. Quite." Yana replied. She turned to her partner, "Get dressed. We cannot stay here long."

Elena shook her head with a bemused expression, accustomed to Yana's bursts of dominance. "Where are we going, Chairman Stalin?" she asked.

"I booked us all a reservation on the 5PM ferry to Split. We can go our separate ways from there."

"Why wait until 5 - if you're so worried about us fucking up?" Kris demanded, her voice dripping with sarcasm and anger.

"It is busy season. No reserved spaces are available before then. I do not want to wait in line on the dock. Do you?"

"So, what is your plan then?"

"We will go to the beach on Jerolim Island. It is a short ride by water taxi."

Elena smirked. Then she tossed off the rest of her covers and stood up, stark naked, spreading her arms wide to welcome the day. "That is a naturist beach. I am dressed perfectly already." Kris and Yana both had to laugh.

"Yes, you are my sweet," Yana said, her eyes devouring Elena's gravity-defying body, as smooth and hairless as the day that she was born. "But, more important, anyone following us will likely stand out."

"And have to show us his gun," Elena joked. With the tension now broken, the three girls sat down for breakfast.

■ ■ ■

Sean O'Keele, wearing his traditional work garb of jeans and a snug-fitting black tee shirt, rapped on the lobby door of the Pharos shortly before noon. He and his three brothers had left Belfast at dawn for the 3 hour flight to the small airstrip in Brac, a neighboring island. Mr. Nakitov had supplied the private jet, a Citation X. Sean had chartered a silver hulled Riva, the Ferrari of Italian speedboats, piloted by a trusted captain and crewman for the trip over to Hvar. The Riva contained three sleeping cabins he hoped that they would not need, capped by a sleek flybridge. The GPS coordinates on Elena's self portrait had led them to Petra Hektorovica Street where Sean had spent the last thirty minutes knocking on doors, trying to find the right hotel, while his brothers circulated around the harbor.

The smile quickly disappeared from Inga Lucic's visage when she opened the door. With dark clothes, hollow cheeks and pale skin, the stranger looked out of place in her vacation paradise. His blue eyes pierced right through her, searching for something or someone. Few young men were so alert here in Hvar, she thought, especially at this hour.

"Can I help you?" Inga asked.

"Yes, ma'am. I'm looking for my cousin, Kris Storm," Sean replied politely, trying to soften his Irish brogue to make sure that the old woman could understand him. "She said that she was staying on this street but didn't tell us where. Her mom has taken ill."

"That is too bad. We do not have anyone here by that name."

"Here, let me show you a picture," Sean said, reaching into his back pocket for the photo on the deck of the Adriana. "She's on the right. Those are her mates. Maybe you've seen them."

Inga looked over the photo, shuffling her feet, then shook her head. "No, I haven't seen these women. But, let me ask my husband, he is inside. Come in, please." She turned, leaving the door open, but Sean did not budge. When Inga returned, not more than a minute later, trailed by Lieutenant Rawlings wearing cargo shorts and an olive v-neck, O'Keele was gone.

Rawlings surveyed the street, but it was empty in the noonday sun. Returning to the Pharos, he texted a brief description of O'Keele to his team, fanned out around Hvar, and then phoned Hayden back in Washington. "The race is on," Rawlings said before detailing O'Keele's arrival and his own efforts to find Kris.

Wearing a now rumpled gray suit and white dress shirt from the day before, Jim Bright patched into the call from somewhere over France, the lone passenger on the government jet commandeered by Hayden for the nine hour flight to Croatia. Jim knew Kris better than anyone, he had reasoned with Hayden, at last convincing the professor to send him to Hvar. He had left for Andrews Air Force Base immediately after their conversation, wheels up at 11:33 PM EDT, not even taking the time to go back to his hotel to change.

Hayden had not asked about his personal relationship with Kris; and, the truth was, Jim really did not know the answer anyway. With the plane to himself, Jim had spent the first hour in the air trying to decipher his feelings. He definitely had an interest. OK, it was more than that, probably much more, but he was not a starry eyed teenager. Kris liked him, he was sure of that, but was it romantic, or just the dreaded platonic attraction? Their working ties unquestionably complicated matters. He accepted that Kris had had some type of relationship with Matt Reilly, a Yankee no less, before the bomb blast at the Stadium. From what he read of the young superstar in the newspapers, he was pretty sure that the relationship was not platonic. Well, there were other women in his life too. But, he wanted Kris. He pushed the image of Kris entangled with Reilly from his mind, preferring to recall her in a more angelic state, head resting on his shoulder after their last hacking session at her apartment, but had slept fitfully nevertheless. Waking an hour ago, Jim was studying the maps of the town, the coast and the surrounding countryside, focusing on what he would have to do to rescue Kris, if she even needed his help, when Rawlings call came through. Kris could be pretty resourceful in her own right, he knew well, but now she had evaded her safety net and was headed right into the arms of a professional assassin. With the cold logic of his FBI experience, Jim surmised that she would be hard pressed to survive on her own.

■ ■ ■

Ilya Nakitov had been awake most of the night as well, waiting for word from the O'Keeles. The call finally came at dawn, while he was in the shower. He had left the burner phone on his nightstand, and had to race for it, naked and dripping wet. With a puddle forming at his feet, Nakitov fumed while Sean recounted their futile efforts so far and his suspicions about the Pharos.

"We can stake out the Pharos and see if the women come back," O'Keele said.

"I do not believe that they will return to the Pharos, and, even if they did, the Americans would be there to protect them. But, there is good news too. The Americans do not have them either. Otherwise, they would have packed up and gone home. Their birds have flown the coop."

"What do you suggest then?"

"Find them."

"Hvar is a big island. I only have my three brothers here and we do not have any clues."

Nakitov paused, ripping the top sheet off his bed and wrapping it around his waist. He laughed silently. Of course. "My friend, Elena Smokina, loves to show off her body. So does her partner, Yana. They will go to the beach."

"That does not narrow it down much. There are many beaches here."

The women could not escape, Nakitov knew. They were amateurs and had no place to go. So, they would either be caught by the Americans or by the O'Keeles. He quickly calculated the risks to himself, his entire operation, and even his country if Elena and Yana ended up in American hands.

"I will make a phone call and arrange for a helicopter to meet you as soon as possible. The pilot will contact you directly to set the pickup point."

"That will help."

"Try the naturist beaches first," Nakitov ordered as he signed off. He shuffled to his closet, opened the safe, and removed his weathered code book. Nakitov had not needed assistance for several years. Now, twice in a week. His superiors in Moscow would not be pleased, but they too would recognize the dangers of failure.

32

Yana bustled the three women through the narrow streets of Hvar towards the harbor. Lathered in sun block, they each slung a daypack and towel over their shoulder, leaving everything else behind. They would not be going back to the apartment. Imagining a Russian agent in every doorway, Kris fought back the urge to peel away. She remained determined to help Yana and Elena, not desert them. But, without a phone, she had no way to contact Jim or anyone else, so she scanned every passerby for a friendly face. No luck. By the speed of their strides, Kris could tell that her friends also could not wait to depart the island. They all sprinted the final thirty yards to catch the water taxi. Elena stumbled, but Yana caught her hand and pulled her onboard.

The ride to Jerolim took only five minutes, but it was enough time for Kris to formulate a plan. Zigzagging through the busy harbor, the taxi skirted an incoming ferry and passed across the bow of a sleek black sailing yacht, two of its crew waving from the deck. They shared the taxi with a family of four including two small girls, blissfully chatting away in Italian. The mother, a full-figured brunette with an overbite of shark-like gleaming teeth, wore a sheer cover-up over a lavender bikini, while the father, dark-haired and olive-skinned, sported a black speedo and matching tank top. Her friends ignored the family, but Kris joined in their conversation, communicating with a mix of English and high school Spanish, and looked for fish in the clear aqua-blue waters of the Adriatic with Sofia, the youngest daughter.

From the map, Kris knew that Jerolim was shaped like a duck swimming towards Hvar harbor. Approaching a protected bay on the near side of the duck's neck, she could see a rocky coastline encircling a modest hillside of shrub and pine trees. The taxi dropped them all off at Amo, the family-friendly destination. Sunbathers were scattered among a colorful array of foam mattresses, lounge chairs and umbrellas perched on the pebbly beach. The Italians headed towards the red pagoda roof of the small restaurant but Yana directed Kris and Elena to a path that led to Kordovan beach on the far side of the island, one of the top nude hideaways in Europe according to the Huffington Post article that Kris remembered reading back in New York. Kris lagged behind, then veered off course. "I've got to pee," she called.

"OK, we will wait here," Yana sighed.

Relieved to be on her own, Kris picked her way through the rocks, catching up with Sofia and her mom just outside the restroom. Once inside, she tapped on the mom's shoulder before she could open the door to one of the toilets. Kris opened her purse and motioned the mom to look inside. "I forgot my telephone in the hotel," she said, performing a pantomime of dialing a mobile and holding it to her ear. "Can I borrow yours - just for one second - to text my boyfriend?" she asks. "He wants to meet us later."

The mother looked indecisive, not sure whether to trust the stranger. Sofia pulled on her hand and opened the stall door. She couldn't wait any longer. "Bene, bene" the mom said to her daughter, letting go of her hand, and then turning to Kris, "OK - one text," she said, holding up her index finger. She opened her bag, took out her phone and tapped in the security code.

"Gracias, thank you, thank you, thank you" Kris replied effusively. She quickly keyed in "**Jerolim. Kordovan beach. Come soon**" and showed it to her benefactor who waited with obvious impatience by her side. Kris just had time to pee herself before hustling back to join her friends. They trudged along the dirt path through the trees, joining a parade of barely dressed young people. Kordovan was obviously not a secret anymore. One couple had decided not to wait any longer, stepping off the path hand in hand to strip. Kris might have been nervous about exhibiting her body, especially the new larger version, in public for the first time, but she was too focused on their predicament to even think about it. Jim was the best hope for all of them, she had decided, wherever he was. A sense of equanimity settled over her now. The next few hours would be tense, but she was ready. Kris thought briefly about Matt Reilly in the batter's box at Yankee Stadium. What would he say? Just swing, dude.

"There's a more private spot," Yana said, pointing left towards a rocky outcropping above a secluded cove.

"No," Kris replied shaking her head. "We should stay with the crowd. It is much safer."

They plunged forward, passing a painted wood sign nailed to a tree pronouncing "nudists welcome since 1896." Kris had to laugh. Still, she wasn't prepared for the display of flesh that greeted them at Kordovan: naked bodies sleeping on beach blankets, reading on folding chairs, climbing on the rocks, swimming in the Adriatic. Mostly nubile, toned, and oiled, but some middle aged flab, and even a little grandfatherly sag as well. Cover that up, please, Kris thought. She slowly scanned the beach for anyone who looked out of place, not really sure what she was looking for but relieved that she didn't find it. This time, Elena selected their resting spot, a flat stretch of fist-sized stones that looked relatively smooth. She rolled out her towel, pulled her top over her head, and wriggled out of her shorts. No underwear to worry about. Kris took a deep breath and got naked as well, quickly lying flat on her stomach on the threadbare towel that she had nicked from the girls' hotel. The stones were more jagged than they looked, forcing Kris to squirm to get comfortable. She deployed her shirt as a cushion for her breasts and propped her head up on stacked fists in an effort to maintain a vigilant watch on the main trail. Kris encouraged Yana and Elena, flanking her on either side, to survey the other directions, but they both quickly fell asleep.

■ ■ ■

"Kordovan Beach - wherever the fuck that is," Jim directed Lieutenant Rawlings, showing him the text from Kris before his feet even hit the deck of Wild Horses. Rawlings was not pleased with Jim's intrusion, but Hayden had been absolutely clear that Jim was now the senior man on the ground in Croatia and had ordered their boat to meet his flight in Split. The price of his failure to safeguard Kris, Rawlings mused.

"When did you get the text?" he asked.

"As soon as I landed. She could have sent it earlier though." Jim replied.

"Are you sure that it's from Kris?"

"Who else would have my mobile?"

"I'll start a trace on the number", Glenn interjected, thrilled to see his partner.

"Do you have any other leads?" Jim asked, unsuccessfully holding back his disdain for the lieutenant.

Rawlings ruefully shook his head. Was Kris kidnapped, or just off on some grand adventure? Either way, looks like she wants out now and had the smarts to communicate her location. Rawlings consulted with the captain perched in the wheelhouse, and returned to the deck. "1630 arrival local time at Kordovan," he told Jim.

33

A puffy white cloud, shaped like a horse's head, drifted across the sun, providing temporary relief from its glare. The cooler air on her bare shoulders woke Kris up. She surfaced to a semi-alert state and checked her wristwatch. Three o-clock. She had slept for almost two hours. Her fellow hackers were still out cold. In another hour, she would rouse them to head back to the water taxi. Kris stood, hesitantly, uncomfortable with her lack of apparel, but determined to take a quick dip in order to stay awake. She strolled down the beach, swiveling her head slowly to reconnoiter but trying not to appear too inquisitive. No Jim yet, but no trouble either. Was anyone staring at *her* body? She really didn't care right now. Kris reached a waist-high wall of stones haphazardly assembled, but quickly reversed course when she saw a couple spooning on the other side, a guttural moan of pleasure escaping the lips of the female form. The bacchanal at Kordovan knew no bounds, Kris thought. Satisfied that all was clear, she waded into the shallows, surf lapping against her knees, shifting rocks underfoot. Her last swim in the nude was senior year in high school, Kris recalled. When the sea finally reached mid-thigh, she dove into a low, rolling wave and swam for thirty meters, aiming at a sailboat in the distance, then pivoted and returned to shore. The water, refreshing but not cold, brought Kris back to a full state of alertness.

A weathered pup tent, prominently displaying the Canadian flag, had appeared next to their position while she was away. The pungent smell of weed wafted from the open flap at its entrance. Confident that their rear was now secure, Kris slipped on a Broncos tee shirt and crawled between her sleeping friends to resume her sentinel position.

The rustle of the crowd on the beach reached Kris before she heard the whir of the helicopter. Men and women arose in anger as the chopper passed overhead, much like spectators doing the wave at a baseball game.

"Fuck off, you rich bastard!"

"Suck this!"

"Kiss my ass!"

Kris didn't possess a robust vocabulary of profanity in multiple languages, but the accompanying obscene gestures did not need any translation. Clearly, the Kordovan beach set did not appreciate the voyeur up above.

I could like this job, Ian O'Keele thought, as he kneeled in front of the open cargo door of the Kazan Ansat military helicopter panning the beach with the long zoom lens of a videocamera. The images fed directly into a laptop operated by a Russian army tech sitting next to him. The computer's software was programmed to identify Kris, Elena and Yana. "Lots of asses down there," he joked. The tech, a pimply faced corporal, barely looked up from his screen. With four years of English at school, he thought that he understood the language, but he did not see any donkeys on the beach. The pilot made one pass along the length of the Kordovan shoreline and then returned for a second pass of the sandy stretch closer to the shrubbery.

"She is here," the tech blurted, pointing to an image that he had frozen on the laptop. "I will magnify it for you." Ian rested his camera on the floor and turned to view the photo. It showed the broken heart tattoo above Kris Storm's ankle.

"Are you positive?" Ian asked, pointing to the laptop.

"Yes," the corporal called up the photo that Dmitri had snapped of Kris on the floor of the rest stop bathroom in the Catskills. "95125, he read the numbers out loud. It is a perfect match."

Ian raised his eldest brother on the walkie talkie clipped to his shoulder. After the brief conversation, Sean retrieved the serrated scuba knife from his pack and hacked off the bottom half of his jeans. He peeled off his black tee, revealing a pale pink chest rippling with muscle. "We don't have to do the full monty boys, but we can't look like visitors from another planet either," he said, passing the knife along. When Padraig and Rory had completed their alterations, the three brothers climbed into the banana yellow zodiac tethered to the back of the Riva and pushed off.

The O'Keeles did not attract much attention when they hauled their boat onto the beach. A blue cooler with stickers from Porcula and Mljet, nearby islands, helped establish their bona fides. Just three more party animals. Sean led the way towards the tent with the bright red flag. About twenty yards away, he stopped, signaling for his brothers to put the cooler down. The set-up was perfect: the three women lying prone, probably sleeping, facing away from them. He reached underneath the ice and beer to extract a clear vinyl pouch containing six syringes. The three with blue marks would inject a high dose of pentobarbital to rapidly induce unconsciousness while the red ones would finish the job with potassium chloride, leading to death by cardiac arrest, the same cocktail used in prison executions. It was just after 4PM now. With all the revelry on Kordovan, no one would even notice that the women were not simply asleep until the sun set by which time the O'Keeles would be safely in the air on the way home. Kneeling, Sean opened the pouch and handed a pair of syringes to each of his brothers, holding up the blue one to remind them of the correct sequence. Anyone watching would have assumed the syringes contained heroin, not exactly an unknown substance here.

■ ■ ■

"We're going to have to detour a bit around the island. Boat traffic is pretty heavy this time of year," the captain of Wild Horses announced, steering towards the open sea.

"How long?" Jim asked urgently.

"Fifteen minutes maybe. You should be on the beach at 1645 now."

■ ■ ■

Yana stirred and rolled over to her back, shielding her eyes from the sun.

"Hey," Kris said, glad to have some company. "Almost time to go."

Yana nodded. "I have to pee," she said, quickly popping up to a sitting position, then standing to scout for facilities.

"Fuck," Sean muttered to himself. The best laid plans...

"Nice bush," Padraig cracked. Sean did not even notice. He had never killed this way before and did not want to leave any variables to chance.

Yana leaned over to stroke Elena's hair. "We'll wake her when I get back," she whispered to Kris before heading for the woods.

"Follow her," Sean directed Padraig. "We'll take the other two right now."

Elena snorted in her sleep, her backside twitching. Kris tracked Yana's progress. She barely felt Sean's icy fingers on her ankle and the prick of the needle into her ass. Rory crouched behind Elena, delivering the barbiturate in the same spot. Sean dropped the blue needle on Kris' towel and reached into his back pocket for the red one. He leaned over Kris body, preparing to cuddle it to camouflage her death throes.

"Bonjour!" Pierre Lincoln exclaimed, flexing his biceps as he burst from his tent through a thick haze of marijuana smoke like a boxer entering the ring for a championship bout. Pierre shook his head energetically sending his long dreads on a wild dance.

Sean retreated back to Kris' feet, not sure what to make of the towering black man, stark naked, now striding towards him. "Hello, mate," he replied, standing. He gently pushed sand over the needle with his foot, motioning with his eyes for Rory to do the same.

"Beautiful day to party, eh?" Lincoln boomed, switching to English.

"Yeah, but our girlfriends have had a few pints too many, I'm afraid."

"They'll sleep it off."

"They will do that. But we need to get them moving." Sean reached under Kris' lifeless arm and lifter her up. He brushed specks of sand from her stomach and thighs. "Her mum is waiting on the boat," he said, pointing to the Riva at anchor in the distance.

"Rich mum, eh?"

"Her family has a bit of money, yes." Rory took the cue from his brother, reaching for Elena's limp body. He could still smell a trace of floral shampoo in her hair.

"Do you need any help?" Lincoln asked.

"I think that we can manage," Sean replied now dragging Kris towards the Adriatic.

"Pierre! Ou es-tu?" a female voice called stridently from inside the tent.

"Ici," Pierre shouted back. "Gotta go," he said to Sean with a knowing smile as he turned around. Sauntering back, Pierre waved to several spectators attracted by his wild looks and strident voice.

"Swaddle her up and let's get out of here," Sean hissed the order to his brother, pointing to the now vacant towel lying in the sand. "We can finish later." The brothers dragged the unconscious girls to the zodiac, arousing surprisingly few stares or comments, puppy-piling them on the deck and hauling it into the shallows.

"Better get moving. Company's coming in," Ian's voice crackled over the radio clipped to Sean's belt. From his vantage point in the helicopter circling offshore, Ian had monitored the arrival of Wild Horses. He did not think much of it at first, but changed his mind quickly when he counted seven men, obviously armed, embark in a light boat of their own.

"Roger that," Sean replied. He immediately contacted Padraig, summoning him back double time, mission completed or not. Two minutes passed at an agonizingly slow pace, Sean constantly scanning the horizon for the arrival of the Americans. As soon as Padraig splashed aboard, Sean flipped on the motor and pointed the zodiac towards their mother ship. He was tempted to salute the Americans as the boats passed within hailing distance, but thought better of it.

Jim Bright, his once crisp business suit now wrinkled like an old newspaper, perched in the bow, the spray from the Adriatic whipping into his face. Rawlings squatted in the stern, steering, with his team huddled between them. While dressed in shorts, the SEALs were prepared for battle and would undoubtedly cause a stir on the beach. Jim was not worried at all, however, about the reaction on shore. It had been more than two hours since he had received Kris' text. The traffic delay had multiplied his anxiety. As they approached, Jim scanned the beach fervently. He did not pay any mind to the zodiac zipping out to sea. Otherwise, he might have noticed the inert body clothed in Broncos' orange.

34

Kris stirred, still smothered by the blanket of sleep induced by the barbiturate, and slowly raised her head. The cabin on the Riva was small, but opulent: twin beds and cabinetry crafted from blonde wood with thick opaque glass and stainless steel fixtures in the en suite bathroom. Kris swung her feet to the floor, wiggling her toes in the taupe carpet. The other bed was vacant, but a man's kit rested on top. She sensed motion, and looked out the porthole to see the Adriatic sailing by. Kris took personal inventory, she didn't feel strong enough to stand just yet. All her body parts were present and in working order. No wounds, no blood, no rape as far as she could tell. In fact, she was now wearing a pair of forest green men's boxers with little puppy dog imprints. At last, head clearing but still groggy, she stood and tried the door. Locked, no surprise. Kris sat back down on the bed. She was a prisoner.

A high pitched scream, it had to be Elena, shattered the silence. Kris shivered and stumbled to the door, unsuccessfully rattling its handle once again. A second hideous wail erupted. Kris placed it in the cabin next door. "No! No! No more," Elena pleaded hysterically. To no avail, evidently, as a third blast of agony shortly bellowed forth. Kris pounded futilely on her door, shouting Elena's name, at least letting her friend know that she was not alone. The cries faded into whimpers as Kris heard an outer door slam. Then silence, the only sounds now the whir of the motor and the waves lapping against the hull.

Kris stewed for the next thirty minutes. She had no phone, no way to contact help. Not even a belt to hang herself, she thought macabrely, dreading what would come next. At last, the latch on her door turned as Sean O'Keele opened it, a black ski mask concealing his face and hair. Kris bolted for him, clawing at his eyes, no point going down without a fight. Kris caught Sean by surprise, tearing at the fabric of his hood, but he recovered quickly, swatting her hands away and then slapping her viciously across the face. Kris fell back to the bed. Sean stepped into the cabin, followed by Padraig, similarly veiled, who closed the door behind them.

"Stupid bitch," Sean snarled. "One more move like that and we'll feed you to the sharks, one limb at a time. Am I clear?" Kris nodded, sliding back towards the headboard, drawing her knees up to her chest. "OK, then," Sean continued after catching his breath. "Your mate, Elena, swears that she didn't tell you anything about their contacts or their operations. Padraig made sure that she wasn't lying." Kris silently thanked Elena for her bravery and deceit. "Now, you may have a chance to get off this boat in one piece," Sean said, reaching into his back pocket and handing Kris his phone.

■ ■ ■

Jim Bright leapt from his seat on the bridge of Wild Horses when his phone buzzed. The ID was unknown, and likely untraceable, but he had been expecting, if not praying, for the call. Yana hung desperately to his arm as he clasped the mobile to his ear. They had collided on the beach earlier, both searching frantically for Kris and Elena. He wasn't even sure who was more distraught at the time. Jim had calmed Yana, finally convincing her that they were on the same side - at least for now.

"Hey," Kris said, determined to maintain a steady keel.

"Hey, where are..."

Sean ripped his phone from Kris' grasp. "Mr. Bright, I need to talk to your superior. Immediately," he demanded.

"OK, OK. Who am I talking to?"

"The man who will kill your friend Ms. Storm slowly, if you do not follow my instructions."

"I understand, but I need a name if we're going to have a conversation. Then I can call in my boss."

"Sean." He couldn't disguise his brogue anyway.

"Good. Now, Sean, you say that you are holding Ms. Storm?"

"She's right here, mate. As good as new."

"Ask her about Elena," Yana whispered. "Elena." Jim shook his head, mouthing "not yet" and steering her to a seat on the festively pillowed bench. "I need proof," Jim demanded of Sean.

"Proof? You just spoke to her."

"Not enough. Take a photo and text it to me. Then I can help you."

Sean thought for five seconds. Stranded in an EU country without any backup, he had a weak hand and three younger brothers to look after. Kris was his ace in the hole. He would have to play the card well if they hoped to return home alive. "Smile, honey," he said, as he flipped his phone around and zoomed in. Padraig expression sagged, the reality of their predicament starting to sink in.

"Got it yet?" Sean asked Jim.

"It just came through, Sean. I need to check it for a second to be sure."

"It's her. Now, patch me through to your boss."

"OK, Sean. It certainly looks like Kris." Looks like you beat her up a bit too, Jim thought, swiping the photo to magnify the red tint and swollen lip on the left side of Kris' face. Stay cool. "I'm going to conference in my boss, Mr. Hayden, right now. He should be standing by."

Jim paced along the bridge, scanning the armada of boats of all shapes and sizes in Hvar's harbor, wondering if Kris was being held on one of them. Yana stalked him as he sat down in the captain's chair to resume the negotiation.

"Sean, it's Harold Hayden here. I work for the United States government. What do you want?"

"We want to trade Ms. Storm here for Yana Lykin. I am betting that she is in your care."

"Sean, the United States government does not trade with terrorists and kidnappers. Those are capital crimes here punishable by death."

"We are not terrorists and we did not kidnap anyone," Sean declared. "Yana Lykin and Elena Smokina are international criminals who have perpetrated a massive financial fraud on their homeland. Millions of dollars. We are here to bring them back to Moscow to face trial for their crimes." Sean took a deep breath. He had pushed all his chips into the center of the table. He calculated that Hayden would recognize his bluff, but he had at least provided a plausible way out of this mess for everyone.

Sean's gambit surprised Hayden. "We would need to confirm that charge through diplomatic channels. Ms. Lykin and Ms Smokina have rights. They could spend the rest of their lives in prison if we let you leave with them," he replied, obviously stalling.

"There is no time for that. We will turn Ms. Storm over to the Soviet authorities instead. Let *her* rot in jail." Padraig smiled as he sensed his brother gain leverage. Would Hayden, or anyone in the US government for that matter, want to face the consequences for the disappearance of a civilian on his watch? Hayden had to fold.

"I'll go," Yana grabbed Jim's hand and shouted into the phone. "I'll go," she repeated.

"This could work out perfectly for everyone," Lieutenant Rawlings chipped in on the other line plugged into Hayden's office. "Remember, those two women *are* criminals who played a crucial part in a terrorist conspiracy. They hacked the credit numbers that provided the cash to fund the bombing at Yankee Stadium."

"Ms. Lykin, are you sure? You are volunteering to return to Russia?" Hayden asked.

"Yes. Yes. Elena needs me. She would not survive in prison alone."

"We have a deal then? Ms. Lykin and your guarantee of safe passage in exchange for Ms. Storm?" Sean pressed his advantage.

"Yes," Hayden replied. "Mr. Bright will work out the details with you."

On the flybridge, the orange and pink pastels of the Adriatic sunset in the background, Sean outlined the rest of his plan to his brothers. They objected, as he knew they would, but there was no other way.

■ ■ ■

The exchange went smoothly. Yana strode defiantly along the dock and stepped into a water taxi that Sean had chartered to bring her to the Riva. Thirty minutes later, Kris appeared in the last pew of St. Stephens, drugged again but conscious. Jim and Glenn supported her on the shuffle to Wild Horses.

The Riva weaved its way through the Adriatic's summer clutter en route back to the airport in Brac. Two deckhands on a black hulled sailboat flashed their middle finger as the Riva cut across its bow. Sean ignored them: he had instructed the captain to steer as close to other craft as possible, although he had not provided any explanation. Yana was locked in the cabin previously occupied by Kris. His brothers were gone, departing safely an hour ago with their two prisoners in tow, but heading in opposite directions. He had hugged each of them tightly as they left.

Now, he sat alone on the bridge scanning the twilight sky, a bejeweled carpet of stars, searching for the American drone that he knew must be tracking him. Sean imagined himself as Leonidas, the ancient Spartan king, waiting at Thermopylae, just on the other side of the Greek peninsula actually, with his three hundred chosen warriors for the onslaught of the Persian horde. A little far-fetched, he knew, but he found comfort in the thought.

As soon as the Riva was securely docked in Brac, the captain hastened ashore. He returned five minutes later behind the wheel of his navy Jeep Cherokee. Sean ushered Yana, head held high and lips set tightly in stoic determination, into the back seat and climbed in next to her for the short drive to the airport. She had followed his directions without comment since coming aboard, but Sean kept his hand on the pistol in his jacket pocket just in case.

"Where is my Elena," Yana asked, as the Jeep pulled adjacent to the wing of the Citation.

"On the plane," Sean replied, opening the car door. He pointed Yana towards the stairs descending from the front of the Citation, glancing skyward before following her up. The Jeep's tires screeched on the runway as the Riva's captain peeled away. The uniformed co-pilot waited at the top of the jetway, pointing them towards the eight cream colored leather seats arranged in facing pairs on both sides of the aisle. Elena sat facing forward in the last row, head bowed. She lifted up slowly when Yana entered, flashing a wan, drugged smile. Yana could see the purple bruise under her lover's eye and two oozing burn marks on her forearm. She rushed forward, almost tripping over the feet of another passenger, sprawled out in his seat. Yana could smell the booze on his breath as she hastened to Elena's side.

■ ■ ■

"Please give me a tally of everyone on board," Hayden asked, viewing the image of the Citation on his screen. He had been watching it for the past hour, but wanted to review the facts one last time.

"I count six passengers, sir, plus two crew," Lieutenant Lance Brockhurst stated from his perch in the bowels of Creech Air Force, just outside Las Vegas. He had piloted combat drones in Afghanistan for six years. The MQ-9 Reaper under his command was cruising 50,000 feet above Brac now, armed with four Hellfire missiles.

"Can we confirm their descriptions?"

"No sir, not everyone. The crew escorted a young woman matching the photo of Elena Smokina aboard at 2100 local time. Three unidentified men followed at 2110. They wore hooded sweatshirts so we could not ID them. Then another male - we have his face and are checking it now - and a female, Yana Lykin, at 2122. That was five minutes ago. The plane door has just closed so I would not expect any more passengers."

"Kris said that she thought there were four men holding her captive. All masked so she did not see any faces," Jim chipped in from the deck of Wild Horses. He and Glenn were staring at the same image as Hayden. Kris was below deck under doctor's care.

"I expect the Citation to go wheels up shortly. Our rules of engagement prohibit any action once it is off the ground," Brockhurst announced.

■ ■ ■

"What happened to Elena?" Yana demanded.

"I'll explain once we're airborne," Sean said calmly, taking the seat across the narrow aisle from Elena. "You can keep an eye on her yourself. Now please sit so that we can depart." He pointed to the seat facing Elena. She obeyed, snapping her seat belt for good measure, then reaching for Elena's hand.

Yana heard a rustle from the drunk behind her. "I want the one with the big titties first," he leered, squirming around in his seat to point to Elena.

"That one's mine. You can have sloppy seconds," his buddy teased.

"What?" Yana shrieked, panic bubbling up from her churning stomach. "We want to leave now." Elena barely moved.

"Sit," Sean commanded, aiming his Glock first at Yana, then at the three drunks behind her. "Everyone sit. The party will start after we take off." He had surmised that Kris would provide a headcount and rough description of his family to Hayden, so he had instructed his brothers to recruit three drunken tourists from the bar at the Adriana to take their place on the plane, luring them with the promise of a sex, drug and alcohol fueled boondoggle to Mykonos.

"Captain!" Yana shouted. "I want to see the Captain." She obviously did not know that Sean had guaranteed the pilot and co-pilot a sizeable bonus, and the first fuck, if they would man the flight. Sean heard the Citation's engines roar to life.

■ ■ ■

"We cross-checked the IRA database at Scotland Yard. It just gave us an ID on the last male boarding the jet. Sean O'Keele. Looks like a bad character. A suspect in several actions going back many years," Brockhurst announced tersely. He could now see the exhaust fumes from the Citation clearly on his screen.

"Please confirm. Sean O'Keele. A known terrorist operative is on board?" Hayden asked.

"Roger that." The Citation began to taxi to the head of the runway.

"Does he have any known associates?"

"Three brothers."

"Bingo!" Jim and Glenn exclaimed simultaneously. Kris had just wandered up on deck to check out the commotion.

■ ■ ■

Glock now resting on his lap, Sean fingered the cross dangling from a silver chain around his neck. If the Americans' software was as fast as rumored, they would have identified him by now. He had posed long enough before boarding the jet. The Citation accelerated on the runway, pinning the passengers to their seats. Sean closed his eyes, memories of his wife and two young sons flooding his thoughts. His brothers would look after them. With a warrior's intuition, Sean sensed the Hellfire's approach a fraction of a second before it turned the plane into a pin-wheeling fireball.

■ ■ ■

Silence.

Kris, Jim and Glenn stared slack-jawed at each other, no one believing what they had just witnessed.

"Elena and Yana?" Kris asked, anguish dripping from her voice.

"Maybe better for them this way," Jim said in a hushed tone.

Soulmates forever now, Kris thought.

"Mr. Ambassador," Hayden's voice crackled from the screen. "I regret to inform you that our satellites have just recorded an accident at your airport in Brac." A long pause. "Yes, an accident," Hayden repeated.

PART 4

"But some just went stir crazy, Lord, 'cause nothin' ever changed."

"Doolin' Dalton"
The Eagles

35

Ilya Nakitov tried to maintain his normal routine while waiting for word from Sean O'Keele: a walk on the beach, a swim, and now paperwork in the back room of Galina's. Lenny Boykin sat across from him, tabulating figures on his laptop. Nakitov glanced out the window at the ocean, his concentration wandering. A small boat, white sail billowing in the breeze, appeared to be chasing a massive ocean liner out to sea. He had employed the O'Keeles several times; they had never failed him. Nakitov's stomach grumbled. He had skipped lunch. Still a few hours until dinner. He buzzed the intercom to order a plate of herring to snack on.

"Sir? Excuse me sir," Lenny interrupted his reverie.

"Yes?"

"A tweet, sir."

"A what?"

"A news flash - a private plane, a Citation X, has just crashed on the runway in Brac, Croatia. All passengers are believed to be dead."

"Brac?"

"Brac neighbors Hvar, sir. Anyone flying privately to Hvar would use the airport in Brac."

"Any identification of the victims?"

"Not yet."

Hvar was a hot spot now. The oligarchs flew in regularly on private jets. Anyone could have been on that plane, Nakitov told himself. O'Keele would call any minute.

"Please leave me alone," he said, dismissing Lenny. Nakitov was no longer hungry. He cancelled the herring, requesting a bottle of his favorite Stoli Elit instead, a necessary comfort for the vigil that awaited.

■ ■ ■

Arnold Klotz turned off the television, he could only listen to the snide comments about his new administration on Fox's 10PM local news show for so long, and hung his burgundy robe on its hanger. Wearing Derek Rose silk pajamas in a matching plaid, he slid between the plum sheets on the four poster bed in the master bedroom at Gracie Mansion. He loved sleeping here. It felt so much more mayoral than the apartment in Stuyvesant Town that he and Stephanie had lived in for the past twenty-five years, raising their two boys, now away at state university in Binghamton. As a lawyer, and then Public Advocate, Klotz had never made much money, certainly not by New York standards, so the trappings of power were a treasured novelty.

Stephanie was moving into the Mansion at a more gradual pace. She had just started to entertain here, an afternoon tea with the women's leadership council from their temple and a dinner party with three power couples, staunch Democrats, of course; but, she wasn't yet comfortable spending the night among the "ghosts" as she called them. Arnold, on the other hand, loved the "ghosts", or at least some of them. He had a stack of biographies on his nightstand - the great liberal mayors of New York City: LaGuardia, Beame, Koch, and Dinkins. He had no interest in two of the Mansion's more recent occupants, Giuliani and Bloomberg, toadies to the rich and powerful, he thought. Klotz had his own plans, but the party brass had convinced him to take a low-key approach during this interim period, honoring the memory of his predecessor, Deion Chamberlain, When the campaign began in earnest, they said, he could step out of the shadows.

Klotz turned off the bedside lamp and sunk back into the feathery pillow. A year ago, he was a bench player on the campaign trail, content to ride

Chamberlain's coattails to victory. This fall, he would be the main attraction. The prospect of the spotlight set Klotz's heart pumping like an open fire hydrant on a summer afternoon. Over the past month, he had hired a personal trainer, a leadership coach, and a public speaking tutor. No more fiascos like his first speech at the reopening of Yankee Stadium. He remembered the fidgeting and even a few Bronx cheers from the crowd. Klotz had no doubt that his proposals would enable *his* people, the middle and lower economic tiers, to narrow the gaps that had fissured *his* city. New taxes on private school tuition, multi-million dollar apartments and luxury boxes would pay for more affordable housing and a long-delayed raise for public school teachers. Klotz had already started to draft his campaign's first speech.

Klotz rolled to his side, kicking off the top sheet. The investigation of the bombing at Yankee Stadium still tormented him. He had shut it down because the perpetrators were all dead, not to mollify Ilya Nakitov or the Russian community. Opponents might accuse Klotz of being soft, but his actions had saved the city millions that were needed elsewhere, he rationalized. Nakitov had never asked for a favor and he would never grant one. They had never even had a direct conversation. All Nakitov had done was set him up with an evening of entertainment in Moscow, Klotz had learned too late. He had never strayed before, but, he certainly wasn't the first politician to have a dalliance on the road. Nothing illegal here. Stephanie would stand by him, if it came to that.

With that night forever etched in his mind, Klotz reached for his phone on the nightstand, the temptation building. He put the phone next to his pillow and rolled over again. He should have known that he was being set up when the girls insisted that they go up to their room, not his. But a threesome? With two beautiful women? Klotz couldn't resist then, and he couldn't resist now. He retrieved his phone, slowly pressing one key at a time to access his cyber vault and unlock the photos that Nakitov had sent. He could almost smell the spiced scent of the slow-dripping candles mingling with the pungent sweat of their interlocked bodies. Two sharp knocks on the bedroom door snapped the mayor back to reality.

"Yes? What is it?" he asked, sitting up. He had not seen any Twitter alerts but, at this hour, the news could not be good.

"The FBI is downstairs, sir. Several agents in fact," the butler replied.

Klotz stood, cinching the belt of his robe and slipping his phone back into its dock.

"Another bombing?"

"No, sir. They have a warrant to search the mansion."

■ ■ ■

The Stoli was almost empty when Lenny knocked on the office door just after midnight, waiting only a single breath before entering. He carried a black doctor's case, as if visiting a patient's bedside. Nakitov, standing by the window, turned and shuffled back to his desk. His face, always lined and weathered, now appeared pale and drawn, like parchment, the mantle of power slipping away.

"Yes?" Nakitov asked, not even bothering to rebuke his subordinate for entering without permission.

"Our friend in the district attorney's office just called. It seems that Yana Lykin provided a full confession on video before boarding the plane in Brac. The police have detained Mayor Klotz. They should be coming for you shortly."

"Thank you," Nakitov replied, slouching into his chair. He poured the last of the vodka into the two glasses on his desk. "*V staryye vremena*," he toasted, downing the shot.

"To old times," Lenny replied, cocking his glass towards his former boss before tossing back the vodka, relishing the burning sensation in his chest. He placed the case on Nakitov's desk and walked out. Ilya fumbled with the lock, his fingers visibly shaking. Finally, after three tries, the mechanism yielded, revealing stacks of twenties, wrapped tightly with red rubber bands. He sunk his hands into the pile, savoring its heft, finally pulling out two bundles and caressing them. Nakitov never tired of the feel, or the aroma, of cash. He inhaled one final time before returning the bundles and snapping shut the satchel.

Nakitov heard the wail of approaching sirens on the street. He would not have much time to ponder his alternatives. After his arrest, he would likely face a solitary life in a US prison, if he was lucky; in Guantanamo if he was not. A show trial? An appeal? Definitely. At best, the evidence was circumstantial right now but the Americans would be relentless. His execution? Possible, but not likely, and certainly not speedy. The Americans would offer him clemency if he provided the details of his operation. He might even be able to negotiate for complete immunity if he betrayed his country. But then he would spend every waking minute waiting for the assassin's bullet and checking every meal for the taste of poison. Ilya Nakitov was a patriot, a general in the Russian army, not a traitor. He thought briefly of Anatoly Turken and his friend, couldn't remember the name. Young fools but patriots too.

Nakitov withdrew his black Makarov service pistol from his desk drawer. He rotated it slowly in his hands, the matted grip familiar, the nicks recalling past campaigns. The police sirens grew louder. He could hear a commotion in the restaurant now. Nakitov swiveled his chair for one last glimpse of his beloved ocean.

36

Although dimmed at this late hour, the lights of New York City never looked so welcoming. Kris and Jim were alone in a black stretch limousine zipping through the sparse pre-dawn traffic in New Jersey on the approach to the Lincoln Tunnel. Rawlings had recovered her suitcase from the Pharos so she had changed into jeans and a simple peasant blouse, but Jim still wore the same rumpled gray suit, now on its third day. They had departed from Split at midnight local time on the government jet along with Lieutenant Rawlings and two members of his team. Glenn and the rest of the SEALs had stayed behind to tidy up. The plane had dropped Jim and Kris off at the executive airport in Teterboro twenty minutes ago before continuing down to Washington. After sleeping almost the entire nine hours over the Atlantic, Kris had at last recovered from the double dosing of barbiturates.

"Nakitov is dead. Looks like he shot himself just before the police arrived to arrest him," Jim said, looking up from the email message on his phone.

"That's fitting," Kris declared without any sympathy. She shifted in her seat. "He was the mastermind behind everything, wasn't he?"

"As far as we know."

"What does that mean?"

"We haven't been able to trace the money flow, at least not yet, so Nakitov had to have some powerful help. That much cash is not easy to hide."

"The Russian government?"

"Maybe. Or maybe just a rogue element within the government. Someone had to have enough influence to get banks in New York, Moscow, the Caymans, Lichtenstein, Iran, wherever, to handle the cash."

"Why plant the bomb at Yankee Stadium though?"

"The target was Mayor Chamberlain. He was pressuring Nakitov here in New York and could have been a serious threat to Russia if he ever became President."

"And Nakitov already had the next mayor in his pocket. Had him by the balls, actually," Kris said, clenching both fists in her lap.

"Klotz is in custody now," Jim replied as he scanned down the rest of his waiting emails. "My guys found the photos of Yana and Elena on his phone and on his computer. Next we'll scour his calls and his calendar to see if he had any conversations or meetings with Nakitov."

"That bastard deserves to go down. How many people have died because of his little tryst?"

"I'm surprised that you didn't ask about the fourth amendment," Jim replied.

"Fuck it," Kris said defiantly. "It's a national security issue - you had to move fast," she added.

"It's tough to make the calls in real-time, isn't it?" Jim asked.

"No instant replays, huh?"

"No," Jim said, chuckling. "But, tonight we had probable cause, and we obtained a search warrant in less than an hour," he continued, reaching out for Kris' hand. Jim's phone buzzed, surprising both of them, forcing him to pull back. Jim listened for a second, then handed the device to Kris. "It's Professor Hayden."

"Ms. Storm, I want to thank you for your service to your country. Your experience was a bit more harrowing than we expected, but the doctors tell me that you are a strong woman and should not suffer any long-term side effects."

"That's good to hear, sir. I am feeling better now." Kris started to return the phone to Jim, but then changed her mind. "Sir?"

"Yes?"

"Did we really accomplish anything?" Kris fixed her gaze on Jim now as she waited for Hayden's reply.

"A fair question. I'd like to think that we slowed down the forces that want to undermine our cherished ideals of freedom; and, we knocked out several of their top players. The metal detectors and the part-timers guarding the gate can stop the amateurs. Please do not misunderstand me - they perform an important service. But, the United States of America needs its best people in the field, armed with the most current and comprehensive intelligence intercepts, if we hope to stop the professionals, like Nakitov and his henchmen."

"Thank you, sir. Good night."

"Good morning, I think," Jim chuckled as the first rays of sunlight slipped through the crevices in the skyline. He put the phone back in his pocket, inching closer to Kris in the same motion. As the limousine swooped through the giant curve of the ramp leading to the tunnel plaza, Kris allowed her body to slide towards center as well. When it dipped into the darkness, Jim reached for her hand again, intertwining their fingers, cementing their bond. They stayed that way for the ride down the West Side of Manhattan to Bank Street.

As the limousine double parked in front of her apartment building, Jim released Kris' hand to cradle his arm around her shoulders, embracing her, swiping a lock of hair from her eyes. He pressed his lips against hers. Not too surprised, Kris responded warmly, but with restraint, pulling back after a brief taste. "Let me help you upstairs," Jim suggested. Kris suppressed a giggle at the thinly disguised attempt at seduction. Jim was finally making his move, but his timing was off.

"Not yet," she replied gently. "Look at me. I'm a mess right now. Let me get back to my fighting weight. OK?"

Jim nodded. "I'll touch base later tonight," he said, retreating but not prepared to yield the ground that he thought he had finally won. Kris had never looked more beautiful.

The driver opened Kris' door and handed her suitcase over as she exited. A red, white and blue banner hung on the rail outside the building: "Welcome home, Kris - Mindy, Joe and Anne." Kris wobbled on her first step from the car, then stumbled awkwardly before regaining her balance. Guess the drugs were still in her system, she thought. Jim had one leg out of the limousine at the first sign of her distress, but Kris waved him off.

"I'm good," she declared.

EPILOGUE

Sidney's Cleaners was the last storefront in Brighton Beach to take down its black bunting, a week after Ilya Nakitov's suicide. The entire neighborhood had mourned its fallen war hero, willfully ignoring the rumors that had circulated about his life and death. Mr. Boykin, no one except his parents called him Lenny anymore and "the Rock" nickname was quickly forgotten, presided over the back table at Galina's flanked by Bill Badenov and Dmitri Remko. A bottle of Elit and a plate of caviar sat in front of them.

Boykin casually thumbed his phone, pausing to read a tweet out loud: *Mayor Klotz to step down at year end citing health reasons. November election could swing to the Republicans.* The FBI obviously didn't have enough evidence to convict Klotz or they never would have let him fade away like this. The little man's only real crime was getting caught naked, sandwiched between Yana Lykin and Elena Smokina.

After closing the Twitter app, Boykin could not resist a playful tap on Sweet Things. It had served him well: both Washington and Moscow were watching him now. More important, both knew that the other side was watching as well. As long as he stayed away from explosives, he might actually be safe. Time to get back to business. Boykin punched up his contact list and dialed Lynne Springer.

"I understand that your boyfriend has left town," he said.

"Yeah, he went out west to coach high school football," she replied vaguely, calculating that Bill already knew as much from the Latourette High alumni circuit.

"That's too bad," Boykin said, stroking his goatee. "We have a new shipment of cards coming in next week. I want you to run the New York crew."

THE END

BIBLIOGRAPHY

ASSANGE, J. (2014, Dec 4). Julian Assange on Living in a Surveillance Society. New York Times.

BAKER, M. L. (2014, Jan 17). Analysis of Obama's N.S.A. Speech. New York Times.

BANJO, D. Y. (2014, Sep 12). Home Depot Upped Defenses, But Hacker Moved Faster. Wall Street Journal.

BULLOUGH, O. (2014, Jul 21). Putinism Thrives on Dirty Money. Wall Street Journal.

COHEN, P. (2013, May 12). Art Proves Attractive Refuge for Money Launderers. New York Times.

COLB, S. F. (2014, Jul 1). The Supreme Court Decides Riley v. California and Updates the Fourth Amendment. Justia.

CROVITZ, G. (2014, Mar 18). America's Internet Surrender. Wall Street Journal.

CROVITZ, G. (2013, Nov 24). Snowden and His Fellow Fantasists. Wall Street Journal.

DWOSKIN, E. (2014, Jan 13). What Secrets Your Phone Is Sharing About You. Wall Street Journal.

ELDER, J. (2013, Nov 24). Inside a Twitter Robot Factory. Wall Street Journal.

ELLIOTT, M. M. (2013, Dec 9). Spies' Dragnet Reaches a Playing Field of Elves and Trolls. New York Times.

FORREST, B. (2012, Aug 23). The Skype Killers of Belarus. Businessweek.

GALL, J. G. (2014, Apr 21). U.S. Promotes Network to Foil Digital Spying. New York Times.

GELLES, N. P. (2014, Aug 5). Russian Hackers Amass Over a Billion Internet Passwords. New York Times.

GOEL, C. S. (2014, Sep 11). Government's Threat of Daily Fine for Yahoo Shows Aggressive Push for Data. New York Times.

GOEL, J. C. (2014, Jun 26). Facebook Bid to Shield Data From the Law Fails, So Far. New York Times.

GOEL, N. P. (2013, Dec 5). Internet Firms Step Up Efforts to Stop Spying. New York Times.

GORMAN, A. E. (2013, Jun 9). Technology Emboldened the NSA. Wall Street Journal.

GORMAN, J. V. (2013, Jul 8). Secret Court's Redefinition of 'Relevant' Empowered Vast NSA Data-Gathering. Wall Street Journal.

GORMAN, S. (2013, Oct 7). Meltdowns Hobble NSA Data Center. Wall Street Journal.

GRIMES, R. A. (2013, Nov 4). 11 Sure Signs You've Been Hacked. Infoworld.

HARDY, Q. (2014, Dec 2). Computing Goes to the Cloud. So Does Crime. New York Times.

LEWIS, P. (2013, Dec 5). Snowden Documents Show NSA Gathering 5bn Cell Phone Records Daily. theguardian.com.

LICHTBLAU, E. (2013, Jul 6). In Secret, Court Vastly Broadens Powers of N.S.A. New York Times.

LOHR, S. (2014, Aug 17). For Big-Data Scientists, 'Janitor Work' Is Key Hurdle to Insights. New York Times.

MACUR, J. (2013, Nov 3). At Marathon, Security Wins. New York Times.

MARKOFF, J. (2013, Nov 27). Researchers Retract Report That Linked Bitcoin Creator and Silk Road. New York Times.

MARKOFF, N. P. (2013, Nov 25). N.S.A. May Have Hit Internet Companies at a Weak Spot. New York Times.

MARTIJN, M. (2014, Oct 14). Here's Why Public Wifi is a Public Health Hazard. Medium.com.

MATTHEWS, C. M. (2013, Nov 12). Art Dealer Admits to Running Gambling Ring. Wall Street Journal.

MOYNIHAN, S. S. (2013, Sep 1). Drug Agents Use Vast Phone Trove, Eclipsing N.S.A.'s. New York Times.

MUKASEY, M. (2014, Jan 20). The President's NSA Illusions. Wall Street Journal.

NIXON, R. (2014, Oct 27). Report Reveals Wider Tracking of Mail in U.S. New York Times.

PALAZZOLO, J. (2013, Nov 18). More Arrests in Alleged ATM Cybercrime. Wall Street Journal.

PALAZZOLO, S. A. (2013, Jan 4). Web Activist's Suicide Highlights Tech Law. Wall Street Journal.

PARKER, N. C. (2014, Oct 31). G.O.P. Ads Chase Voters at Home and on the Go. New York Times.

PERLROTH, D. H. (2014, Jul 2). Cybercrime Scheme Aims at Payments in Brazil. New York Times.

PERLROTH, J. M. (2013, Mar 26). Online Dispute Becomes Internet-Snarling Attack. New York Times.

PERLROTH, M. G. (2014, Oct 31). Luck Played Role in Discovery of Data Breach at JPMorgan Affecting Millions. New York Times.

PERLROTH, M. G. (2014, Nov 9). On the Hunt for Wall St. Hackers, but Not the Spotlight. New York Times.

PERLROTH, N. (2014, Dec 2). Hacked vs. Hackers: Game On. New York Times.

PERLROTH, N. (2014, Apr 7). Hackers Lurking in Vents and Soda Machines. New York Times.

PERLROTH, N. (2014, Dec 1). Hackers Using Lingo of Wall St. Breach Health Care Companies' Email. New York Times.

PERLROTH, N. (2014, Dec 1). Hackers With Apparent Investment Banking Background Target Biotech. New York Times.

PERLROTH, N. (2014, Aug 27). JPMorgan and Other Banks Struck by Hackers. New York Times.

PERLROTH, N. (2014, Nov 20). Malicious Software Said to Spread on Android Phones. New York Times.

PERLROTH, N. (2014, Oct 9). Phone Hackers Dial and Redial to Steal Billions. New York Times.

PERLROTH, N. (2014, Jun 19). Tally of Cyber Extortion Attacks on Tech Companies Grows. New York Times.

PETERS, C. S. (2014, Nov 18). Bill to Restrict N.S.A. Data Collection Blocked in Vote by Senate Republicans. New York Times.

POPPER, N. (2013, Nov 18). Regulators See Value in Bitcoin, and Investors Hasten to Agree. New York Times.

POPPER, N. (2013, Jul 25). Wall Street's Exposure to Hacking Laid Bare. New York Times.

RAPOZA, K. (2013, Dec 4). Kaspersky Lab Names This Year's Top Cyber Security Threats. Forbes.

ROSEN, J. (2014, Jan 18). Madison's Privacy Blind Spot. New York Times.

SANGER, D. E. (2013, Dec 19). Obama Weighing Security and Privacy in Deciding on Spy Program Limits. New York Times.

SANGER, D. E. (2014, May 19). With Spy Charges, U.S. Draws a Line That Few Others Recognize. New York Times.

SAVAGE, C. (2014, Nov 4). Appeals Court Is Urged to Strike Down Program for Collecting Phone Records. New York Times.

SAVAGE, C. (2013, Nov 7). C.I.A. Is Said to Pay AT&T for Call Data. New York Times.

SAVAGE, C. (2013, Sep 17). Extended Ruling by Secret Court Backs Collection of Phone Data. New York Times.

SAVAGE, C. (2014, Feb 7). N.S.A. Program Gathers Data on a Third of Nation's Calls, Officials Say. New York Times.

SAVAGE, C. (2014, Mar 24). Obama to Call for End to N.S.A.'s Bulk Data Collection. New York Times.

SAVAGE, C. (2014, Jan 23). Watchdog Report Says N.S.A. Program Is Illegal and Should End. New York Times.

SCHARR, J. (2014, Mar 7). Blackphone vs. FreedomPop's Privacy Phone: Security Showdown. Tom's Guide.

SCHECHNER, S. (2014, Jan 8). Online Privacy Could Spark U.S.-EU Trade Rift. Wall Street Journal.

SCHMIDT, E. S. (2013, Sep 29). Qaeda Plot Leak Has Undermined U.S. Intelligence. New York Times.

SCHMITT, M. S. (2014, Apr 10). Russia Didn't Share All Details on Boston Bombing Suspect, Report Says. New York Times.

SCHWARTZ, R. (2013, Apr 23). Feds Dissect Boston Marathon Bombs. ABC News.

SCOTT, A. C. (2014, Nov 5). British Intelligence Official Says U.S. Tech Companies Offer Terrorists 'Networks of Choice'. New York Times.

SCOTT, M. (2014, Jun 16). British Spy Agencies Are Said to Assert Power to Intercept Web Traffic. New York Times.

SENGUPTA, S. (2013, Jun 19). In Hot Pursuit of Numbers to Ward Off Crime. New York Times.

SHANE, S. (2013, Sep 10). Court Upbraided N.S.A. on Its Use of Call-Log Data. New York Times.

SHANE, S. (2013, Nov 2). No Morsel Too Minuscule for All-Consuming N.S.A. New York Times.

SIDDIQUE, H. (2013, Apr 25). Boston Bombing Suspect Was Put on Terrorist Database 18 Months Ago. theguardian.com.

SILVERGLATE, H. (2013, Oct 6). How Prosecutors Rig Trials by Freezing Assets. Wall Street Journal.

SOLTANI, B. G. (2014, Mar 18). NSA Surveillance Program Reaches 'into the past' to Retrieve, Replay Phone Calls. The Washington Post.

STANTON, J. (2013, JUL 7). Meet The Chief Justice Of America's Secret Supreme Court. Buzzfeed.com.

STEWART, C. S. (2013, Mar 3). As Pirates Run Rampant, TV Studios Dial Up Pursuit. Wall Street Journal.

VALENTINO-DEVRIES, J. A. (2012, Sep 29). New Tracking Frontier: Your License Plates. Wall Street Journal.

VALENTINO-DEVRIES, J. (2014, Jun 2). Sealed Court Files Obscure Rise in Electronic Surveillance. Wall Street Journal.

WINGFIELD, J. R. (2013, Jun 19). Web's Reach Binds N.S.A. and Silicon Valley Leaders. New York Times.

YADRON, C. L. (2014, Jan 21). Card-Theft Software Grew in Internet's Dark Alleys. Wall Street Journal.

YADRON, C. L. (2014, Jan 13). What Secrets Your Phone Is Sharing About You. Wall Street Journal.

YADRON, E. G. (2014, Oct 2). J.P. Morgan Says About 76 Million Households Affected By Cyber Breach. Wall Street Journal.

YADRON, J. V. (2013, Aug 3). FBI Taps Hacker Tactics to Spy on Suspects. Wall Street Journal.

YADRON, P. Z. (2014, Feb 5). Before Target, They Hacked the Heating Guy. Wall Street Journal.

YADRON, P. Z. (2014, Feb 5). Target Breach Traced to Heating and Air-Conditioning Contractor. Wall Street Journal.

YOON, S. (2011, Jun 20). North Korea Recruits Hackers at School. Al Jazeera English.

ABOUT THE AUTHOR

SM Smith has longed to write fiction since high school, but needed to "detour" through a career in the investment world first. As one of the first Wall Street analysts to specialize in the information industry, and then as the co-founder (along with his wife) of a successful hedge fund, Smith has researched and invested in the technology sector for the past thirty years. The Fourth Amendment is Smith's debut, but he is already at work on the next novel involving Kris Storm and her cybersleuthing crew. If you are interested in receiving updates, please email brooklyn25518@gmail.com.

19544398R00174

Made in the USA
Middletown, DE
25 April 2015